THE TATTOOED DUCHESS

OTHER NOVELS BY VICTOR GISCHLER

Suicide Squeeze

Gun Monkeys

The Pistol Poets

Shotgun Opera

Go-Go Girls of the Apocalypse

Vampire a Go-Go

The Deputy

Three on a Light

A FIRE BENEATH THE SKIN SERIES

Ink Mage

THE TATTOOED DUCHESS

A FIRE BENEATH THE SKIN: BOOK 2

VICTOR GISCHLER

47NORTH

Text copyright © 2015 Victor Gischler
All rights reserved.

Published by 47North, Seattle

www.apub.com

Amazon, the Amazon logo, and 47North are trademarks of Amazon.com, Inc., or its affiliates.

ISBN-13: 9781503948228
ISBN-10: 1503948226

Cover design by Megan Haggerty
Illustrated by Chase Stone
Interior maps by Tazio Bettin

Printed in the United States of America

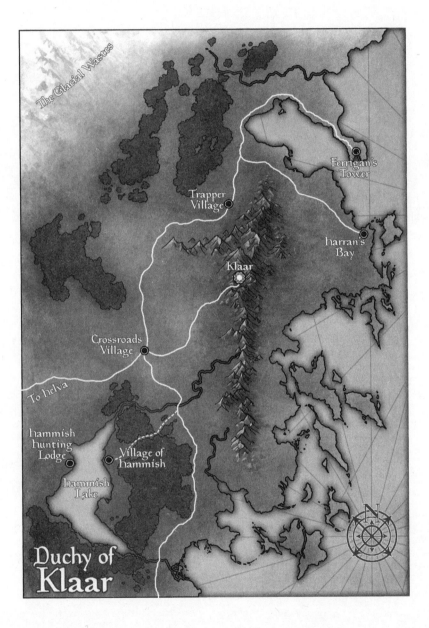

The Glacial Wastes

Ferrigan's Tower

Trapper Village

Klaar

harran's Bay

Crossroads Village

To helva

hammish hunting Lodge

Village of hammish

hammish Lake

N

Duchy of
Klaar

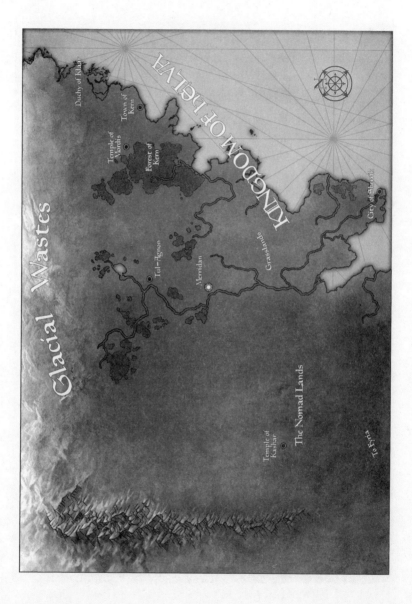

City of Sherrik

The Red City

The Scattered Isles

FYRIA

EPISODE ONE

PROLOGUE

Two lesser priests of the Order of Mordis leaned into the bitter wind, sleet lashing their wrapped faces as they sluggishly climbed the narrow stone steps of the Skyway of Eternity, the treacherous path that twisted up and up, past the tree line, to the glacial heights where the air thinned to almost nothing.

Skull shrines dotted the trail as they ascended, and the lesser priests stopped at each one to make their obeisance, kneeling and reciting a prayer to the dead. The further up they climbed, the less their enthusiasm was for each prayer. The Skyway wore down even the most devout.

They hunched in their white bearskins, thick wool robes beneath, the bones of their ancestors sewn into the fabric like insignia of rank. Hoods up. Faces wrapped with thick cloth, only a small slit for the eyes.

Priests and greater priests were exempted from this duty, having already hiked the Skyway many times in their younger days. The Skyway provided good motivation for the lesser priests to seek promotion. Often, lesser priests newly promoted from the masses of initiates eagerly looked forward to hiking the Skyway as some kind of rite of passage. One trip was usually enough to dispel any youthful notions they had of glamorous piety.

The trail took them into a narrow crevasse, cold stone rising high on either side. They trudged in a slow curve, close now, almost to the end. The stone walls fell away quickly, the wind picking up again as they emerged into an open space. This was the summit.

They trudged past the empty outbuildings, stone structures that once housed monks who trained and studied and meditated year-round. The buildings had been abandoned more than a century earlier, when recruitment into the order had dwindled to a trickle.

The Temple of Mordis, perched at the highest point on the summit, was a wide, low pyramid of rough black stone, cracked and pitted. It had weathered the eternal wind, the blizzards, the sleet and freezing cold, for more than twenty-six hundred years. There were other temples, naturally, wilderness outposts and other more convenient places of worship in more hospitable climes. Even a few village chapels remained from the order's more popular days. The ornate consulate temple in Tul-Agnon endured the derision of the citizenry, but the temple at the Summit of the End of the World in the Glacial Wastes was *the* temple, the origin of the entire order, and the burial tomb of Mordis himself.

Into this most holy of places limped the lesser priests, who shoved open the mighty stone doors, stumbled into the sudden warmth of the eternal flame within, and collapsed, panting and groaning.

The fat one, Glex—who had against all logic remained fat despite months of hard labor and a limited diet of lentils and turnip greens—drew a ragged breath and said, "This is bullshit."

Glex's sullen companion, Bremmer, made no comment.

Glex turned over, sat up, started rubbing his ankles. "I am so numb. You just know in a minute the feeling will come back and my feet are going to hurt. Damn, I hate it. As soon as I'm promoted to priest I'm going to ask for missionary duty in the south, at one of those seaside places with sun and those trees. What do they call those trees?"

"Palms," Bremmer said.

"Yeah, palm trees and sun."

"It's a thousand miles away."

"Everything's a thousand miles away from somewhere," Glex said. "Sure, it would be a long trip, but it would be all rum and suntans after that."

"Is that why you joined the order?" asked Bremmer. "Rum and suntans?"

"Hey, hey, don't go getting all holy on me." Glex stood and stretched. "I'm devout. I recite the tenets and all that, but I still have some ideas about how to get out of the Wastes. I'm not built for cold weather."

"What *are* you built for?"

"Is that a fat joke?"

"No, *this* is a fat joke," answered a new voice from the shadows. "What's a big tub of goo and never shuts up? Answer: Glex."

Glex squinted into the shadows as two lesser priests stepped into the light of the eternal flame. "That you, Horst?"

"Who else?" Horst said. The lesser priest was lanky and pale, with a hooked nose and alert blue eyes. "Thought you guys would never get here."

"Hey, we're on time," Glex said. "You get a week just like everyone else."

"A week lasts a lot longer up here," said Morrisan, the lesser priest with Horst. Morrisan was as lanky as his friend but had the dark, olive skin of the Fyrian folk. "Not a lot to do up here. Tend the eternal flame, sleep, and pray. That's about it."

"Tending the eternal flame is the only reason they even need us up here," Horst said. "I keep telling the prefect they should just get a mage to cast a self-fueling fire and save us all a shitload of trouble."

"It's not the only reason." Bremmer had propped himself up on one elbow.

Horst's gaze shifted to the man on the floor. "What?"

"It's not the only reason," repeated Bremmer.

Horst blinked, slowly turned his head back to Glex. "Who's this guy?"

"He's new. Bremmer. First trip up." Glex rolled his eyes as if that explained it.

Bremmer stood, dusted himself off. "The Great Reconstitution. You've forgotten?"

Horst shuffled his feet and nodded. "No, no, of course. Yeah, I mean . . . sure."

"It's sort of hard to think about a once-in-a-lifetime event like that. I mean, when most of your routine is keeping warm and tending fire," Morrisan said. "I mean, *of course* the Great Reconstitution. I mean, there's no other point, right?"

"If no one is here to perform the Reconstitution ritual, then hundreds of years of devotion are for naught," Bremmer said gravely. "It is the ultimate, ongoing act of faith."

"Hey, hey, no problem," Glex said. "The guys weren't thinking of the ritual when they said there was nothing to do up here. Horst, if you needed to do it, you'd be right there ready to go with the ritual, right?"

"Damn right."

"And me," Glex said. "If I'm on duty when the Reconstitution thingy goes down, I'm all over the ritual. Don't even think about it. So it's all good, okay? We're all faithful here."

"I suppose." Bremmer turned away from the others and began to pull items out of his pack, preparing to settle in for the week.

"I'm going to pull out a jug," Morrisan said. "We can all have a friendly drink and tend the fire. Horst and I pull out in the morning."

"That's the most civilized suggestion I've heard today," Glex said.

Horst and Morrisan brought wood for the fire while Bremmer and Glex found spots for the night and spread their bedrolls. Morrisan's jug came out and they enjoyed the warm glow of liquor in their bellies and lively conversation.

Except for Bremmer.

The wide-eyed lesser priest explored every inch of the temple, the anteroom, and prayer chambers. He inspected each shrine and idol with grim reverence. He lingered especially over the altar and the tomb. At last he joined the others around the fire and deigned to take a single sip from Morrisan's jug, contributing minimally to the conversation. He was first to sleep when the party finally broke up in the wee hours.

They awoke early the next morning. Horst and Morrisan grabbed their gear, donned their furs, wished Glex and Bremmer good luck, and headed down the mountain.

Glex sighed. "One week. Man, it's going to creep by, I tell you. Might as well get comfortable."

"Shouldn't one of us go down to the tree line for more wood?" Bremmer asked.

Glex glanced at the pile of wood along the far wall, enough for several days. They wouldn't run out any time soon. However, there wasn't much else to do. "Couldn't hurt. You want to go first or me?"

"I'll go." Bremmer pulled on his furs and left with the wood axe on his shoulder.

Glex tossed a few small logs into the fire pit just to have something to do. He prodded and arranged the fire for a minute with the long poker before he sat on a step between the altar and the fire pit, pulled out a bundle of prayer scrolls, and began reading carefully. He'd need to demonstrate that he'd memorized the prayers to pass the tests that would allow him to be promoted to priest. Within the scrolls were common prayers he would use often when leading his future flock in weekly services.

He read for maybe half an hour, stood, yawned.

It was going to be a long week.

The long, thin windows of the temple began to dim. Glex blinked. He thought thick clouds were momentarily passing overhead, but the light continued to drain from the windows until it was as dark as night.

"Uh . . . Okay."

Glex went to the temple entrance, cracked open the big doors, and looked outside. An eerie darkness had settled over the snowscape. Glex knew it was midmorning at the latest. He could not possibly have lost track of the time so badly that it was dusk already.

He cautiously crept outside, down the front steps off the temple. He turned.

He looked up.

"What. The. Fuck?"

Instead of the sun, a great black orb hung in the sky. It was ringed entirely with blazing white light that stung his eyes.

Glex's heart beat against his chest. He had never seen this before. Was it harmless? Was it the end of the world, some attack on the temple? Worse yet was Glex's nagging feeling that he should have known what was happening. As strange, disturbing, and outrageous as the spectacle was, Glex could not escape that feeling that it was somehow . . . familiar.

And ye shall know his coming . . . something, something *and the day shall be as night* . . . something, something.

The half-remembered scripture popped into Glex's brain.

The Great Reconstitution!

"Oh, shit!" Glex yelled. "It's happening!" He ran for the steps. "It's happening right now!"

Panic gripped him.

The ritual!

He slipped on a patch of ice on the last step, cracked his knee on the stone, pushed himself up again, and hobbled inside. Heat washed over him. He stood, eyes wide, mouth agape.

Impossible! It was happening, actually *happening*, after all these centuries.

The fire from the eternal flame had grown, expanded, the flames twisting and spiraling into a long tentacle of fire toward Mordis's tomb. The flames surrounded the tomb, the fire splintering apart, the tentacle becoming two hands with long fingers, gripping the tomb like some animal trying to rip into a piece of fruit.

The temple rumbled. The floor shook beneath Glex's feet. He was thrown down again, palms scraping the rough stone. He got to his hands and knees, eyes wide with terror. The flame hands tore into the stone tomb with an earsplitting crack, the fire pouring inside, filling the small structure with white-hot flame.

The temple shook as if it might cave in any minute.

The fire within the tomb expanded until it shattered, shards of stone and dust flying in every direction. Glex went flat, covered his head with his arms, flying bits of stone stinging his back and legs.

When Glex lifted his head again to look, his fear was such that it threatened to catch in his throat and choke him.

The flame swirled over the broken tomb. Mordis's remains, bones and dust, mixed and turned in the fire like some hellish tornado. The ash and fire came together in a mass. A torso formed, then limbs expanded from it. A black figure emerged with skin cracked all over from the flames lighting it from within, hands with long, curved fingers, and a head with a gaping maw that roared fire. The flames held the figure like some kind of prison, both bringing it to life and keeping it trapped. The roar of the flame and the bellow of the creature blended into a deafening cacophony.

Mordis, Glex realized. His god had returned.

Panic and fear and disbelief spun Glex's head. He fought the urge to throw up.

The ritual! Holy shit, Glex could suddenly not remember the words to the ritual. What was the opening line? How did he segue into the refrain? This was unbelievable. Every time he tried to concentrate, the sight of the howling deity before him sent fresh shock waves of terror down his spine.

A flash of memory, something significant enough to momentarily distract him from Mordis and the temple shaking to pieces around him. The blood offering. It was why lesser priests were sent two at a time to the remote temple. One priest recited the ritual while the other's blood was offered to Mordis to finalize his passage back into the realm of the living.

Bremmer! He had to find that little turd and put a dagger in him fast, or—

Glex turned just in time for the blade of the wood axe to lodge itself with a meaty crack in his forehead—right between the eyes.

Glex fell backward, landed flat on his back, arms spread, the axe sticking out of him. His legs twitched, his mouth opening and closing with awkward, choked pleas. A look of wide-eyed shock froze on his face.

Bremmer stepped on Glex's throat to hold him still, yanked on the axe handle until he'd tugged it free. He'd started chanting the ritual the second he'd seen the sky darken, knowing immediately what was happening. A ferocious joy had seized him as he'd sprinted through the snow and up the mountain. He'd left the firewood but had clung to the axe.

When Bremmer got to the ritual's finale of blood offering, he lopped off Glex's head with the wood axe. The blood gushed unnaturally from his neck, like it couldn't wait to escape Glex's body. It ran bright red down the steps of the altar.

Bremmer backed away from the blood, down to the bottom of the steps, went to his knees, supplicated himself.

Mordis raised his hands above his head, stretched, the flames licking his body. The blood on the steps began to boil. Red droplets lifted into the air, spun around Mordis faster and faster, soaking into him, filling in the fiery cracks of his skin.

When Bremmer looked up, it was into the eyes of his god made flesh.

A thousand miles away, the wizard Esthar Talbun awoke with a gasp, shivering in the early morning darkness. She always slept nude. Her magic was powerful and old, and seeing to her own comfort was a matter of simplicity. She was never any warmer or colder than she wanted to be.

But now she shivered, sweat soaking her sheets.

She blinked, slightly disoriented. "Fire."

The braziers in Talbun's personal chamber atop the tower failed to ignite.

Something's happened.

She touched her upper lip, and her fingers came away sticky. Was her nose bleeding? She needed light.

She muttered the words to a simple light spell, and an orb the size of a fist blazed into existence, hovering midair a few feet away. She examined the tips of her fingers. Wet and red. She had a nosebleed.

Talbun realized she could no longer sense the Kashar temple at the top of the mountain. She was charged with guarding the priests there through the hundred years of the long sleep. Something had swept through, a force pushing aside spells, shattering wards.

Something's wrong. There's nearly two years to go on the Long Dream. Nothing should disturb those wards.

Esthar Talbun was one of the most powerful living wizards in Helva, but for the first time in a century, she felt panic.

She rushed to the window, leaned out to look up at the dark mountain.

A bright-orange glow flickered at the summit. Talbun gasped.

The Temple of Kashar burned.

CHAPTER ONE

Bland dawn light leaked gray between the cracks in the shutters and woke her.

Rina stretched and sat up in bed. She stifled a yawn, not wanting to wake Alem, who was buried beneath the bed furs next to her. He'd been sneaking up the secret stairs every evening, often to make love for hours, other times simply to curl next to her.

Secret stairs. The duke's old bedroom—hers now—had stairs leading down, exiting behind a secret door behind a set of shelves in the pantry. What else didn't she know? What other secrets had her father kept?

Rina had her own secrets. She looked down at the white silk glove on her left hand. She always wore it to bed. The idea of some horrible accident terrified her. If she rolled over one night, touched Alem while he was asleep . . .

You made a bad deal with that priest, Rina Veraiin. Now you've got to live with it.

She didn't wear the other glove to bed, so she could touch Alem, caress him, trail fingers down his flat stomach, and then work him until he was ready to enter . . .

Ahem.

She felt herself flush. Best to shift to other thoughts before she over-heated herself. She had a lot to do today.

And so did Alem.

Alem.

Loving him was a problem. He was a commoner. Promoting him to stable master was like saying he was the *best* grubby, unimportant ser-vant as opposed to an ordinary grubby, unimportant servant. In a back-water duchy like Klaar, the affair would likely draw only a few raised eyebrows and dirty looks. Rina was duchess, after all. She could pretty much do as she liked. But in places like Tul-Agnon and Merridan, the capital, such behavior courted ruinous scandal.

It was easier for men. For some reason, women were expected to hold themselves to a higher standard.

I don't want to hold myself to a higher standard. I want Alem.

Okay, that came out wrong.

That nobility might indulge in a brief dalliance with the lowborn was hardly unheard of, but as of last week, Rina had reached marry-ing age, and a single duchess of marrying age was a rare commodity. The matchmakers would be coming for her. And soon. Alem simply wouldn't fit their equation.

She'd been over this in her mind a hundred times already. *Burn that bridge when it comes*, her father had been fond of saying.

She caressed Alem's cheek with her ungloved hand, tucked a lock behind his ear. His hair was getting long, down past his shirt collar. Rina's own hair had been completely scorched off during her battle with the other ink mage—a duel she barely escaped alive, thanks largely to luck.

Rina ran her hand through the new growth on her head. Her hair had come back, jet black as always, but it was still short, spiky in all directions. It gave her a wild, windblown look that she couldn't quite decide if she liked. She really hoped it would grow back faster so she could braid—

You're stalling.

I don't want to be duchess today.

Too bad.

She reached under the furs to rub Alem's bare back. He grunted, burrowed deeper into the bedding.

"Get up, Alem."

He grunted again.

She smiled but prodded him more insistently. "Come on. We both have a lot to do today."

"The new boys can handle the horses," he mumbled from beneath the furs.

"You can't be here when the servants come to clean," Rina said.

He sighed and sat up, throwing aside the furs, shivering in his nakedness. "I thought it was getting warmer."

Rina smiled, eyes lingering on his body. "It is. A little."

A little more than two months since the Perranese had fled their shores, and spring was coming even later than usual, but the bitterest part of winter had passed. The wind off the sea was now merely cold instead of biting. The thaw wasn't far off. The castle folk—as the common people called Rina and her people—could sleep straight through until morning without the servants needing to sneak into their bedchambers in the middle of the night to stoke the fires. When spring came, it brought with it new duties for Rina. The trade roads would open. She needed to renew the relationships with her neighbors that her father had forged years ago. A hundred little tasks.

Dumo, help me. I don't know how to be a duchess.

Alem pulled on his breeches and boots. Shirt. Vest.

The heavy green cloak of thick, expensive material had been a gift from Rina. It clasped at the front with a silver buckle wrought in the shape of a horse's head. She'd meant it as a badge of honor. She'd been pretending, she realized, trying to make believe Alem was something he wasn't. The gap between stable master and noble was as wide as the sea.

No matter how I dress him up, he'll never be good enough for some people.

Alem kissed her on the cheek. "See you tonight."

"Not tonight," she said quickly.

He blinked at her, surprised.

"It's getting close. We need to sleep apart a few nights. Like last month."

"But why . . ." His eyes shot wide. "Oh! Yes, okay. Right."

He looked away as he blushed red, something Rina didn't think still possible after all of their nights together.

Young ladies of good birth were expected to abstain from sexual relations until marriage, as was only proper, of course. It was also the only sure way to prevent an unplanned child. But Rina's mother had been a pragmatic woman and had taken Rina aside once Rina had gotten her blood at age thirteen. She'd taught Rina to keep count of her days each month. It wasn't a foolproof system, but it was better than nothing.

"I might take a horse, then, and see my grandmother. The roads are clear enough now." He smiled. "I mean, if I have the duchess's permission."

She returned the smile. "Of course."

He kissed her again, on the lips this time. Her mouth opened to take his tongue, her arms going around him. They let go of each other a few seconds later, breathless.

"How many days?" Alem asked.

Rina laughed. "You'd better go now or you'll never escape."

Alem went to the full-length mirror on the wall and pulled it open on well-oiled hinges, revealing the narrow stairs behind it. Alem paused a second, shot Rina a final grin, then entered the secret passage, pulling the mirror shut behind him.

She went to the large cedar wardrobe across the room and threw the doors open. On the lower shelves sat the black armor the wizard Esthar Talbun had given her. She hadn't worn it since the slaughter in the castle and the streets of Klaar. It was still bloodstained from those she'd cut down with her own blade, still damaged and scorched from her battle with the other ink mage. The wardrobe was probably the wrong place for it. Maybe she should hide the armor under the bed or have it taken away.

She hated to think that she might need it again.

Her eyes shifted to the dresses in the wardrobe. She selected one of sapphire blue that buttoned all the way to the throat. No cleavage today. Long sleeves. Matching blue gloves. She'd told her personal servant she wanted matching gloves for every outfit she owned. The white glove was fine for bed, but people would think her odd going around with only one glove all the time.

She peeled the white glove off of her left hand, and as always her eyes were drawn to the ugly tattoo on her palm, a skeletal hand. Rina had come to think of her other tattoos as quite fetching, even making her look a bit exotic, especially the ones around her eyes. But the sight of the skeletal hand always turned her stomach, stole whatever warmth was left from Alem's kiss.

Rina quickly pulled on the blue gloves, dismissed the horrid tattoo from her mind.

She opened the door to an anteroom next to her bedchamber—a small place with a modest desk, a table, chairs, a room in which she could rest or read or converse quietly and privately with confidants. The warmth hit her immediately. The fire in this room had been recently stoked.

Her maidservant rose quickly from her stool in the corner, knitting needles and a half-made scarf in her hands. Lilly had a round, sweet face and wide hips. She'd just turned sixteen and was the daughter of one of the other castle servants. She'd been offered to Rina as a personal maid, and Rina had accepted without thinking. A duchess needed servants, right?

Normally, the maidservant would have entered Rina's bedchamber to help her dress, but Lilly held back, allowing Rina her privacy.

Because she knows about Alem. They all know. It's the worst-kept secret in the castle.

Lilly curtsied clumsily. "Some breakfast, milady?"

"Yes, and hot tea, but have it sent to my office," Rina said. "I have too much to do today to dawdle."

CHAPTER TWO

The four boys gathered around Alem in the castle stables. They were streaked with mud and stank of horse and boy sweat. One scratched his head incessantly. Probably fleas.

Was I as filthy as that when I was a stable boy?

Probably. Alem would address the subject of baths upon his return. It would help if the weather turned warm a little faster.

Alem pointed at the smallest stable boy, a lad of perhaps eleven. "You. Pip, isn't it? Saddle the white mare. I'm leaving for a few days on an errand."

"Yes, sir!" Pip flicked him a two-finger salute and scurried to obey.

Alem told the next two boys—twelve years old, a pair of twins named Hamm and Jak—to get about the business of feeding and watering the horses.

The last boy, Vohn, was fourteen, tall for his age and lanky, a shock of red hair and freckles, a gap between his front teeth.

"You're head stable boy, Vohn. You're in charge while I'm away," Alem said. "You up for it?"

Vohn grinned. "Yessir."

"Have you been cuffing the stable boys on the ear again?" Alem asked.

Vohn's grin dropped. "They don't always listen. My old man says a slap learns 'em quick."

"Don't do that anymore."

Vohn frowned.

"Look, if they give you any back talk you can cuff them," Alem said. "Otherwise, show a little patience. That's part of being a leader."

A nod and a shrug. "Yessir."

Pip brought the mare, and Alem mounted. "Back in a few days."

He trotted out of the stable.

It felt good to be on the back of a horse again. There were few things Alem could do well enough to claim expertise. He'd been practicing with the crossbow but was hardly a marksman or any kind of warrior. He had no formal education.

But he could ride better than anyone else he knew, nobleman or commoner. Alem could ride fast and ride well. He had a good rapport with horses, could get the most of them.

Mostly he just enjoyed it.

He spurred the mare faster, and it sped with rapid *clop-clops* across the cobblestones and through the narrow streets toward the front gate. Alem's green cloak flapped behind him. It was still early morning and cold, and the streets were mostly deserted. A few times he had to dart around a startled pedestrian, but Alem maneuvered the horse easily.

When he rounded a corner to the wide courtyard in front of the city's main gate, he slowed the mare to a walk. The gate stood open, light foot traffic coming and going as the makeshift repairs on the bridge continued. Alem fell in with the others going through the gate.

He stopped upon reaching the other side, standing up in the stirrups to take a look at the repairs. Thick wooden planks were being fitted into place across the gap in the stone. It had been Rina, during her duel with the other ink mage, who'd blasted the huge gap in the Long Bridge. Travel to and from Klaar always dwindled to a trickle during the thick of winter, but even those few intrepid trekkers who still traveled had been forced days or weeks out of their way to enter the city through the back gate. Rina had ordered the bridge fixed, but options had been limited.

"Craston," Alem called.

A little man with bright eyes and a pointed beard turned, waved when he saw it was Alem, then jogged over to stand next to the mare. He shook hands with Alem.

"How goes it?" Alem asked.

"I am ashamed," Craston said. "A wood span is all I can manage. The Long Bridge used to be a beautiful achievement. One of the man-made wonders of Helva."

When Rina had asked who had the best chance to repair the Long Bridge, everyone had mentioned the same name: Craston.

"You're the best stonemason in Klaar," Alem said.

"Yes," Craston agreed. "And the best carpenter. The best builder of any kind."

Alem could tell the man wasn't bragging, merely acknowledging a fact.

"But Klaar is not the world," Craston continued. "The Long Bridge was built by university engineers with precise mathematical measurements. Every arch, every supporting buttress and stone, fit one to the other exactly. I can bring the stone from the quarry and put it back together in my own way. And maybe the first caravan of trade wagons comes across and the whole thing falls down again."

Alem tsked. "I don't think Duchess Veraiin would like that."

"No, I think not."

"What's the answer?"

Craston grinned. "Duchess Veraiin sponsors me to attend the university in Tul-Agnon, of course. I learn the secrets of the ancient builders and return in ten years to fix the bridge."

Alem scratched his chin. "Some scheme that can be achieved sooner than a decade might be more acceptable to all involved."

Craston shrugged and gestured at the bridge where the workman labored. "As you can see, I can fill the gap with a wooden span, narrower than before, but strong enough. People can pass each other without problem, but wagons will have to go one at a time. We'll have to establish some rules—right-of-way, that sort of thing. It won't be as good as before. I am not satisfied, but I know my limits. I can do better with more time, but I have been told to hurry. The thaw is coming and that means traders arriving. The duchess wants what she wants."

Yeah, I know what you mean.

"So is your bridge open for business, Craston?"

"Two more days," Craston said. "But for Klaar's master of horse, I can make an exception. Tread carefully. The guardrails are not up yet."

"Thank you, Craston," Alem called over his shoulder as he galloped toward the bridge. "Good luck!"

Craston whistled loudly at his workers, and they stepped aside as Alem crossed the bridge. He looked down as he crossed the narrow, unfinished wooden span. The sight made him dizzy, the floor of the canyon nearly a mile down.

I'm glad the horse is more sure-footed than I am.

Once across the bridge, Alem spurred the horse into a run. There was still snow on the road, but it wasn't deep. If he kept to the road, he'd reach the village of Crossroads at the bottom of the mountain in a few hours, and then he'd turn south toward his grandmother's village of Hammish.

But he had one errand before seeing her.

He patted the parchment in his vest pocket to make sure it was still there. Rina had sent a runner who had found him in the barn. The runner had given it to Alem with Rina's instructions.

And so Alem rode hard for the Hammish hunting lodge to deliver a message.

CHAPTER THREE

Rina sat at the desk in her official office. The anteroom off of her bedroom was for meetings and informal chats with friends. The ducal reception hall was for meeting other heads of state and similar diplomatic occasions. The daily grind of running a castle and a city was handled in this office, the same room her father had used. The conquering Perranese general had also used it for a time. Klaar's coat of arms had been found in storage and returned to its place on the wall behind her desk.

Rina poured tea into a delicate cup from a pot and set it back on her desk. She sipped, closed her eyes. Warm.

Her secretary entered, and Rina's brief moment of calm evaporated. Time to get to business.

"Bruny to see you, milady," said Arbert.

Arbert was young and pale with sandy hair and thin bony fingers. The man had spent some small amount of time studying to be a scribe. The simple fact Arbert could read and write and had good penmanship was what had gotten him drafted as the duchess's personal secretary.

He kept a strict log of her schedule, scribbled notes when needed, and recorded the business of the day.

"Send her in, Arbert."

"Yes, milady."

"Arbert?"

"Milady?"

"About a hundred years ago, Lilly went to the kitchens to arrange some breakfast. Can you send somebody to check on that? If Lilly's wandered off again, just have them send somebody with something. Anything hot will do."

Arbert bowed slightly. "Of course, milady."

Arbert left, and a split second later, Bruny walked in and approached her desk. The woman was sturdy, hair streaked gray, ruddy cheeks.

Rina glanced at the brief schedule Arbert had organized for her. The first appointment of the day said *Bruny: Kitchen and pantry.*

"Good morning, Bruny."

Bruny dipped a brief curtsy, the effect somewhat spoiled by the woman's hands nervously wringing the apron she wore. "Milady."

"I understand you have some kind of complaint."

Bruny's eyes shot wide. "Oh *no*, milady! Not a complaint. Never a *complaint*. I love it here in the castle, of course."

Rina smiled tolerantly. "Perhaps *complaint* is not the right word. You want to bring a concern to my attention, yes?"

Bruny nodded. "That's it exactly, milady. An important concern."

"Go on, then."

"The winter stores have held well," Bruny reported. "But with the thaw coming, we obviously need to make the usual preparations."

Rina rubbed her eyes and muttered, "If I have to hear about the damn thaw one more time . . ."

"Milady?"

"Nothing." Rina pasted a fake smile to her face. "Please continue."

"Continue?" Bruny blinked. "Well . . . that's it."

Rina blinked back at her. "What's it?"

"As I said. Preparations. If we keep going as we are, we'll be fine another three weeks," Bruny explained. "Six if the thaw is delayed and we go on half rations."

One of Rina's eyebrows shot up impatiently. "And?"

"Well, we need to restock the pantry, milady."

"Oh. Well." Rina shrugged. "Fine. Restock it. You have my permission."

Bruny wrung the apron with renewed vigor. "Thank you kindly, milady, but it's not a matter of permission. It's a matter of money. I can make the lists, but the purchases . . ."

"Arbert!" Rina called.

The secretary rushed into the room, stood next to Bruny before Rina's desk. "Milady."

"Is there money in the treasury?"

"Certainly, milady."

"How much?"

"Should I . . . I mean, is that the sort of information . . ." Arbert's eyes darted to Bruny and back swiftly to Rina.

"Is there enough to replenish the castle pantry?"

"I would think so, yes, milady."

Rina looked at Bruny. "Problem solved."

"But . . . I mean . . . it's just . . ." Bruny had gone red, looked like she might dissolve into some kind of fit.

"It's okay, Bruny. Just explain yourself. Go slowly. Take a breath."

"Well, the Perranese were murdering savage bastards, of course— begging your pardon, milady." Bruny paused to look embarrassed. "But General Chen did retain a proper chamberlain. I mean, he was slain, naturally, when you took back the castle, not that we'd want one of those foreign sons of—"

Rina slapped a palm to her forehead. "A chamberlain. Of course."

"The chamberlain always knew which merchants offered the best prices," Bruny said. "And for some things he'd make them put in bids. I wouldn't even know where to begin."

Rina nodded. Giffen had been a devious traitor, but he had kept the castle running smoothly. The whole place had been operating with a skeleton crew since they'd taken the duchy back from the Perranese. Something would have to be done.

"Thank you for bringing this to my attention, Bruny. I'll take care of it."

Bruny nodded, backing away. "Milady."

Arbert followed her out of the room.

The door had barely closed behind them when it swung open again, an old man with a tray of food.

"Thank Dumo," Rina said. "What is it?"

"Eggs, milady. Sausages. Biscuits."

"I've not seen you before."

"Lots of new people coming to the castle for work," he said. "Word's out you're shorthanded."

"I don't suppose you'd like to be chamberlain."

The old man chuckled. "Such things are beyond my ken, milady." He set the tray on her desk and began to unfold a napkin.

Rina smiled. "I've been thinking the same thing all morning. Maybe if—"

A glint of metal. From beneath the napkin as the old man's hand came up fast.

Rina screamed, flinched back, and barely had enough time to tap into the spirit.

Immediately the world slowed. Or rather, it went along as it always did, but Rina's reflexes and perceptions were now lightning fast. She felt the Prime tattoo humming with power down her spine. Each of her other tattoos gave her a specific ability, but none of them would be possible without the Prime, the tattoo that allowed Rina to unlock the full potential within her, the one that let her tap into a well of spirit that fueled her powers.

The point of the dagger was a half inch from Rina's left eye when she dodged aside, the blade thrusting past her. She grabbed the old man's wrist and twisted, the strength of the bull tattoo kicking in. There was a sickening wet snap. The old man grunted, and the dagger clattered across the desk.

The old man was fast. His other hand came around quickly with a small gentleman's blade that had been hidden in the waistband of his breeches.

Rina blocked the strike easily, rose from her chair, and thrust her head forward.

The head butt flattened the old man's nose. Blood exploded from his nostrils.

Rina struck the man's chest with the heel of her hand. He flew back, landed hard, and skidded along the stone floor, his mouth working for breath.

Rina vaulted over the desk after him, her dress billowing and flapping.

The old man tried to sit up as he held the broken wrist tight up against his chest. The other hand had already dipped into his boot. It came out with yet another blade. He cocked it back to his ear, then let fly.

The stiletto tumbled end over end toward Rina's face. She snatched it midair and tossed it back without thinking.

It buried to the hilt in the center of the old man's forehead.

His head bounced off the stone floor as he sprawled back. One foot still twitched as the door flew open and Tosh rushed inside, Arbert behind him, peering with concern from the safety of the hallway.

Tosh held a short, broad-bladed sword in his hand, but his eyes shifted from Rina to the dead man on the floor. "Ah. You've handled it then."

CHAPTER FOUR

Alem climbed the steps of the front porch of the large hunting lodge that faced Hammish Lake. On the other side of the lake was the village of Hammish, where he'd visit his grandmother after completing his errand.

He'd been scared to death last time he'd been here, on the run from the Perranese with a duchess in exile by his side.

He knocked and waited.

And waited.

Alem was about to knock again when the door swung open, and he was greeted by a young blond woman, slightly built, fair skin with fresh pink in her cheeks, pretty. Her hair was mussed and she seemed slightly out of breath.

"Sorry to keep you waiting . . ." She looked Alem up and down. "Sir."

"Alem. Stable master of Klaar," Alem announced with mock haughtiness. "Here to call on Baron Hammish." He bowed deeply.

The maid's eyes widened. "Oh."

"Is that Alem?" came a voice from within the lodge.

Brasley Hammish appeared behind the maid, his hair equally tussled, loose white shirt unbuttoned halfway down his chest. "It *is* you! Elza, go fetch us some wine."

"I'm just here to deliver a message," Alem said quickly.

"You'd let me drink alone? I expect better manners from Klaar's master of horse," Brasley grinned crookedly, flashing perfect white teeth.

Elza half curtsied and turned to go fetch the wine. Alem saw that the laces up the back of her dress were half undone.

"I hope I'm not interrupting anything, Baron."

"Nonsense. I always have time for a friend," Brasley said. "And knock off this *baron* rubbish. We've been through too much together."

Alem smiled and followed Brasley into the lodge.

When Alem had first met Brasley, he'd been determined not to like the man. Brasley was spoiled, a rake, drank too much, and avoided anything resembling work, danger, or responsibility. But the man had a seemingly effortless charm that won everyone over eventually. Brasley could have a monk of Dumo, sworn to vows of silence, drunk and singing bawdy tavern songs in an hour.

The lodge's great hall was much as Alem remembered it. Weapons—mostly spears and bows for hunting—entirely covered one wall. An enormous bearskin rug covered the floor in front of the huge stone fireplace, where a modest blaze warmed the room. A chandelier of elk antlers hung low, but none of the candles was lit, a few oil lamps sufficing to illuminate the room.

Brasley gestured Alem to a stuffed chair covered with some animal hide, and Brasley flopped into a similar chair just as Elza brought a pitcher of wine and two goblets. She set them on a table between the two men before scurrying away.

"What's it like being baron?" Alem asked. "Does it suit you?"

Brasley frowned and shrugged, reached for his goblet of wine.

Brasley's uncle, father, and older brothers had all been killed defending Klaar during the Perranese invasion and subsequent occupation. The title of baron had fallen to him. The loss of his family had hit Brasley hard, and he'd handled it in his own typical way—by drinking and whoring until Alem had literally found the man in the gutter, picked him up, cleaned him off, and had one of the castle kitchen girls spoon chicken broth into him until he felt almost human again.

Brasley still drank too much and liked his women, but at least he paced himself now, walking the path to self-destruction instead of sprinting down it at full speed.

"With the inheritance I was at least able to pay off my gambling debts," Brasley said. "So I have something of a clean start. Not everyone gets a second chance. I suppose I should put my mind to making the most of it."

"You're not upset with Rina?"

Another shrug. Brasley sipped more wine, smacked his lips.

When it came time to drive the Perranese from Klaar, the gypsies had sent a small force to help Rina sneak into the castle and take it back. In return, Rina had promised the wandering gypsies a permanent homeland. Accomplishing this meant Rina had confiscated a small portion of the holding from three different barons—including from Brasley Hammish.

"She's duchess and within her rights," Brasley said. "And anyway it's not such a bad deal. The gypsies will manage the timber across the lake and send me a tithe. Also, Rina plans to reopen the silver mines up in the mountains, and I've been offered a share as compensation."

The abandoned mines were largely thought to be played out, but Alem decided not to bring that up. Instead he said, "What about the miners? I hear they won't go near the place because of the snow devils."

"Rina is sending hunting parties to drive them back into the wilderness. I'm sure it will all work out."

"Yeah." Alem hoped so, but even if it didn't, Brasley wasn't going to suffer. Anyway, it wasn't Alem's job to worry about the man.

Alem reached into his pocket and came out with the message, handed it to Brasley.

"Do you know what's in it?" Brasley asked.

"It's sealed."

"Yes. But do you know what's in it?"

Alem smiled. "The castle will have some visitors soon. I imagine Rina wants you there to class up the place and impress everyone."

"Uh-huh."

"Also the visitors include a delegation from the gypsies," Alem said. "You'll probably need to sign something with a big feathery quill and make proclamations of a new lifelong friendship between our two peoples and other such horse dung people like to hear at ceremonies."

"Dumo help me. Anything else?"

Alem spread his hands. "That's all I got."

Brasley ran a finger under the edge of the folded parchment, breaking the wax seal. He unfolded the message and began reading. "'Baron Brasley, your presence is requested at Castle Klaar to help welcome the gypsy blah, blah, blah.' Yes, you were right, Alem. Let's see what else Rina has to say." Brasley kept reading down the page. "Ah, here we go. 'Brasley, I wanted to give you fair warning. My sources tell me' . . ." Brasley's eyes moved more slowly down the page as he read to himself.

Brasley went pale before Alem's eyes.

"Are you okay?"

"I'm . . . I'm not sure," Brasley said.

"What is it?"

"The king is sending a delegation to Klaar. Some nonsense about renewing old ties and becoming closer allies with the crown's country cousins."

That was a surprise. Alem hadn't heard a thing about this. "Well, I mean, is that so bad?"

"One of the members of the delegation is Count Becham."

Alem searched his memory for the familiar name. Ah, yes. When Brasley had been in the capital, Rina had tasked him with getting her an audience with the king. Brasley decided the quickest way to do that was to seduce the daughter of one of the city's most important men. What was the woman's name again?

"Fregga," Brasley said, reading Alem's face.

Alem snapped his fingers. "That's it! I'd have thought of it if you'd given me another second. Do you think Becham being part of the delegation has something to do with her?"

"She's pregnant."

Alem threw back his head and laughed loudly.

Brasley shot him an angry look. "You think that's funny?"

Alem sobered immediately. "Sorry." Now that Alem thought about it, the situation could be quite serious. Men had been murdered for less.

Brasley drained the wine from his goblet, grabbed the pitcher, and filled it again.

"What are you going to do?"

"I'm doing it," Brasley said, draining the goblet again.

"That seems like a short-term solution at best," Alem said.

Brasley returned to the parchment, read further.

"It might not be so bad," Alem said. "Marrying Count Becham's daughter puts you in powerful company."

Brasley's eyes came up from the parchment to meet Alem's. "There's more."

Poor bastard. Still, Brasley made his own bed. Now he has to lie in it.

"The delegation also includes Sir Ferris Gant."

The name meant nothing to Alem.

"Sir Ferris Gant is King Pemrod's grandnephew and only living heir. Which means he's heir to the *throne*," Brasley said. "Pemrod wants to wed him to Rina Veraiin."

Alem blinked and swallowed hard. "Oh."

It was Brasley's turn to laugh at Alem, but he didn't. He simply sighed in a commiserating sort of way and said, "I'm sorry."

Alem nodded, tried to summon a weak smile, and failed. Something cold and leaden formed in the pit of his stomach.

What did you think, thicko? That you'd marry a duchess, have children, and grow old together?

Alem reached for the other goblet. "I think I will have that drink after all."

CHAPTER
FIVE

"It was a mistake to kill him," Rina said.

Servants had already taken the body away, and Rina stood, hands clasped behind her back, watching the maid scrub the blood off the floor.

"You feel bad about it?" Tosh leaned against the wall behind her, arms crossed and looking sour.

"I feel bad that now we can't *question* him," Rina said.

"Good point. I suppose we could take a guess who'd bribe a servant to kill you."

"He was too fast to be a servant," Rina said. "Even for an old man. Some kind of professional, I think. If I hadn't . . ."

If she hadn't tapped into the spirit, she was about to say, but she didn't want to discuss such things in front of the maid. There were a few—Alem, Brasley, Tosh—who knew about her tattoos and her powers, but it wasn't something she talked about openly. And only Alem knew the complete horror of the skeletal hand tattoo on her palm.

Rina had unburdened herself to him one tearful night. The tattoo was a mistake, a constant source of guilt, a reminder of the consequences of a hasty decision.

"Servant or professional, does it make a difference?" Tosh asked. "We know who sent him."

"Giffen," Rina said.

The man who betrayed Klaar to the Perranese. The bastard who'd murdered her father and ordered the execution of her mother in front of Rina's own eyes.

"If he's still hanging around, that's bad," Tosh said. "And if he has people helping him and hiding him, that's worse."

"And he apparently has resources if he can afford to hire an assassin," Rina said grimly.

"What should we do about it?"

"What *can* we do?" Rina asked.

"Not much," Tosh admitted. "I'm grateful you made me captain of the guard, but I don't have a lot to work with. Old men and boys mostly. We're spread pretty thin."

Putting Klaar's army back together after the departure of the Perranese had been something of a mess. Many had been killed during the initial invasion. The surviving soldiers had been organized into labor gangs, and many had become malnourished and had perished. When the remaining soldiers had at last been freed and nursed back to health, there were barely enough troops and officers to man the walls, walk the watch, and rotate shifts.

Tossing Tosh back into the army as one of the enlisted men seemed a poor way to thank him for all he'd done, but making him an officer would likely rankle the other officers. She remembered her father talking at length about military code and officers not socializing with the common grunts. It had all seemed unbearably dull at the time.

You'll need to know these things, Rina, her father's voice echoed in her mind.

Making Tosh captain of the castle guard seemed a good way to reward him with a cushy job. What was there to do, really? Make sure there was a man standing at every entrance to hold a spear and look official, right?

Apparently there's more to it than that. Somebody needs to keep the assassins out.

Still, she was glad about her decision to give Tosh the job. She wanted at least one trustworthy person close by who knew how to handle a sword. Alem was as brave as any man, Dumo bless him, but he was no swordsman. Although he did seem to be getting better with his crossbow.

Rina sighed. "Barely an army, no chamberlain, not enough men for a proper castle guard. I don't seem to be duchessing very well, Tosh."

"It probably takes practice."

"Well, I hope I get the hang of it before the whole city falls down around our ears."

Tosh cleared his throat, scratched behind one ear, and shuffled his feet.

Rina raised an eyebrow. "You want to say something?"

"Oh . . . I don't know."

"Out with it."

"I can't raise an army for you," Tosh said. "But I might have an idea how to solve your other problems. Although as solutions go, these might seem a bit . . . uh . . . creative."

"Go on then," Rina said. "Let's be creative."

◆ ◆ ◆

The area of Back Gate had come alive in recent weeks. Darshia supposed the closure of the Long Bridge was the reason. With the bridge and front gate useless, some of the more intrepid tradesmen and merchants had elected to take the long way around, up the Small Road to Back Gate.

For years the abandoned buildings of Back Gate had been home to the city's criminals, beggars, and outcasts. The Wounded Bird brothel had been the only honest place of business in the neighborhood, but now a fledgling market had sprung up among the desolation.

I hope it's not just something temporary until they fix the Long Bridge, Darshia thought. *I like the idea of Back Gate getting a second chance.*

It was a cold day, but not *so* cold. She wore her heavy cloak open and thrown back so people could see the leather armor underneath. She let her hand rest on the hilt of her sword as she walked. When people passed—men and women both—they nodded to her with respect.

Respect. It was something new, and she liked it.

I'm not the tall redheaded whore with the big tits anymore. I'm . . . what?

She wasn't sure. Darshia and Prinn and the other girls had talked about it. Most of the ones who'd taken up arms against the Perranese agreed—the ones who'd lived through the battle anyway—weren't going back to whoring. Never again. A few did go back. The idea of a man's cock inside them was more appealing than sticking a blade in his belly and watching his guts spill out. A couple of the girls didn't want to follow either path and had packed their things and vanished into the night.

That left fourteen women, good with swords, taking charge of their own destiny.

She hoped. It was a plan anyway.

Darshia entered the Wounded Bird, and a half dozen faces turned to consider her a moment before going back to the business of drinking and whoring. Even this early in the afternoon, there were always at least a few customers. Darshia didn't recognize the new girls flirting with them.

Mother is already replacing us. Business is business, I guess. I wonder if the new cook is any good.

Since Tosh had taken his position as captain of the castle guard, the Wounded Bird had gone through three cooks. Two simply couldn't measure up, the food they'd prepared barely edible. The third thought freebies with the girls were a perk of his new job. Bune and Lubin had disabused the man of this notion—with their fists—then thrown him and his belongings into the snow.

"Darshia."

Darshia turned her head to see Prinn coming down the stairs.

"Did you find a place?" Prinn asked.

Darshia frowned. "Not a place big enough for all of us. Not that we could afford."

Mother had been generous. She'd told them they could stay in their old rooms until they'd found another place to live. For a while. The women had thought they might find someplace to all live together, just like at the Wounded Bird . . . but they'd be their own bosses this time.

"Tosh is up there talking to Mother now," Prinn said. "He might have a solution to our problem. It's . . . interesting."

"Tell me."

Prinn shook her head. "Better if Tosh explains."

"Fine," Darshia said. "I'm open to anything. As long as I'm not working for Mother anymore."

Prinn grinned. "Hold on to that thought."

CHAPTER SIX

They day had begun with the killing of an assassin.

It hadn't gotten better.

Running a castle was a huge pain in the ass. As a spoiled girl, Rina had simply enjoyed living in the castle and gave no thought to how the laundry was done or who prepared the meals or fixed the damage on the roof after a long winter or how the servants were paid or what needed to be done to prepare for important guests. She was abysmal at all this and completely fed up with being a duchess.

Rina sat at her desk and massaged her temples.

I need a goblet of wine. No, a hot bath.

Okay, both.

A knock on the door. It creaked open, and Arbert stuck his head inside. "Tosh to see you, milady?"

Rina nodded. "It's okay."

Arbert stepped aside. The door swung wide, and Tosh entered. A handsome middle-aged woman followed him in. She wore a fine dress.

Her hair pulled back into a tight bun. Both of them stopped in front of her desk. The woman didn't curtsy. Somehow it didn't fit her. Instead, she clasped her hands in front of her and offered Rina a half bow.

"Thank you, Tosh," Rina said. "If you'll excuse us, please."

The expression on Tosh's face made it clear he hadn't expected to be dismissed. "Oh. Yes. Of course."

He bowed perfunctorily and backed out of the room, pulling the door shut behind him.

"Would you like to sit?" Rina asked.

"Thank you," Mother said.

She pulled up a chair, sat with her hands in her lap, waited for Rina to start.

"Tosh says everyone calls you Mother," Rina said. "I hope you understand I need more than that."

Mother nodded. "My name is Stasha Benadicta."

"An exotic name," Rina said. "The Scattered Isles?"

"The Red City," Mother—Stasha—said. "Obviously."

Obviously—the Red City was the only place of civilization in the Scattered Isles, a place of trade and culture. The other inhabitants of the Scattered Isles were all primitive savages. At one time, the Isles had been united, but some catastrophe had occurred in the ancient past. Only the Red City remained, a feeble remembrance of a once sophisticated and mighty empire.

"You're far from home," Rina said.

A smiled flickered briefly to life on Stasha's face then died away almost as fast. "My husband was the fifth of five sons. He asked for his inheritance early, determined to travel as far away from home as possible and make his fortune. He died our first winter here."

"That's when you started the brothel?" Rina asked.

Stasha let out a long sigh, shook her head. "No. There were a few false starts. I finally discovered there were girls who would rather whore for me than for some man. The Wounded Bird was a safe haven for them, in an odd sort of way. But I circulated the rumor I was running the place for some man. That seemed easier for everyone to believe, and most left us alone, thinking they'd have to answer to some mysterious stranger."

"Tosh thinks you might make a good chamberlain."

Stasha shrugged.

"We're all busy people," Rina said. "There's no time to spare for false modesty."

"I know budgets and organization," Stasha said. "I know the local merchants and can get the best prices. I can run the kitchens and the maids, the whole household. I can't claim to know everything about a castle, but begging your pardon, I think I can do a bit better than what's happening now."

"I see."

"I don't mean to give offense."

"None taken," Rina said.

"Tosh told me what you needed. I can do it."

"I know," Rina said. "But there's more. I need somebody I can trust."

The silence stretched between them.

"I knew your father," Stasha said. "I organized the effort to avenge his death. If I can't serve him, I will serve his daughter."

Rina stood, bowed, and said, "I accept your service gladly, Lady Chamberlain."

♦ ♦ ♦

Darshia and Prinn led the other women into the barracks. It was a floor below the castle's main level but not quite at the depth of the dungeons. Low ceilings. Two rows of narrow bunks, ten on each side, a wide path down the middle. A wooden chest at the end of each bunk for personal possessions. Dim embers glowing in a sunken brazier provided the room's warmth.

At the Wounded Bird, each of them had had a private room. For obvious reasons. It would be odd for all of them to sleep in a group like this.

But I'm not a whore anymore, Darshia thought. *I'm a soldier.*

Was that even true? She hadn't signed on to any army, hadn't taken any oaths. Tosh had told them they were charged with guarding the castle and protecting the duchess. It wasn't ceremonial. Darshia and Prinn and the others weren't here to be ornamental. Tosh had made it clear. There were real dangers, even here in the castle.

That's soldiering as far as I'm concerned.

Prinn sighed, looking around the barracks. "What do you think?"

Darshia tossed her pack onto the nearest bunk. "I think it's home."

CHAPTER
SEVEN

Alem and Brasley rode side by side north up the mountain from the village of Crossroads. They'd stopped to check in on Alem's grandmother and endured the gossip of the small fishing village on the north shore of Lake Hammish.

How can people have so many different stories about fish?

Listen to yourself, thicko. Alem from the stables. When did you get so worldly?

He rubbed his temples again and moaned.

"First hangover?" Brasley asked.

"And last," Alem said. "I'm *never* doing that again."

Brasley threw his head back and laughed loudly.

"Now why the hell is that so funny?" Alem asked.

"Dumo keeps a long list of famous last words," Brasley said. "And *never again* after a long night of drinking is in the top three."

"What's number one?"

"I'll tell you when you're older."

Alem frowned. "Hilarious."

Upon hearing that a royal suitor was en route to Klaar to sweep Rina off her feet, Alem had decided to try the Brasley method of problem avoidance, which involved crawling into a bottle and diving deeper until you found the bottom. They had ended up drinking long into the night, signing the filthiest tavern songs Alem had ever heard.

Around dawn there had been some earnest vomiting.

And the worst part is that I'm just right back to where I started anyway. Did I really think I had a chance? Of course Rina will marry somebody important, not some jerk from the stables.

"He could be hideously ugly," Brasley said. "And then maybe Rina would send him packing, eh?"

"It doesn't matter."

"No?"

"If it's not this guy, it'll be somebody else," Alem said. "Rina's a young, unmarried duchess. Do the math."

"You've got a point there. Sorry."

"What about you?" Alem asked. "Are you going to marry Fregga?"

"I've been thinking about that," Brasley said. "I mean, think about who I am. A drunkard, a gambler, a womanizer. Who'd want that for a son-in-law?"

"An excellent point," Alem said.

"Well—*ahem*—yes. The point actually being that it's likely old Becham doesn't want me to marry his daughter at all. He probably just wants some sort of compensation, a bag of gold or something. I mean, it happens all the time, doesn't it? They pack the girl off to have the baby with some distant relatives and give it to a farmer to raise or something and then the girl returns home after some extended traveling to see the world and everything is back to normal."

"You're kidding yourself."

"I just want a little hope to hang my hat on," Brasley said. "You don't have to throw brutal reality in my face."

"I am too hung over to throw anything except up."

Brasley laughed. "Look, your problem isn't so bad really. You'll feel bad for a time, but there are other women. I promise you, there are *lots* of other women out there. I mean, okay, they're not all duchesses, but that's—"

Brasley reined in his horse suddenly, looking off into the woods. "Who are they?"

Alem followed Brasley's gaze and caught the movement, a flash of metal. He recognized the style of armor, the overlapping bands of metal, the helms that flared wide.

"Perranese!"

The two Perranese warriors saw they'd been spotted and turned their horses into the woods, the beasts breaking into a run.

Brasley spurred his horse into motion. "After them!"

Alem blinked. "After them? Run *toward* the men with swords?"

"If they're spies, we've got to shut them up." Brasley called back to him.

Alem rode after him.

What could spies tell? The details of the Long Bridge repairs. That more traffic was coming up the Small Road. Was that useful information for another Perranese invasion force? Maybe. It didn't matter. Brasley was right. On the chance they knew something, they needed to be silenced.

Alem leaned low and rode hard, ducking tree branches. He was a much better rider than Brasley, and he caught up and passed him in a few seconds, keeping the two Perranese in sight ahead of him. The forest grew thicker, and Alem deftly dodged trees as he closed on the warriors.

He reached behind him for the light crossbow hanging from his saddle and brought it around one-handed. He'd practiced shooting the thing from horseback, but he hadn't practiced reloading. He'd get one shot.

Alem aimed, held his breath, tried to compensate for the bouncing motion of the galloping horse, and squeezed the trigger.

The bolt flew and struck one of the Perranese warriors in the meaty part of the thigh. The man screamed and tumbled from the saddle.

Alem rode past the fallen man a second later. He turned his head to grin back at his work, absurdly proud of himself.

Okay, yeah, that was lucky, but the practice paid off too. Maybe I'll enter the crossbow competition at the spring fair and—

When he turned back, he barely had enough time to get his hands up to keep the low hanging branch from smacking him in the face. He was knocked backward out of the saddle and landed hard in the snow.

Alem lay groaning as Brasley reined in his horse next to him. "Anything broken?"

"I don't think so," Alem said. "The other one?"

"Too far ahead."

He got away. I was gloating over a lucky crossbow shot and got my stupid self knocked off my horse, and the other one got away.

"I wounded one," Alem said. "We can take him back for questioning."

"That's something at least," Brasley said.

They retrieved Alem's horse and backtracked to the spot where the Perranese warrior had fallen. They found him sprawled awkwardly, head cocked at an odd angle, neck broken.

"Well." Brasley sighed. "That's a damn shame."

CHAPTER EIGHT

Prinn lived by one governing thought: Whenever life seems to be going surprisingly well, just wait ten seconds and everything will go back to shit like normal.

A warm, safe place to sleep in the castle. A good job that wasn't whoring. Respect and friends. All too good to be true, obviously. And so she wasn't really surprised when the man came along with the message, both an offer and a threat. She'd been given instructions and warned that if she didn't follow them to the letter, then the worst possible people would take great delight in carrying out the threat.

On the other hand, if she was a good girl and did what she was told, she'd be given a bag of silver and a horse, and she could take off and start life anew wherever she pleased.

It wasn't difficult to decide which option she liked better.

Prinn padded down the stone steps to the dungeon, where she found the little jailer's room. There was no jailer at the moment, and as soon as they'd found somebody trustworthy, they wouldn't have to send one of Tosh's women down to guard the place.

Tosh's women. That's what the castle folk called the new female guards. *We really do need to think of a better name,* Prinn thought.

No. It won't matter. I'll be gone.

She knocked once and then entered.

Viriam looked up from where she was sitting on the jailer's bunk against the wall. She was sharpening a dagger with a whetstone. The woman had plain brown hair and bland skin but also the large soft curves that many of the Wounded Bird's patrons preferred. Those curves had lost some of their softness since she'd taken up the sword.

"I thought Carrine was my relief," Viriam said.

"She's got a man in town," Prinn said. "I'm doing her a favor."

"Sit back and prepare yourself for six hours of solid boredom," Viriam told her. "Not sure why we have to guard this door. It can't be opened from the outside."

"Do you want to take that chance?"

Viriam shrugged. "I guess not. Have fun."

Prinn counted to a hundred after Viriam left before shoving the bunk aside and depressing the stone on the floor that triggered the unlocking mechanism. There was a dull *clunk* from the depths of the dungeon, and a four-foot-high door swung open in the stone wall.

Three men emerged. Two were ruddy and unshaven, short and stout, greasy hair and daggers hanging from belts. One carried a large canvas sack. The third man, obviously the leader, was a few inches taller, with a braided black beard and a receding hairline. He wore an eye patch, and the way his other eye rolled around in his skull gave Prinn the creeps. She knew from the description that this was Garth.

"Lord Giffen sends his compliments," Garth said.

"I don't want his compliments," Prinn said. "I just want this over with."

"It soon will be," Garth assured her. "And as promised, no harm will come to your aunt or cousins."

"And the money?"

A snorting laugh from Garth. He reached into a satchel slung over his shoulder, came out with a heavy bag that clinked with coin and tossed it to Prinn. "You brought something from her?"

Prinn handed him three strands of black hair. "From her brush."

"Good enough." Garth took the strands and nodded to the henchman who carried the canvas sack.

He carefully set the sack on the ground, opened it, and lifted out a large earthenware pot. The lid was sealed with wax. The henchman set the pot on the floor and then backed away quickly as if it were a coiled snake.

Garth knelt next to the pot and flipped open a small gentleman's blade. He cut open the wax seal and removed the lid. He dropped the hairs into the pot and then slowly stood and backed away.

At first nothing happened.

Prinn wasn't sure what to expect. All she knew was that they were all standing around looking at a pot.

A black glow grew from the open pot.

Black light? Is that even possible? It's dark and glowing at the same time.

Prinn blinked and flinched. The light was hard to look at. It hurt her head.

An oily black smoke rose from the pot, swirled, and began to take form.

Prinn took in a sharp breath. She tried to back up, but something stopped her, and she realized her back was already against the wall. Her eyes darted to the door. She contemplated making a run for it, but her feet were frozen to the floor.

The oily smoke congealed and became nearly solid for a split second. It was long enough for Prinn to glimpse it.

A huge figure emerged, its head almost touching the ceiling. Long arms with gnarled claws. Its face was stretched out, lower jaw showing curved tusks, horns like a ram sprouting from its head. Its eyes seemed to leach away all light and warmth.

A palpable and immediate dread filled the room.

Prinn opened her mouth to scream but nothing came out. Terror's cold grip immobilized her. She had the overwhelming urge to pee and was surprised when she didn't. Her arms and legs felt numb and leaden.

As quick as the creature had formed, it dissolved back into roiling smoke and bled away beneath the door and into the castle.

Prinn's heart beat so hard her chest hurt.

"The stalker demon is unleashed and off on its fell errand," Garth said grimly.

Prinn trembled.

Dumo save us. What have I done?

EPISODE TWO

CHAPTER NINE

A knock.

"Come in," Rina said.

Arbert entered the private anteroom adjacent to Rina's bedchamber. He carried an armload of large, rolled parchments. "I wasn't sure which map you wanted, milady," he said, "so I brought them all."

"That's fine, Arbert. Bring them to the table."

Alem and Brasley gathered around the table. Rina sorted the maps until she found the one she wanted. She unrolled it and looked at Alem. "Show me."

"Here." Alem tapped a spot on the map just north of Crossroads. He trailed his finger west across the map. "And they fled in this direction."

Rina *tsked*. "A pity you couldn't get the other one."

Alem cleared his throat and shrugged awkwardly. "Sorry."

"You know I didn't mean it like that."

"Perhaps some refreshment while we discuss this?" Brasley suggested.

Lilly leapt up from her stool in the corner. "I could fetch a pot of tea, milady."

Brasley cleared his throat pointedly. "I think we could all use something a little stronger, don't you?"

Lilly's eyes shifted from Brasley to Rina.

"A pitcher of wine," Rina said. "A big one."

The maid dipped a quick curtsy then scurried away.

"What's that area here?" Alem tapped the area west of Crossroads. "I came home south of there when I returned from our little vacation. It's not part of Klaar. Does some other duchy claim it?"

"Some scattered flatland villages," Rina said. "Unclaimed, I think. There's nothing much of value there. A lord might claim it for the farmlands. On the other hand, a lord might ignore it if he didn't want a bunch of extra peasants to feed."

"I can't imagine why the Perranese would want to go there, but that's the way the rider was headed," Alem said.

Rina tapped a different part of the map. "Or he could have doubled back and turned north up past Trapper Village and on to the coast. If the Perranese have landed another force, it would make sense that they'd send out scouts."

"You've got coast watchers," Brasley pointed out. "Have any of them seen anything?"

"No, actually," Rina admitted. "And I sent Zin up to spy on Ferrigan's Tower, but all seems well."

"Who's Zin?" Alem asked.

"The falcon." Rina's hand came up automatically to the tattoos around her eyes. Most of the castle dwellers were used to seeing them by now, the tiny feathers at the corners of her eyes like dark teardrops and the tight, neatly printed runes under each eye like garishly applied makeup. New people still did double takes, not sure what they were seeing.

The tattoo bound the falcon to her, a familiar. She could see through its eyes.

"You named the falcon Zin?" Brasley looked amused.

"No. It's his name."

"How do you know that?" Alem asked.

"I—" She realized she hadn't thought about it before. "I don't know. One day I just knew his name. Look, the point is that I sent him to check the tower, and we haven't heard anything from the coast watchers. I think we can rule out problems coming from that direction."

"Can we?" Brasley asked. "I mean, we don't really know *anything*, do we? There are miles and miles of coastline. That rider could have gone off in any direction once we lost sight of him. He could be scouting for an invasion force, or he could be a deserter who was left behind. We can guess and wonder, but we *know* nothing."

The hard truth hung in the air a moment.

He's right, Rina thought. *If Father were here, he'd know what to do. But it's just me.*

"What would you suggest?" Rina asked.

Brasley pointed at himself, eyes going wide. "Me? I have no idea. Did I accidentally give you the impression I was helpful? I'm just waiting for your girl to return with the wine."

Alem scowled at him. "At least he admits it."

"Okay, shut up, the both of you," Rina said. "I'm sending a dozen men to sweep south and west through the forest in the direction the solider was fleeing—and *yes*, I know he could have turned off in any direction, but I don't have enough men to search the entire duchy. Anyone object to that?"

Alem and Brasley looked at each other and then shook their heads.

"Okay, then," Rina said.

"I know the spot. I can lead the men on the search if you want," Brasley said.

"You most certainly will not." Rina offered him a tight smile. "We have guests coming. Remember?"

Brasley suddenly looked ill. "Oh yeah."

Lilly entered, carrying a tray with a pitcher and goblets. "Sorry it took so long, milady."

"Never mind," Rina told her. "Just set the tray over—"

Rina gasped, stepping back. All heads turned. Brasley muttered a startled oath and drew his sword.

The oily black smoke loomed over Lilly and formed briefly into a hideous shape, a black figure with tusks and horns, long gangly arms, fingers ending in razor claws. For a split second, the smoke creature looked almost solid.

Lilly looked up and dropped the tray, terror seizing her. She opened her mouth to scream.

The grotesque figure dissolved into smoke again and plunged into the maid's open mouth.

"Lilly!" Rina screamed.

Lilly went rigid as the dark smoke filled her up. Her eyes went completely black, a dark light boiling out from within her. The maid's expression changed from terror to fury in an eyeblink.

She tossed her head back and vomited the dark smoke into the air.

The smoke circled the room once then headed straight for Alem.

"Shit!" Alem threw himself on the floor and rolled under the table.

The smoke turned abruptly, split into two streams, and stabbed deep into Arbert's eyes like black daggers. His scream turned into a guttural growl as his eyes turned black, his face a savage mask.

Lilly and Arbert advanced on Brasley, growling like animals, hands up to claw him.

"I'm sorry, Rina, I'm going to have to kill your maid," Brasley shouted.

"It's not her anymore!" Rina said.

Brasley thrust his rapier through Lilly's gut. The strike had no effect. The wild maid drove the blade deeper as she pressed forward trying to grab Brasley, teeth snapping to bite him.

"She won't die!" Brasley backed against the table, brought a foot up to kick her away.

Arbert leapt at him from the other direction, but Alem slammed into him with a flying tackle, both going over in a heap.

Rina tapped into the spirit and in less than a heartbeat was across the room, where her rapier hung on the wall. She drew the sword and spun, swinging in one smooth motion.

The blade passed through the smoke creature, leaving swirling eddies in its wake.

A black hand formed solid and latched onto her wrist with strength as cold as iron. Rina gasped in surprise.

It's fast!

When tapped into the spirit, Rina had full control of her body, every reflex. The lightning-bolt tattoos on her ankles made her faster than a running horse. In battle, the quickest, strongest warrior seemed no more than a stumbling toddler to her. But this smoke monster was every bit as quick as she was.

She swung her sword at the hand holding her. The blade bit deep, and she felt resistance as if striking flesh, but the resistance immediately vanished as the hand melted back into smoke.

It has to turn solid to get me, but then it's vulnerable.

She swung the sword wildly in front of her to keep the thing at bay.

Across the room, Brasley and Alem struggled to fend off Lilly and Arbert. Rina's maid and secretary had become mindless killing machines. Arbert was on top of Alem on the floor, clawing at his face and trying to bite him. Alem had a forearm jammed in Arbert's throat, trying to push him away.

Brasley managed to kick Lilly off of his blade, and she stumbled back. He swung again, cutting a deep gash across her cheek. She didn't flinch, seemed not even to feel it.

"Any guesses how to kill them?" Brasley shouted. "I'm open to suggestions."

Rina had no time for Brasley's question. Two hands formed solid from the smoke and latched on to her throat, the claws digging into the flesh of her neck. She felt hot blood flow and trickle down her back. Her skin sizzled where the claws pierced her skin.

Some part of her felt panic, but she locked it away.

She swung the rapier, but only the creature's hands were solid, and she didn't have an angle to strike at them. She dropped the sword and grasped the hands choking her, using the strength of the bull tattoo to pry away the fingers around her throat.

Rina couldn't budge the hands at all. The monster was every bit as strong as she was. Stronger.

Lilly screamed animal fury and leapt at Brasley again.

Brasley thrust high, the tip of his rapier sinking into her left eye. He drove it in another six inches.

One of Brasley's strikes finally seemed to have some impact.

Lilly went rigid, mouth working soundlessly. She slid off of Brasley's blade and hit the floor with a thud. A thin tendril of black smoke oozed from her wounded eye and drifted away into nothingness.

Brasley spun and rushed to Alem. He kicked Arbert off him, and the secretary rolled onto his back, hissing up at Brasley. Arbert's eyes seemed to drink the light and give back some impossible black glow.

Brasley stabbed him through one eye, driving his sword tip to the back of the man's skull.

Arbert arched his back violently in a shock of pain, froze that way for a moment before going limp. Brasley withdrew his blade, and again the smoke rose from the wound like the remnant of some black soul.

Rina tried again to pry the hands away from her throat, but it was impossible. He mouth worked for breath. She felt her face going hot, and her vision began to go dark, bright dots flashing in front of her eyes.

Since she was tapped into the spirit, she had perfect control, perfect calm. *I can't breathe. I have maybe twenty seconds left. Do something. Anything.*

She peeled the glove off her left hand and tossed it aside.

Rina grabbed one of the monstrous hands holding her throat and held on tight.

The skeletal tattoo made contact and Rina's entire body exploded with dark energy. She felt herself fill up with darkness, her insides painted with some greasy coating. A hard, cold knot grew in her chest. It spread like ice through her limbs, to the tips of her fingers and toes. She felt sick, stomach pinching, mouth going dry with some bitter taste.

Rina was vaguely aware of Alem and Brasley yelling to her, but their voices seemed distant, trying to reach her through some cottony haze.

Darkness swallowed her eyes, and she felt herself falling down an endless dark pit and finally plunging into cold and formless depths, screaming, trying to claw her way back, kicking against the currents that pulled her down below the surface of reality.

CHAPTER TEN

Jariko's eyes popped open. It took him a moment to realize he was on the floor of his room in the shabby inn, the side of his face scraping against the rough, unpolished wood.

He sat up and blinked, rubbed something red and sticky beneath his nose. Blood. It had flowed down into the braided white moustaches that fell to the middle of his chest. The old wizard was thin and bony, so he wore extra layers of fur against the cold, which had helped cushion his fall when he'd passed out.

He was aware of somebody pounding on the door, Prullap's voice shouting for his attention. "Jariko! Jariko, what's happening?"

Jariko rose on unsteady legs and stumbled to the door, slid the bolt back, and swung it open.

Prullap rushed inside, puffing, round face red. "I heard you scream. I was about to call soldiers to come knock the door down."

"My bond with the stalker demon was cut abruptly," Jariko said.

Prullap nodded. "That would do it. You're okay?"

Jariko stumbled back across the room and plopped down onto a hard wooden chair. "Shaken but fine. The demon has been destroyed."

"And what of its mission?" Prullap asked. "Is the duchess dead?"

Jariko closed his eyes and tried to recall what he felt before the link was severed. He'd summoned the demon and so had a bond with it, but it wasn't like a bond with a familiar, nothing so deep or permanent. He couldn't see through the demon's eyes or hear through its ears. The wizard could get a sense of it, though, the gist of emotions and feelings. What had the demon felt before it had been destroyed?

Fear. Confusion. Pain.

Failure.

Jariko sighed. "Rina Veraiin lives."

Prullap *tsked*, scratched absently at his neatly trimmed black beard. "I suppose the commander will have to be informed."

Jariko knew what the younger wizard was thinking. With the stalker demon's failure, Commander Tchi might want them to try something else, something more up close and personal.

Something *dangerous*.

Jariko and Prullap had heard the reports of Duchess Veraiin's powers.

An ink mage. I'd thought such things had faded into legend until I met Ankar. He was powerful, yet the duchess killed him.

The two Perranese wizards were formidable, but who could guess what the girl might be capable of? Jariko wanted nothing to do with her. He wished he'd never crossed the sea to this frozen shit hole. Not that he'd had a choice. Jariko served at the pleasure of the emperor, like everyone else.

Jariko stood, his knees creaking. The weather the past week had begun to warm, but he still hated this place.

"Come," he told Prullap. "Let's see if we can talk some sense into our young Commander Tchi."

Commander Tchi stood at the second-story window of the small room he'd taken as his office and watched the wizards come, crunching through the dirty snow. Their posture and demeanor indicated they were bringing a headache. He was inclined to dislike and distrust their sort anyway. Wizards were schemers. At least that was their reputation.

Tchi's room was in the village's town hall, the largest—and the only two-story—building in the village. He and his officers had taken the building for themselves after the wizards had blasted open the gate to the village's palisade. The gate had been repaired, and Tchi and his men had ridden out the long winter in relative—*very* relative—comfort. Better than bivouacking on the open plain and being constantly lashed by the bitter wind.

The minor lord who'd led the defense of the village had been executed, his men put into chains. The rest of the population had been routinely subjugated. As ordered, Tchi had subdued the flatlands west of Klaar.

Not that it mattered.

When a breathless rider had arrived to say the Perranese garrison at Klaar had fallen, Tchi had realized his efforts had been for nothing. The invasion had failed, and the Perranese had lost their foothold in Helva. Tchi and his men couldn't make it back to Harran's Bay to escape with the rest of the army.

With nowhere else to go, they'd stayed put, eventually making contact with their agents who were still at large in Klaar.

Tchi watched the wizards enter the building. A moment later, one of his junior officers ushered them into the room. The wizards nodded their heads, not quite a bow but an adequate show of respect.

"Your spell was successful?" Tchi asked.

"The summoning was flawless," Jariko said. "And the demon was delivered to your agents in Klaar without incident."

Tchi narrowed his eyes. "But?"

The two wizards looked at each other, and finally Jariko said, "The stalker demon was destroyed. Before it could kill its prey."

Tchi frowned. "I see."

Prullap cleared his throat. "I've been discussing it with Jariko, and he agrees." Prullap shot the older wizard a look.

Jariko nodded.

"Jariko agrees," Prullap continued, "that it's again time to broach the subject of withdrawing from the field."

"That's what you think?" Tchi said.

"Yes."

"And Jariko agrees?"

"Yes."

"And by *withdrawing from the field*," Tchi said, "I take it you mean running away?"

"Well . . . I mean, I'm not sure putting it that way . . ." Prullap shuffled his feet, looked at his colleague for help.

"If we were engaged in battle, that might be the way to phrase it," Jariko offered. "But do we serve any purpose languishing here? Our forces in Klaar have been defeated, and the remainder have fled back to the Empire."

"And where would we go?"

"Home," said Prullap. "We're no longer wintered in. Most of the roads are clear."

"We have a fighting force sufficient to make our way to the coast and capture a ship," Jariko said. "If we are fast and stealthy, it can be done. The longer we remain here, the better the chances Helva eventually galvanizes a force to root us out. Nobody came for us in the thick of winter, not in this remote location. But with the thaw comes risk. It's only a matter of time."

Tchi paced, considering. It was tempting. Tchi and his men had been abandoned without orders for such a contingency. That left matters to his judgment as an imperial officer.

The thought of returning back to the Empire with nothing to show for his efforts rubbed him the wrong way.

"We still have agents in Klaar who need our support," Tchi said. "Our armies will return. In a week? A year? We don't know, but we *must* stand ready. We're here behind enemy lines with brave, battle-hardened men and two capable wizards. I feel confident we can figure out a way to contribute to the war effort. In short, gentlemen, we aren't going anywhere."

The two wizards wilted. Their disappointment was so palpable, Tchi almost threw back his head and laughed.

CHAPTER ELEVEN

She awoke with a gasp, sitting up in bed, eyes darting around the room.

Rina looked down at herself. Both gloves were back on. Someone had dressed her in a warm flannel nightgown and had put her in bed, covered her with furs. Embers glowed orange in the fireplace.

She remembered the attack, the horrible smoke creature, and her hand went to her neck. She imagined she could still feel its razor claws piercing her flesh, but the skin was smooth. No wound. The healing rune had done its work. When the wizard Weylan had inked the Prime onto Rina's back, he'd included the extra rune as an experiment. Now whenever she was injured or wounded, the rune healed her. The magic had saved her on more than one occasion.

Rina sensed another presence in the room, turned her head abruptly to look at the woman in the corner. Stasha Benadicta sat quietly, working needlepoint by the low light of an oil lamp.

"About six hours," Stasha said, anticipating Rina's question.

"You've been here the whole time?"

"Yes."

No wonder they called the woman Mother.

"There are two of Tosh's women in the anteroom and two more in the hall," Stasha said. "There have been two attempts on your life. Everyone's braced for a third."

"What happened?"

"Arbert and Lilly are dead. I'm sorry," Stasha said. "Their bodies were taken out and burned."

Rina winced. "Was that necessary?"

"I wouldn't know. They told me the bodies had been corrupted in some way. They didn't want to risk it."

"What happened to me?"

"They said you defeated the demon," Stasha said. "But it knocked you out."

"Demon?"

Stasha shrugged. "That's what they started calling it."

"I need some water."

Stasha stood, crossed the room, and took a pitcher from the vanity and filled a goblet. She brought it to Rina.

"Thank you."

The inside of Rina's mouth tasted awful, and she drank deeply, washing away the flavor of bitter ash. The skeletal tattoo on her palm was meant to leach away a person's spirit to replenish her own. When she'd drained the demon of its spirit, she felt as if she were filling herself with something vile. She didn't know what it was, but it had overwhelmed her.

Stasha returned to her seat, quietly working her needlepoint.

Rina sat still for a moment, thinking. The silence stretched.

Finally, Rina said, "I need help."

Stasha looked up. "How do you mean?"

"I don't know how to run this castle, let alone a duchy," Rina said. "My father knew how, but he still had advisors. Even Giffen was useful before he turned traitor. I need people to help me. An inner circle."

Stasha turned back to her needlepoint, steadily working the neat pattern a little at a time. A few moments later she said, "I can come up with a list of names, if you like."

"Thank you."

"I'm keen to help any way I can, milady."

They lapsed again into silence.

"I don't want to go back to sleep. I want tea, but I don't have a maid anymore."

"I can get it," Stasha said.

"No," Rina told her. "You're the chamberlain. Chamberlains don't fetch tea."

"None of the girls in the castle volunteered to be your maid, milady. Not after what happened to Lilly. We can simply appoint one of them."

"No. Thank you."

I don't want anyone else dying for me. Or because of me. Or simply because they were near me.

It had started with her bodyguard, Kork. The man must have known how severely wounded he was, vital organs punctured, losing blood. Instead of stopping to bind himself and rest, he'd pressed on through the driving snow, leading her to the wizard Weylan as was her father's last request.

Who would be next? Brasley? Stasha? Tosh?

Alem?

"Send someone for the tea," Rina said. "I don't want anyone serving me if they're afraid. I don't need a maid. I can dress myself. It's not like it's difficult."

Stasha stood. "As you wish."

"And food. Stasha?"

"Milady?"

"Can you have that list of names by the time I'm finished with breakfast?"

"Absolutely," Stasha said.

"Good." Rina threw back the furs, swung her legs over the side of the bed. "It's time to get to work."

CHAPTER TWELVE

Tosh felt slightly out of place.

No. That wasn't quite true. Tosh felt *very* out of place.

The formal meeting hall had high vaulted ceilings and wide windows to let in the light. Rich tapestries hung on the walls. It was the sort of hall that was meant to convey the message *this is an important place where important people are doing important things.*

Tosh sat at a wide, circular table with six other people, and as far as he could tell, they were all more important than he was. The bishop of Klaar was Dumo's representative for the entire duchy. Mother—he was still having trouble thinking of her as Stasha Benadicta—was his boss and a formidable woman even before Rina had made her chamberlain. The general of Klaar's army was a man named Kerrig. He'd been a captain before and was one of the few officers to survive the Perranese occupation. Tosh was glad he hadn't served directly under the man, since that could have made the current situation a bit awkward. Yes, Tosh was in charge of the castle guard, but he didn't really feel like an officer. Most officers he'd known had been pretty snooty.

The man sitting directly to Tosh's right was Borris Dremen, head of the merchants' guild and likely the most economically powerful man in the city. On Tosh's left sat Baroness Caville. If Tosh understood correctly, the Caville family had been close with the late Duke Veraiin. Baron Caville had been killed the day Klaar had fallen, and now the baroness ran the holdings.

Brasley Hammish, the final person at the table, offered Tosh a reassuring nod.

I'm glad to see at least one friendly face.

The empty chair was, of course, for the duchess.

A servant made the rounds with hot tea, and just when everyone's cup had been filled, Rina Veraiin came through the door.

She swept in, long blue gown trailing behind her, chin up, eyes bright. The gown was long-sleeved with a high collar, a style she'd taken to wearing to cover her tattoos. Obviously, there was no practical way to cover the tattoos around her eyes. They gave her a tribal look, which contrasted strangely with the elegant gown.

She looks regal and exotic, Tosh thought. *I wonder if she feels it or if she's just putting on a brave face.*

Everyone around the table stood and nodded respect. Rina gestured for them to please be seated. She sat too, back straight, hands on the table in front of her. She met the gaze of each person at the table before beginning.

"Thank you for coming," Rina said. "Some of you are here at my request. Others at the suggestion of our new chamberlain."

She paused momentarily to exchange courteous nods with Stasha.

"And while you all have some basic idea of why I've asked you to attend this unofficial meeting," Rina continued, "I'd prefer you hear it all together directly from me, so there will be no doubt what I'm asking."

Rina gave them a moment to jump in with a comment or question. When nobody did, she went on.

"You all know what happened," she said. "When I came back to Klaar, I waded neck deep in blood to drive out the Perranese. I fought their ink mage and went so far down a hole toward death that I almost didn't make it back. I now look back on those events and think of them as the *easy* part."

Those assembled shifted in their seats and offered weak smiles, not sure if they were meant to react to some joke.

"Yes, I am duchess of Klaar," Rina said. "And I intend to always do what is best for my people. Most of you knew my father. I won't insult your intelligence by trying to convince you that I can step in and rule as well as he did. I mean, it's laughable. But what I can promise you is that I'll never stop trying to do my best. I will never give up. I'll never stop fighting for Klaar."

Tosh glanced at the faces around the table. None seemed especially impressed by Rina's words. On the other hand, they didn't seem disapproving either. They all listened intently.

"Here is my last promise to you. I'm not so vain I can't recognize my own shortcomings," Rina said. "That's why you're all here. I want your help. My father had advisors, and that's what I'm hoping you will be to me. And we're all obviously aware that his closest advisor, Giffen, betrayed him. So the fact that you're here at this table right now is not only a sign that I think you can contribute to our duchy and make it a better place but also my declaration that I find you all to be trustworthy. I hope I can earn an equal trust from you."

Tosh surveyed the faces again. Most seemed to be nodding approval, although the bishop remained stone faced. *Still, it was a pretty decent speech. Sounded natural, not overly rehearsed. She probably scored a few points for sincerity.*

Baroness Emra Caville was the first to break the silence. She was gray and wrinkled, and her skin hung loosely from the weight she'd lost during the occupation, but her eyes gleamed alert and intense. "I can only speak for myself, Duchess Veraiin, but my husband was a devout supporter of your father. It would be an honor for me to act in my husband's stead on your behalf." She chuckled lightly. "Although what service this old woman might offer, I'm sure I don't know."

Rina smiled warmly. "Don't sell yourself short, Emra. You still have cousins in Merridan, yes?"

The baroness nodded. "We correspond frequently."

"Then, my dear baroness, you are *essential*."

"Obviously, I'm with you one hundred percent," General Kerrig said. "Most of my men and I would still be in chains if you hadn't come back and run those savages back into the sea. But our forces are badly undermanned and poorly supplied. If this is to be your cabal of advisors, then now would seem an opportune moment to raise these issues."

"I might be able to help with that."

All eyes turned to Boris Dremen, head of the merchants' guild. He was one of the smallest men Tosh had ever seen, without actually being a dwarf. The man was bony to the point of seeming frail, fingers slender and delicate. Even his pale hair was thin.

"By all means," Rina encouraged.

"The increased traffic on the Small Road has invited a surprising influx of trade through Back Gate," Dremen said. "Klaar's economy is reasonably stable at the moment. But more to General Kerrig's point, I think we need to be shrewd about resupplying his army. Cash is in short supply, so I would encourage bartering whenever possible."

Rina leaned forward, hands clasped on the table. "Example?"

"The best blacksmiths in Helva are in Sherrik," Dremen said. "The best swords and spears. But the timber around Sherrik is inferior, and building with stone is expensive. I think some sort of arrangement could be reached that would benefit both parties without biting into Klaar's cash flow."

"Sherrik is a long way south," Brasley said. "Our city could be sacked five times by the time we haul lumber down there and returned with fresh steel."

Dremen offered Brasley a tight smile. "An astute observation, Baron Hammish. Fortunately, the main trade routes north run up the coast to Kern. The baron keeps a warehouse for Sherrik's trade goods for which the baron earns a modest fee. I'm sure he'd be happy to set up a lumberyard with some similar arrangement. For a nominal fee, I'm more than happy to make all of the contacts and supervise the arrangements."

It was Rina's turn to smile tolerantly. "I hope there hasn't been a misunderstanding, Master Dremen. I've called you all here hoping to appeal to your sense of patriotism as a citizen of Klaar. I can't offer special titles or privileges or compensation to anyone. Perhaps that might change in the future, but at the moment we're just trying to get back on our feet. I'm sorry if I led anyone to believe any differently."

Dremen looked abashed. "I'm the one who should apologize, your grace. Old habits of a lifelong businessman. Naturally, I will do anything in my power for the betterment of Klaar. May I venture a final bit of advice?"

"Of course," Rina said.

"It's my understanding you plan to open the silver mines again."

"Yes. If we can do it safely. There's some concern about snow devils that high up in the mountains."

"I think we should open it up to toughnecks," Dremen suggested.

Rina blinked. "Open it up to who?"

"The unaffiliated prospectors and miners," Dremen explained. "They work a claim and pay the landowner a tithe. The rest they keep for themselves. When a claim is played out, they move along."

"I'm afraid I don't see the advantage," Rina said.

"First, we can't be sure we'll find a new vein after we open the mine," Dremen said. "If we let toughnecks work the mine, it reduces Klaar's risk. Very little investment on our part. It's the toughnecks' gamble. If they do well, then word spreads and more come, and they all pay a tithe. But there's a further benefit, I think. Generally speaking, Klaar is isolated. Toughnecks would come from all over. They'd bring news. They'd bring outside money to spend with local merchants on food and supplies."

Rina nodded. "I like the sound of what you're saying. We'll definitely be talking more about this. Thank you, Master Dremen."

Dremen nodded, seeming pleased with himself.

Rina turned to the bishop.

Bishop Feridixx Hark was a broad-shouldered man with a florid complexion. In his early fifties, bulky without quite being fat, he looked like he'd be more comfortable in full plate armor rather than the gold-trimmed white robes of Dumo. White was fast overtaking the red in his hair.

"Bishop Hark, there are other temples in Klaar, but the majority worship Dumo. I'm hoping you can tell us the mood of the people," Rina said.

"Indeed, we are fortunate to live in an epoch of Dumo's ascendance, and I'm happy to report what I've observed, your grace," Hark said. "As you know, I am not native to Klaar. Ten years ago, the mother temple sent me to take over when the old bishop passed away. I've grown fond of the people in that time. They're a hearty and determined lot. Many still grieve loved ones who died at the hands of the Perranese, but on the whole I sense a gritty optimism." The bishop paused, looked slightly uncomfortable. "There's something else I've noticed about the people of Klaar, something that concerns what I need to say next."

Rina raised an eyebrow. "You're hesitating. I have a feeling I might not like this."

"Yes, I'm worried about that too," the bishop said. "But you opened this meeting with an emphasis on trust, so I'm hoping I can be honest."

"Please. Speak freely," Rina said.

"Klaar is an isolated and independent place," Hark said. "I think these facts have shaped the people in a special way. I have seen wealthy merchants sit side by side with pig sloppers in a tavern. I'm not saying we live in a classless society, and there is certainly a healthy respect for authority—especially for *you*, your grace—but there's not an ugly animosity between those classes. There is little envy among the poor for the nobility—not to the point of hostility anyway, and for the most part, the upper elite don't hold the peasantry in contempt as they do in other places."

"I'd think this would be a point in Klaar's favor," Rina said.

"I heartily agree," Hark said. "I would even venture to say that the people of Klaar are so tolerant and amiable that someone of high birth could carry on an intimate relationship with a commoner, and the local nobility wouldn't even bat an eye."

People cleared throats and averted gazes around the table. Rina went pink in the cheeks.

The bastard's talking about Alem and Rina. Tosh had a sudden urge to smash his fist into Hark's smug fucking face, bishop or not.

Hark held up a hand, placating, reasonable. "But this isn't the point. In almost every way the people's attitude in these matters is commendable. But as Dumo's representative in the mortal realm, I must think of the souls of my flock and their moral health. Even in a place like Klaar with its relaxed attitudes toward societal norms, there must be . . . well . . . a line. I have to be able to tell my flock that even tolerance has its limits. Otherwise, what is Dumo's church for, if not to show the difference between right and wrong, proper and improper?"

Rina let out a long sigh. Her smile fooled nobody. "And in what way do you believe we've crossed some line?"

"May I speak freely?"

"I've already said so."

"Your personal castle guard are whores," Hark said. "And your new chamberlain is their madam."

Stasha Benadicta choked on a gasp before it had completely escaped her mouth.

Tosh stood abruptly, his chair falling back and hitting the floor loudly. He made fists and shot dagger eyes at the bishop.

"Please sit down, Tosh," Rina said calmly.

After a tense pause, Tosh righted his chair and sat.

Rina turned back to the bishop, her eyes hard, meeting his. "Those ladies helped free Klaar of the Perranese. I couldn't have done it alone. And whatever you think, they aren't whores any longer. I trust them, and I need them."

Hark held up his hands again, shaking his head. "I know, I know. I don't doubt their courage." He turned to Stasha. "And you have my word, that was not meant as an attack on you as a person, but I've spent a good part of my time here trying to keep the people of Klaar out of establishments like the Wounded Bird. If there's one thing parishioners can't stand, it's hypocrisy among their church leadership. It's about setting the proper example, you see." He stood slowly. "This should not be interpreted as an act of disloyalty to Klaar. It isn't, I promise. But fair or not, we're judged by the company we keep. I can't in good conscience serve on this council even if it is informal. I hope you understand, your grace."

"You've made yourself clear." Rina's voice sounded strained. "If you wish to excuse yourself, I understand. Your honestly is blunt but appreciated."

He nodded again, something a little closer to a bow this time. "Your grace."

With that the bishop left. Rina sighed, wilted slightly in her chair. She smoothed her hair and tried to force a smile, but her face wasn't going for it.

"Well," Rina said. "I want it clear nobody is *forced* to serve on this council. If anyone else feels they need to depart, then by all means let me know." She glanced quickly around the table. "No? That's a relief. Now there are some other issues I'd like to—"

Baroness Caville cleared her throat, a sound midway between embarrassment and shame.

Rina looked at the old woman. "Emra?"

"I . . . I'm sorry," the baroness said. "It's just. Well, I attend Hark's service every High Day. My husband and I were regulars. I still go when I can, and I observe all of the first-tier holidays and holy stations. If the bishop can't . . . well . . . I don't see how I can . . ." There seemed to be genuine anguish on her face.

"Oh." The word left Rina breathlessly as if the air were being squashed out of her. "Obviously you need to do what you feel best."

The look on Rina's face almost made Tosh cry.

◆ ◆ ◆

Two hours later they all stood and stretched.

"Thanks, everyone," Rina said. "We did good work tonight. I'd like to meet again in a week or maybe ten days."

She made a point to spend a moment with each person as they made their way out of the hall, sharing assurances or gratitude. She'd seen her father do this, shake a man's hand, single him out, let him know he was an important part of the team. She felt a sudden pang at the thought of him.

Father, I've only glimpsed what it's like to be in charge. I never knew. I wish you were here. I wish I didn't have to do this.

She shook her head and tsked. Selfish thoughts like that solved nothing.

When the council had gone, she turned to see that Stasha had lagged behind. The woman was visibly troubled, and it didn't take a genius to guess why.

"Don't let Hark bother you," Rina said.

Stasha laughed but it was obviously forced. "I was going to tell you the same thing."

"I must admit, he did take me by surprise," Rina said. "I should have paid better attention when Mother and Father dragged me to temple on High Day. I didn't realize Dumo was such a prude."

"I should have known," Stasha said. "I took the job as chamberlain because I knew I could do it. It didn't occur to me that having somebody like me around could reflect poorly on you."

"Forget it," Rina said. "The bishop was right about one thing. People around here don't go out of their way to look down on others."

"It's not people around here I'm worried about, your grace," Stasha said. "The king's delegation arrives in two days."

Rina swallowed hard. "Oh yeah. Shit."

CHAPTER
THIRTEEN

It was old snow and tightly packed, crunching beneath her feet with each step. Soon the thaw would come. Some said it had already started, just a bit slowly, the weather warming so gradually most people failed to notice until one day they'd look up and realized they were simply miserably cold instead of in dire peril of freezing to death or losing a foot or a hand to frostbite.

Not that it mattered at this altitude, where snow reigned eternally.

Still, the day was bright and the sky was blue, and Rina Veraiin had to get away from the castle before she killed either herself or everyone else. Servants scurried from nook to cranny, dusting and polishing anything that would hold still. Fresh flowers—where they'd found those, Rina couldn't possibly guess—had been put into the best rooms for the coming guests. Cupboards and larders had been plundered throughout the city to prepare the best possible meals for the king's representatives. Klaar was a simple place, but they were all determined to put their best foot forward.

But damn it, it makes me nervous. Everyone making a fuss as if Dumo himself were coming. Everyone needs to calm the fuck down.

Including herself. But knowing she needed to calm down and being able to do it were two entirely different things.

She looked back at the semicircle of men following her up the hill. A dozen of them with long spears. This was normally how a snow devil would be hunted, men taking the beast from all sides with long spears to stay out of reach. Tusks and claws. Both were deadly. The problem was when the expedition encountered a full hunter pack high on blood-lust. But they were well past the mating season, and so far that hadn't happened. Rina had killed three lone rogues.

Anything to get away from that damn castle for a few hours. Besides, we need to clear the way for the miners.

Silver or no, even the heartiest toughneck would balk at the thought of a hungry snow devil. Drive them farther into the mountains, and send out word that the way was clear. Klaar's mines were open for business. That was the plan anyway.

Rina also had other reasons for coming up the mountain.

She came to the stone marker and the steps winding upward. She was surprised that the last time she was here had become such a faded memory. Her bodyguard, Kork, had been dragging her through the driving snow. She'd been stunned by violence, crushed by grief as she left her dead parents behind. Her father had given Kork his final instructions: to take his only daughter into the mountains, where the reclusive wizard Weylan dwelled. Kork had completed his mission. It had cost him his life.

The snarl and the sound of crunching snow drew Rina's attention back to the present.

The snow devil loped down the slope toward her, running hunched over like an ape, using the knuckles of its hands like another set of feet. Its fur was completely white, long tufts curling up from its eyebrows in the shape of horns. Tusks grew from its bottom jaw. Its eyes were red coals sizzling in its skull.

Rina tapped into the spirit, and the world slowed.

She watched the snow devil come toward her, measured its speed, calculated when it would leap. It was fast, vicious, and strong, but Rina felt no fear. There was only cold cunning as she visualized how she would meet it. Her hand was already moving back to the two-handed sword slung across her back.

When Kork died, she'd taken up his enormous two-handed blade. It was a ridiculous weapon for her, longer than she was tall, and under normal circumstances she'd barely been able to lift it. But with the strength of the bull tattoo, the sword had become flashing death. She'd lost the sword in her battle with the other ink mage but had found another in the castle's armory, this one somewhat shorter so she could wear it across her back.

The snow devil growled and leapt.

She pulled the sword from its scabbard and in the same smooth motion sliced down through fur and flesh just to the left of the beast's head into the meat of its shoulder, its growl twisting into a scream of surprise and agony.

The two halves flew past her on either side, landing a dozen feet away, blood staining the snow garish red.

The men with spears had arrived on the scene, and one knelt while pulling a long curved knife from his belt to remove the tusks. They'd fetch a nice price as curiosities in places like Merridan and Tul-Agnon.

"Up these stairs," Rina told them. "We're almost there."

They followed her up the mountain.

She paused at the mouth of the cave. Kork's body was still there, crusted with ice. She went to one knee, reached out with a shaking hand to touch the cold armor on his shoulder. She hadn't expected such a sudden emotional response, but her eyes misted and a lump grew in her throat.

She paused a moment, composed herself, and then called back to the men behind her. "Build the pyres in the clear space at the cliff's edge."

"Yes, milady."

The men sprang into action, unpacking tools and wood they'd carried on their backs up the stone stairway.

"And somebody light me a torch," Rina said.

A few minutes later, she carried the torch into the depths of the cave. The dead wizard sat where she'd left him, frozen, looking more like a pale sculpture than someone who'd ever been alive. Rina knew little about Weylan. The wizard had been dying. His last act was to gift her with the magical tattoos that had changed her entire life.

She moved past the dead wizard and raised her torch to examine the shelves and tables behind him. Books, old and leather bound. Vials and jars containing . . . Well, who could guess? Powders, herbs, a container that seemed to be filled with dried eyeballs. Another sealed jar contained a pink mist that swirled within. Ingredients for fell and exotic potions.

In addition to laying Kork to rest, these items were the reason she'd come. Perhaps somewhere in the wizard's books or other paraphernalia lay a clue to the ink mage tattoos. Rina had once been told that hundreds of different tattoos existed, maybe thousands. With just a few tattoos, Rina felt impossibly powerful. What must it be like for an ink mage with a score of tattoos? Or a hundred?

She considered the skeletal hand on her palm.

Some power is too much and too dark for anyone. I don't want this.

Rina recalled Weylan's warning that the power could be a warning. He'd asked her if she'd be able to step away, if she could let go of the spirit before she burned herself out.

I don't know. I hope so.

Most of the tattoos had been lost to time, but even one or two more could help her.

It's not because I'm greedy for power. I just need to defend my people.

Rina hoped she wasn't kidding herself.

She returned to the mouth of the cave. She dipped a hand inside her furs and pulled out a chuma stick from the inside pocket. She lit it with the torch, puffing, taking the smoke into her lungs, feeling a vague and mild calm ease through her limbs. The leaves were grown in the bottom lands. The chuma sticks were a habit Rina hadn't tried very hard to shake.

Rina watched six of the men gently lay Kork's body on the first pyre.

One of the men broke off from the group and approached Rina. "We've finished the pyres, milady."

Rina stuck the chuma stick into the corner of her mouth, motioned with her chin toward the cave. "The other body's in there. Send men to fetch him."

"Yes, milady."

"One more thing," Rina said. "Take some men and pack up all of the wizard's things, especially the books. Be careful. There's magical stuff in there, and Dumo knows what might explode or turn you into a cockroach or something."

The man squinted into the darkness, a worried frown on his face. "In there?"

Rina puffed the chuma stick. "In there."

"Yes, milady."

Alem shaded his eyes from the sun, squinted up the mountain at the flicker of orange light. "Do you think that's it?"

Brasley lowered the wineskin from his mouth and smacked his lips. He followed Alem's gaze up the mountain. "The pyres?"

"I don't know what else it could be."

They stood atop one of the keep's corner towers, one of the places that let them view the duchy in every direction. Just a week ago, they wouldn't have lasted a minute in the frigid wind, but now the day was pleasant, sky clear, visibility going on for miles.

"She's found the bodies, then," Brasley said. "Why didn't you go with her?"

"I offered," Alem said. "She said she wanted to do it alone and had to get away from all the craziness. I sort of got the feeling *I* was lumped in with all the craziness."

Brasley chuckled. "Don't take it personally. She's got a lot on her mind, not least of which is a future husband she's never met."

Alem frowned. "That hasn't been decided yet. She probably won't even like him."

"Of course she won't like him," Brasley said. "Pressured into marrying some fellow she's never met? Our Rina? I'd rather breast-feed a snow devil than try to get that woman to do something she doesn't want to do. That's not the point. Women in her position marry men they don't like all the time. There's too much at stake for the kings and queens of the world to leave such matters in the fickle hands of love. You're lucky you're lowborn. You can do as you like."

"Lucky?" There was an edge to Alem's voice. "How about you take over running the stables and give me the title and the money and the hunting lodge. Take your turn at being lucky for a while."

Brasley waved him away. "Oh, you know what I mean. There's a certain responsibility that comes with being part of the nobility. It's not all drinking and womanizing, you know. I mean, for *me* it mostly is, but still."

"Not so much womanizing when you're married to Fregga," Alem said.

Brasley made an annoyed noise in his throat. "You're only saying that because you want me to be in as bad of a mood as you are."

"Yes."

"And anyway, who says the womanizing stops just because I marry Fregga?" Brasley took another long pull at the wineskin.

Alem looked so genuinely shocked that Brasley laughed, spitting out wine. It dribbled down his chin and onto his heavy fur cloak.

"Oh, grow up, you ridiculous stable boy."

"If you love somebody—"

"Love," Brasley scoffed. "I've never known it, and you're drowning in it."

"If you've never known love, I feel sorry for you," Alem said.

"Quite the reverse, I'd think," muttered Brasley, lifting the wineskin again.

Alem frowned and looked back up the mountain.

Brasley was looking back the other way at the road leading up the mountain to the Long Bridge.

A long moment passed, and finally Brasley sighed heavily. "Do you believe in luck, Alem?"

Alem turned back to him, a curious look on his face. "I don't know. Do you?"

"Yes," Brasley said. "All bad. Do you see that line of men heading for the bridge?"

Alem crossed to the other side of the tower, leaned against the parapet, and squinted down at the road. He counted forty riders, most of them in full plate armor. Banners streamed behind them, and a herald out front bore some nobleman's house colors.

"I can't quite make out the coat of arms from here," Alem said.

"It's the king's delegation from Merridan," Brasley said with an air of dread. "The bastards are a day early."

CHAPTER FOURTEEN

Eastward across the sea and sharply south lay the heart of the Perran Empire, a long, thin island surrounded by numerous smaller islands. Such a people, as one might imagine, were good with boats and sailing and shipbuilding and the art of navigation by the stars. They quickly found the continents to their east and south and subjugated the people there. Fearless, ruthless, and efficient, the Perranese Empire was forged in fewer than fifty years and stood for nearly four hundred.

But nothing lasts forever.

The aboriginal tribes of the eastern continent had united to overthrow the Perranese, who'd become complacent over the centuries. The Perranese had been driven back into the sea, many ships left to burn at the piers before they'd had a chance to launch. The day would go down in Perranese history as the Red Retreat.

The southern continent was made up of rich farmland and had become the breadbasket of the Empire. The locals had been enslaved to work the fields, but those lands were now entering their twentieth straight year of drought. The harvest ships that had once sailed the seas by the hundreds had dwindled to a trickle.

The Empire had receded to its home islands, overflowing with an out-of-control population, one the Empire could no longer feed. The emperor had cast his eyes west toward Helva. To him the equation was simple. Conquer or starve.

The emperor concocted a cunning plan with his generals to send a small invading force to gain a foothold in Helva. Once dug in, like a tick behind a dog's ear, he would gradually send more troops until the Empire's presence on the Helvan mainland was an undeniable fact of life.

When the Perranese fleet had returned in disgrace, defeated by the least significant duchy in Helva, the emperor clutched his chest and dropped dead in the middle of the imperial throne room.

His wife, Her Imperial Highness Empress Mee Hra'Lito, had put down nine coups in the ensuing weeks, the last of which was so bloody and brutal that all other pretenders had decided to shelve their ambitions until better opportunities presented themselves. Bodies had been removed and burned. Lesser ranks promoted. The hierarchy restored. Now that internal matters had been settled, Mee turned her attention again to problems of empire.

She stood in her room atop the Imperial Tower of the Heavens, the highest point of the imperial palace. She stood on the balcony, looked at the sprawling city below. According to imperial mathematicians, the city of Klaar would have fit inside the imperial city limits fourteen times over, and yet the empress's citizens lived on top of one another in the most crowded conditions imaginable.

The footsteps echoing behind her drew her attention.

Mee turned to see her chief advisor crossing the high-ceilinged chamber, his boot heels clacking on the polished floor. Hanging lamps lit the area.

Mee gathered her silken robe in one hand, and her long braid in the other. The robe was aquamarine with a pattern of sea waves, adorned with little blue fish around the belt and sleeves. It was her family pattern, her people having originally come from the fishing fleet hundreds of years ago. Her braid, even draped over one arm, still dragged across the smooth floor. She was young, just thirty, and her hair was still jet black, white skin perfectly smooth, dark eyes deep and mysterious. Her lips and eyelids were stained a blue that matched her gown. She appeared regal and lethal and cold.

The emperor had been eighty-one when he'd died. If Mee planned to make it that long, she would need all of her skill and intelligence.

Her advisor stopped five feet from her and bowed in half from the waist. He held the bow until addressed.

"Rise, General Thorn."

The general stood straight. He wore no armor or weapon here in the imperial palace, only a simple black robe with the emblem of the imperial army over his heart, a golden serpentine dragon wrapped around a silver sword. "Your imperial majesty."

"The preparations?"

"Precisely as intended and on schedule," Thorn told her.

"Excellent. Your service to the Empire will not be forgotten."

"Thank you, highness, but my own glory means nothing. I do all for the throne and the Perranese people."

"General Thorn, if this invasion fails then the Empire fails."

"I know," Thorn said. "I promise you it will not fail."

"Then there is nothing more to be said," Mee told him. "You sail with the tide?"

"At first light, highness."

"Then go," Mee said. "And take my blessings with you."

Thorn bowed low again, held it for a moment, then rose, spun on a heel and stalked away.

Mee went back out onto the balcony. A cool wind struck her from the north, raising goose bumps on her skin. She turned her gaze toward the Golden Harbor, named for the way the sunlight hit the water at dusk.

A chill went down her spine. She'd not gotten used to the sight of ten thousand ships. The harbor was practically choked with them. Men swarmed the docks loading last-minute supplies. Every ship in the Empire. Every soldier, save her household guard. Everything.

"Everything." She said the word out loud to taste its weight.

If this endeavor failed, nothing would be left.

She was too afraid to say the word *nothing* out loud.

CHAPTER
FIFTEEN

Castle Klaar found itself in an uproar of sudden hospitality.

Servants scurried to prepare bedchambers and bring refreshments. The visitors explained that fair weather all the way from the capital had hastened their arrival. Count Becham was the official head of the delegation, and he'd dragged along with him a klatch of barons and other nobility, all of whom needed accommodations befitting their stations.

The slow-roasting suckling pigs would not be ready until the following evening, and there was no help for it, but a number of fat geese were identified for the chopping block. Sailors deserting a sinking ship could not have moved faster or with more purpose than the cooks in the castle kitchen. Casks of the second-best wine—the very best being held in reserve to accompany the suckling pigs—were brought up from the cellar.

Stasha Benadicta had assured the count that it was no trouble whatsoever, that everyone in Klaar welcomed the opportunity to bask in the count's presence an additional day. Inwardly, she hoped Dumo would strike the man with a bad case of the runs and that the count would be locked in the privy his entire visit.

Stasha had sent a kitchen boy to the stables to find Alem. He needed to know Rina would want to see him just before her return from her trek up the mountain. Alem would know to use the secret stairs. This was all accomplished using code language, of course. The last thing Rina needed was to meet her guests while still covered in travel grime and snow devil blood.

Alem had dutifully arrived with Rina in tow, and the chamberlain barely had said thank you before Alem was sprinting back down the stairs muttering something about forty new horses to feed and water.

Stasha stood behind Rina Veraiin, tugging like mad on the laces of the duchess's corset.

Rina grunted. "It's been a while since I wore one of these, and frankly, if I didn't wear one now or ever again, it would be just fine with me."

"One never gets a second chance to make a first impression," Stasha said.

Rina rolled her eyes. "Wisdom of the ages."

"Are we in a cross mood tonight?" Stasha asked.

"Why do women wear these damn things?" Rina struggled against the corset.

"Men, I suppose." Stasha tugged harder on the laces.

"Just stop," Rina snapped. "Any tighter and I can't breathe."

"I'll fetch your gown."

"Thank you."

The gown was a deep and vivid purple, cut in Rina's preferred style: high collar, long sleeves, and matching gloves.

Stasha frowned at the dress. "That's wonderful fabric, but fashion today is to show a little more skin. Especially in Merridan, where cleavage is all the rage."

"Fuck what they do in Merridan."

Stasha cleared her throat and took a step back, waiting patiently.

"I'm sure you've heard worse language at the Wounded Bird," Rina said.

Stasha, stoic, didn't respond.

"Oh, fine. I'm sorry," Rina said. "To answer your earlier question, you're fucking right. I'm—*ahem*—that is to say, yes, I am cross. Very."

"Try to control yourself. You have guests."

"The damn guests are half the reason I'm cross! A day early, and dragging the king's stupid grandnephew along to look me over like I'm a hog at market."

"It's the way of things," Stasha said calmly, bending to place Rina's shoes in front of her.

"I almost told Alem all about it." Rina stepped into the shoes. "But . . . well, I didn't want to upset him until I found out more."

"Alem already knows."

"That's impossible. Wait, does he? How could he?"

Stasha shrugged. "I know men, and I see the way he looks at you and how he's been sulking. He knows."

"No, he . . ." Rina snapped her fingers. "Brasley. Son-of-a-bitch idiot."

"And how did Baron Brasley Hammish know?"

"Because I . . . uh . . . told him."

Stasha said nothing in that exact way that says everything.

"Okay, so *I'm* the idiot."

"I said no such thing, your grace."

"Forget it," Rina said. "You'd better go get changed while there's still time. They'll be serving the wine soon."

"Actually, uh . . ." Stasha looked away awkwardly. "I hadn't planned on attending the dinner tonight."

"Are you kidding me? I need you there."

"There's such so much to do around the castle. The guests and all the—"

"Horseshit!"

"Your grace, please. I don't think it fitting—"

"I'm a fucking duchess in my own fucking private room of my own fucking castle, and I'm about to have a panic attack," Rina shouted. "I can't face the king's delegation without some backup. I don't need you to face a hunter pack of snow devils, but for *this*, I do need you."

Stasha flushed, her feet shifting nervously. "I'm simply concerned that my presence might do more harm than good."

"I just told you I need you. I don't see . . . oh." Rina calmed herself. "This is about what the bishop said."

The chamberlain opened her mouth then shut it again, simply nodding.

Rina put a hand on her shoulder. "I am Klaar. *We* are Klaar. You're my choice. We do things *our* way here. I might be so nervous I'm going to sweat through this gown, but that's okay. Because you are going to get dressed and come with me. We'll face these people our way on our terms, or at least fake it the best we can. Yes?"

Stasha nodded again.

"Good."

"Thank you, your grace. It . . . it means a lot."

"Thank *you*. Count Becham will have his people there. I need you and Brasley to be *my* people."

"Oh, uh . . ." Stasha looked embarrassed. "As you might guess, Baron Hammish had his own misgivings about Count Becham."

"What are you saying?"

"I believe it's quite possible Brasley won't be joining us tonight," Stasha said.

"Are you fucking kidding me?"

♦ ♦ ♦

Brasley Hammish walked fast down a dim castle hallway, saddlebags thrown over one shoulder, as he pulled on his riding gloves. It was a hallway generally used by servants, and it led to a door that opened to a courtyard near the stables. Then it would be simplicity itself to hop on his horse and steal away for an extended holiday. Some place obscure and far away.

Some place *warm*.

And Count Becham could just chew on that.

He rounded a corner, and big hands grabbed him from all sides.

Brasley kicked hard, caught one of the men in the balls, and heard an anguished grunt. He threw an elbow, tried to pull free of the hands holding him.

A punch in his gut doubled him over, then something heavy hit him in the back of the head, and he dropped to the floor, trying to blink away the stars in front of his eyes. The hands picked him up again and dragged him down the hall and into a storeroom half filled with sacks of potatoes and grain. They dropped him on the stone floor. He heard a door slam, rolled over, his eyes trying to adjust to the dim light. Somebody held a small oil lamp.

"Sit up and look at me, boy," said the man with the lamp.

Brasley did as he was told, sitting up and scooting back against a stack of flour sacks. He squinted past the gleam of the oil lamp to see who was speaking.

Count Becham.

Shit.

Brasley's eyes darted quickly around the room. Five other men, all big and all wearing Becham's livery.

"Count Becham." Brasley attempted to muster some charm. "I was just about to come pay my respects."

"With your saddlebags and riding cloak?"

"I must ride to some minor errand." Brasley smiled. "After I came to talk to you, of course. Naturally, I've been eager to ask about the welfare of my beloved Fregga."

Becham scowled. "You're smiling, Baron Hammish. Evidently you find something amusing." The count turned to one of his men. "Remove the smile from the baron's face, please."

The man leaned in, punching down hard across Brasley's mouth, snapping his head around. Brasley tasted blood. Bells rang in his ears.

"Your beloved Fregga is swelling rapidly with your child," Becham said. "She's been wearing her clothing looser and looser to cover up, but soon everyone will know the shame on my family. Do you really believe I intend to suffer such shame quietly without exacting retribution from the one responsible?"

"I promise you, sir, my intentions—" Brasley coughed, spit blood. "Nothing but . . . honorable . . ."

"Baron Hammish likes to spread his seed around," Becham said. "I think we can do a favor to all the women of Helva to make sure that doesn't happen."

Brasley blanched. "Wait—"

Two of Becham's men grabbed Brasley's arms. Another two grabbed his legs and spread them. The fifth man drew his dagger, the point aimed at Brasley's groin.

Brasley struggled. "Wait. There's been a mistake. Count Becham, please." A pathetic edge of cowardice had crept into Brasley's voice. "We can fix this. Please!"

Becham grinned. "Say good-bye to your balls, Baron Hammish."

Brasley's desperate screams echoed down the castle hallways, but nobody else heard them.

EPISODE THREE

CHAPTER SIXTEEN

Brasley screamed again.

"Will you cease your wretched caterwauling, please?" Count Becham said. "Nobody's even done anything to you yet."

The man who held the dagger against Brasley's balls turned back to Becham. "You want I should slice him, milord?"

"No!" Brasley screeched.

"Hold a moment," Becham said. "Baron Hammish, if there's some convincing reason we *shouldn't* cut off your balls and feed them to you, I'm all ears."

"It's true that you caught me trying to sneak out," Brasley said. "But that's because I was rushing home to fetch my dead mother's ring. My intent, as it has always been, is to beg for Fregga's hand in marriage . . . for which, I'd like to point out, I would *very* much need my testicles."

Becham scratched his chin, considering. "To fetch your mother's ring, you say. A lie, obviously, but the sort of lie I can warm up to. Go on."

"A quiet ceremony," Brasley said hurriedly. "She can stay with me at my lodge, away from prying eyes until the child is born. Put the word around Merridan that she's off with her new husband, and she can come home later at some appropriate time."

Count Becham nodded slowly. "Put him on his feet."

The count's men obeyed, set Brasley on his feet. His knees were watery, and for a moment, Brasley thought he might collapse. His heart was still hammering away inside his chest at the thought of the dagger cutting into his scrotum. His hair was matted with fear sweat, damp under his arms and behind his ears.

Becham stepped forward, smoothed the wrinkles down the front of Brasley's tunic with the palm of his hand. "Now there's a bright fellow. I knew you had it in you. There's also the matter of the line of credit you opened with the Royal Bank to open Klaar's consulate in Merridan. We don't really like it when people skip out on their debts."

Brasley swallowed hard. His reason for seducing Fregga had been to get to Count Becham and his connection with the Royal Bank. The line of credit Brasley had established had enabled him to open the Klaar embassy, all part of the ultimately successful plan to get Rina in to see the king. Brasley had felt pretty clever and pleased with himself at the time.

And now I'm just trying to save my balls.

"But never mind the debt for now," Becham said. "There are ways around such things."

Brasley managed a sick smile. "That's most generous, Count Becham."

"Now, here's what I think best," Becham said. "You ride off and get your mother's ring. I think Fregga will be delighted. But there's no hurry. Tomorrow is soon enough. Duchess Veraiin has arranged a dinner. What a wonderful opportunity to announce your engagement."

Brasley turned green. There was a very real danger he would vomit.

"They'll be serving the wine just about now, so we should probably move along," Becham suggested.

Brasley nodded, tried to speak but was still too stunned. *Dumo, yes, wine. All I can get.*

"I thought you might come you to your senses." Becham put a fatherly arm around Brasley's shoulders. "She's following by wagon and should be here in two days. Your idea of a quiet ceremony sounds perfect. Welcome to the family . . . *son.*"

CHAPTER
SEVENTEEN

Not bad for short notice, Rina thought.

Rina stood at the head of the long dining table in the formal dining hall. The table had been laid with the best silver. Servants circled the table with wine pitchers, making sure goblets stayed full. The chandeliers glittered with hundreds of tiny candles in glass globes. Everyone wore their best finery. In the corner, a trio of musicians—mandolin, pipe, fiddle—played soft music that just about everyone ignored.

This would actually be a pleasant evening if I weren't having a suitor shoved down my throat.

Rina reminded herself that Ferris Gant was not the only reason for the king's delegation. King Pemrod had taken an interest again in Klaar and wanted to renew relations. That could either be very good or very bad. A renewed relationship with the capital might mean more trade, better cultural exchange, and other unforeseen benefits. On the other hand, Klaar had been independent for years, part of the kingdom of

Helva in name only. The people wouldn't take it well if "renewed relations" translated into interference with how they lived their lives.

For that matter, I wouldn't take it well either.

She saw that everyone had taken their places, standing next to their chairs, all eyes turned toward her at the head of the table. *Time to play the gracious host.*

Rina spread her arms in a welcoming gesture. She'd rehearsed with Stasha what she might say, something bland and noncommittal, yet friendly and welcoming.

"Lords and ladies, welcome one and all to the duchy of Klaar," Rina began. "Our humble holding is made brighter by your presence. I'd especially like to welcome Count Becham and his retinue, who traveled all the way from Merridan as King Pemrod's representatives."

Rina gestured to the count. As guest of honor, he'd been placed at the table directly to Rina's right. A modest smattering of applause rippled along the table in appreciation of him. The count smiled and nodded in acknowledgment.

"We look forward to a much closer relationship with our cousins in the capital," Rina continued. "I'd also like to welcome new friends." She nodded to the three people sitting at the complete opposite end of the long dining table.

The three gypsies had arrived quietly while most of the castle had been in a tizzy trying to provide the best rooms in the castle for Becham and his party. The gypsies had taken the lesser accommodations offered them without complaint. As chief, Gino was ostensibly the leader of the gypsies, but the two women with him were arguably more powerful. The handsome middle-aged women with the tattoos on her face was Klarissa. The tattoos were identical to the ones on Rina's own face. It had been Klarissa's mother who'd put them there. Rina would need to find a quiet moment later to apologize for seating them so far down the table, but while the three gypsies were the most important people in their own tribe, they weren't considered nobility by Helvan standards. Gypsies were generally known as thieves and swindlers, and seating them at the table at all may have offended Becham and his party.

Then they'll just have to be offended.

The gypsies had been useful. When it came time to recapture Klaar, they'd shown up to help. The king hadn't. And anyway, Rina *liked* Klarissa.

That was more than she could say for the third gypsy.

Maurizan was Klarissa's daughter. Rina and Maurizan had little affection for each other. Mostly because they'd both set their sights on Alem. Rina had won.

Okay, that's petty, but I don't care.

It was time to wrap up her opening remarks. Rina lifted her goblet, and the guests did likewise. A traditional toast.

"To his royal majesty, King Pemrod of Helva," Rina said.

"His majesty!" replied the gathering

"Now please be seated, my friends," Rina said, "and enjoy the feast!"

The applause this time seemed a little more enthusiastic.

They kept to polite and inconsequential topics through the soup and the main entrée. Brasley sat next to the count, and Rina thought his contributions to the conversation a bit perfunctory. She'd been counting on him to carry some of the weight and wondered what was wrong with the man.

Stasha sat on Rina's left, and next to her sat Ferris Gant. Rina had faked as much warmth as possible when they'd been introduced.

Gant was a bit older than Rina but still short of thirty, Rina estimated. Tall, broad shoulders, wavy auburn hair, beard neatly trimmed along his jaw. Smooth skin, a bit tan from outdoor activity, probably something gentlemanly like riding or hunting. Gant's eyes were a deep, rich brown.

At least he's good-looking. That helps. Or maybe it makes it worse?

Rina startled herself with this line of thought.

Dessert came and went, and the servants brought out the thick liqueur called musso in small glasses. Musso was expensive and imported from the Red City, and it had been Stasha's suggestion to serve it. The liqueur signaled the end of the feast, and now was usually when additional toasts and announcements were made. Rina prepared her final words, to thank the guests for coming.

I just want to get out of this damn corset, so I can breathe again and—

She blinked, not sure what she'd seen. Had Count Becham just leaned over and nudged Brasley in the ribs with his elbow?

Brasley stood slowly, tapping a spoon against his glass for everyone's attention. All heads turned toward him, the conversation in the room falling away.

Brasley opened his mouth to speak, and for a second he froze. He cleared his throat, mastered himself, the practiced charm returning.

But something's wrong with him. What's going on?

"Lords and ladies, I beg your attention," Brasley said. "I have an announcement to make, and as we've all been served this excellent liqueur"—he paused to nod politely at Rina—"now would seem the appropriate time to share the joyous news."

The dinner guests were rapt. They were full of wine and food, and a surprise would be an amusing way to cap off the evening.

"After relentless pleading, I have finally convinced our most excellent count"—he put a hand on the count's shoulder, giving him a wink and really playing it up—"to give me his lovely daughter Fregga's hand in marriage."

The dining hall erupted in applause. Everyone loved somebody else's wedding.

Rina shot a look at Stasha.

The chamberlain offered a bewildered shrug as if to say, "Don't look at me."

Brasley gestured with one hand for the crowd to hush, and they quieted.

"I am happy to say that the wedding will take place in a few days as soon as my lovely fiancée arrives," Brasley said. "Sorry, ladies, but this side of beef no longer hangs in the butcher's window."

The comment instigated a good-natured round of laughter, which summoned more applause and shouts of congratulations from the guests.

Count Becham gave Brasley a hearty pat on the back.

Rina stared at Brasley, her mouth hanging open, stunned.

Oh, you poor bastard.

◆ ◆ ◆

Rina stood in the large archway of the dining hall and offered each guest a few parting words. Her feet were killing her. The shoes were almost as bad as the corset—almost.

And you get to do it all over again tomorrow night, you lucky duchess.

How long were these guests staying again?

As the final guests trickled out, Rina realized she'd actually made a useful decision by seating the gypsies at the far end of the table, because this meant they were the last to leave. Rina would be able to have a quiet moment alone with them. Well, not *entirely* alone. Stasha hovered in the background in case her duties as chamberlain demanded she leap into action, and guards stood unobtrusively in the corners. As duchess, Rina found that it was difficult to be truly alone anywhere in the castle these days, as there were always servants or guards or some functionary hanging about. Her office and private quarters were the only exceptions.

Rina clasped one of Klarissa's hands in both of hers, smiled warmly. "It's good to see you again, Klarissa. I'm sorry we didn't have a chance to visit during the feast. It was horrible, seating you so far away like that."

"Nonsense, your grace," Klarissa said. "You had a count to deal with. We understand completely, don't we, Gino?"

Gino bowed, a tight smile straining his face. "Of course."

"And you remember my daughter, Maurizan."

Rina faked a smile. "Maurizan."

A half bow from Maurizan. The girl didn't bother to fake a smile. "Your grace."

"You youngsters run along," Klarissa said to the other gypsies. "I want to indulge in a little gossip with Duchess Veraiin. Nothing important enough to interest you, Gino."

The look on Gino's face made it clear he knew he was being dismissed. He and Maurizan left. Klarissa and Rina walked slowly down the wide hallway, the chamberlain and guards following at a respectful distance so as not to intrude.

"How are you getting along, your grace?" Klarissa asked. "Now that you're duchess, I mean."

"Please, I can't handle anyone else calling me *your grace*. Rina works fine. At least when we're alone," Rina said. "And being duchess is a huge pain in the ass. Thanks for asking."

Klarissa laughed. "Maybe the gypsy system isn't so bad. I make most of the decisions, but Gino is chief. Everyone takes their problems to him."

"Maybe you can lend him to me," Rina said. "I'm tired of other people's problems. I have enough of my own."

"I have a feeling you'll do just fine."

"What about your people?" Rina asked. "Are they ready to settle along Lake Hammish?"

"The caravans are being prepared," Klarissa said. "We're waiting one more week to make sure the thaw has taken, and then we'll bring everyone."

"Brasley is ostensibly lord of those lands, but he knows to leave you alone," Rina said. "Go to him if you need anything."

"I'm sure we'll get along with Baron Hammish just fine," Klarissa said. "There's another reason I wanted to speak with you, Rina, if you don't mind."

"Of course."

"You've been very kind to me and my people. I was hoping I might offer you a gift."

Rina braced herself. Gypsies didn't strike bargains with friends. Rather, they offered gifts and hoped they were offered another gift in returned. It seemed like splitting hairs, and Rina suspected it was some sort of test of friendship and loyalty. If Klarissa gave her a gift, then she'd expect something in return but wouldn't ask for it. It was up to Rina to decide whether she would return the gesture.

"I hope I can be worthy of any gift you might give," Rina said carefully.

A knowing smile spread on Klarissa's face. "It's late, and you've been playing host all night. I'll bet you're tired. I don't want to keep you up. May I beg some of your time tomorrow to explain more fully?"

Rina's day was slammed full, but for Klarissa she'd make time. "Can you join me for breakfast?"

"Happy to."

"Good," Rina said. "And welcome to Klaar. I'm glad you and your people are here."

Klarissa kissed Rina on the cheek. "See you at breakfast. Good night."

"Good night."

Rina stood a moment and watched Klarissa go. She sensed her chamberlain coming up behind her.

"Stasha."

"Your grace?"

"What did we do with all the books and wizard paraphernalia we brought back from Weylan's cave?"

"Locked in the prayer tower as you instructed," Stasha said.

"Who knows?"

"You and I," Stasha said. "And the two men I handpicked to carry it all up there. They're sworn to secrecy. I trust them."

"Thank you," Rina said. "Are you turning in now?"

"Soon enough. There's still plenty to do. You should head off to bed. I'll see to everything."

"Thank you, Stasha. I'm glad you're here."

"I wouldn't be anywhere else, your grace."

CHAPTER EIGHTEEN

For the first time, Rina missed having her own maid. It took longer than usual to pry herself out of the corset on her own, but she eventually managed it, and breathed deep with relief. She kicked off her formal shoes and stepped into soft slippers. She donned a heavy robe, tied it in the front. She felt human again.

Her body ached for her feather bed, but her mind raced. She knew she wouldn't be able to sleep, not yet.

She was considering sending a servant for a pot of herbal tea when there was a tentative knock at the door.

Rina took a step toward the door. "Yes?"

"Sorry to disturb you, milady, but there's a guest to see you."

The voiced sounded like one of Tosh's women, the big redhead. What was her name again? Darshia. "At this hour?"

"I told him, milady," Darshia said through the door. "He's quite insistent."

Rina sighed, pulled the bolt back, and opened the door. There was another woman on guard duty with Darshia, but Rina didn't recognize her. A man stood waiting beyond the two women.

Ferris Gant.

Two goblets hung by the stems from the fingers of one hand. In his other hand he carried a wine pitcher.

"Forgive the late hour, your grace." He smiled, half charm and half apology. "But I was hoping we could share a drink. And some conversation."

Rina's mouth fell open. *You've got to be fucking joking.*

Darshia leaned toward Rina and whispered, "I don't care whose grandnephew he is, milady. Say the word, and I'll escort him out of here. As roughly as you like."

Nobody, not even King Pemrod, would be able to hold it against her if Rina sent the man away. It was rude and presumptuous to come to her private chambers in this way. On the other hand, she'd take all the goodwill she could get. It was simple enough to invite the man in, exchange some conversation, then send him on his way without hurt feelings.

Rina stepped aside and gestured into her sitting room. "Please come in, Sir Gant."

"Are you sure about this, milady?" Darshia whispered.

"Do you really think he can do anything to me?" Rina said.

"Well, no, milady. But it's *improper*," Darshia said. "Forgive me, but I know a little something about improper."

"I'll trust to your discretion," Rina said. "And I promise that if he gets out of line, I'll call for you to come fetch his body."

A grin flickered briefly across Darshia's face. "We'll be right outside."

Gant nodded at the guards as he entered. "Ladies."

Darshia scowled at him but said nothing.

Rina closed the door but didn't slide the bolt back into place.

Gant gestured at the table with the wine pitcher. "Do you mind if I sit?"

"Please. Be comfortable."

Gant sat. He set the goblets on the table in front of him and filled each. He motioned to the other chair across the table. "Join me."

Rina stood, back straight, hands clasped primly in front of her. "I've just come from the same feast as you. I've had quite enough wine, thank you."

"No you haven't," Gant said. "The servant filled your glass for the toast and then once more between the entrée and dessert. I watched what you were drinking. I didn't want to pass out before we had a chance to talk, so I took it as easy as you did."

"By all means, say whatever you came here to say."

"Could you sit, please?" Gant said. "You're making me nervous."

"Somehow I doubt that," Rina said, but she took the chair across from him.

He slid one of the goblets across the table toward her, lifted the other in a toast. "To mutual interests."

"And what might those interests be?"

"Friendship, I hope. And a better relationship between Merridan and Klaar, obviously," Gant said. "And marriage."

Rina didn't reach for the goblet.

"You're much prettier that the last one," Gant said. "The king has been trying to set me up for years. Some bucktoothed girl from Tul-Agnon, daughter of the Royal University chancellor. I like the tattoos around your eyes. Makes you look . . . a bit . . ."

"Exotic," supplied Rina. "Or so I've been told."

"Yes," Gant agreed. "Exotic."

"Am I supposed to be flattered?"

"Certainly. Why not?" Gant sipped wine. "May I be frank?"

"Please."

"You're not keen to marry me, I take it."

"Such talk is a bit premature, don't you think?"

"Yes, but we all know where this is headed," Gant said. "The king sends me along with Count Becham to get a look at you. And if we don't object too strongly to each other, maybe you come to the capital for a visit in the spring, and we're seen walking together or attending a concert. Who cares? Whatever. Word gets around that there might be a wedding on the way. That's how the king tests the water. If the nobility seem in favor, then things proceed, and a year from now we're walking down the aisle. Events unfold slowly, but not too slowly, when the bride and groom are the future king and queen of Helva. Pemrod is getting old. His health is good, but nobody lives forever."

Hearing things spelled out like that made Rina's stomach twist. She could barely tolerate being duchess. She certainly didn't want to be queen, and she had no intention of marrying a man she'd known only a few hours. Now she did reach for the goblet and took a long drink.

"I'm Pemrod's heir," Gant said. "Sooner or later I'm going to have to marry *somebody*. If it can't be for love, then it might as well be a good match."

"*Why* can't it be for love?"

"Ah." Gant paused to sip wine. "Again. Mutual interests. I'll turn the question back to you. Why can't you marry the one you love? Stable boy, isn't it?"

Rina's eyes narrowed, and her voice became icy. "Excuse me?"

"To be honest, I didn't believe it at first," Gant told her. "I mean, a stable boy? Really? It sounded like something from a troubadour's bawdy tavern song."

Rina pushed the goblet away, face tight with anger. "Did you come here to insult me?"

"I came here to *commiserate* with you," Gant said. "You can't marry the one you love because he's . . . let's say *inappropriate* in the eyes of society. Has it occurred to you I might be in the same fix?"

No. It hadn't occurred to her, but of course, why not? It's not like Gant had been saving himself all his life waiting for Rina Veraiin to show up. *How common could she be*, Rina wondered. Chambermaid? Kitchen girl? Rina brightened suddenly at the thought they were both in the same situation. Maybe they could figure a way out of it.

"Your granduncle is the king," Rina reminded him. "Just have her raised to the nobility."

"It's a bit more complicated than that."

"Does it have to be?" Rina asked. "Grant her family some lands far away. *Very* far away. Make her father baron of the swamp or something. It's cheating a bit, but then she'd be nobility."

"That's not the problem." Gant set his goblet aside, a serious look on his face. "He's already noble."

"Then what's the problem? You can—" Her eyes widened as she replayed Gant's words. "He?"

Gant nodded.

"Oh."

Rina grabbed the goblet again, took a long drink to give herself time to think.

"I hope what I've said isn't offensive to you," Gant said.

"No. I'm just . . ."

"Disappointed?"

"Surprised," Rina said.

"He means a lot to me," Gant said. "But obviously not what King Pemrod had in mind."

"That's not a secret someone shares lightly," Rina said. "What makes you think you can trust me?"

"We should probably trust each other if we're going to be married."

"I think you lost me there. I thought we were figuring out how to get *out* of being married."

"Think about it," Gant said. "I'm stuck, right? Sooner or later I'll be expected to produce an heir. That's down the road, but it's coming.

So I need a wife whether I want one or not. Better one who knows what she's getting into than some poor girl who can't understand why her new husband has no interest in getting under her skirts. We'd make a good-looking king and queen, Rina Veraiin. We'd attend royal functions, smile and wave, then adjourn to our separate bedrooms at night."

"But don't forget," Rina said. "Sooner or later people will be expecting an heir."

"Ah, yes." Gant tugged at his ear nervously. He seemed embarrassed. "I was thinking . . . uh . . . that might be where your stable boy could be useful . . . I mean . . . you know."

"What?"

"I would raise the child as my own," Gant said. "He would want for nothing. And of course you would be there to mother him."

Mother him? Suddenly she was queen with a child and married to a man who wasn't the father.

"Stop," Rina said. "You're forgetting something. Not even the king can force me to marry against my will. All I have to do is say no."

"True. Up to a point."

"Meaning?"

"Pemrod is brilliant and experienced," Gant said. "He is also devious and vindictive. Really the worst combination of personality traits. It means that he'll get back at anyone he thinks has wronged him, and he's good at it. With a wave of his scepter, Klaar might as well be a plague zone. All trade will stop. You won't be able to buy anything, or sell your timber anywhere in Helva. If you get your mines going again, nobody will take your silver." Gant shrugged apologetically. "These are just the measures that occur to me off the top of my head. Pemrod will likely think of worse."

"All because I won't marry you?"

"Because you'd be *defying* him," Gant said.

"Is he really so vain?"

"Oh my, yes."

"This is madness."

"I can't disagree."

"I don't *want* to be queen."

"That's refreshing," Gant said. "You can't swing a cat at court without hitting some dizzy girl who'd stab her sister in the eye to become queen herself."

"Choose one of them."

Gant chuckled. "I know the marriage will be a sham, but I'd still prefer it be to somebody I can stand. Anyway, none of those women would satisfy King Pemrod. He's looking for more than just a broodmare. You've proved yourself a capable woman. As a duchess, you outrank most other women at court. And then there are the tattoos. You're powerful, but the king isn't sure *how* powerful. You intrigue him, Rina."

"It sounds like I'm just one more thing he wants to control."

"Doubtless," Gant agreed. "But there's more. In his own way, he truly does care about Helva. He wants to leave a strong kingdom behind him when he passes. That his heir should marry well is a part of that."

The silence stretched between them for a long moment. It was a lot to take in. Rina's head swam with the implications.

Gant pushed back from the table and stood. "It was rude to barge in at such a late hour, but I hope you can see it was important to talk to you alone. And I hope we can keep each other's secrets."

Rina stood. "Of course. We should trust each other. As you say . . . we're in the same fix, aren't we?"

Gant smiled politely, turned, and went to the door. He paused before opening it, looked back at her. "One final thing. I hesitate to alarm you needlessly, but I've come this far, so you might as well know it all."

Rina sighed. "Dumo save us, there's more?"

"As a duchess you have rights and protections a commoner doesn't," Gant said. "If your stable boy got in the way of Pemrod's plans, the king would simply make him go away. I think you know what I mean."

Rina felt her stomach twist.

"You said we should keep each other's secrets, and I agree," Gant said. "I don't mean to be harsh, but you don't keep your own secrets very well. Your people love you, but they whisper. Peasants love their gossip. Sooner or later those whispers always reach the wrong ears. Look to your own, Duchess Veraiin."

"Thank you for your advice, Sir Gant." The words felt leaden in her mouth. She could hardly breathe.

"I hope we can speak again soon." He turned without another word and left.

Rina followed slowly, sliding the door bolt shut.

She turned and sagged back against the door, sighing long and tired.

CHAPTER NINETEEN

Torchlight cast jagged shadows on the rough cobblestone alley.

Prinn was looking for a tavern called the Drunken Imp. She caught site of the sign, a pop-eyed, pointy-eared imp with a mug in his hand and a silly look on his face. She ducked under the low arch and found herself in a small courtyard.

As had been described to her, the tavern was off to the right, and the small stable was on the opposite side of the courtyard to the left. Prinn was here for the second half of her payment. The bag of silver had been the first part. The horse was the second. Horses were in short supply in Klaar. It would have cost her entire bag of silver to buy one for herself, and she needed that horse to follow through with her plan to flee the city.

I can't stay around here after releasing that thing in the castle. Thank Dumo it didn't kill the duchess. But if people find out I had anything to do with it . . .

Laughter and boisterous conversation spilled out of the tavern. She turned her back on it and headed for the stable. She still hadn't decided if she'd ride out over the recently repaired Long Bridge or take Back Gate and the Small Road.

Prinn swung open the stable's wide wooden door. It creaked on rusty hinges. She stepped inside, let her eyes adjust to the shadows within. Three empty stalls. Old, dry hay in the corners. A cracked leather saddle hung on the wall.

No horse.

Sons of bitches.

"Boss wants to see you, Prinn." A voice behind her.

She turned slowly and saw Garth standing there. He had a wicked grin on his face and a tankard in his hand. She understood now. He'd been waiting for her in the tavern, probably keeping watch at the window. There'd never been a horse. Her hand fell to her sword hilt.

Gut him, then run for it, a voice in her head screamed.

Three more men came out of the tavern, cudgels leaning lazily on shoulders. Two more stood in the archway of the courtyard, leaning there and grinning. She suspected they were all greasy alley bruisers, not trained swordsmen. Still, six of them. As plans went, drawing her blade was probably a loser.

"Where's my horse?" Prinn asked.

"Never mind that now," Garth told her. "Boss wants to see you."

"Maybe I don't want to see him," Prinn said. "I fulfilled my part of the bargain. I'm done."

Garth shrugged. "You'll have to ask him about it."

Fight or play along? She scrambled to think of a third option but came up short. "Where?"

Garth jerked a thumb over his shoulder at the tavern. "In there."

"Lead on, then."

Garth headed back inside the tavern, and Prinn followed. The other men closed ranks behind her, and Prinn tensed. She didn't like feeling surrounded but didn't let the fear show.

The dank interior of the tavern smelled like stale beer and man sweat. The only light came from a small oil lamp over the bar and a modest blaze in the stone fireplace across the room. The ceiling was low, the room smoky. Men sat at tables drinking, their heads turning upon Prinn's entrance. All faces unfriendly.

"By the fireplace," Garth said. "He's waiting for you."

The drinkers went back to their tankards and their conversations as Prinn headed for the fireplace. There was a figure there in a cushioned, high-backed leather chair. She circled around, looked down at the man sitting there.

She'd never met the traitor Giffen but recognized him from his description. A pushed-in face, sparse but pointy beard with no moustache, thin and greasy hair spread across a sweaty pate. Prinn hadn't expected Giffen to look so gray and shrunken. It looked as if the man had been ill for a while.

"What is it you want, Giffen?"

"*Lord* Giffen." He sneered up at her. "And I'll ask the questions, thank you. Now pull up a chair, you stupid slut, and pay attention."

Prinn's grip on her sword hilt tightened.

It would be easy. Draw the blade and lunge. Right through the throat.

Her eyes spun once around the room, counting men and looking for other exits. If she killed Giffen, she'd never make it out of the tavern. She swallowed any retort she might have made, pulled up a wooden chair, and sat.

"I need an informant in the castle," Giffen said without preamble. "You."

"We had a deal," Prinn said. "I kept my end."

"You'll do as you're told," Giffen said. "The king has sent a delegation to Klaar. So have those miserable gypsies. I need to know what's going on. You will be my ears and eyes in the castle."

"No."

Giffen sighed. "Don't be tiresome. How is your aunt, may I ask? Her bones still ache? We can put her out of her misery, if you'd like. And your cousins, the oldest is Loreena, yes? Thirteen and fast becoming a ripe young woman. I can arrange to have her passed around to every man in this room, and if there's anything left of her afterward, maybe she can follow in your footsteps at the Wounded Bird. Have I made my point? I grow weary of wasting time."

Prinn trembled, half from fear and half rage. Her stomach felt sick. "You've made your point."

"Good," Giffen said. "Now listen closely."

Giffen was especially interested in anyone coming and going from the castle. He wanted to know why the gypsies were relocated to the shores of Lake Hammish and what the duchess expected in return. He wanted confirmation of a rumor that Rina Veraiin was carrying on with a servant, what was the lad's name, and what was the best way to get to him. Anything that might be used as leverage against the duchess interested him keenly. The king had sent a delegation. What *really* was their mission here in Klaar? Who was this woman from Merridan that Baron Hammish was marrying?

To Prinn, Giffen seemed like a man frustrated that he had to rely on a spy for this sort of information. *He was close to the duke for years, had his finger on the pulse of castle intrigue. Now he sulks in some low-class tavern, snatching at whispers and rumors. A rat trying to remain relevant.*

"And try to get close to the servants," Giffen said. "They hear everything."

Giffen dismissed her, and Prinn stood to go.

"One more thing," Giffen said. "I have hiding places all over the city, so I'm seldom here. Nevertheless, if we see any of the Duchess Veraiin's soldiers here or any of those whores she's deigned to give swords, if you disobey or attempt to cross me in any way, then all the terrible things you imagine and more will come to pass. Prove useful to me, and you can expect more bags of silver. Is this clear?"

"Yes. Perfectly."

"Just remember that I own you." Giffen's words dripped contempt. "You're still a whore as far as I'm concerned, selling yourself at the Wounded Bird. I've bought and paid for you."

And that's when Prinn decided she'd have to kill him.

CHAPTER TWENTY

They'd pushed the dishes of half-eaten eggs and potatoes, a pot of strong, hot tea, to one side of Rina's desk. They hadn't lingered over breakfast. They both wanted to get to the business of Klarissa's gift.

Klarissa unrolled the parchment, spread it on the desk. A map.

"The Scattered Isles?" Rina looked up at the gypsy woman.

"Precisely," Klarissa said. "Do you know how they became scattered?"

Rina searched her memory. There was a vague recollection of a tutor boring her numb as a young girl. Her father had been right. She should have paid better attention to her lessons.

She was tempted to tap into the spirit. Doing so would give her perfect control of herself, inside and out. If she'd ever been taught the history of the Scattered Isles, she could search through the corners of her mind to find the memory. Rina felt herself reaching, eager to tap into the spirit, to feel the power and control.

No! The more you do it, the more you'll keep looking for excuses. Weylan was right. You'll want more and more until you'll burn yourself out.

"I think you'd better remind me," Rina said.

"It happened in the ancient times," Klarissa said. "During the Mage Wars. It had all started with so many factions, petty spell casters, all trying to grab power and get the upper hand. Eventually, two opposing wizards rose to dominance. The lesser wizards across the land made their choices, flocking to one banner or to the other. As you can imagine, many wizards were slaughtered. That's what happens when you toss around so many dangerous spells, I guess. Anyway, the wizards began to wise up. They wanted to send others to do their fighting for them, so they invented ink mages. They tattooed spells into the skin of their warriors and sent them into battle."

"This sounds familiar now," Rina said. "I thought most of it was legend."

"I'm sure fact and legend have become tangled over the centuries," Klarissa said.

"You were explaining how the Scattered Isles became scattered," Rina reminded her.

"They didn't used to be islands at all," Klarissa said. "It was the southern part of the continent where one of the wizards ruled. The other wizard won the war by calling a great fiery rock from the sky. It smashed the southern lands, and the ocean rushed in. The islands were created."

"A great fiery rock from the sky?" Rina's face was deadpan. "Seriously?"

"I'm just telling you the story as it was told to me," Klarissa said. "What was left after the rock smashed the land became known as the Scattered Isles. There are three main islands and about a dozen lesser islands and thousands of other tiny islands. Some are not really islands at all, just clumps of rock to rip the bottom out of a ship."

The gypsy woman gestured at the map where a dotted line threaded its way in a roundabout way from a city on the northern coast, past a number of the smaller isles to an obscure island in the middle of the cluster. "This map has come to us after years of searching, chasing rumors, and trading favors. The wizard who ruled this place was a master of inking the tattoos of power. There is a fortress on this secret island, long abandoned. A stronghold of the master wizard. If there is a place in all the world where we might find more tattoos, it is here. Clues, ink, stencils, scrolls. They may have survived the ages."

"Or maybe they didn't," Rina said. "It was a long time ago. And it's a faraway place."

"Nothing like this is ever easy."

Rina thought about it. Both she and Klarissa had the Prime tattoo down their spines, both put there by the same wizard. Weylan's death meant one fewer person in the world who knew how to ink such a tattoo. It made the women rare individuals. All the other tattoos of power were useless unless a person had the Prime also. Thinking about it that way, Rina almost felt like having the Prime was a responsibility, like searching for this secret fortress was an obligation.

Almost.

"What do you plan to do?" Rina asked.

Klarissa gestured to the map. "My gift to you. And all the knowledge that comes along with it."

Rina had been afraid of this. Now it did feel like some kind of obligation. "I have no gift worthy to give in return."

"It is a gift, Rina Veraiin, not a trade," Klarissa said. "Nothing is expected in return."

Rina kept herself from sighing. Stupid gypsy customs. Of course the woman wanted something in return. Why did they have to go through the motions of friendship? Or maybe they weren't just empty gestures. Maybe Klarissa believed in the custom, actually thought this was a legitimate way to strengthen her relationship with Rina.

"I'm not sure what to do with a gift like this," Rina said. "It's a long way to go just because somebody found an old map."

"There are legends among the Red City fishermen," Klarissa said. "The fishermen sometimes venture into the waters of what they call the Lost Islands, where nobody goes unless the fishing is poor and they're looking for a catch. The fishermen say they've seen something swimming with the dolphins just below the surface of the water. Something in the shape of a person. This person never surfaces, and streaks away before they can get a better look."

"Sailors are always seeing mermaids," Rina said.

"But we can think of other answers, can't we?" Klarissa said. "If a tattoo can let you see through the eyes of a falcon or wield your sword with the strength of a bull or run faster than a horse, then I have to believe that anything is possible."

What she means is that there could be anything on that island. She's dangling the idea of limitless power right in front of my nose. She doesn't realize I'm not interested in that sort of thing.

But was that true? When Rina tapped into the spirit, there was a definite thrill, and it wasn't just physical. The idea that she could somehow be . . . what?

More.

That was it, she realized, the idea she could be more than who she was, achieve things, control destiny itself. In the entire world, only she could—

Listen to yourself, girl. You're almost drunk with the thought of all that power.

On the other hand, do I trust somebody else to have it? At least I know I'm a good person. Or is that how tyrants are made, thinking such things? Wanting power so much is probably the first sign a person shouldn't have it.

"Why didn't you go searching for the island yourself?" Rina asked.

"As you've pointed out, it would be a long journey, dangerous and expensive," Klarissa said. "I don't have a ship, and I can't spare the men. For that matter, I can't spare myself either. My people are settling in a new place, and they need my leadership."

Rina bit her bottom lip, thinking. "I don't think I could go either. I'd have to send someone." And with those words she realized she was considering it. The Perranese had burned most of Klaar's boats, but they were too small anyway, coast huggers for fishing. She'd have to send someone south to Kern to hire a proper ship and crew. As Klarissa said, it would be expensive. Rina wondered whether Borris Dremen might be useful. The merchant probably knew something about hiring a ship for a good price.

"Still." Klarissa picked up the teapot and refilled her cup. "I wouldn't mind sending one of my people as a representative." She sipped from her cup, turning her head to look out the window as if this suggestion were something she was only just thinking of, no big deal.

Which means it actually is a big deal.

"Did you have someone in mind?" Rina asked.

"Maurizan has an adventurous heart," Klarissa said. "But I sometimes feel she lacks . . . direction. I think it would do her good to see something of the world."

Rina frowned, her mind racing to understand. Such a journey would be dangerous. Klarissa had admitted as much. Why send her only daughter into harm's way?

Klarissa must have sensed Rina's struggle. The gypsy woman decided to spell it out.

"The thaw has begun," Klarissa said. "Maurizan would have gone up to see Weylan this summer . . . if the wizard hadn't passed."

Of course! How could I be so stupid?

Weylan had inked the Prime onto Klarissa's mother and then onto Klarissa herself. Maurizan had been in line to be inked next, but the old wizard had died before it could happen. In fact, Maurizan held a bit of a grudge against Rina. Inking the Prime along Rina's spine had been Weylan's final act, and in an odd way the young gypsy felt something had been taken from her. It wasn't accurate to say Rina had stolen Maurizan's birthright, but she could see how it might seem that way to a young girl.

All her life she's dreamed of those powers, and then I came along out of nowhere.

But Rina still felt she was missing something. Klarissa wanted the Prime for her daughter, and that was understandable. But she wanted something from Rina too. It was almost as if she were asking . . . permission?

Yes, that was it, Rina realized. For some reason, Klarissa thought she needed Rina's blessing, as if Rina wouldn't want Maurizan to have—

Rina gasped.

Klarissa's eyes widened. "What is it?"

It was true. The thought of Maurizan having the Prime made Rina clench her fists. Rina had known two wizards in her life—Weylan and Talbun—and both had made similar comments about how jealously wizards guarded their secrets. They were a petty and competitive breed, and Rina was ashamed to admit that apparently ink mages were no better. The more people who had the powers of the ink mage, the less special Rina would feel.

So what makes me so special? I'm a duchess? So what? That's an accident of birth. Who am I to keep somebody else from having what I have? These tattoos are not my identity. They are not the sum total of who I am.

"I'm sorry," Rina said. "I was just . . . thinking."

I have to prove that I'm not like that. That I'm not that petty. No, it's not just about being petty, is it?

"I'm going to arrange an expedition to the Scattered Isles," Rina said.

If I don't obsess, if I'm not letting the power control me, that proves something, doesn't it?

"And I think Maurizan should go also," Rina continued.

I don't care if Maurizan has the Prime. It means nothing to me. I am a duchess, and that has nothing to do with the tattoos. Alem loves me, and that has nothing to do with the tattoos.

"And if we find the lost fortress of this ancient wizard, if the secrets of the ink mage are there," Rina said, "then I will do everything in my power to make sure your daughter Maurizan gets the Prime."

Saying it made her stomach clench, and Rina hated herself for it.

"I hope you'll accept this as my gift to you."

CHAPTER
TWENTY-ONE

Having important guests was supposed to be an honor. Really, it was a pain in the ass.

Rina remembered when her father had entertained visiting nobility. It had seemed all parties and flirting with young lordlings and, well, relentless entertainment. Now that it was her duty to keep these tedious people entertained, it was a lot less fun.

Brasley had come along with Rina to accompany the count and his retinue on a morning hunt. Gant had bagged a large buck, and that had seemed to be enough to declare the expedition a success. A luncheon followed with plenty of wine, and then the guests were allowed to retire and refresh themselves so they could summon the energy for more eating and drinking at the evening feast.

Only Rina seemed to notice that Brasley's good humor was clearly forced. As an adolescent, Rina had thought Brasley dashing. Later, she'd found the man brash, full of himself, and immature. Now she thought of him as a friend, but she saw no way to help him.

Rina used the afternoon pause in the hospitalities to steal away to the prayer tower. It wasn't a place that anyone would stumble into by accident, which was why Rina had elected to store all of Weylan's things there. The only people who went to the prayer tower were those willing to climb a tight spiral staircase up ten stories to a barren room meant for quiet meditation and prayer. Rina and her family had been only perfunctorily religious, so the tall, narrow tower was visited only occasionally by those looking for a panoramic view of the valley below.

Rina felt out of breath and slightly dizzy by the time she reached the top. More than ever, she refused to tap into the spirit for everyday tasks. It was a way to assure herself that she was in control.

She took the key ring from the inside pocket of her cloak, found the door key, and entered.

She briefly surveyed the small room with its rough floors and unadorned walls. A plain wooden chair and table with books stacked atop it. There were padlocked chests against the wall, containing the wizard's other possession, the keys to the padlocks on her ring. A brazier and a stack of wood for warmth, flint and steel. Rina reminded herself to bring a kettle and tea next time. Perhaps a narrow cot and bedding.

My home away from home for the foreseeable future.

Rina was determined to go through the wizard's books. She would make his secrets her own.

She stacked kindling and wood in the brazier, and lit a modest fire. When it was warm enough, she took off her cloak and hung it on the back of the chair. She went to the windows. It really was a fantastic view, the snowcapped mountains in one direction, the valley stretching in the other, a glimpse of Lake Hammish beyond.

You're stalling. Get to work.

The problem was that she really didn't know what she was looking for. Lore about the tattoos, yes, obviously, but what would that mean? Did Weylan own a book titled *Everything You Need to Know about Magic Tattoos*? Rina doubted it. She was educated, but she wasn't a scholar.

The only thing to do was dive into the books and find whatever she could find.

She sat in the chair and scooted it up to the table. She examined the stack of books. A thick leather-bound volume caught her eye. Tight gold lettering down the spine doubtlessly made it clear what the book was about . . . if one spoke the language.

Rina did not.

Not the best start, is it? Okay, just open it up and have a look anyway.

She flipped the book open to the middle and squinted at a random page.

The letters—no, not letters, but symbols, foreign and impossible to read—swam before her eyes, her vision going blurry, her head light. She tried to avert her gaze but couldn't. The symbols swirled on the page, making her dizzy. Then there was a roar in her ears, the sound of the ocean, the sound of screaming. She found it hard to breathe.

The symbols tried to worm their way in through her eyes, into her brain. They seemed suddenly too bright to look at, and yet she couldn't turn away. She opened her mouth to scream, but only a strangled croak came out. The bright light seared her eyes. She couldn't even blink.

Rina set her jaw, drew a deep breath and held it. With everything she had, she wrenched her eyes from the page.

She tumbled off the chair and onto the hard, wooden floor. She stood on wobbly legs, reached for the book, her gaze averted, and slammed it shut. She immediately fell back to the floor, dizzy and dis-oriented, the roar in her ears slowly fading. She panted, drawing in cool, ragged breaths.

No matter how many times she blinked, red spots kept exploding in front of her eyes.

Rina stuck a chuma stick in the corner of her mouth. She leaned into the brazier to puff it to life. The heat on her face was sobering. She sat on the floor again, and scooted back until she felt herself up against the stone wall beneath one of the windows. Her hands shook. She blew out a long plume of gray smoke.

Okay, that didn't go so well. What the blazes did you think was going to happen, fucking around with a wizard's magic books?

She took another long pull on the chuma stick. The mildly narcotic effect began to seep into her limbs. Her vision cleared.

This isn't going to work. You don't know anything about all this wizard shit.

She puffed and sat, looking at the pile of books and the chests. Anything in there could get her killed. What she really needed was someone like Talbun. In some ways the woman was terrifying, but she'd helped Rina by giving her the lightning-bolt tattoos on her ankles. If anyone could make sense of Weylan's books, it would be her.

Too bad she's hundreds of miles away.

Rina drew in a lungful of chuma smoke, held it, then let it out. The smoke drifted to the center of the room and hung there.

A moment later, the cloud of smoke began to turn as if it had caught a draft. Instead of drifting away, the smoke began to swirl around itself a little faster. Rina blinked. The ball of smoke spun faster around itself, and it was obvious now it wasn't the result of an errant breeze. A pinprick of blinding light sparked to life in the center of the cloud and slowly began to grow.

Rina scrambled to her feet, scooted around the glowing smoke ball with her back against the wall until she came to the door. She put her hand on the door handle, ready to flee if necessary. Her other hand came up to shield her eyes from the growing brightness.

The tower began to vibrate, shutters rattling, dust falling from the rafters.

The smoke was a blur now, revolving at impossible speed around the light.

Had she somehow unleashed one of Weylan's spells when she'd been flipping through his book? An instinct told her to run, but she stood transfixed.

The glow began to take shape, elongate. Rina saw it was now the shape of a person, legs and arms. It was a woman.

The light pulsed one last time so bright that Rina had to turn away. An explosive rush of air nearly knocked her off her feet.

Smoke and light had both vanished when Rina turned back. A naked woman stood in the middle of the room. She teetered, a moment of wobbly legs, then fell to the floor with a loud thump.

Rina rushed to her side, went to her knees but stopped short of touching her.

The woman's skin was red down the side of her left arm and leg as if from a burn. Dark bruises were scattered along the rest of her body. The woman lifted her head. Blood streamed from her nostrils and the corners of her eyes.

Rina almost didn't recognize the face for all the blood and the matted hair. "Talbun!"

Talbun turned wild eyes on Rina. "The gods are at war."

♦ ♦ ♦

Talbun sat at the table atop the prayer tower staring into a bowl of weak broth. When Rina had first met Talbun, the wizard had been beautiful and glamorous, her spells keeping her eternally young. Now she seemed pale, strain showing around her eyes.

The wizard hadn't recognized Rina had first, had babbled about the gods a few more seconds before passing out.

Rina had tapped into the spirit and flown down the stairs, sure-footed and fast. She'd grabbed the first servant she'd seen and had calmly and clearly issued instructions—she needed two female servants at the top of the prayer tower immediately, at least one with nursing skills. Salve for burns. Food. Water. A simple, clean dress. Shoes. Underthings. "Tell them we've got a hurt woman. And she needs to be cleaned up too."

She'd paused only long enough to confirm the servant had understood before streaking back up the stairs to the top of the prayer tower.

When Talbun's eyes had finally flickered open again, a young girl with a warm, wet cloth was tending to her, wiping the blood from her face. When the wizard had been sufficiently cleaned, they'd dressed her in a simple dress, but Rina had been forced to cut the left sleeve off with a knife, so the girl could attend to Talbun's burns.

They'd sat the wizard in a chair, and the girl had lightly rubbed a greasy salve down her left arm. They'd hiked up her dress to apply more salve to her thigh.

"Is it bad?" Rina had asked.

"No, milady," the girl had said. "These burns are the mildest kind. The salve will ease the pain."

Talbun endured the ministrations stoically, grunting answers to questions, still stunned or perhaps in some kind of shock.

The girl had just finished with the salve when another girl had arrived from the kitchens with a basket—chicken broth, brown bread, cheese.

Now Talbun sat there, sighing and looking down at the bowl of broth.

Rina had a thousand questions for the woman but forced herself to be patient. Whatever Talbun had been through, it had taken its toll. Rina would let Talbun gather herself before pestering her for information.

The kitchen girl filled a mug with water, and set it on the table next to the bowl of broth.

Talbun picked it up, drank. "Do we have anything stronger?" It was the first thing she'd said since raving about the gods.

"I'm sorry," Rina said. "I didn't think of it."

"Begging your pardon, milady." The kitchen girl went into the basket and came out with an earthen jug, the lid sealed with wax. "Bruny packed this. Just up from the cellar."

Rina laughed, relieved and grateful. "Thank Dumo for Bruny."

Talbun's eyes shifted to Rina. "Bruny?"

"The ranking servant," Rina explained. "She runs the kitchens."

Talbun finished the water and held the cup out to the kitchen girl. "Please."

The girl broke the seal on the jug and filled Talbun's cup.

Talbun lifted the cup. "To Bruny." She tilted the cup back, drained it. She closed her eyes, sighed.

When she opened her eyes again, she looked at Rina. "You should join me."

"It's okay," Rina said. "I don't need any."

"You will."

"I'm sorry, milady." The kitchen girl looked pained. "There's only one cup."

Talbun held out the cup for a refill. "We'll share."

The kitchen girl filled the cup again.

Talbun took a more modest sip this time, then set the cup on the table and slid it toward Rina, who picked it up and drank.

Talbun's eyes flicked to the servants than back to Rina again. "We need to talk."

"Thank you," Rina said to the girls. "You can go now. Our guest needs her privacy. Tell no one she's here."

The servants exchanged looks then said, "Yes, milady," as they dipped hasty curtsies and left.

Rina slid the cup back to Talbun, who drank.

"Where am I?" Talbun asked.

It seemed an odd question. Didn't she know? "Klaar."

Talbun nodded, drank again, and gave the cup back to Rina.

Rina drank.

"How do you want to do this?" Talbun asked. "Shall I just start talking, or would you prefer to ask questions?"

"Why are you here?" Rina asked. "What happened?"

"What happened is . . . a bit of a story," Talbun said. "I'll answer the why-am-I-here question first. It's simpler. It will get us started. Tell me, were you talking about me or thinking about me right before I arrived?"

Rina was startled to realize she had been. "I wished you were here to help me figure something out."

Talbun nodded, drank more wine. "That explains it. That's what the magic latched on to."

"A spell?"

"A defensive spell. Something I never expected to use," Talbun said. "I escaped to a place between worlds and was held there outside of place and time. The magic would not allow me to be called back until I could go someplace safe. It latched on to your thoughts, this place, and brought me here."

Rina was shaking her head. "I don't understand. A place between worlds? That doesn't make any—"

"Between realities," Talbun said. "It's hard to explain."

"But why did you have to escape?"

"Because I was going to die."

"But—"

This doesn't make any sense. She's probably the most powerful wizard in Helva.

"What day is it?" Talbun demanded.

"What day?"

"Damn you, what day is today?"

Rina told her. A week before the thaw festival. Almost winter's end by the calendar in Helva.

"Blast. Three weeks," Talbun said. "Nearly three weeks."

"You've been hiding for three weeks?"

"Time didn't exist for me," Talbun said. "I was outside of time."

"Outside of . . . but how could—"

"Quiet," Talbun said. "Listen."

Rina shut her mouth.

"I was in peril, and the spell allowed me to hide," Talbun explained. "Your thinking of me was the final element needed to bring me back from my hiding place. That's all you need to understand. I don't have the energy to explain further." She drained the cup and set it back on the table.

Rina cleared her throat. *Well, okay, then.* She picked up the jug and refilled the cup.

"I don't mean to try your patience," Rina said carefully. "I'm just trying to understand."

Talbun sighed and drank. "No, I should apologize. My nerves are frayed. It's been a couple of centuries since I thought I was going to die. I'd forgotten what fear felt like. I don't fancy it."

"It's okay now," Rina said. "You're safe here."

Talbun laughed.

"You were guarding the priests, yes?" Rina said. "During the Long Dream?"

"Yes."

"What happened?"

Talbun blew out another tired sigh and shook her head. "I can't say for sure. I think I know. It's guesswork."

Rina filled her cup with wine again, fixed her with a stare she hoped was supportive and encouraging. "Then take a guess."

CHAPTER TWENTY-TWO

Three weeks earlier . . .

Talbun screamed for the captain of the guard.

Captain Joff burst into Talbun's quarters, sword and armor rattling, helm carried under one arm. The man seemed ever ready, as if he never ate or slept. His eyes popped with alarm when he saw the smear of blood beneath Talbun's nose. "Milady! You're hurt!"

"Never mind that," the wizard said. "The temple is under attack. Gather every man. Saddle the horses. I can't wait. Follow as fast as you can."

Joff nodded briefly, spun on his heel, and departed, already yelling for his men to make ready.

Talbun grabbed a dress of sturdy material. Boots. It was one thing to lounge around half-naked, sipping wine, under normal circumstances. She liked to be comfortable, and she liked the way she looked, but going into battle that way didn't strike her as a good idea. She briefly lamented giving away her armor to Duchess Veraiin. She'd hadn't expected ever to wear it again, and anyway, she'd already cast magical wards that were better protection than any armor could be. She buckled around her waist a thin belt from which hung a modest dagger in a leather sheath. There always were those rare occasions when a bit of mundane steel was the answer to a problem instead of a spell.

She wished she could wait for her guards to accompany her, but every moment of delay brought her closer to failure—if it wasn't too late already. Her job had been to guard the Temple of Kashar while the monks within slept the hundred years of the Long Dream. Talbun's tower had been built at the bottom of the mountain to watch over the only road leading up to the temple. Whatever was up there hadn't come past the watchful eyes of the tower.

Talbun closed her eyes and took a deep breath. The spell she was about to attempt took a lot of energy and concentration. She'd cast it before, but only a few times. She began to speak the arcane words, and in moments the spell became a torrent of blurred syllables trying to get out of her. She couldn't have stopped the spell now even if she'd wanted to.

She opened her eyes and saw the tower being stripped away a layer at a time, like watching an artist add color to a painting but in reverse. Talbun reminded herself it wasn't the tower that was fading away. It was her. She closed her eyes again and pictured the top of the mountain, the temple, the wide courtyard with its broad flagstones, ancient and cracked. She'd never been there, but she'd seen the place before through scrying spells.

She felt herself go light, and lift. In almost the same moment she had weight again, her feet firm on the ground.

She opened her eyes . . . to the sight of a blazing hellscape.

The temple's wooden outbuildings had been almost completely consumed, the flames rising high and creating a hellish glow in the still-weak early morning light. Black smoke roiled across the courtyard.

Bodies littered the flagstones, singed and smoking. Talbun identified the green robes of the Kashar monks. Other bodies were burned beyond recognition. The way the bodies were arranged suggested the monks had been fleeing the temple. None had made it. Scores lay dead, burned and blackened. The smell brought back a long-forgotten fray a century ago. The wizard had done her best to stay *out* of battles.

Talbun stepped around the bodies, heading for the temple itself. It was a wide, two-story stone building. Stone steps led up to fluted columns lining the ground floor. An enormous set of closed double doors fifteen feet high. The second story was lined with high, arched windows. Black smoke billowed, a flickering fiery orange glow visible beyond the smoke. The temple was built of stone, but whatever was within burned freely. Just below the temple's peaked roof was a stone carving of Kashar, the serpent circling the eye.

I've failed, Talbun thought. *For nearly a hundred years I've guarded these monks through the Long Dream, only to fail here at the last.*

With trepidation she began to climb the steps up to the temple. *I have to look. I have to know for sure.*

She'd just put a boot on the second step when the huge double doors exploded outward with a deafening blast. The doors flew at her, fire belching from the open doorway. Talbun flinched and turned, felt the heat, hot and stinging, chase after her.

The doors weighed at least a ton each. One tumbled down the steps, cracking stone and bouncing at a perilous angle past Talbun. She threw herself down as the second door flew over her head, coming within a foot of taking her head off.

Talbun rolled back down the steps, slapping at her sleeve and trying to put out the flames where her dress had caught fire.

She looked back up at the temple. Not only had the doors been blasted off their hinges, but much of the facade had been destroyed, leaving a gaping hole in the front of the temple. The interior was a storm of flame. Two gigantic figures battled within the fire.

One of the figures was a gigantic serpent. Talbun recalled Rina's experience with the temple guardian, a stone statue of a serpent that came to life and attacked her. Perhaps this creature was something similar, a guardian to repel the intruder.

The other figure was a huge man—or at least the shape of a man. He looked to be wearing bulky spiked armor, but only his silhouette was visible, the details of his appearance lost amid the flames. The enormous serpent coiled around the figure, mouth open to strike. The other being grabbed the serpent by the jaws, prying its mouth open.

The great serpent's tail thrashed, and the ground shook. It felt like the entire mountain might shake to rubble. A cold fear gripped Talbun she hadn't felt in decades. She hastily mumbled protection spells even as she knew they wouldn't be enough.

The hulking dark figure in the flames managed to get a powerful arm around the serpent's throat. The huge snake redoubled its thrashing, but the dark figure spread its legs, taking up a wide stance to steady itself. It twisted sharply, wrenching the snake's neck.

There was a snap so sharp and loud it made Talbun flinch.

The figure flung the snake corpse aside with contempt.

The serpent's body flew out of the flames, through the wrecked temple doorway and toward Talbun. She swallowed a panicked scream and dove to the side.

The serpent's body crashed down the steps, singed and limp. It was impossibly long, its tail stretching back into the temple. Its dark-green scales glistened in the firelight. A golden ichor oozed from its wounds like blood. In the center of the serpent's face was a single glowing eye.

The glow faded, then went out completely.

Talbun stumbled to her feet, gawked at the beast.

This isn't some guardian. This is Kashar himself. A god slain right in front of me.

She raised her terrified eyes again to the temple.

Another god stood there in all of his terrible glory. His armor was fashioned from some jagged dark metal. Talbun still couldn't make out details through the flames, just gleaming eyes from the slits in his helm. The god raised an arm toward Talbun.

I'm going to die.

The god clenched his fist, and a brilliant green light shot out from his hand and struck Talbun. A hot-pink globe of light blazed into existence around the wizard, shielding her from the attack. The protective globe was Talbun's strongest ward, but with a single strike from the god, she already felt the globe shudder on the edge of collapse.

The god still stood amid the flames inside the temple, visible only as a hulking silhouette.

If I knew which god it was, maybe I could guess a weakness or at least try to understand what's going—

Another stab of eldritch light lanced out and shattered Talbun's shield. The blast lifted her and tossed her back thirty feet. She smacked into one of the large boulders that ringed the clearing, felt and heard bones snap, then tumbled to the ground hard, twisting an ankle.

Pain shocked though her, tears blinding her. She summoned the will to ignore her injuries and mumbled the words to a spell. Immediately a healing warmth spread though her body, bones mending, bruises fading.

That's my only healing spell. If he hits me again—

The green light blazed, and Talbun dove out of the way. The boulder behind her was blasted to pieces. Talbun threw herself to the ground, her arms going over her head as dust and rubble rained down.

The wizard heaved herself to her feet, coughing and wiping dust from her eyes.

The god stirred within the temple.

He's staying inside. Why doesn't he come out?

The god roared, went to one knee, and slammed a fist into the floor of the temple.

It sounded like a crack of thunder. The ground shook beneath Talbun's feet, almost knocking her over. The earth still shaking, Talbun widened her stance to keep upright. Everything shook apart around her. The burned-out buildings collapsed in on themselves, sending swirling sparks into the air along with black smoke.

The earsplitting sound of fracturing stone drew her attention back to the temple.

From the strike of the god's fist, fissures spread rapidly down the stone steps. The fissures glowed a bright red, branched, and branched again, like a hot bright spiderweb spreading out from the burning temple and across the flagstones of the courtyard. Wherever the web intersected the body of a fallen monk, a blinding flash of red swallowed the corpse, red lines circling the body as if wrapping it in a cocoon of pure light.

In a matter of seconds, the body of every monk was wrapped in a brilliant red glow, sixty or seventy in all.

And suddenly the glow ceased. The ground stopped shaking. The only sound was the lick of flame from the burning temple, the snap and pop of shifting lumber as the last of the temple's outbuildings fell over.

Talbun stood completely still.

Is that it? Is it over?

She could just make out the sound of something like a boot scraping on stone. A second later, she heard a similar sound come from another direction. Soon the entire courtyard crawled with the sound. She blinked. The ground was moving.

No, of course it wasn't. It wasn't the ground that was moving. It was what was on the ground.

The corpses.

The bodies of the monks quivered, hesitantly at first, as if they were trying to remember how to move again, feet twitching, hands scraping along the flagstones, fingers flexing and struggling for purchase.

Well, this is . . . interesting.

She readied herself, summoning a spell to the surface of her mind.

The corpses lurched to their feet, took halting steps toward her. Smoke still rose from many of them. Their eyes raged with the same red glow that had enveloped them seconds before. They moved as one mass slowly but steadily toward the wizard.

Talbun's eyes made a quick scan of the courtyard. The only path leading back down the mountain was on the other side of the corpse horde that was moving toward her.

She muttered arcane words, and a sword of pure light appeared in her hand. The blade was straight and thin and glowed a cold blue. It had been years since she'd wielded a weapon of any kind, but her old reflexes returned quickly as she swung at the closest corpse.

Talbun wasn't particularly strong, but that hardly mattered with the spell sword. The blade sliced through the corpse's neck like soft cheese. The light blinked out of its eyes as the head went flying.

The dead monks crowded closer, and Talbun swung the spell sword wildly, hacking the limbs reaching out for her. The corpses didn't even flinch, the armless dead still pressing in, mouths working like grotesque predatory fish. She swung again, took off another head, and the monk collapsed inanimate into a heap.

The heads! You've got to decapitate them.

Talbun swung hard, lopping off a head, the backswing taking off another. If the spell sword had been heavy steel, Talbun would have been fatigued quickly. But the weapon was no heavier than a willow switch. Talbun kept swinging, and heads rolled.

A few seconds later, a pile of monk corpses lay in a semicircle at her feet. She was panting now, a cold trickle of sweat down her back. The dead continued to press in relentlessly, and she was no closer to breaking through and escaping.

A corpse snatched at her from the side. Talbun flinched back, but a monk had hold of her sleeve. She lashed out with the sword and cut the monk's hand off at the wrist. More of the dead crowded her from all sides.

Too many. I need to try something else.

She scrolled through the spells in her head but none fit the situation.

Idiot. You're the most powerful wizard in Helva, and you're going to die because you memorized the wrong spells.

One of the monks latched on to her left wrist, grip like iron. She lifted the spell sword to strike, but two more corpses grabbed her arm. She struggled as they started to pull her down.

Talbun bit the inside of her lip. Hard. She spit blood, and the red splatter landed at her feet. She muttered the words of her spell and stepped back, yanking her sword arm from the dead monk's grip, slashing through the middle of the monk's face.

She finished her spell, and the droplets of blood began to bubble and expand in front of her. Five of the blood droplets were substantial enough to catch the magic. In a matter of seconds, they grew into gelatinous mounds and then elongated and took shape. All five were perfect duplicates of Talbun herself, except they were nude, and red as the blood the wizard had spilled.

The duplicates pushed forward into the corpses, heedless of their own safety, the dead monks clawing and grabbing at them. Talban stumbled back against one of the perimeter boulders, chest heaving as she gulped breath. The duplicates would keep the corpses at bay for only a minute. Her mind raced for some plan.

A horn sounded.

Beyond the mass of corpses, Talbun saw two dozen mounted soldiers riding fast, spears lowered in a charge. Joff sat astride the lead horse, spear tucked under one arm, his other hand bringing a curved horn to his mouth, blowing hard to sound that rescue was on the way.

Talbun's heart leapt. *Bless you, Joff, you loyal old hound.*

The horsemen crashed into the rear rank of corpses with a deafening clamor of armor, spears, pierced bodies, and horses tromping singed monks into the flagstones.

The attack had a mixed effect. A dozen corpses fell, jabbed clean through the chest with spears. Others went down, trampled by the horses. A few of the monks attempting to push past the duplicates turned to face the new threat instead.

Half the corpses that went down stood up again, moving awkwardly with spears through their chests. Joff's men rode among them, hacking down with swords, slicing away random chunks of monk.

"The heads!" Talbun yelled. "Take off the heads."

Joff nodded, shouted the instructions back to his men. Immediately the soldiers began the decapitations, swords rising and falling with meaty *thwaks*.

The corpses swirled around the men and horses, heedless of their own safety. The soldiers continued to hack and slash, heads tumbling and rolling along the ground. Moments later, the sounds of slaughter died away, until only the armor clank of dismounting soldiers, the snort of horses, and the crackle of flame from the temple could be heard.

Talbun looked around the courtyard. Piles of bodies littered the flagstones, heads everywhere, many with expressions of pain and terror etched across their faces. The wizard gaped at the macabre scene, not completely understanding what had happened. Her eyes darted to the gaping hole in the temple and the fire beyond. No sign of the hulking god who'd menaced her.

A god. Is that possible?

Her eyes shifted to the great serpent Kashar. Dead.

She waved her hand absently, and the duplicates dissolved into puddles of dirty blood.

Joff leapt from his horse and ran to her. "Milady, are you all right?"

"Just bruised, Joff."

Joff gestured to the carnage around him. "This . . . this is madness."

Talbun shook her head. She didn't have an explanation. All she knew was that she'd failed to protect the monks during the Long Dream. And yet she couldn't quite fault her efforts. For nearly a century she'd kept brigands and petty thieves from molesting the monks while they slumbered. How could she have known . . .

What? What did she really know about anything? Gods? At war?

"We've got to get out of here," Talbun said.

"Of course," Joff said. "I'll gather the men and—"

A sudden, piercing howl shot through Talbun's brain, a cry of fierce brutal hatred.

Joff and the rest of his men grabbed their heads, eyes shut tight, pain clear on their faces. She looked at the temple.

The god had returned.

No!

Twisting flames shot out of the temple and engulfed Joff's men. Screams of pain and horror. The flames consumed Joff and were mere feet from her.

She turned to run, felt the flames blister her on one side. Talbun opened her mouth to scream, but instead the words of a spell poured out, and the entire world went white.

◆　◆　◆

Talbun drank wine. Telling the story had made her thirsty again. "It was an *automatic* spell. It casts itself when all seems lost and hides me in a nowhere place between realities . . . as I've already made clear."

Rina blinked. *Uh . . . yeah. Clear as mud.*

"What about the spell that let you travel instantly to the top of the mountain?" Rina said. "What did you call it?"

"Teleportation," the wizard said.

Rina mouthed the word, tasting its strangeness. "Why didn't you use it again to escape?"

Talbun sighed. "When you cast a spell it's gone. Like pouring water out of a bucket. The bucket's empty. To get it back I need to study the spell again. But that's in my spell book. And *that's* in my tower."

Rina realized again how special her tattoos were. The magic was hers to command anywhere and anytime. Wizards spent years learning how to read and understand magic. Rina didn't have to. She didn't need to keep a spell book. On the other hand, she used up something within herself whenever she wielded the magic. Too much, and she could destroy herself, or at least that had been Weylan's warning.

"Maybe it wasn't a god," Rina ventured. "Perhaps some other being—"

"It was a god."

Ah. Okay, then.

"Why didn't the god come out of the temple to attack you?" Rina asked.

"I've been thinking about that," Talbun said. "My theology is rusty. I'll try to keep it basic."

"Please."

"The gods live on a different plane than we do . . . a different spiritual realm," Talbun began. "They only come to our plane under extraordinary circumstances. Most scholars agree that they affect humanity only indirectly, and mostly through their priests and other servants. That's why when we pray to a god to strike an enemy dead or save us from a flood, it hardly ever happens."

Rina glanced down at herself. When she was fourteen, she'd prayed for bigger breasts. It hadn't happened. Probably not high on Dumo's priority list.

"Many years ago an elder priest explained it to me like this," Talbun said. "A god's temple is the place where that god touches our plane. As a result, the temple is half in and half out of both realms. Oh, I don't mean every country chapel or city church. I'm talking about the mother temple, the cradle and origin of every sect. The Kashar Temple at the top of the mountain was such a place."

"You're saying that for gods, the temples are like little portals between realms?"

Talbun shrugged.

"Then . . . this god—the one who killed Kashar—he could hop from temple to temple, picking fights with other gods?"

Talbun shrugged again.

"You don't *know?*" An anxious edge in Rina's voice.

"No."

"But this could mean—" Panic rose within Rina. "What could this *mean?*"

Talbun frowned. Her eyes went hard. "I. Don't. Know."

Rina put a hand on her stomach, exhaled raggedly. "Dumo help us."

"For all we know," Talbun said, "Dumo is already dead."

EPISODE FOUR

CHAPTER
TWENTY-THREE

"And so, here in the sight of Dumo and before the good nobility of Klaar," intoned Bishop Feridixx Hark, hands raised toward the temple's vaulted ceilings, "I pronounce you, Baron Brasley Hammond, now in a state of joyous matrimony to Lady Fregga Becham. You may begin your new lives together with your first kiss."

First kiss. That's a laugh, Rina thought. She doubted there was any part of Fregga that Brasley had left unkissed.

Rina sat in the first pew along with some of the other Klaar nobility. Count Becham and his retinue also sat in the front row but across the aisle. The dozen pews behind them were packed with the important people of Klaar, and the standing room behind the pews was packed shoulder to shoulder with those not quite important enough to rate a seat.

Everyone loves a wedding, I guess. Or maybe everyone just loves a party.

Brasley's wedding day had turned out to be even warmer than expected, and the main castle courtyard had been set up for a magnificent reception, huge braziers lit to fend off any lingering winter chill.

Barrels of wine and beer tapped. In the tradition of Klaar, they'd laid a banquet of simple food but plenty of it: roasted meats and potatoes, and fresh vegetables, hard to come by after a long winter, but they'd managed to scrape up some carrots and onions.

Not that anyone would care once the wine was flowing.

Rina had told Stasha to spare no expense when making the arrangements. Count Becham had mentioned to Rina that he just *might* be able to convince the Royal Bank to forgive Klaar's debt, and she was going to do everything possible to keep the man happy.

Brasley lifted Fregga's veil and set it back on her head. Fregga smiled so widely that Rina was worried her face might split in half. But she did have a certain glow about her. Pregnant *and* a new bride, after all. That would probably set any woman glowing. Rina had to admit Fregga looked good. She was an ample woman with lots of soft curves. Some might say she was fat if all that ampleness had been arranged poorly, but her father had obviously hired the best dressmakers in Merridan to make damn sure Fregga looked her best on this special day. The wedding gown was nothing short of magnificent, with a thirty-foot train.

Brasley leaned in and kissed Fregga gently on the lips.

The temple erupted with enthusiastic applause.

Bishop Hark stood on a step behind the newlyweds and raised his arms again. "I present to you Baron and Baroness Hammond of Klaar!"

The applause surged.

Arm in arm, Brasley and Fregga descended the steps from the altar and slowly walked down the temple's center aisle, smiling and nodding to the congregation. Two boys in velvet finery darted from nowhere to pick up the ends of the gown's train and follow dutifully behind the newlyweds. As they passed each pew, those seated there rose and continued to applaud.

Brasley's smile probably convinced almost everyone. Rina knew better. *Trapped like a rat, poor bastard.*

Once the bride and groom had passed, the congregation fell in behind them to follow the couple out of the temple. Rina found herself walking next to Count Becham.

"They make a lovely couple," she said.

Becham blew out a relieved sigh. "Last daughter out of the house. Thank Dumo."

At the mention of Dumo, Rina glanced up at the temple's high ceiling. She half expected a god to show up and pick a fistfight with Dumo, but of course this was not Dumo's mother temple, which was miles away in Tul-Agnon.

The wedding procession spilled out into the street, Brasley and Fregga leading the way. The young couple waved at the citizens who hung out of windows, cheering and waving banners. Brasley and Fregga were stars for a day. The rest of the processional strolled along behind, socializing and patiently enduring the short walk from temple to castle, where the party would soon begin.

A moment later, Borris Dremen was walking next to Rina.

"Eager for the reception, Borris?"

"Too busy, I'm sorry to say, your grace," said the head of the merchants' guild. "A few very minor loose ends to tie up on the little favor you asked."

And by "little favor," Dremen meant a huge, time-consuming effort.

"Are we all set?" Rina asked.

"It was a tall order," Borris said, "but the ship will be waiting in Kern, fully provisioned. A reliable captain and crew."

"Excellent. Thank you, Borris."

"It was . . . expensive, your grace. There were a lot of things to pull together at the last minute."

"Don't tell me how much it cost until later," Rina said. "I'm on my way to a party, and I don't want to spoil the mood."

Dremen excused himself to see to the final details.

They finally arrived at the reception, and the newlyweds took the place of honor at the high table, flanked by Becham, Rina, Gant, and a few other important nobles. Lesser nobles sat at lower tables facing the high one. Servants scurried to fill wine goblets. As the ranking person in attendance, Rina gave the first toast, then Count Becham, then a bunch of other tedious people, until proceedings dissolved into a general sort of merrymaking, food, drink, and laughter.

A sideways glance at Fregga made Rina smile. The new bride was laughing at something so hard, her face had gone red, wine spilling out of the goblet in her hand and over her white fingers. Brasley had an arm around her shoulder, pulling her close.

This party is moving along just fine. They don't need the duchess anymore.

Rina excused herself and slipped away.

After the noisy party, the silence within the castle settled over her like a balm. *Just for a little while. I know, I'm hostess, but just a quick break. I need to think.*

Someone behind her cleared his throat.

She turned, saw Gant standing there.

So much for a moment to myself.

"Can we talk?" Gant's eyes darted up and down the hallway. "Someplace private."

"I'm going to my quarters," Rina said. "Come on."

He followed her upstairs, and before she had a chance to enter her rooms, she spotted one of Tosh's women hovering at the end of the hall. She felt bad for them. Rina had made it clear to Tosh she needed her space, but at the same time the ladies had been tasked with guarding her. The compromise had been the women lingering always just at the edge of her peripheral vision, close enough to rush in and save the day if needed, but not so close as to crowd her. She'd even spotted a few of the woman at the edge of the wedding processional on the walk from the temple.

She nodded curtly at the guard, then went into her room, motioning for Gant to follow.

"I can send a servant for wine if you like," Rina offered.

"No," Gant said. "I've already had quite a lot at the reception."

"Tea?"

"Nothing. Thank you."

"You seem . . . distracted."

"I'm bloody terrified."

"Tell me."

"I need you to marry me, Rina."

His abruptness made her want to throw up. *I have gods at war with one another. I don't need this right now.*

The shock must have been plain on her face because Gant hurriedly said, "I'm so sorry. I know that this isn't the way any girl ever daydreams about being proposed to, but I find myself in a situation."

"What kind of situation?"

"The word *dire* comes to mind."

"Talk."

"I've had word from Merridan," Gant said. "And King Pemrod has threatened to disinherit me."

"What?" Rina's face scowled with incomprehension. "You've had word? From the *capital*? But . . . how did you do that?"

"Let's just say I have my methods," Gant said. "The important thing is that I need to send word tonight we're going to be wed."

"But—"

"I swear, I don't want to pressure you like this, but it's *urgent*."

"But—"

"My life is in your hands, Rina Veraiin."

"Stop." Rina took a deep breath. "Just please stop talking."

Gant stopped.

"I'm going to ask questions. You'll answer them. Right?"

Gant nodded.

"How did you get a message from the capital so fast?"

Gant frowned. Shook his head.

"Fine," Rina said. "Your secret. You keep it. Let's try something else. Why is this mess suddenly so urgent?"

"He knows?"

"Who knows what?"

"The king," Gant said. "About me and my . . . significant other."

"Oh. That's . . . that's bad, isn't it?"

"Yes, I would describe it as a bit bad," he said dryly. "A bit totally, utterly, catastrophically bad."

"How does marrying me help?"

"King Pemrod is a proud man and vain in all the worst possible ways," Gant said. "He hates the thought of one of . . . one of *my* kind in the family. According to my source, Pemrod seemed torn between *pillow biter* and *sword swallower* as his favorite term for me. And the disgrace of having me actually sit on the throne? Forget it. If I can send word to him immediately that I'm engaged, it might help."

Rina shook her head. "It would be an obvious sham."

"But it would be *his* sham," Gant said. "Yes, he'd know the truth, but he's the king. He says what the truth is, and if anyone contradicts him, he can point at you and say 'There's the man's wife right there. How dare you accuse him of perversion.' Much harder to defend his grandnephew if I give him something to hang his hat on, and a beautiful wife isn't a bad start."

Rina blew out a sigh. "It's thin."

"I know. And I'm sorry. This hasn't gone at all like I'd hoped when I came to Klaar. But deep down, I think Pemrod wants to defend me. Oh, not because of any special affection, but simply because I'm his blood and how dare anyone slander me. It's the same as slandering him. But we've got to give him something to work with. I know the king. He won't stand for being embarrassed. He'll simply arrange for me to go away and never be seen again. 'What ever happened to the dashing

Sir Gant?' people around court will ask, and everyone will shrug and go on with their business."

She liked him, Rina realized. He was amiable and seemed honest and charming without being overbearing. There was something of a Brasley quality about the man, but with Gant, unlike with Brasley, she never felt he was undressing her with his eyes. Not that Rina really held that against Brasley. It was the man's nature. He couldn't help himself. Maybe Marrying Fregga would cure him. Probably not.

Hey, pay attention. You're wandering.

"I . . . I don't know what to say," Rina said.

"I've already told you how matters can improve greatly for Klaar if you marry me. And one day you'll be queen. You're an intelligent woman. You know what that could mean," Gant said. "Saving me from being brutally murdered by the king is just a bonus."

In some ways, he makes sense. Marriages are arranged all the time. Sometimes between two people who haven't even met, but . . .

Even when she was in bed with Alem, limbs intertwined, dozing in the afterglow of lovemaking, a part of her knew. They would never be married. There was no real future for them. Her father had tried to explain it once, what it was like to be duke.

"I'm the most powerful man in Klaar," her father had told her. "And in many ways that means I have the least freedom. I am really chief among servants. I have the well-being of an entire duchy to consider. The needs of every peasant are ahead of my own. No, it doesn't have to be that way, but it should. It's called responsibility. If a common soldier or cobbler or herdsman gets drunk and falls down in the street, then the man's only human. If I do it, it's a disgrace, because I'm supposed to be better."

And now she was duchess. For all intents and purposes, she was Klaar.

Gant cleared his throat. "Rina Veraiin, will you please marry me?"

Rina opened her mouth to answer him.

◆ ◆ ◆

The stables were full, so many horses from all of the guests, and Alem had the stable boys hopping, making sure all the animals were watered and fed and brushed. Fortunately, some of the guests would be leaving first thing in the morning, and more still later in the day after recovering from hangovers.

Tosh's party would be leaving at dawn, so Alem needed to make sure the stable boys were up before first light. Tosh plus five, Alem had been told, so they'd need to ready six mounts. Alem hadn't asked, but he'd been led to believe Rina was sending Tosh on some important task. He'd been instructed to pack the saddlebags with enough provisions to get them to Kern.

And then things get back to normal, Alem thought. *Whatever* normal *means around here.*

Vohn entered the stables, a goofy, lopsided grin on his face.

"Where have *you* been?" Alem asked.

"Went to the, *hic*, reception like you, *hic*, told me," Vohn said. "To see if any of the nobles, *hic*, wanted their horses tonight."

"Have you been drinking?"

Vohn grinned.

"Seriously?"

"The kitchen help was, *hic*, giving out beer behind the drink tent," Vohn said. "It's quite a, *hic*, party."

"So did they?"

"Did who what?"

"Did any of the nobles want their damn horses tonight?" Alem asked.

Vohn scratched his head. "I don't remember."

"Go soak your head in the water trough," Alem told him. "Or I'll throw you in there myself."

Vohn looked abashed, started to shuffle away. "I'll splash some water on the back of my neck."

"Wait," Alem said. "Did the guests seem to be having a good time? Was the duchess . . . enjoying herself?"

"She wasn't there."

"What? Where was she?"

Vohn shrugged. "She wasn't at the high table."

Alem considered. He hadn't had a moment alone with Rina since her guests had arrived. Not that he held it against her. It was her duty to play the attentive host, and the visitors were important people, but he was lonely for her. Stealing even five minutes of her time would go a long way toward brightening Alem's evening.

Even before he'd finished the thought, Alem found himself jogging out of the stable and toward one of the castle's servant entrances.

He was a fairly common sight in the kitchens now, and none of the cooks gave him a second look as he passed through on the way to the main pantry. He paused in the hallway, glancing about to make sure nobody saw him. When it was clear, he ducked into the pantry, closing the door silently behind him.

By now, Alem could find the secret lever even in the dark. He reached between two shelves, stretching his hand around back of one until he felt the small lever with his fingertips. He stretched just a little more, pulled the lever down, and with a *clunk* the simple mechanism unlocked. He swung the shelf out smoothly and quietly on well-oiled hinges, stepped inside, and pulled the shelf closed behind him.

The narrow stairway spiraled up and up, finally terminating at a narrow hallway. Again, he made his way in the dark. It was all familiar territory. He'd tried to figure out once where he was, and his best guest was that he was in a passage built behind the rooms in the ducal wing of the castle. He wondered idly if there were other secret doors that emptied into this hall.

He arrived at the end of the hall, and pulled another lever, and a second later he was in Rina's bedchamber. It was dark here too, but yellow light seeped from under the door leading into Rina's sitting room. Alem couldn't be sure, but he thought he heard voices.

Alem reminded himself to step lightly. Nobody was supposed to know he was a frequent visitor in the night.

He tiptoed to the anteroom door, cracked it just enough to peek inside with one eye.

Rina looked troubled, thoughtful. There was a man with her. A far-too-good-looking man.

Don't be stupid. He's probably somebody important, and she needs to speak to him. Alone. In her personal quarters.

He thought he recognized the man as one of the guests from Merridan. Yes, definitely somebody important.

The conflict in Rina's expression was clear. Alem knew her well by now, knew when she was mentally wrestling with something. It made sense. She was duchess. She made important decisions every day. Suddenly, Alem felt like a first-class fool, spying on her like some child. The smart thing—the *mature* thing—to do would be to go back the way he'd come and catch up with Rina some other night.

Alem kept watching.

The man cleared his throat. "Rina Veraiin, will you please marry me?"

Alem's eyes shot wide. He suddenly couldn't draw breath.

A long pause, and for a moment it was as if she hadn't heard him.

"Send word to King Pemrod," Rina said. "Tell him we're engaged."

A hole opened in the world, and Alem fell into it.

CHAPTER
TWENTY-FOUR

Alem was halfway down the secret staircase when he realized he had no memory of getting there. He was dizzy, felt like he couldn't breathe, a cold weight on his chest.

He put a foot wrong, tumbled down the last few steps, and landed in a heap against the secret door to the pantry.

Alem lay there a while. His world was over. Why bother to get up?

He understood he was being childish. There had never been a future for him and Rina together. He'd been kidding himself.

But it would have been nice to kid myself a little longer. I'm not ready for it to be over.

It didn't matter. Nothing mattered.

Over.

He stood up slowly, rubbing a sore spot at the small of his back.

Nobody saw him leave the pantry. Nobody spoke to him as he waffled leadenly though the kitchen and out of the castle.

Back inside the stables, Pip ran up to him. "All of 'em watered and rubbed down, Alem."

"Good."

"Anything else?"

Alem shook his head. "Go to bed. Tosh and his people leave early. We need to see them off."

Pip scampered away.

Alem went to his shabby room, stood there a moment looking at it, numb. A narrow bunk. A stool. A small potbellied stove. The room had always been just the place he waited until it was time to see Rina again. Now it was home. Forever.

No. No it's not.

He knelt and pulled a wooden chest from beneath the bunk. He opened it, withdrew the contents and lined them up on a bunk. A dagger in a sheath. A bag with a small collection of coins. A travel cloak and a floppy hat. Two spare shirts and two pairs of breeches. A silver engraved gentleman's blade Rina had given him, the handle wrought in the shape of a horse's head. He took his crossbow and a quiver of bolts from where they hung on the wall and dropped them on the bunk next to the other items.

An hour earlier, Alem had lived in a very different world, bigger, filled with Rina, filled with possibilities. Now his world had been reduced to a barren room and a meager collection of possessions that wouldn't fill a pair of saddlebags.

Or he could go *find* the world. He could just . . . go.

It occurred to Alem that he'd stood in this exact room contemplating something similar not so long ago.

That's not really true, is it? The last time, the city was overrun with Perranese. I was fleeing for my life.

This time, Alem was fleeing *from* his life.

He shoved his belongings into a saddlebag. Dawn would arrive soon enough.

◆ ◆ ◆

Ferris Gant blew out a relieved sigh. "You've made me a happy man, Rina. I mean, not in the usual way a man's happy when a woman accepts his proposal, but still."

"I didn't accept your proposal," Rina said flatly.

One of Gant's eyebrows shot up. "What?"

"I said to send word to the king we're engaged," Rina corrected. "I didn't say I'd marry you."

Gant cleared his throat. Frowned. "And that helps me how?"

"It buys you some time," Rina said. "And when it comes to fish or cut bait, I'll back out. You can blame me."

"You'll regret it, Rina."

"You don't seem the vindictive type, Sir Gant."

"Me?" Gant shook his head. "No, you've nothing to fear from me. It may be *my* wedding, but it's Pemrod's plan. It's *him* you'll be thwarting. And he won't let something like that pass without payback."

"I'm sorry," Rina said. "It's the best I can do."

Gant scratched his chin, thought about it for a minute. "Okay. As you say, it will buy me some time. *However.*" He thrust a finger into the air for emphasis, grinned. "I'm going to keep reminding you why marrying me would be a good arrangement. I'll win you over sooner or later."

Rina's smile was half-tired and half-amused. "You can try."

◆ ◆ ◆

The sounds of merrymaking dwindled behind her as Prinn left the main courtyard, rounding a corner and taking a side alley toward one of the servant's entrances. The diehard revelers were still going strong when Prinn had been relieved. The bride and groom had finally retired, but that hadn't stopped the party.

It's sure as blazes over for me, Prinn thought. *I'm bloody exhausted. All I want is bed.*

"Don't walk so fast, missy," came a voice from the darkness.

Prinn's head spun, hand going to the hilt of her sword. Garth lurked in the shadows up close to the castle wall. How had that worm gotten inside the walls?

Giffen, of course. He'd lived in the castle for years, knew all of the ins and outs.

"You shouldn't be here, Garth."

"And the boss should have heard from you by now," he said. "He's invested in you and expects a payoff."

"These things take time."

"What are the king's folk doing in Klaar?"

"No idea," Prinn said.

"Not good enough," Garth said. "Earn your silver, missy."

"Shove the silver up your ass."

"I'll take care of that little cousin of yours," Garth said acidly. "Do her myself."

"Don't."

"Then give us something, damn you. Who's the duchess screwing on the sly?'

"Alem," Prinn said. "His name is Alem."

Prinn felt ashamed as soon as the name had left her mouth. She'd needed to tell the man something, and she'd panicked.

"Who's that?'

Prinn swallowed hard. "He runs the stables."

"Stable boy? Is that a fucking joke?"

"Not a stable boy." Prinn felt sick, something heavy in the pit of her stomach. "He's in charge."

"Whatever." Garth sneered. "He must be some pretty boy." He squinted at the sky. "Dawn soon. Most of that lot will be in bed by then."

He meant the revelers. "Should be nice and quiet then. Me and a few of the boys will ease in sneaky-like to the stables and snatch him."

"But why?" Prinn asked. "He's nobody."

"If he's slipping it to the duchess, he's not nobody, is he?" Garth said. "We get him, then the duchess does what the boss says or else, eh?" He drew a thumb across his throat to make clear what he meant.

Prinn tried to think of something to say, something that would reverse what she'd done. Nothing came to mind.

"You go about your business, missy. You done fine," Garth said. "For now. Just keep feeding us, and you won't have any problems."

Prinn nodded, turned, and walked away, feeling leaden and queasy.

Tosh grabbed at the pitcher, eyes bleary, found the handle, and poured water into the shallow basin by the light of a single candle. He splashed water on his face. He'd learned to get up early in the army. And as cook at the Wounded Bird, he'd had to get up early to prepare breakfast. Now he was up before the dawn again.

He fucking hated getting up early.

Tosh dressed himself in simple warm clothes: a sturdy brown travel cloak with a hood. High boots, well worn and broken in. He buckled his belt, short sword hanging from one side, a dagger on the other. He slung a crossbow over his shoulder. A servant was already taking some armor and his saddlebags and other gear down to the stable.

Servant. In a million years, did Tosh ever think he'd have a servant? Did he think he'd have any of this? The two adjoining rooms he'd been given were the old captain of the castle guard's quarters. They were small, and on a lower level, but compared to his old army barracks, they might as well have been a palace.

Something stirred in the other room. Tosh waited.

Emmon walked out a second later, rubbing her eyes. In her other hand she clutched a collection of rags that loosely resembled a doll. She looked innocent and beautiful, and every time Tosh looked at the little girl, he saw her mother, Tenni, and his heart broke a little bit all over again.

"Are you going now?" Her voice like some toy musical instrument.

"Yes."

"Don't go."

Damn. "I have to, Emmon. Like I said last night. It's my job now to do things for Duchess Veraiin. We have a nice place to live with the castle people, but that's only if I'm a good helper."

"I'll miss you."

Tosh wanted to cry.

"Me too, honey. But Aunt Darshia and Aunt Prinn will look after you. Make sure you go to the tutors with the other castle kids."

"I don't like them. They call me whore child."

Tosh squeezed his eyes shut. *Why are kids such fucking assholes?*

He opened his eyes again, forced a smile. "Those kids don't even know what they're talking about."

"I hate them."

"Pity them, Emmon," Tosh said, "because the world they live in is small, and when it gets bigger fast, they won't know what to do. And talk to your Aunt Darshia. She's tough, isn't she?"

Emmon nodded.

"Okay, then. If anyone knows how to cope, she does. Now give me a hug."

She threw herself on him and hugged him tight.

"I'll be back before you know it," Tosh said.

He hoped it was true.

Prinn slipped into the barracks, kicked off her boots and unbuckled her sword belt, and lay down in her bunk. Darshia snored lightly in the bunk next to hers. The brazier in the center of the room burned low. Prinn's limbs ached. Her heart ached. Her head spun.

Go to sleep and forget about it. There's nothing I can do anyway.

But she couldn't sleep.

She sat up. She got out of her bunk and went to the footlocker at the end. Prinn dipped two fingers into her shift, down between her breasts, came out with a string, a key dangling from the end. She unlocked the footlocker and took out two bags of silver, all the money Giffen had paid her.

She nudged the woman in the next bunk. "Darshia."

Darshia snorted once, and her eyes popped open.

"I need you," Prinn whispered.

Darshia sat up immediately. "What is it? Is there a problem?"

Prinn shushed her, looked around the barracks, but none of the other women woke. "I need a favor, and I need it fast."

Darshia rubbed her eyes. "It's the middle of the—"

"It's almost dawn, and I need your help *now*," Prinn hissed.

Darshia stood, a serious expression replacing sleepy eyes. "Are you in trouble?"

"There's no time." Prinn shoved the bags of silver into Darshia's hands. "You've got to take this to my aunt in Eastside. Tell her to get her family out of Klaar. Now. Don't pack anything. Just take the money and go."

Darshia's eyes shot wide. "This is a fortune."

"Please, there's no time."

"Prinn, if you're in trouble, you've got to tell—"

"Damn it, Darshia, are you my friend or not?"

A stunned pause, then, "Yes. Yes, of course."

"Then do this for me, but it has to be *now*."

Darshia glanced down at the money in her hands. "Okay."

"Thank you. Oh, Dumo, thank you," she said and told Darshia the address.

Prinn grabbed her sword belt and extra daggers and walked fast toward the barracks door as she glimpsed Darshia hurriedly pulling on clothes.

Outside, the sky was just lightening from black to a dull gray with the coming dawn. She hoped she wasn't too late. Her fast walk turned into a jog then a full sprint as the stables came into view.

She burst in through one of the side doors, eyes alert, hand on the hilt of her sword. Prinn still favored the long, curved Perranese blade she'd trained with.

Four heads turned her way, Garth and three of his thugs. Alem crawled on all fours at their feet. A bright smear of blood from one ear down the side of Alem's face, eyes glazed. Fairly easy to guess he'd resisted and taken a fist to the side of the head.

"Step away from him." Prinn's voice was flat and low. No heat in it, just a cold resolve.

"Enough of us here to handle this, Prinn," Garth said. "Move along now."

"No."

Her against four. That might be tough, although they had only short daggers and cudgels. Not the weapons of a soldier. Street thugs.

Garth's frown deepened. "You know what this means for you and yours, don't you? Burnard, give her a taste."

The one called Burnard was big running to fat, a dull, round face. He raised his cudgel and moved toward her, clumsy and lumbering like a bear.

Remember your footwork, Prinn.

She lunged and swept the sword from its scabbard, swinging across Burnard's midsection in the same motion. He moved well for a big man, fast, but there was too much belly to miss. The tip of the sword sliced a two-inch-deep gash across his stomach, blood splattering from Prinn's follow-through.

Burnard clutched his gut, stumbled back, and grunted. "Bitch cut me."

Garth's other two ruffians surged past Burnard, daggers ready, pissed looks on their faces.

Prinn slashed at one, but that left her open to a quick lunge from the other. He drew a red line down her shoulder. She hissed at the pain and jumped back, swinging her sword widely from side to side to keep them at bay. They rocked back and forth in front of her, waiting for an opening.

"You're a stupid whore, and now you're going to die," Garth said.

He might be right. But I can't just stand here and wait for all of them to rush me.

She made a quick feint at the one closest, and he stumbled back off balance. He was still recovering when Prinn changed directions for the other one. She went at him full speed, using the sword's longer reach to get past his dagger. She thrust the blade straight through the middle of his gut. The blade sank in six inches.

He grunted, face frozen in a contortion of pain, slid off the blade, and landed with a thump on the floor.

Prinn turned to face the other one but was too late, the dagger already coming fast for her midsection. She tried to turn and took the blade in the side. It bit deep, and hot blood flowed. Prinn's adrenaline carried her through the pain.

She brought the Perranese sword down in an overhand swing. There wasn't much strength in it, but the blow was aimed right at the man's head. He tried to duck to one side.

And almost got away clean.

The blade sliced flesh down one side of the man's face. Sliced off an ear. Gore and blood and screaming.

She moved forward to finish him with a sharp thrust through the middle then kick him off her blade. He spun away, trailing blood.

Prinn turned to face Garth. She held the sword in front of her one-handed. Her other arm hung wounded and limp. She panted, blinked sweat from her eyes. The wound in her side flared pain. She needed to finish this fast. When the battle rush faded, she'd wilt like a cabbage leaf. She was losing blood fast. Already she felt dizzy.

But Garth wasn't moving in to engage her. He held Alem by the hair, the point of his dagger at Alem's throat.

"Feisty lass." Garth sneered. "Don't know what this boy is to you, but I'll open him up right quick if you take even one step in this direction."

Prinn froze, didn't lower the sword, her mind racing for ideas. Waiting favored Garth. The more Prinn bled, the more she wanted to simply fall down and close her eyes. Her mouth felt dry, heart thumping in her ears.

"Now why don't you just back on out of here?" Garth suggested. "Let's all just take it easy and—"

Garth screamed.

Prinn's eyes shifted to his feet.

Alem had unfolded a short gentleman's blade and had stabbed it straight down into the top of Garth's foot, straight down through boot and bone. Garth kept screaming, trying to balance on one foot, his dagger hand coming away from Alem's throat.

Prinn rushed forward, slicing down with her sword. Garth's hand came off at the wrist and flew away still clutching the dagger. Blood spurted from the stump.

She lifted the sword high again to bring it down on Garth's head.

Garth threw himself on her, and they both went down, Prinn's sword flying back behind.

Garth ended up on top, jamming a handless forearm against her throat. "Fucking bitch. Kill you for that."

She raked her fingernails across her face, drawing four red lines, but Garth didn't let up. All his weight was against her throat, his forearm pressing down, his leering face inches from hers. Spots in front of her eyes. Her mouth worked for breath that wouldn't come.

And in the next second he was off of her.

She drew in breath, throat raw, coughed and gagged. She blinked away the spots, saw Garth and Alem wrestling and rolling across the stable floor.

Prinn drew a dagger from her belt, tried to stand but couldn't, the room spinning, face hot, stomach queasy. She crawled toward them on her belly, smearing the floor with blood. She suddenly could no longer move one leg, as if it were caught on something. She tried to yank it free without success. She looked back.

The fat Burnard had an iron grip on her ankle. With his other hand, he was clutching his sliced belly. His fingers were completely red, his tunic soaked with blood. He lay on his side trying to wriggle along after her. His face was ashen, hair matted with sweat, but his expression was fierce with hatred.

"You get back here, whore." Burnard's voice was hoarse, strained with the pain in his belly. "Think you can slice me and not pay for it, do you?"

"Go fuck yourself." She tried to kick him away, but he wouldn't let go.

But he couldn't crawl after her either, not awkwardly lying on his side, one hand still clutching his gut. Burnard finally figured out he was a strong man, and she was a relatively small woman. He began pulling her toward him.

Prinn tried to find purchase somewhere on the floor with her fingertips, anything to grab on to, but she felt herself being dragged backward. From five feet away she heard the grunts and struggles of Alem and Garth still locked in their own struggle.

Burnard released his own belly to pull her toward him with both hands. When he'd finally dragged her close enough, he slammed a fist into the side of Prinn's head. Bells went off and the world began to tilt and spin. She fumbled at her belt for the other dagger, and the big man's fist slammed her again, this time across the mouth. She felt her teeth crack and she spat blood. Her vision blurred but she drew on every bit of strength she had left to keep from passing out.

She drew the dagger and rolled toward him, stabbing blindly. It sank deep into his belly and he screamed. She pulled it out and stabbed a second time. She yanked it out again and blood sprayed. She stabbed a third time and couldn't pull the blade out—stuck between two ribs, she suspected, and she didn't have the strength to pry it free.

Burnard lay still.

Prinn pulled herself along, stomach dragging and bloody. Her senses reeled, eyes a dark blur, head pounding, bells loud in her ears. Blood and snot and sweat streamed down her face.

Burnard twitched, pawed at the dagger in his chest.

Just keep . . . going. Don't . . . stop.

Crawl away. Don't . . . look back.

Burnard pulled the dagger free, rose up, and lurched at Prinn, falling on her hard, bringing the dagger down between her shoulder blades. Fire exploded along her spine, and she went rigid.

Oh no.

Oh . . . no.

◆ ◆ ◆

Alem found himself on top of the leader. He'd heard the others call him Garth. He punched down hard and connected high on the man's cheek, but Garth bucked him off and soon they were rolling around and grappling again.

Garth had just lost a hand, but he was a veteran of countless back-alley brawls. No rules. Just life and death. He smashed a knee into Alem's groin. Hard.

The breath left Alem all at once. His face went red as he toppled over, groaning and clutching himself.

Garth laughed as he crawled away. "Sorry about your stones, lad. I was going to make it quick, but things got complicated."

Alem tried to say something but was able to squeeze out only an urgent croak.

Garth retrieved his dagger, staggered to his feet. "The boss said either grab you for a hostage or, if that didn't work out, kill you and send a message to her grace. And I really hate to say it, lad, but this isn't your night."

Alem rolled over, willed himself to get up, but his world had been reduced to a bright ball of pain radiating from his groin throughout his whole body. He felt he might vomit any second.

Garth stood over him. He cradled his stump against his chest, held the dagger awkwardly in his other hand. "I'd like to take you back alive, but I can't chance it now that I'm . . . shorthanded." He waved the stump and chuckled.

Alem couldn't bring himself to see the humor.

Garth lifted the dagger. "Again, nothing personal."

A crossbow bolt sprouted from the center of Garth's forehead. His eyes crossed as he looked up at it. A moment of silence stretched before Garth twitched once and fell over backward, scattering a stack of watering buckets.

Thank Dumo, Alem thought and passed out.

CHAPTER
TWENTY-FIVE

It only seemed like a second later that Alem's eyes flickered open. He was flat on his back. Tosh stood over him with a crossbow in his hand. Next to him stood one of the women turned sword maidens from the Wounded Bird. Alem couldn't remember her name.

His balls were still on fire, but not quite so bad now.

"Are you okay?" Tosh asked. "Where are you hurt?"

Alem's eyes shifted briefly to the woman standing next to Tosh, then back. "Just . . . shaken up. I'll be fine."

Alem sat up quickly, remembering. "Prinn."

"They're looking at her now," Tosh said.

Alem staggered to his feet, the ache flaring in his groin, and went to a group of people a few feet away. Stasha Benadicta sat on the stable floor, Prinn's head in her lap. Three other women knelt in a circle around them. There were bloody rags all over. The women pressed more rags against Prinn's wounds, the blood seeping through so fast. A pool of blood spread slowly out from her. The women trying to help her were kneeling in it. It seemed impossible one girl could hold so much blood.

Prinn's face was ghost white. She twitched, eyes blinking, mouth working, trying to speak.

"Don't talk," Stasha said. "Stay still. Let us help you."

Prinn shook her head. She must have known she was almost gone. She lifted a hand, bright and slick with blood, and weakly gestured to Stasha. The chamberlain bent her head, and Prinn whispered in her ear.

From a few feet away, Alem couldn't quite make out Prinn's whisper, but the chamberlain's eyes grew larger at the dying woman's words.

Prinn suddenly went rigid. A long sigh leaked out of her as she deflated slowly and went limp in Stasha's arms.

Alem heard a sniff behind him, turned to see Tosh wiping his eyes.

Tosh saw him looking and said, "She was one of the first after Tenni. That I trained, I mean. They all wanted to learn how to fight. I wish I'd never shown them. I wish—" He turned away, rubbing his eyes with his palms.

Alem looked back at Prinn. *She saved me. It cost her everything. How had she known? Or was it a coincidence? Maybe she'd come down to the stables on other business.*

Alem might never know.

Stasha stood. Her eyes were red and glistening. She clasped her bloodstained hands in front of her, back straight, chin up. All eyes went to her immediately.

"Listen to me," she said calmly. "There's been a terrible tragedy, but we must set our grief aside for the moment. Duchess Veraiin wanted Tosh's expedition away at dawn before too many prying eyes were awake. We're late, but still, the sooner they're off the better."

Alem glanced at the stable's doorway, where a small group of people hovered, looking inside. He hadn't noticed them before, but obviously this was the team setting out with Tosh. He looked up, saw the stable boys watching the scene wide-eyed from the hayloft. They were supposed to be saddling horses.

Guess I can't blame them for gawking.

Tosh shouldered past Alem. "Mother, under the circumstances, perhaps we'd better—"

Stasha shot him a fierce look.

"Your pardon," Tosh said. "Lady Chamberlain."

Stasha's expression softened, but only slightly. "No more delays. We have our duty to do, and we'll all carry on as best we can." She pointed at one of the women still kneeling in Prinn's blood. "You, go and fetch a blanket and two men to carry Prinn to the lower crypts. We'll bury her honorably after our work here is done." She pointed at one of the other women. "You, round up men to build a fire. I want the bodies of these street toughs burned, but make sure they're searched first. Listen, all of you. No one says a thing. Do you understand? The events that have transpired in this stable this morning are to be treated as an official state secret. Even a hint of a whisper gets out and Dumo help you."

They all stared at her dumbly.

"Get to it," she shouted.

The stable erupted with activity. The two women Stasha had appointed bolted from the stable, running into those who entered with baggage.

Stasha looked pointedly at Alem. "Horses."

Alem gulped.

"Get down here now," Alem shouted at the stable boys. "I want these horses saddled and ready to go in three minutes."

The stables boys nearly fell down the ladder as they scurried to obey, some leading horses from stalls, others fetching saddles and gear.

Stasha approached Alem, stopped when she stood next to him, pitched her voice low. "Are you okay?"

Alem nodded. "I will be. Just a few bumps and bruises. Thank you, Lady Chamberlain." His eyes drifted to Prinn. "I just wish . . . I wish I could thank her."

She patted him briefly on the shoulder, then turned to supervise the two men who'd arrived for Prinn's body.

Alem found Tosh. He wished he could leave the man alone with his grief, but this couldn't wait. "I want to come with you."

Tosh looked confused. "Rina's orders?"

Alem hesitated then shook his head.

Tosh frowned. "I don't get it."

"You don't have to take me on your mission," Alem said. "I don't want to get in the way. As far as Kern will do. I just want to ride along. I'm leaving either way, but I'd prefer not to be out on the road alone."

"But why?"

"I just need to leave. There's nothing in Klaar for me."

An expression crossed Tosh's face like he understood, or could at least guess. "Okay, why not? Sure. Happy to have you ride along."

"Absolutely not!"

Both men turned their heads, startled.

A slight figure, short, concealed in a travel cloak. She threw back her hood, scowling, eyes blazing. "He is *not* coming with us," Maurizan said.

Alem flinched as if he'd been struck, partly because of the surprise, and partly because of the naked hostility radiating off her. And her red hair had always been so striking, and those eyes, and the glowing skin and the freckles—

What, am I crazy? She looks like she wants to murder me.

"His coming along isn't part of the arrangement," Maurizan said sharply. "We don't need him."

"The arrangement is that I bring you," Tosh said. "Other than that, I pick my own team. You don't have anything to say about it."

The gypsy girl opened her mouth to say something, then snapped it shut again. If evil looks could kill, Alem would have fallen dead on the spot. She turned on a heel and went to her horse.

Tosh rolled his eyes. "This is going to be just one long, fun trip, isn't it?"

"Sorry," Alem said. "I wasn't looking to cause trouble."

"Forget it," Tosh said. "But I'd sleep with one eye open if I were you."

CHAPTER TWENTY-SIX

A shape came for her in the darkness.

Rina ran.

From shadow to fog.

The shape pursued her.

She tried to tap into the spirit and failed. Panic seized her. She was lost in the fog, barefoot, the ground wet and cold. Where was she? A forest, it seemed, but she couldn't be sure. The fog swirled around her, thicker, cold, clinging to her hair and thin nightgown. She felt the shape at her back, an icy sensation of dread.

She ran faster.

The forest opened into a clearing.

A temple. A high wall with the gate smashed open.

Wait. I recognize this place.

It was the Temple of Mordis. There had been a terrible battle here. She'd slaughtered nearly a hundred Perranese warriors who were attempting to storm the temple. She blinked, looked again. The slain Perranese littered the ground all around her as if summoned by the memory. Somehow they seemed older, skeletons, as if the corpses had been here for centuries. The battle had been the first time she'd used the skeletal tattoo on her palm. She looked down at her hand and gasped.

The tattoo was gone.

She looked at her ankles. The lightning-bolt tattoos were gone too. They were all gone.

She turned abruptly and looked back at the tree line at the edge of the clearing. The dark shape still loomed there in the fog, only its vague bulk discernible and two eyes like glowing red coals. She sensed it no longer pursued her, but it loomed in the darkness, ready. If she turned back, it would be waiting.

When she faced the temple again, someone was there.

A shriveled, emaciated figure in a black robe stood between the temple's shattered gates, his hood pulled forward to obscure the face. He stood barefoot.

But Rina knew who he was. She went to him. "High Priest Krell."

He pulled back his hood. His skin stretched too thin over his skull, complexion chalky, grin an obscene collection of yellowing teeth. Frail as a bundle of dry sticks, but his eyes were bright and knowing.

"How nice we should meet again, Duchess Veraiin."

She'd forgotten how unpleasant his voice sounded, like rough stones scraping across rusty metal.

Rina showed her blank palm to the priest. "The tattoo is gone."

"Don't worry," Krell told her. "The Hand of Death will be waiting for you when you awake."

"I'm dreaming."

"Of course."

"Then this isn't real?"

Krell's laugh was halfway between a wheeze and a hiss. "It most assuredly is real, Duchess. I'm here as a reminder."

"Of what?"

"You owe the Cult of Mordis," the priest reminded her. "We have a bargain."

"What if I don't honor it?"

A mild shrug. "Break the bargain if you dare." He gestured behind her. "The consequences await."

She looked back. The figure in the darkness was still there, eyes glowing. "What is it?"

Another shrug, even vaguer and more noncommittal this time. "Your conscience, perhaps?"

"Don't toy with me," Rina said sharply.

"I wouldn't think of it," Krell said. "But while my message to you is real enough, this conversation is transpiring in your dream, your own mind, filled with all the pitfalls that entails. We are adrift in the sea of your own misgivings, fears, hopes, worries, and anxieties. For those I am not responsible. Again, I am here only to remind you of your obligation."

Rina took one more look at the sinister, glowing eyes. "You know what it is and you won't tell me."

"There is also that possibility, yes," Krell admitted. "But the more likely answer is that while I have suspicions, I know very little with an absolute certainty."

"But you have the sight." When she'd first met Krell, Rina had been informed the priest was a seer.

"I see what the gods allow," Krell said. "They show me only what furthers their purposes."

"You sound more like a puppet than a seer," Rina said.

The priest smiled thinly. "I serve as I can. It isn't for me to decide how. I am simply an instrument. But I do know one thing, and I think you do too. Things are changing. This epoch is fading into history. We find ourselves amid the birthing pains of a new one. The gods battle, maneuver, entice, and attempt to outwit one another. Which will be dominant is yet to be determined. The game plays out even now, here, with the two of us, two pawns who play our small parts."

"I'm not a pawn," Rina said. "And I don't want any part of this game."

"You don't have a choice," Krell said. "None of us does. If a pawn chooses not to move, then another piece will. The game goes on." He shook his head, sighed. "But this sort of talk is academic. Pawns don't get to see the end game of the gods. I did my part and made sure you received the Hand of Death. Now you must do your part. Fulfill your obligation, Rina Veraiin. Are you not a person of honor?"

"*Honor* is a word men use to justify duels and wars," Rina said. "My only concern is doing the right thing."

"History will decide what is right," Krell said. "Return to this temple. Come back, and I will give you what you need to fulfill your destiny."

"No." Rina shook her head slowly, her eyes not leaving his. "I don't want anything to do with destiny. I make my own choices and live with them."

"Or die by them," Krell said. "I would reconsider if I were you, Duchess. Time is running out." Krell waved his hand.

The fog rushed in from all sides to surround her. Rina's world was reduced to gray mist, no sign of clearing, temple, or priest. She was turned around in seconds, clueless as to which way to go.

The red eyes came toward her.

She turned and ran, cold fear gripping her, bare feet splashing in mud. Rina didn't dare turn to look. Whatever pursued her cast a sense of dread ahead of it. Her legs and arms felt heavy. The harder she ran the slower she went, and the thing chasing her was upon her now, right behind, within arm's reach. She couldn't turn to look, wouldn't allow herself to see it, braced herself to be struck from behind, torn apart. She could barely move. She opened her mouth to scream but couldn't.

I'm going to die. It's going to catch me.

She opened her mouth to scream one more time. It caught in her throat. She couldn't breathe. Something heavy pressed down on her chest. The sense of dread was overwhelming her, everything going black . . .

◆ ◆ ◆

Rina sat up in bed, gasped, gulped for air. She was drenched in sweat. Her gloved hand went to a spot between her breasts. Her heart beat so hard, it hurt her chest. She shook, panted, eyes blinking to adjust to the darkness of her bedchamber. The embers burned low in the fireplace.

A dream, but of course Krell had admitted as much.

But not *just* a dream.

She reached out to the empty space in bed next to her.

Where's Alem?

She'd drifted off the night before, waiting for him. After several nights apart, she'd hoped to have his company for the evening. She just wanted him next to her, to sleep peacefully. Gant, Klarissa, even the *king* all wanted something from her. With Alem she didn't have to be duchess. She was just Rina.

And now this dream with High Priest Krell? What do I know about the gods? Dumo help me, how did I get into this? Where are you when I need you, Alem?

Then she remembered.

He'd be helping Tosh and the others with the horses, seeing them off. The king's envoy and most of the other nobility would still be sleeping off last night's revelry, and that's just what Rina wanted. The fewer who saw Tosh leave the better. Not that a small group of people leaving Klaar on a short journey was particularly noteworthy, but the fewer who knew, the better. Innocent questions often led to more awkward ones.

A soft light flickered into existence across the room, pale and cold and blue.

For a second Rina thought something had followed her from her dream. She stepped back, tapped into the spirit, and calmly regarded the expanding light. It slowly took shape becoming a person. A woman.

Talbun hovered like a ghost, a transparent apparition, her edges drifting into mist. Rina felt sure she could pass a hand right through her.

"I always wondered what Weylan had in his spell books," Talbun said. "I couldn't resist trying out a few things. Also, we need to talk, and this is easier than going up and down all those stairs in the prayer tower."

Rina released her hold on the spirit. "If you have something to tell me, go ahead."

"It's something I need to *show* you," the wizard said. "Weylan kept a journal of his research. I think you should come up here."

Great. So I have to climb all the stairs instead.

"Let me get dressed, and I'll be up as soon as I can."

CHAPTER TWENTY-SEVEN

"There are instructions and likely a stencil for a tattoo in the Great Library of Tul-Agnon." Talbun gestured at the book on the table in front of her. "If Weylan is to be believed."

"What?" Rina rapidly circled the table to read the book over the wizard's shoulder. She squinted at the pages. They were unreadable, at least to her. At first she thought simply that Weylan's penmanship was unreadable, but she looked again and saw the entries were written in some unfamiliar foreign tongue.

"It's ancient Fyrian," Talbun explained.

"And of course you're fluent in ancient Fyrian," Rina said.

"Of course," Talbun said with no hint of irony. "The mystic arts are said to have originated in Fyria. All wizards read and write it, so we can communicate with one another."

"You talk shop in ancient Fyrian."

"That's a tad glib," Talbun said, "but yes."

"What does it say?"

"It's a little hard to follow," Talbun said. "These are obviously notes to himself. It's not a book meant to be read by others. Studying the tattoos was obviously his passion for many years. He'd been collecting rumors and stories and legends, anything that might lead to another tattoo or hint at its location. It makes sense, really."

"Why would he be so obsessed?"

"Because Weylan could ink the Prime," Talbun said. "There are other wizards like me who have power tattoos. Or your gypsy friend who put those feathers at the corners of your eyes. These tattoos are rare enough, but they mean nothing without the Prime, and Weylan might have been the last wizard alive who knew the secret." She cast her eyes over the pile of books. "I've only just started going through his possessions. I was hoping to find something about inking the Prime. No luck so far, and I have to go slowly. A number of the books are spell-trapped."

"Yeah," Rina said flatly. "I've unfortunately had some experience with that."

"I'm pretty sure if we studied Weylan's books carefully, we could locate a half dozen power tattoos."

Rina's heart skipped with excitement, and that excitement worried her. She didn't *want* to want more tattoos.

But she did.

Weylan warned me. He said the power was seductive.

"Not that we have the time to chase them to the four corners of the world," Talbun continued. "But *this* tattoo is different." She tapped a word in the middle of a page.

Rina squinted at it. *Kataar.*

The word meant nothing to her.

"You'll have to translate that for me."

"I can't," Talbun said. "It's not Fyrian, and I've never seen the word before. But it's what Weylan calls one of the tattoos."

"What's so special about it?" Rina asked. "Would it let me fly or something?"

"It's not that it grants some specific power. That's not what caught my attention," Talbun said. "It's more that it seems very relevant to our current problem."

There's a tattoo that keeps the king from wanting me to marry his grandnephew?

No. Obviously not. Wait, did she mean . . . ?

"I had a dream last night," Rina said. "More of a visitation, really. From a high priest of the Cult of Mordis."

Talbun's eyes narrowed. "Tell me."

Rina related the dream, every detail. Talbun interrupted a few times for clarifications. When Rina had finished, the wizard looked troubled. She stood, walked to a window, looking out of it silently.

Finally, Talbun turned and asked, "Are you sure? It wasn't just a normal dream?"

"I'm not *sure* of anything," Rina admitted. "But I had an . . . awareness. I knew I was in a dream, and the priest admitted as much. He told me one epoch was ending and that another was about to begin."

Then Rina saw something she'd never seen before. Talbun afraid.

"What do you know of the Mage Wars?" the wizard asked.

"What everyone says." Rina shrugged. "Powerful wizards dueling for power. Does it ever change? One crown and too many men who want to wear it."

"Some think the Mage Wars were all about the gods," Talbun said. "Some say there were those who invented a new magic to oppose the gods themselves. And they were in turn opposed by those *loyal* to the gods. The entire war was religious, some think."

Rina shook her head. "That's . . . impossible." The tattoos made her powerful, fast, strong, but mighty enough to take on a god? Ridiculous.

"It will take more study," Talbun said. "But the great library of Tul-Agnon is more than just a repository of books. It's an ancient structure from the last age. The lower levels housed works used mostly by university scholars and students. The upper levels are off limits to all but select researchers. If there's anywhere in the world one might find an ancient relic powerful enough to battle the gods, it would be there."

"Thank you for that bit of trivia," Rina said. "I'm sure it will be very useful information. For somebody else."

"Count Becham and the royal envoy leave tomorrow for the capital," Talbun said. "We can travel with them that far then continue on to Tul-Agnon ourselves."

Rina groaned. This was all too much. "Why is it up to *us* to do anything about this? I didn't ask for any of this. I don't want—"

With a crack like thunder the tower's roof was ripped away in a ball of flame.

Rina and Talbun dove to the floor, hands and arms going over their heads as debris rained down on them, fragments of stonework and dust and splintered wood. A scorched roof beam landed with a clatter six inches from Rina's head.

The women staggered to their feet in the center of a circle of ruined stonework. A cold wind whistled past them, tugging at hair and clothing, smoke swirling.

"What happened?" Rina shouted over the wind.

Talbun scanned the sky then pointed. "There."

It dropped out of the clouds, the morning sun glinting off its scales. It wheeled, spreading its wings, and Rina got a good look at it. The head was long like a horse's, but flatter, with rows of spiky teeth. A long snake-like body with two short legs at the back end, a long barbed tail trailing behind. A three-fingered claw at the end of each wing. A ridge of stumpy spikes down its spine. Its scales gleamed like metal, bright green along its back and fading to white on its belly. It was bigger than a wagon.

Bigger than some cottages she'd seen in lowland villages.

It finished its turn and dove for them.

"A dragon," Rina said in awe.

"No. The great dragons are extinct," Talbun said. "This is a mountain wyvern from the west."

Rina shot her a scowl. "This is no time to split hairs!"

The wyvern pulled up at the last moment, its great flapping wings buffeting the women, almost knocking them over. It opened its mouth, hunched up its back.

"It's going to breathe fire again," Talbun said.

"What?" Rina shrieked. "That sounds bad."

"It is."

Talbun flung out a hand and mumbled quick arcane syllables. Scorching pink light flew from her fingertips and struck the wyvern in the face. The beast's head flinched back and up as it belched fire, the gout of flame shooting straight up into the air.

From below, the wyvern's barbed tail swung up fast like the tip of a coachman's whip. It crashed through the tower's stonework and wooden floor. Both women lost their footing and found themselves tumbling through the air, screaming, the ground coming up at them so very fast.

EPISODE FIVE

CHAPTER TWENTY-EIGHT

Even with the late departure, the streets of Back Gate were nearly deserted. Few saw them, the horses clopping along the cobblestones in the early gray, a somber pall still hanging over them after Prinn's death. Alem had known her slightly, but Tosh and the other women had known her since the Wounded Bird days, and they sat in the saddle, shoulders slumped, heads down. The guards waved them through the Back Gate, and they started the slow, winding journey down the Small Road.

The seven of them traveled single file and in silence. Tosh rode at the head of the line, followed by Maurizan and Alem. The woman behind him was named Viriam. Alem knew her only vaguely. The other three women were new to him. Lureen was tall, slim hips, almost boyish but with a striking face, clear skin, and eyes so blue and bright they seemed to glow. Her hair, black as midnight, was woven into a tight braid and fell to the middle of her back. The twins were called Kalli and Nell, blond and pretty in an ordinary way. Alem was given to understand they were something of a tag-team attraction when they'd worked at the Wounded Bird, although they were no longer quite identical, Kalli bearing a scar down the left side of her face from the battle to drive out the Perranese.

The solemn troop rode without talking for another hour, the wind and the quiet clank of armor and weapons the only sounds.

When the road widened enough for two horses to walk side by side, Alem spurred his mount and pulled alongside Maurizan.

"I didn't invite myself along just to upset you," Alem said. "I promise."

She kept her eyes forward, chin up. "You can't upset me. Not anymore because I don't care what you do or where you go."

"All I mean is that if we're going to travel together, it's probably best for everyone if we get along," Alem said. "We can be courteous."

Now she did turn to him, eyes hard. She pitched her voice low for just the two of them to hear, but there was an intensity that made Alem wince. "Listen to me, stable boy. If I say something or act in a way that seems impolite to you, then that's just too fucking bad. I'm not interested. I don't have any cordial small talk for you. No pleases or thank-yous. Are we clear?"

Alem swallowed hard. "Clear."

He spurred his horse ahead to ride beside Tosh. "You catch any of that?"

"Enough," Tosh said. "You must've done a number on her."

"It's a long story," Alem said.

"Never mind. I can guess most of it anyway," Tosh said. "You know what I said about sleeping with one eye open?"

"Yeah."

"Better make it both eyes."

Alem forced a smile. "Great."

"I *would* give you some advice about women."

"But?"

"But I don't know shit." Tosh shrugged. "Sorry."

"Okay if I change the subject?"

"Please."

"How far do we go today?"

Tosh tugged an earlobe, thinking. "I don't want to camp in the mountains. Warmer down below. We'll see how much daylight is left when we hit the valley floor."

The road circled back along the mountain and afforded a partial view of Klaar, the tops of the tallest towers. Alem wondered if he'd ever return, then reminded himself not to be so melodramatic. Maybe all he really needed was some time away to think, time to let it sink in that Rina was getting married and that was just how it was going to be. What he'd do in the immediate future was still a toss-up. Maybe in Kern he could find work or—

He blinked. Something had move rapidly across the sky over Klaar, but he'd only seen a blur. Too big for a bird. Too fast for a wisp of cloud. Maybe his eyes were playing tricks on him.

A ball of fire followed by a distant *boom*.

All heads turned at once, looking back toward Klaar.

Tosh stood in the saddle, eyes squinting. "What in blazes was that?"

"The prayer tower," Alem said. "It just exploded."

CHAPTER TWENTY-NINE

Rina and Talbun tumbled among the debris from the ruined prayer tower and plunged, the ground below spinning and approaching far too rapidly, cold wind whipping past them. Rina tapped into the spirit, and her mind cleared, the panic caused by her imminent impact evaporating.

Okay, assess the situation. What can you do?

The short answer was not a damn thing. She was falling and would keep falling until she hit with a splat. Part of her urgently wanted to feel pure stark fear about this fact, but she kept fear at bay. If she survived the fall, the healing rune would eventually put her back together, but the odds of surviving a fall from the prayer tower—the tallest tower in the city—were outlandish. The obvious conclusion was that she would now die.

I always think that I'm about to die these days. It's getting old.

This entire thought process blazed through her mind in the merest fraction of a second.

Rina felt a hand grab her wrist. She turned to see a wide-eyed Talbun, the wizard's mouth working rapidly to spit out some spell.

The world blurred for a moment, and their descent slowed to almost nothing halfway down the tower. They were still falling but like a feather now. "That spell. You made us lighter somehow, didn't you?"

"No." Talbun's face was still a mask of fear. "We're in a time bubble. We're still falling just as fast. When we hit, we're dead."

"I don't understand."

"There's no time to explain."

"We're in a *time* bubble, but there's not enough *time* to explain?"

"Shut up and listen!" Talbun shouted. "It's the only spell I thought might help. I've bought us time—a *small* amount of time—to think of something. So think of something!"

"Take off your dress," Rina said. "Rip it into strips. Not too thin."

There was slight hesitation, but then Talbun obeyed. Rina did the same, and soon both women were falling in their shifts. As Rina tied the torn strips of her dress together, she searched the face of the tower until she found what she wanted, an outcropping with a gargoyle carved into the stone.

She finished tying the strips of the dress together. She tied a loop in one end. Rina pulled Talbun close to her. "Hang on to me and don't let go."

"The spell is about to give out," Talbun warned.

"Just do it!"

Talbun held on tight.

As they passed the gargoyle, Rina tossed the looped end of the makeshift rope over it. She wrapped the other end of the fabric around her arm three times and gripped it with all of her strength. Her other arm went around the wizard.

"Brace yourself for a jolt," Rina said.

Talbun opened her mouth to say something, but that's when the spell expired. They were immediately falling at full speed again.

The rope yanked tight. Agonizing pain lanced through Rina's shoulder. She would have screamed if she hadn't been tapped into the spirit.

She felt and heard stitches pop, but the fabric held. They swung wide, out and around and then back toward the tower, slammed into the rough stonework. Talbun grunted but held on to Rina. Slamming into the wall knocked Rina's grip loose and they fell, hitting the roof of the castle's east wing eight feet below. It was a peaked roof, tiles slick with morning dew, and they both slid toward the edge, the wizard slightly ahead of the duchess.

Rina was mildly aware of her left arm hanging limp at her side, but most of her attention was focused on not sliding off the roof and crashing into the courtyard three stories below.

Talbun slid over the edge and just barely managed to latch on to the edge of the gutter. She clung by her fingertips and shouted, "Help!"

Rina slid after her. There was nothing to grab on to. She summoned all the strength from the bull tattoo and squeezed her fist tight. Her feet just started to clear the edge of the roof, and she punched down hard through the tile and wood beneath, smashing a hole through the roof. She heard and felt bones and knuckles crack and break but held on to the new hole she'd made, feet dangling in midair.

"Grab my ankle," Rina yelled at the wizard. "I can't move my other arm. You'll have to grab my leg and pull yourself up."

Talbun grabbed her ankle. "Do you see it?"

"See what?"

"The wyvern."

Rina craned her neck, turned her head from side to side, trying to see every inch of the sky at once. "I don't see it."

Talbun pulled herself up using Rina's leg then lay panting on the slanted roof next to her. "There's a balcony and a window over there. If we can ease ourselves along the roof without slipping and busting our asses, I think we'll be okay."

Talbun looked at Rina's dangling arm. "You're hurt."

"The arm's out of its socket," Rina said. "Don't worry. I won't feel it until later." Already she felt the healing rune doing its work. Her hand had stopped throbbing.

They made their way slowly along the roof, and Talbun helped Rina over the stone railing and onto a small balcony. They threw open a pair of shutters, and Talbun helped Rina crawl through the window. They found themselves on the other side in an unused sitting room.

Rina had used a lot of the spirit, but she just needed to stay tapped in a few more seconds. With her good hand, she reached around and wrenched her limp arm, popping it back into its socket.

She released the spirit, pain flooding in white-hot, and passed out.

CHAPTER THIRTY

"Well?" Commander Tchi looked at Jariko with impatience. "Is it done?"

Both of them looked across the table at Prullap. The young wizard blinked, coming out of his trance, looking slack jawed and sleepy.

"The commander asked you a question, Prullap." Jariko tugged at one of his long, braided moustaches. "Is she dead?"

"I . . . I don't know."

Jariko made a disgusted noise and turned away, rolling his eyes.

"You wanted the wyvern to attack the tower. It did," Prullap said. "It was a long flight from the mountains, a long time to control such an animal. I made it obey as long as possible. It destroyed the tower. I don't know after that. I lost control."

Jariko turned to Tchi. "See, I told you. If the demon I summoned couldn't do the job, then something as clumsy as this was bound to fail."

Prullap frowned but kept his mouth shut.

"My spy in the castle told us Veraiin goes to the tower," Tchi said. "I will have her confirm or deny the duchess's death. We will know soon enough." He waved them away, fatigued by their presence. "Go now. I will send for you if I need you."

The two wizards rose from the table, bowed perfunctorily, and left.

A moment later, Tchi stood also, clasped his hands behind his back and paced the little room. His thoughts refused to congeal. He went to the window and threw open the shutters. The cool wind on his face felt good, crisp and bracing.

The village below went along in the usual way, peasants going about their business. They'd grown somewhat used to the Perranese presence but still went out of their way to avoid the warriors.

Beyond the palisades, patchy snow still clung to the plain. Spring was coming. The road that led out from the town gate twisted eventually into the tree line of a forest. A figure on a horse emerged, riding toward the town. He couldn't see who it was at this distance but suspected it was the overdue spy, not from Klaar but from Merridan.

Tchi watched the rider approach, observed the men open the front gate and question him briefly before sending him through. A moment later there was a knock at Tchi's door.

"Come."

The spy entered, bowed, and closed the door behind him. He was the most unmemorable-looking man Tchi had ever seen.

An asset in his line of work, I'd imagine.

"Something warm? Tea?" Tchi offered.

A lopsided grin from the spy. "Something stronger, if it's not too forward, sir. Been a long ride."

Tchi retrieved a pitcher and two cups from the cabinet behind him. "Brandy? It's not very good, I'm afraid."

"Good enough for me, sir."

Tchi set the cups on the table and began to pour. "What news from Merridan?"

"Pemrod is sending out a force," the spy said. "Five thousand men. I rode hard out of the south gate just ahead of them."

Tchi's head came up abruptly, eyes wide. He spilled some of the brandy. "Five thousand? Coming here?"

The spy shook his head. "South to Sherrik. There's a staging area near the river just south of Merridan. They're loading the army onto barges. They'll take the river as far as the white water then go overland from there."

"Why?"

"Don't know, sir," the spy said. "But riders came in from Sherrik four days ago, important types by the look of the fancy livery. Whatever they told the king has the whole court buzzing. Some of my boys are trying to get the story, but I thought I'd better get out here and let you know."

Tchi chewed his bottom lip. A second later, he shouted for one of his junior officers, who then entered the room and saluted.

"I want five hundred men ready to march in twenty-four hours," Tchi told the officer. That would leave a handful of men to hold the town in case they needed to fall back. He didn't relish the thought, but it was his job to consider every contingency. "Tell the men to pack light so we can move quickly."

"Yessir." The officer saluted again and left.

"Begging your pardon," the spy said. "But what are you going to do with five hundred men against five thousand?"

"Not a thing," Tchi said with an indulgent smile. "I'm extremely *brave*. Not extremely *stupid*."

In fact, Tchi had little idea what he was going to do at all, but some instinct told him the time for sitting still was over. Could his small force affect upcoming events in some significant way? Maybe or maybe not. But he wanted to put himself in a position to try. Opportunities often fell from the sky.

"Get something to eat and some rest," Tchi told the spy. "I might have another job for you soon."

◆ ◆ ◆

Rina held the chuma stick in a trembling hand, leaned forward to light it from a candle flame. She drew in a lungful of smoke, held it, then exhaled. Her entire body hurt. Her hand ached. Her arm felt like it could not properly be connected to her shoulder, but the castle physician confirmed she'd popped it back into its socket.

She sat and smoked. Bruny and Stasha and a handful of other woman buzzed around the room like panicked nannies. Mostly they attended to Talbun's scrapes and bruises. Rina had stayed tapped into the spirit as long as possible to let the healing rune do its work, but eventually she'd had to let it go. She'd used a lot, almost too much.

Now she felt the full impact of her remaining injuries.

"Bruny?"

The servant looked at her with wide eyes. "Your grace?"

"Brandy."

"At once, your grace."

"Wait," Rina said. "Do we have anything stronger?"

"There's a jug of that foul stuff Tosh favors in the pantry," Bruny said. "It'll knock a horse on its . . . pardon, grace. Yes, it's quite strong."

"Bring it."

Bruny brought the drink. Other women brought in fresh dresses for Rina and the wizard.

Rina took the chuma stick from her mouth and gulped down half the cup Bruny had poured for her. She coughed, fire burning her throat and nostrils, her eyes watering. *I remember this stuff.* She'd only sipped before when she, Tosh, Brasley, and Alem had sat on the ruined Long Bridge contemplating the future.

She took another gulp. A peaceful, warm feeling spread through her limbs. It numbed the pain slightly.

"More." She held the cup out to Bruny. "And where's Alem?"

"I'm sure I don't know, your grace." Bruny refilled the cup.

Rina puffed, then drank again, sipping this time.

When Stasha came back into the room, Rina asked again. "Have you seen Alem?"

"Yes, your grace," Stasha said. "He's off with the others. They should be halfway down the Small Road by now."

Rina froze, the cup almost to her mouth. "What?"

"With Tosh and his people," Stasha said. "I haven't had a chance to tell you about the trouble in the stables. Alem wasn't injured too badly."

Rina stared blankly for a long second. "What?"

"But it's okay," Stasha insisted. "Alem was still able to go with them."

Confusion clouded Rina's face completely. "What?"

Now the chamberlain looked confused too. "I've told you. Alem is . . ." Her eyes slowly widened. "You don't know."

Rina shook her head.

"I'm most dreadfully sorry, milady. It never occurred to me—I mean, I never thought Alem would go off without asking . . ."

"Let me see if I'm understanding this correctly," Rina said. "Alem is gone. With Tosh. He's *left* Klaar."

"Yes."

"But *why?*" She realized she'd raised her voice. All the heads in the room turned to look at her.

"I'm sorry, your grace," Stasha said. "I assumed you'd sent him as part of some plan."

"Never mind. We'll talk about it later."

Rina turned away, puffed the chuma stick thoughtfully. It didn't make any sense. Had she done something to him, maybe said something he'd taken the wrong way? What could possibly have compelled Alem to suddenly undertake such a journey? It was just Tosh, and a few of his guardswomen, and . . .

Maurizan.

No. That was over before it had really even begun. Alem had chosen Rina. And anyway, the gypsy girl was more likely to slip a dagger between Alem's ribs than try to lure him away with a few batted eyelashes. No, Alem and Rina were happy. He wouldn't choose to go with Maurizan. Unless . . .

Was it possible he'd heard about Ferris Gant's proposal? But that didn't make any sense. She'd refused Gant. *None* of this made any sense.

Rina realized her chamberlain was still standing next to her, waiting for orders.

"I'm raising you to steward," Rina said.

Stasha raised an eyebrow. "Your grace?"

"I need to leave Klaar, just for a while," Rina said. "I have to do something." The chamberlain ran the castle. But as steward, Stasha Benadicta would have the authority to run the whole duchy in Rina's stead.

Rina's eyes met Talbun's. There was the briefest moment of consideration, and then the wizard nodded.

It's settled, then. Good. Might as well get on with it.

"Stasha, is Count Becham's party still scheduled to depart in the morning?" Rina asked.

"Yes, milady."

"Then please convey to him my best wishes and ask if I and a very small retinue might accompany him as far as Merridan."

CHAPTER THIRTY-ONE

A servant woke Rina just before dawn, and she rose, grumbling.

It had been a poor night's sleep. It had taken her too long to drift off. She was nervous the glowing red eyes would chase her again in another dream. When she finally did fall asleep, she'd started awake several times, reaching for the empty space where Alem should have been, only to remember a second later that he'd abandoned her.

That's how she felt: abandoned. She alternated between sick confusion and anger.

In the stables, she kept looking for him as if it had all been a mistake. No sign of him. Only bucktoothed stable boys tossing saddles onto mounts. Talbun already sat astride a tall black stallion. She looked odd to Rina in the conservative brown riding dress with the split skirts and forest-green cloak. When Rina had first met the wizard, she'd strutted around topless like some exotic foreign queen supervising an all-male harem. She'd been beautiful and glamorous, and there had been a bright aura around her.

Talbun was still quite a beautiful woman, but she now seemed . . . ordinary.

Rina mounted her horse, looked at the wizard. Talbun grinned.

"What's the joke?"

"No joke," Talbun said. "I was just noticing again how much the armor suits you."

Rina had donned the black armor again. It was tailored to a woman's body, fitting close, not heavy and bulky like a man's armor. "I hope you don't want it back."

Talbun shook her head. "It was a gift."

Rina draped the fur-collared cloak around her shoulders. It was the same cloak she'd taken from Kork, but she'd had it hemmed for her shorter stature. "What about you? Any luck?"

The grin fell from Talbun's face. "No." She'd taken a dozen servants and had scoured the courtyard and circled the outside of the prayer tower, hoping to find any of Weylan's books or scrolls that might have survived the attack. "Shredded, scorched, and scattered to the wind."

"Not even the spell book?"

"Especially not the spell book," Talbun said bitterly. "I only have the few spells still in my head. When they're gone, they're gone."

A wizard without spells. Not very helpful. Still, she knows more about these things than I do. I need her.

"Come on," Rina said. "Let's catch up with the others."

They took the cobblestone streets at a trot and minutes later entered the grand marketplace's courtyard, in front of the city's main gates. Becham and his party prepared for departure, heralds lining up in front, supply wagons bringing up the rear. Rina and Talbun reined in their horses next to Gant and Becham, and Rina made introductions.

"Your steward said your entourage would be small, but I expected more than just this young lady." Becham bowed to Talbun as well as he could from horseback. "Obviously quality makes up for lack of quantity."

Talbun nodded and smiled. "You're most gracious, Count Becham."
Rina rolled her eyes.

Gant saw her and grinned. She returned the grin then immediately frowned. *I'm in no mood for your charm*, she reminded herself.

"The Hammish estate is a short detour," Rina said to Becham. "I'd like to break off and ask Brasley to join us. It's rather a long story, but he's a valuable retainer, and I find I suddenly have need of him." The words *valuable retainer* in connection to Brasley weren't words she'd ever expected to utter. More surprising still was the fact it was the truth. "With your permission, of course."

"It's not *my* permission you need," Becham said. "If you can pry him away from his new bride, then my son-in-law is welcome."

"Thank you."

The count raised his voice, doing his best to sound like an old campaigner. "Very well, then. Let's get started, shall we? There's a reasonably serviceable inn a day's ride from here, and I'm too old to camp in the damp wilderness. Heralds, lead the way, and . . ."

The sound of a galloping horse distracted them.

A man in full plate armor on an enormous white steed rounded the corner. A big man, barrel chested, broad shoulders made broader by the bulky armor. A white cloak trimmed in gold draped across his shoulder. No sword hung from his belt. Instead, there was a thick and murderous-looking mace. The face guard was down on his helm. Rina had no idea who the man could be. Another rider on a smaller brown gelding followed him, a skinny lad of maybe sixteen, with the look of a gawking squire.

The white steed clattered to a stop in front of Rina, and the man in plate dismounted. He took off his helm.

It was Bishop Feridixx Hark.

If he seemed an unlikely bishop in his fine clerical robes, he looked every bit at home in the plate armor, powerful and strong, like he might knock the castle down with a single blow of his mace. He tucked his helm under one arm and bowed low.

"Duchess Veraiin, I owe you an apology," Hark said.

She regarded the bishop with a raised eyebrow. "Oh?"

"You needed help. *Klaar* needed help, and I turned my back on you," Hark said. "At the time, I thought I was doing the right thing, that the pious among us needed to set an example to . . . well . . . offset your choice of chamberlain."

"Steward now," Rina told him.

"So I've heard," Hark said. "I wanted to send a message that Dumo did not approve of certain behaviors, but such matters seem petty now, and I feel obligated to offer my assistance."

"You're no good to me if your loyalty comes and goes on a whim," Rina said. "What changed your mind?"

"Dreams," the bishop said. "And wicked red eyes watching me from the shadows."

Silence descended over the courtyard.

Rina cleared her throat, turned to Count Becham, and forced a smile. "It seems my retinue will be slightly larger than expected."

◆ ◆ ◆

The journey down the mountain was quick and uneventful, and by the time they reached the village of Crossroads, the temperature had warmed enough that Rina removed her cloak and packed it away into a saddlebag. By Klaarian standards it was practically a heat wave.

Rina, Talbun, and Bishop Hark broke off from the main group and left Crossroads, heading south. They promised Becham they'd catch up with him on the King's Highway after they'd fetched Brasley.

The road was wide enough for the three of them to ride side by side. Hark's squire rode several yards back to give the trio privacy.

"Now that it's just the three of us, Bishop Hark, I'd like to hear more about those dreams," Rina said.

Hark glanced at Talbun.

"She knows," Rina said. "I've already told her about my own dream."

"You've had them too, then," Hark said.

"I thought you knew that already."

"I suspected," Hark said. "I don't know anything. May I be frank?"

Rina laughed. "You mean you've been holding back all this time?"

Hark reddened and looked abashed. "Again, I apologize, your grace. I'm embarrassed by my behavior."

"Forget it," Rina said. "With gods throwing tantrums, we all agree we've got bigger worries."

Hark cleared his throat. "Tantrums, you say. I was thinking world-shaking catastrophe, but I will of course yield to your grace's assessment."

Rina turned her head to hide a grin. She couldn't help it. She was warming up to the burly bishop.

"I believe you were about to get frank," Rina reminded him.

"There are only seven bishops in the Church of Dumo in all of Helva," Hark said. "I rank least among the seven, but as you can imagine, I keep rare company within the hierarchy."

"If you're trying to tell me how important you are, I believe you," Rina said.

"No, that's not quite what I mean."

"He means he is more in touch with his god than the average parishioner," Talbun said.

Hark nodded acknowledgment to the wizard. "Perhaps a bit oversimplified, but yes. As the fifth son of a lesser noble, I was trundled off to the priesthood at age eleven. I'd resented it actually and had planned to run away but soon found I had an aptitude for religion."

"They don't groom you for bishop just because you show a knack for the clergy," Talbun said.

"No," Hark agreed. "I see milady has some knowledge of church hierarchy."

"When you've been around as long as I have, you pick up a few things."

"I imagine I have a few years on you, milady," Hark said.

"You'd be surprised." A sly smile.

Curiosity briefly passed over Hark's face before he went on. "When I was fifteen, I blessed a village well in which the water had turned sour, and it cleared the next day. Things I did seemed to always go right. As a priest, my sermons seemed to lift the masses. Often when I touched the sick, they seemed to heal more quickly. Please understand that I had no control over these things. Months or years would pass as I went about my normal duties at the temple, and then out of the blue, Dumo would guide my hand."

Rina and Talbun traded looks.

Hark saw the exchange. "Yes, I know how it must sound. Please trust that I have no interest in self-aggrandizement. But miracles aren't the important thing, not really. For as long as I have served Dumo, I have always *felt* his presence. And that feeling has always provided a confidence that I was doing Dumo's work."

In another time or place, Rina might have scoffed at Hark's claims, but she remembered how High Priest Krell had magically etched the Hand of Death tattoo onto her palm. If Mordis could grant special powers to his servants, then Rina supposed Dumo could do the same thing.

Rina guessed what Hark was getting at.

"Something's changed," Rina said. "Hasn't it?"

Hark sighed. "For the past couple of weeks I've felt that Dumo has withdrawn from me, that he's no longer close and isn't listening when I pray. There's no way to prove this, obviously, but when you live with a feeling for years and then it's no longer there, you notice. I thought

I'd displeased Dumo in some way and he was punishing me, but then I had the dream."

They rode a few moments in silence, and Rina wondered whether the bishop had changed his mind about sharing the dream with them.

"A shadow within a fog," Hark said at last. "Large but shapeless with glowing red eyes. I ran, but you know how it is sometimes in a dream. The faster you try to run, the slower you go. Quite frustrating, really. Just when I felt that this shapeless dread was upon me, I burst through the fog into a clearing. Across the clearing I saw a temple with wrecked gates. You were there, your grace, talking to a priest in a black robe."

Rina and Talbun exchanged looks again, no hint of amusement this time.

"I see I've hit on something," Hark said. "Your grace, my dream. It felt, well, almost as if Dumo had been in hiding but showed himself briefly to guide me in this dream. I've done a good bit of traveling in my years, and I think I recognize a temple of Mordis when I see one. I also note that our road to Merridan takes us fairly close to this temple." A noncommittal shrug. "You know the rest of the story. I quickly climbed into my armor and hastened to offer your grace my services. I hope we strive in common cause."

When Rina and Talbun exchanged looks this time, the wizard said, "Tell him."

Rina told the bishop about her own dream. Her visitation from High Priest Krell. The eyes in the fog. Everything. She related her story in flat, businesslike tones, avoiding drama, and Hark grew more ashen with each word she spoke.

"It's changing," Hark said gravely. "The whole world is going to be different."

"You said it was as if Dumo were hiding," Talbun said. "You might be right."

Hark sighed heavily. "When your god runs and hides, what hope is left for mere mortals?"

"Come on," Rina said. "The path splits off from the road just ahead. Through the forest in the fastest way to the Hammish Lodge. Let's surprise the baron, shall we?"

◆　◆　◆

Fregga kissed the back of his neck, scooted right up against him underneath the blanket, one soft hand reaching around to find him, rubbing and then tugging until he was fully erect.

Brasley turned over to face her. "This will make four times."

"Are we newlyweds or not?"

She threw a leg over him, positioned herself, and guided him in as she lowered onto him, taking him in all the way. They found a steady rhythm. His hands gripped her plush backside. Fregga was soft all over, and it hadn't taken Brasley long to appreciate it. Fregga tended toward the plump anyway, and the pregnancy wasn't showing yet. He wondered what she would look like at nine months, huge and ready to pop. Well, in the meantime . . . it wasn't like she could get any *more* pregnant.

"You feel . . . *so good*," Brasley said.

She laughed. "I'm a good cook too. I'll make you something later."

"We have a cook."

"I sent her away."

"Oh, well . . . wait . . . what? You sent away . . ." *Damn it, what's that girl's name again?* "You sent away the cook?"

"And the maid. They were both a little too pretty," Fregga said.

The maid too? Brasley hadn't even had a chance to try her yet. "You fired them?"

"I made other arrangements in Klaar for them," Fregga said. "Don't worry. They won't starve."

"We still need servants," Brasley insisted. "You're a baroness."

"You do intend to let me run the household, don't you?" Fregga redoubled her rhythm, her ass making slapping sounds against his thighs.

"Of course." Brasley grunted. "What's there to run?"

"I have a new cook coming from Crossroads. She's seventy."

"I'm sure she knows her way around a kitchen."

Fregga threw her head back. "Oh. Oh, Brasley. Oh, yes."

He moaned and she did too and they finished at the same time. She fell across him, panting, their hearts beating together. Brasley closed his eyes. The woman had taken a lot out of him the past twenty-four hours.

The distant sound of a neighing horse popped Brasley's eyes open again.

He eased out from under Fregga and went to the window, peeked through a crack in the shutters. Four people on horses headed straight for the lodge. Too far to make out whom they might be, but Brasley was definitely *not* expecting company.

He quickly pulled on his breeches and tied the laces. He snatched a shirt off the floor and put it on. He sat on the edge of the bed and grabbed his boots.

"What is it?" Fregga asked from the tangle of sheets, voice sleepy and content.

"Somebody's coming. Don't worry. I'll go see who it is."

He went downstairs and past the great stone fireplace. A modest fire within had burned low. He opened his mouth to shout for the maid to bring more wood but then remembered the maid had been sent away. Somehow, in a day, Fregga had taken over his whole house.

And she'll take over me *next!*

Yeah, and what was really so bad about that? The woman did any-thing—*anything*—he wanted in the sack and seemed actually to enjoy it. So maybe having a woman in his life to keep him organized and on the right path was exactly what he needed. Maybe settling down with Fregga was the key to Brasley's happiness.

But the maid did have great tits. I wish I'd had the chance to—

He shook his head, banishing such thoughts, and went out through the front door. He stood on the front porch, hugging himself in the cool air, and watched the riders approach. He only had to watch another few moments before Rina came into focus.

She's wearing that sinister black armor. That can't be good.

The woman riding next to here was stunningly beautiful. He'd never seen her before. Brasley would certainly have remembered.

The third rider was . . . *Bishop Hark?* And in full plate armor. The youth riding behind them seemed to be a servant.

I like the look of this less and less every second.

He waited until they'd reached the lodge before offering a half-hearted wave.

"Hello, Brasley," Rina said.

"Dare I ask?" Brasley said.

"Something's come up," Rina said. "I need you."

"Me? That's probably some kind of mistake because nobody ever needs me for anything. I'm sure you'll sort it all out," Brasley said. "As you know, I'm on my honeymoon, so I'm sure you'll forgive me if I don't jump into a full suit of armor and ride off to whatever dangerous thing you've got going this time."

"Don't be ridiculous, darling," Fregga said coming up behind him. "Invite them in, for goodness sake. I'll brew us all a nice pot of tea."

Somehow Fregga looked perfectly put together, hair neat and combed, dress smooth and unwrinkled. Brasley marveled. The woman had just been sweaty and breathless two minutes ago, hair mussed. Now she looked ready to attend a royal dinner.

Fregga nodded to Hark. "Lovely to see you again, Bishop Hark. Your ceremony was just wonderful."

Hark managed a smile. "Only too happy to be of service."

Brasley took his wife's hand and gave it a little squeeze. "Fregga, my dear, I was just telling Duchess Veraiin I would have to decline her offer to take me on a little camping holiday."

"Don't be silly, Brasley."

Brasley blinked. "What?"

"She's your duchess," Fregga said. "If duty calls, then you must obey."

Brasley blinked again. "But we were *just* married. I thought that—"

"Now, don't trouble yourself with a bunch of thinking, Brasley." She brushed past him and gestured to Rina and the others. "Please do come in. You can have your tea while Brasley packs."

"You have my thanks, Baroness Hammish," Rina said. "If we can get back on the road quickly, we should be able to catch up to Count Becham and the others before nightfall."

"Even better," Fregga said. "Brasley, you get to travel with Father."

"Yes," Brasley said. "Even better."

CHAPTER
THIRTY-TWO

As steward, Stasha Benadicta decided to set up her office similar to Rina's. It was smaller, naturally, and didn't have a window, but she'd found a small, rectangular table, highly polished and sturdily built to serve as a desk. It was important that she project the right sort of authority. In Rina's absence, Stasha represented the duchess and Klaar itself.

The air of power she'd hoped to project seemed entirely lost on the young army officer standing before her.

"Madam Steward." The officer's voice cracked, nervous. "General Kerrig sends his compliments and asks what service he might do for you."

"He need not trouble himself personally," Stasha said. "I simply asked for a squad of men."

"Regretfully, the general must remind the steward how shorthanded the military is at the moment." The young officer said this as if he'd rehearsed it. "He says if you'd like to tell him what task you need accomplished, he can tend to it. Keeping the men directly under his command will expedite whatever it is you need done."

He means that General Kerrig doesn't want to take orders from the woman who runs the brothel. She'd reached the highest rank in Klaar possible for someone without noble blood, but to many she would always be Back Gate scum.

She lifted her chin, giving no sign that anything the officer had said flustered her at all. "Please tell the general . . ."

What?

If she gave him a direct order and he refused, what would happen? He was the man with all the soldiers. If he refused, it would only highlight Stasha's weakness. If he resigned, it would hamper the military's recovery. Rebuilding the army was a slow process. She could report the general to Rina upon her return, but that would only make Stasha look like a little child running to her mommy.

She needed to handle this herself.

"Please tell the general that I thank him for his offer and will let him know when I need him."

The officer bowed low and left in a hurry, apparently relieved to be on his way.

Stasha sent a servant to fetch Darshia. She'd already made up her mind how she would handle the situation. Some of the puzzle pieces were already in place.

A knock at the door.

"Come in."

Darshia entered and shut the door behind her. Her red hair had been woven into two tight braids that hung over her shoulders. She wore her sword belt with the Perranese blade. Darshia and the other women from the Wounded Bird never seemed to be without their swords. A symbol of their liberation perhaps.

Or maybe they just wanted to be ready for anything at any time. Stasha could understand that.

"You wanted to see me, Mother. Sorry, I mean, Madam Steward."

"It's okay," Stasha said. "When we're alone I don't mind."

"Okay."

"Prinn sent you on an errand the morning she was killed."

"A favor for her," Darshia said.

"What was it?"

She hesitated a moment, then: "She wanted me to take some money to her family. And to tell them to leave Klaar. Prinn was in a hurry and didn't explain, but I guess they were in some kind of trouble maybe."

"And did they? Leave, I mean."

"Yes," Darshia said. "It was a lot of money, and I think it frightened them. They didn't have much. It didn't take long for them to pack up."

"Do you know where they went?"

"I didn't ask," Darshia said. "I didn't want to know."

Stasha nodded. "Probably for the best. Would you like to help me get those responsible?"

"Prinn was my best friend."

"I'll take that as a yes," Stasha said. "I want you to pick two girls and tell them to be ready. Take them off guard duty rotation. Send somebody to the Wounded Bird to bring back Bune and Lubin."

"I can fetch them myself."

"No, I have something else for you to do," Stasha said. "There's a drab little tavern down a dark alley. There's a panhandler there in rags. You will put a copper coin in his cup. If there is a folded piece of parchment in the cup, bring it to me. If not, go about your business. Do this once in the morning and once in the evening every day until I say to stop. Try not to be seen, but if you are, then you're just a generous passerby giving to a beggar."

"Who's the beggar?" Darshia asked.

"My eyes and ears," said Stasha. "I need you to be ready, Darshia. When it's time to move, it will happen fast. And it will get bloody."

CHAPTER THIRTY-THREE

The *Witch of Kern* sliced the foamy waves, bobbing in the emerald sea, its square sails full and white against a bright blue sky. Alem knew nothing about sailing but guessed they were making good time.

In fact, he'd never even seen an ocean before even though Klaar sat on the icy Northern Sea. He'd never left Klaar before his adventure with Rina and Brasley, and that had taken him west, not east toward the water. He found, much to his pleasant surprise, that he loved the smell of the salt ocean, the breeze in his face, the immensity of the ocean stretching vast to the horizon.

Alem leaned against the railing, breathed in the air, and sighed with pleasure.

"Could you at least not sound so fucking happy?" Maurizan said. "I'm trying to die in peace over here."

The gypsy girl sat cross-legged, hunched over a bucket in her lap. A second later she vomited into it. She'd felt nauseous almost immediately after the ship left port in Kern and had stood at the railing giving the contents of her stomach to the fish for two hours, before becoming too fatigued to stand anymore. She'd been convinced to sit, and Alem had brought her the bucket. He emptied it over the side for her periodically. She'd tolerated his help but hadn't actually said thank you.

Not that I'm expecting an outpouring of gratitude any time soon, Alem thought.

Each new swell of the ocean pulled another moan out of her. Maurizan vomited again.

"I'm throwing up things I don't even remember eating," she said.

"Tosh is sick too," Alem said. "If that makes you feel any better."

"As sick as me?"

"Nobody is as sick as you."

Maurizan vomited again.

The trip from Klaar to Kern had been a quick and uneventful four days. They'd spent another day in the town of Kern itself, making sure the *Witch of Kern* was properly provisioned and to comb drunken sailors out of the dockside taverns in time enough to sober them and set sail. Spending a day in Kern revealed to Alem that the town was not significantly any more interesting than Klaar, the chief difference being that he didn't know a soul.

And really, what was the point of running away from Klaar only to end up in a place exactly like Klaar? Likely he'd end up getting some drab job shoveling shit in a stable. When Tosh said he could come south on the *Witch of Kern* to Sherrik, Alem jumped at the offer. An exotic city in warm climes? Why not?

"I'm sorry you're not feeling well," Alem said.

Maurizan looked daggers at him. "If there were any justice in the world, you'd be the one puking, not me."

"Can I get you some water or something?"

"No," Maurizan said. "Just let me sit here."

Right.

Alem moved down the deck where the captain stood at the railing, hands shading his eyes as he looked back north and east. To Alem, Captain Barazz looked less like a sea captain and more like a pit wrestler, powerful arms and legs, thick neck, tall and broad shouldered. Black skin, head shaved except for a black topknot.

It occurred to Alem he'd never met a sea captain or a pit wrestler.

But he'd heard stories.

"What are you looking at, Captain?"

"A ship." Barazz's voice sounded like something from the bottom of a deep well, with a strange accent Alem had never heard before.

"I don't see it," Alem said.

"That's because it's far away."

"But then . . ." *Never mind.*

"Is it another merchant ship using the same shipping lanes we are?"

"Maybe," the captain said.

Alem scanned the horizon for a full minute but still couldn't see it. "Could it be a pirate?"

"Maybe."

"You don't know?"

"How would I know?" the captain asked.

Alem frowned. "Because . . . you're the captain?"

Barazz turned his head slowly until his tired eyes met Alem's. "Boy, go away."

Alem went away.

He met Tosh coming up from belowdecks. He looked green and drawn but better than he did yesterday.

"You okay?"

Tosh nodded. "Not so bad nothing coming up at least. Have you thought about what you're going to do when we reach Sherrik?"

It was *all* Alem had thought about. The *Witch of Kern* would stop at Sherrik for provisions and news and to offload cargo before heading due south to the Red City, and the Red City was as far as Alem could go. Tosh hadn't told him what errand they were on for Rina, and Alem hadn't asked. He was just along for the ride.

And anyway, if Rina needs favors she can damn well ask her new husband.

Alem winced at his own pettiness. He couldn't help it. Thinking of Rina put a knot in his gut every time. Instead he thought about the sea and the salt air, what he might do in Sherrik, and the Red City. He would go out into the world and make something of himself.

Yeah, and how do I do that exactly?

He really had no idea.

"I thought I'd wait until we hit port," Alem said. "Sort of size the place up."

"I've heard it's a sizable city," Tosh said. "Oh, not like Merridan or Tul-Agnon, but big. Twice as big as Klaar, I guess. Anyway, like you said, you'll see it when we get there."

"Yeah."

Alem emptied Maurizan's vomit bucket again. She mumbled something that might have been "thank you" but could just as easily have been "fuck you."

He returned to the railing, where the captain was still looking back at the other ship. This time, Alem strained his eyes and made out a vague dot on the horizon that might have been a ship or could have been his eyes playing tricks on him.

"It's probably just a merchant following the same trade route, right?" Alem said.

"No," the captain said. "It's following us."

Alem frowned. "How do you know that?"

"I changed course, and it changed course to match ours," Barazz said. "It is gaining but slowly. Tomorrow afternoon. Before supper, I think."

Alem swallowed hard. "That's rude. They could at least let us eat first.

The hint of a smile tugged at the corner of Barazz's mouth.

"Master Nork," Barazz shouted. "Front and center."

A wiry little man, shirtless, ran barefoot across the deck and came to attention in front of the captain. First Mate Nork's skin looked like a withered brown apple. His arms and legs looked made of old rope. "Sir?"

"Tell the master-at-arms to open the weapons locker and pass out spears and cutlasses," Barazz ordered. "Tell the men to keep their weapons close but not to get jumpy. Who has the best eyes?"

"Bosun Figg," Nork said.

"Into the crow's nest with him, if you please, Master Nork," Barazz said.

Nork saluted and ran off screaming for the bosun.

"Can you fight, boy?" Barazz asked.

No. "I'm okay with a crossbow."

"Do you have one?"

"Yes."

"Draw an extra quiver of bolts from the master-at-arms," Barazz said. "And pass the word among your friends."

◆ ◆ ◆

Three days of dropping copper coins into the beggar's cup, and Darshia still had nothing to show for it. A dank little alley, an archway into a courtyard and an even danker tavern beyond called the Drunken Imp. That's what the beggar kept an eye on, sitting just outside the archway in his rags, holding his little keep.

And he smelled.

Yeah, well, you were a whore, Darshia. Nobody's perfect. Let's be a bit more tolerant, shall we?

She bent to drop another copper into his cup and was surprised to see a small, folded piece of parchment. She palmed it and moved on even as the "Thank you, generous lady" followed her down the alley.

She paused at the other end of the alley, stopped and pretended to adjust a boot to give her a chance to glance backward. Nobody followed her. The alley was empty, save for the beggar, motionless in the same spot.

Darshia left the alley and strolled along with the flow of pedestrian traffic, glancing back a few times but seeing nothing amiss. She considered the folded piece of parchment in her closed fist. Stasha Benadicta hadn't actually said Darshia couldn't read it.

She unfolded it and read. One word: *Tonight.*

Darshia couldn't remember the last time a single word had made her so nervous.

◆ ◆ ◆

Rina sat astride her horse, eyes closed, tapped into the spirit.

Brasley, Talbun, Hark, and the squire sat on their horses twenty yards away so as not to disturb her. They were in a quiet glade just inside the edge of the forest, the only sound the leaves rustling in the cool breeze.

The day had turned gray with the gathering clouds.

They'd caught up with Count Becham and his party after picking up Brasley but had broken off again to detour to the Temple of Mordis.

"Explain to me again what she's doing," the bishop said.

"She has a familiar," Talbun said. "That's what the tattoos on her face are for. A forest falcon. She can see through its eyes. She's sent it to scout ahead."

"Please don't take it as disrespect, but the tattoos make her look a bit like a jungle savage," Hark said.

Talbun smiled. "You have a wide experience of jungle savages, Bishop Hark?"

"I have a wide experience of many things," Hark said. "I've also been known to read a book now and then."

"Sailors have tattoos," Talbun said.

"So I've observed," Hark said. "Although I've never seen them on faces. Seems an awkward place for one."

"I think it's quite exotic and attractive," Talbun said. "Wouldn't you agree, Baron Hammish?"

"I suppose," Brasley said.

"Pardon me for saying so, Baron," Hark said, "but you seem a bit sullen."

"Could you both call me Brasley, please?" he asked. "Whenever you say *baron*, I keep looking around for my uncle. And yes, I am sullen. Also anxious, nervous, unhappy, and *afraid*. You weren't at the temple last time around. It was a *slaughter*. I've never seen anything so bloody in my life."

"But you were victorious, weren't you?" the bishop asked.

"Yes."

Hark frowned. "Then why—"

"I'd rather not talk about it," Brasley said. "And anyway, here she comes."

Rina approached, reined in her horse next to theirs.

"Zin circled the temple three times," Rina told them. "It looks deserted. And the gates haven't been repaired."

"That's a shame," Brasley said. "Nobody home, you say? Looks like we'll just have to turn around and head home."

"No," Rina said. "We've come this far. I want to see for myself."

Brasley sighed. "I just *knew* you were going to say that."

CHAPTER THIRTY-FOUR

She'd always wanted to be the prettiest.

Except now.

It was because Darshia was competitive. When she'd worked at the Wounded Bird, it had never much mattered what the men thought, but she'd always been competitive with the other women, the best clothes, the best hair, the best makeup, the best figure. She realized now how small her life had been at the brothel. That trying to outshine the other girls was the only way she could feel good about herself was proof of this.

Now there were other ways. She was good with the sword and getting better every day. She had a purpose she was proud of. She didn't need to be the prettiest anymore.

But Stasha, Carrine, and Becca all agreed she looked best in the dress. A vivid green, cut low enough to be fashionable without going overboard. Her ample figure, bright white skin, and red hair against the dress made her irresistible bait.

I don't want to be bait. I want to strap on a sword and armor and cut open the bastards who killed Prinn.

But a sword and armor would ruin the effect. She walked down the alley in a white fur cloak, hood thrown back and red hair loose and flowing, gleaming like a beacon. There was a thin stiletto tucked into her fur-lined boots, her only weapon.

She turned into the courtyard of the Drunken Imp.

Yellow lights and bulky shapes in the tavern windows. Raucous laughter from within signaled the night's festivities were already well under way.

Darshia drew a deep breath, gathered herself, and entered.

The laughter died away immediately, all eyes turning to her.

She scanned the place. No other women. Darshia thought there might at least be prostitutes, but no. It would work to her advantage, but it still made her feel uncomfortable. She tried to remember how the noblewomen carried themselves around court.

Darshia smiled. "Gentleman, please go about your business and don't let me disturb you. I took a wrong turn, and I've just popped in to your establishment briefly to refresh myself."

There was an empty table across the room, and Darshia went to it, not too fast, head up, confident, like she came to this squalid place every day. She felt the eyes on her and ignored them. She sat herself at the table, took off her cloak, and hit them with the dress.

An emerald tossed into a pile of cow shit. That's how she must have looked sitting there among the denizens of the Drunken Imp, shining and clean in an expensive dress and smelling of Stasha Benadicta's best soap. Even with a roaring blaze in the big fireplace across the room, the dress's thin fabric did little to fend off a chill, and Darshia's nipples strained against the material. When she'd worked at the Wounded Bird, she'd pinch her nipples before entering the common room to achieve just such an effect, but now she felt only self-conscious.

Get over yourself. They're just nipples.

She waved a handkerchief at the squat brute behind the bar. "Barkeep, could I have something warm? A pot of tea perhaps?"

Every man in the room gawked at her, none trying to hide it.

Nobody in the tavern noticed the two others who entered quietly and took the seats in a darkened corner.

Darshia made a quick count. Eight men in the tavern, nine if you counted the barkeep. Another door just to the right of the fireplace was the only other exit besides the main entrance. Low ceiling, a gray layer above them from pipe smoke. A cramped place for a fight. Knives and fists better than swords.

A greasy man with a five-day beard plopped down in the seat across from her, splashed purple wine into a wooden cup and slid it across the table to her. "Can't let a pretty thing like you drink alone. Have a cup of this then. Do you better than tea."

Darshia fluttered her eyelashes, one white hand going delicately to her chest. "Oh my. How . . . generous."

A man twice as big and twice as greasy came up behind the first one, swatted him on the shoulder. "Shove off, Rory. Real woman like this wants a real man."

"Shove off, yourself," Rory snarled over his shoulder.

"You've got pox on your cock."

"That's a damn lie!"

There was the scrape of chairs as others rose to come join the scene or gawk at it. Men crowded closer from all sides, the sweating smell of them cloying and foul. Darshia wondered how fast she could draw the stiletto from her boot.

"Enough." A voice from across the room, high-pitched and piercing.

The greasy men slunk back to their tables like whipped dogs.

The new voice had come from the direction of the fireplace, and Darshia craned her neck. Two upholstered high-back chairs faced the fireplace. From one an arm gestured "over here."

"Bring her to me," the voice said.

A man standing next to the fireplace walked toward her. He looked a half cut above the greasy ruffians, clean shaven, with simple clothes that were neat and clean. A short, fat sword hung from his belt.

He stopped at Darshia's table, nodded politely. "My lord asks that you join him by the fire. Milady might find it more comfortable."

She returned the nod. "Most gracious."

He escorted her to the fire, and she sat in the other armchair.

The man sitting across from her fit Giffen's description exactly. His smug, leering face made Darshia want to stab him in the eye. And Stasha had been correct that he would not be able to help himself if a pretty girl caught his eye . . . although the same proved true for most men in Darshia's experience.

"My gratitude, my lord," she said.

"You're too fine a lady for those brutes. Too fine to be in the Drunken Imp at all," Giffen said. "I felt it my duty as a gentleman to come to your rescue."

Go fuck yourself.

"Yes, I do seem to have wandered down the wrong street," Darshia said.

"Your face is not familiar to me, and Klaar is a small town," Giffen said. "May I ask your name?"

"Lady Elris Gant," Darshia said. "I arrived with the party from Merridan." The story had been prearranged. Elris was Ferris Gant's sister, although she hadn't come to Klaar.

"Odd," Giffen said. "I thought I knew everyone who'd come with Count Becham." Was there some doubt in his voice? Or possibly slime and suspicion were his usual demeanor.

Darshia was suddenly worried the story might not hold together. Giffen obviously had a better spy network than they'd figured.

"Also, didn't Count Becham and his retinue already leave to return to the capital?" Giffen asked.

Now Darshia found herself on firmer footing. "I'm of little significance, so it's no wonder you hadn't heard of me, and yes, the count and the others are on their way. I've stayed behind to keep the new Baroness Hammish company while she settles into her new home. Likely you heard news of the recent nuptials."

"Ah, yes." Giffen nodded. "That does ring a bell."

"As you might know, the Hammish lodge is off in the wilderness somewhere," Darshia said. "I thought it best to stay in town and shop for a few necessities before making the trip."

"Lady Gant, I hope you'll allow me to offer you some refreshment. I understand you're used to a better sort of place than this, but as I happen to do some business in here from time to time, the barman keeps a bottle of a tolerable brandy just for me." Gant gestured to his servant. "Bring the bottle and two glasses."

Darshia watched the man with the short sword leave and return with the bottle and two glasses. He might also have been some sort of bodyguard, and Darshia realized she'd have to take him out first.

The servant filled two glasses and handed one to Giffen and one to Darshia.

She tossed back the whole glass in a single gulp, remembering only after she'd swallowed that a proper lady sipped brandy. No guzzling.

She faked a cough. "Oh my, it's going right to my head."

"That's strong stuff, my dear," Giffen said.

She used the cough as her opportunity to give the signal. No point in waiting anymore. Everyone should be in position.

She brought her handkerchief to her mouth, coughed some more.

"My dear, perhaps a glass of water," Giffen offered.

Darshia held the handkerchief out to one side.

And let it drop.

A split second later the tavern erupted in screams of pain and the sound of furniture overturning. Darshia didn't need to see it. She already knew the sound of mayhem induced by Bune and Lubin.

Her hand went down to her boot.

Giffen and his bodyguard turned to look at the uproar.

Giffen's eyes shot wide. "What the bloody blazes is—"

His bodyguard's hand fell to the hilt of his sword. His other hand still held the brandy bottle.

Darshia was already coming out of her chair. She thrust the stiletto into the bodyguard's gut. His eyes shot wide, breath catching. She pulled out the blade and slammed it home again, hot blood washing over her hand. The bodyguard tumbled to the floor and dropped the brandy bottle. It clattered and rolled under the chair but didn't break.

Giffen was fast. Much faster than Darshia had anticipated.

He grabbed the wrist holding the stiletto and twisted. She screamed and dropped it, and his other open hand came down hard, slapping her across the face. She blinked stars, and they grappled, tangled, and went down.

He ended up on top of her.

"Bitch, who are you?" Giffen demanded.

One of his hands found her throat and squeezed.

EPISODE SIX

CHAPTER THIRTY-FIVE

Darshia's mouth worked for air, Giffen's crushing grip on her throat squeezing tighter.

With one hand Darshia pried at the fingers around her throat. With the other she reached up and raked her nails across Giffen's face, drawing three red lines. He grunted pain, grabbed her wrist, and pulled the hand from his face.

She felt her face going hot, lungs begging for air.

Some part of her registered the altercation going on in the rest of the tavern, furniture being tossed around and broken, shouts of pain and panic and anger.

She abandoned the hand around her throat. She wouldn't be able to pry it loose. She felt blindly along the floor. Maybe she could find the dropped stiletto.

Darshia's hand closed around something.

She brought it up hard, striking out, desperate.

The brandy bottle smashed against the side of Giffen's head. Glass and brandy rained down on her. Giffen loosened his grip but not enough.

Darshia still held the broken bottleneck. She jammed the jagged end into Giffen's hand and twisted. Giffen screamed but held on. Blackness clouded her. She was blind, brandy stinging her eyes. She twisted the broken bottle again, and Giffen's scream went up an octave.

And he let go.

Darshia rolled away, coughing, gagging, trying to suck breath. Every gulp of air was like hot daggers down her throat. She started to crawl away on her belly, aware of Giffen behind her. There was a thump and a thud.

She felt a strong hand under her arm and began to jerk away.

"It's me." Lubin's voice. "Let me help you."

Darshia let the big bruiser help her up and wiped brandy from her eyes with the back of her hand. She looked around the tavern. The place was a wreck, bodies and broken chairs and overturned tables littering the floor. Some of the tavern patrons on the floor groaned and tried to move. Others would never move again.

"Giff—" When she tried to talk, pain erupted white-hot in her throat.

"Don't worry." Lubin jerked a thumb over his shoulder at his brother. "Bune's got Giffen."

Bune hoisted Giffen's limp body over his shoulder. Giffen's wrists and ankles had been bound with rope, and a bag had been tossed over his head and cinched tight. Stasha Benadicta had ordered that he be taken alive. If Darshia had been given the chance, she would have jammed the broken bottleneck into the man's throat.

She stumbled to the door, and Lubin moved to help her. She waved him off.

Darshia met Carrine and Becca in the courtyard. They were cleaning blood off their swords. Three dead men lay at their feet. None had been allowed to escape. They might have raised an alarm or brought reinforcements. Darshia was just glad the men were dead.

Bune and Lubin followed her out of the tavern.

It was late, and the yellow moon was high. Not so many people would be on the streets, but if anyone became too curious about the limp body over Bune's shoulder, one scowl from the big man would send them scurrying.

She gently cleared her throat. Her voice slipped out as a scratchy whisper. "Let's get him back to the castle. Mother already has a cell in the dungeon waiting for him."

♦ ♦ ♦

They left the forest and crossed the open ground, leading their horses at a walk. They approached the temple slowly, watching and listening. Rina scanned the walls. No guards or movement of any kind, no signs of life.

Appropriate for the Temple of Death? Or maybe they've just abandoned the place.

They paused at the ruined gates. Rina puffed quietly on a chuma stick as the bishop and Talbun appraised the damage.

"These are the gates I saw in the dream. What happened?" Hark asked.

"The Perranese knocked them down with a battering ram," Rina said.

"They overran the temple?"

"No."

"You stopped them," the bishop said. Not a question.

She sucked on the chuma stick, blew out smoke. "Yes."

Hark nodded as if that confirmed something he'd been thinking. "Let's have a look, then."

Hark and his squire passed through the gates and Talbun followed. Rina turned to see Brasley hanging back. "Are you coming?"

"I don't like this place."

"There's not much to like," Rina said.

"Rina, let's just go."

"You know I have business here," she said. "I struck a bargain with the priest."

"Shit on him," Brasley said. "Break the bargain. What can he do?"

Rina puffed the chuma stick. *What indeed? That's the big question, isn't it?* The feeling of dread from her nightmare was still a palpable thing in her chest. An intuition from some deep part of her warned against crossing the priest. She'd made the deal willingly, and the evidence was the obscene skeletal hand on her palm. The Hand of Death, Krell had called it.

Rina didn't know what would happen if she backed out of the bargain. Something bad? Obviously. But maybe what the priest wanted would be even worse. Choices. Forks in the road. And no turning back once the choices were made.

She sucked the chuma stick, held the smoke in her lungs a long moment before exhaling.

"Stay out here if the place make you uncomfortable," she told Brasley.

"It's not just the temple," Brasley said. "It's you. It's what happened to you here."

He didn't need to say more. Armed with the Hand of Death, Rina had slaughtered nearly a hundred men until the ground had become a bog soaked with their blood. She'd been red from head to foot with it by the end, and the look on Brasley's face had made her sick. In that moment, in his eyes, she'd become something less than human, some dark force reaping all life in her path. He'd been revolted and he'd been afraid.

"I'm sorry that it was ugly," Rina said. "I'm sorry you had to see it."

"I'm sorry for you."

She shifted the chuma stick from one corner of her mouth to the other, turned, and led her horse past the gates.

When she'd been here last, there's been a small village, bland unhappy people tending scrawny animals and living in dilapidated shacks. There was no sign of them now, nor any sign of the small garrison of black-armored guards who served the temple.

But there was an old cook fire that had burned out, the remaining smoke drifting across the compound. Someone had been here recently, maybe was still around. Talbun and the bishop waited for Rina at the bottom of the steps leading up to the temple, a squat stone building topped with a black dome.

Just as Rina arrived, a bedraggled man emerged from the temple's arched doorway. A dusty guardsman with dented black armor. He carried an open-faced helm under one arm. "Welcome back to the Temple of Mordis, Duchess Veraiin."

Rina recognized the man from her last visit. She'd forgotten his name, had likely never known it. He looked more haggard now, worry lines deep at the corners of his eyes and mouth.

Rina took a last puff of the chuma stick and flicked away the butt.

"What happened to the village?" she asked.

He shrugged. "Peasants have a sense of things. Like forest animals fleeing before a storm."

"And your men?"

"Some deserted," admitted the guard. "Others have escorted the acolytes to other temples. Only High Priest Krell remains . . . and I to serve him."

"I want to talk to Krell," Rina said.

"He knows. I've been sent to fetch you." The guardsman's eyes drifted over the others. "Just you alone, I'm afraid, Duchess Veraiin."

Talbun moved to stand next to Rina. "I could go with you. He couldn't do anything about it," she whispered.

"It's okay," Rina whispered back. "I'll go."

"How long should we wait?" Talbun asked.

"I don't know. Do what you think's best."

She handed her horse's reins to Talbun and climbed the steps. The guardsman ushered her into the temple.

Once inside, the guardsman gestured her on. "You remember the way, yes?"

She did.

Rina proceeded on her own down a hallway of rough stone. Candles in iron sconces lit the way, a mound of wax drippings on the floor beneath each candle indicating long decades. She arrived at a stairway of black stone. The place felt ancient and cold and unfriendly. She climbed the stairs reluctantly, feet leaden.

The top of the stairs opened into a wide room with a high ceiling. The sudden space had caught her off guard last time. Now she knew she stood underneath the temple's great dome. She'd been ready for the sight, but it was still impressive. It looked and felt bigger on the inside than it did looking at it outside.

As before, the inside of the dome didn't look like a ceiling at all but more like the inky sky at midnight, stars swirling magnificently overhead. The effect was dizzying. A red planet rose from the dome's horizon and plied a lazy course across the cosmos. She felt small and wondered whether that was one of the intended effects.

"Good of you to come, Duchess Veraiin," said a dry, reedy voice. "Welcome again to the Temple of Mordis."

She recognized Krell's voice, turned to look for him.

High Priest Krell oozed from the shadows as if the darkness itself were spitting him out, and suddenly he stood before her, yellow smile grotesque against chalky skin. Krell was as withered and frail as she remembered. Barefoot. Black robe with the hood up. He seemed more wraith than man, almost as if he were made of smoke.

But Rina remembered the surprising strength in his hands when he'd grabbed her wrist and had magically drawn the tattoo on her palm, his bony fingers like iron. She shivered.

"What do I have to do to keep you and your evil eyes out of my dreams?" Rina asked.

"Not *my* evil eyes, Duchess," Krell said. "We all have our own evils to contend with, watched by powers beyond our ken. The world is full of perils seen and unseen, and I am your friend."

"You're no friend of mine."

He smiled, an old uncle tolerating a precocious child. "You cannot insult me. I am but an instrument of my master. There is a peculiar freedom in completely giving oneself over to service to a god. All I need to do is tell you what is required of you. I need not understand it. You need not even heed my words. I will still be content knowing I have done as my god has asked of me."

"You sound like a puppet."

"A faithful servant," Krell corrected.

"Tell me what to do to fulfill my part of the bargain," Rina demanded. "So I can be rid of you and your god."

Krell spread his arms. "Then let us consult the cosmos."

The stars above swirled and expanded, and the entire world seemed to tilt. The night sky surrounded her, spread out above and beneath her feet. Rina felt dizzy. She felt as if she were floating in space, but she knew her feet were planted on something solid.

It's an illusion. I'm still standing on the floor in the temple.

Or was she?

Rina was too frightened to move her feet, as if she might lose touch with the floor and float off into space, drift away, lost forever among the stars. A comet streaked by, its tail bright and white. Stars floated below her and above. Krell hovered a few feet from her, perfectly at ease in his surroundings. Only his face seemed strange, eyes suddenly glassy, mouth hanging open.

He began to chant strange, foreign words in some rhythm that seemed to pulse in time with the surrounding stars. If drifting freely in the vastness of space disturbed him, he didn't show it.

A pale light the color of the moon grew in the priest's eyes.

"I open myself to the immensity of everything, to the totality of all knowledge of what has been, what is, and what will be." Krell's echoing voice filled the room, filled the universe.

The stars spun around them in a wild blur, planets and moons coming and going. Time itself seemed caught in the maelstrom.

And in some unexplainable way, Rina understood the high priest's words. It was as if everything in existence flowed around and through them. Rina felt connected to every person, animal, river, the sky, the mountains, every idea anyone had ever thought. There was nothing to do, no way to control it or make meaning from it. Her only choice was to let herself be overwhelmed, to let the cacophony of everything wash over her.

"You will be offered two paths, Rina Veraiin," Krell's voice echoed. "One north and one south."

Forks in the road again. The old man really is a charlatan, isn't he?

And yet Rina knew Krell was offering her raw truth. Not simple truth or plain, but a truth straight from where all truths were born. Krell had the sight. His words would need interpretation, but an instinct told Rina they were *not* lies.

"The northern path fills the empty palm," Krell said. "The southern path pays a debt."

Rina blinked, and just like that she stood on a solid stone floor again, the stars back in their proper place overhead. She felt hollow, relieved, and let down. She knew with a surprising disappointment she would never be able to describe to anyone else what it felt like to connect to the entire universe. Or maybe it was one of the priest's parlor tricks, though she thought not.

Krell looked shrunken and stooped, as if using the sight took much out of him.

"Heed the words, Duchess Veraiin," Krell said. "Few people in the world have been the subject of the sight even once, and yet *twice* has the universe delivered a message to you through me."

"I don't understand," Rina said.

"That is not my concern." Krell waved a hand as if dismissing her. "I have passed along the message. The dice are cast. I must trust my efforts have pleased Mordis."

"You're not going to tell me what it means?"

"I was not told what it means."

"Then how the fuck am I supposed to know what to do?" Rina snapped. "I came all the way back to this wretched temple so you could tell me how to clear my debt. The southern path pays a debt. Is that it? Do I go south when given the choice?"

Krell laughed, the sound of fingernails on stone. "You will pay the debt whichever way you choose, Duchess. I told you. Just coming here has set it into motion. There remains only the *manner* in which events unfold."

"I take it one way is preferable to another."

"Without a doubt," Krell said. "But preferable for whom? For you? For my master? Or for some other god?"

"What other god are you talking about?"

"Any of them," Krell said. "Do not pretend ignorance. One epoch fades as another one is born. The gods vie for dominance, and pawns such as we are caught in the middle. We catch only the vaguest glimpses of their machinations."

"You know more than you're telling me," Rina said.

"I have no reason to withhold anything."

Rina's hand fell to the hilt of her rapier. "Maybe a foot of steel through that black lump you call a heart will loosen your tongue."

Krell *tsked*. "How tiresome. You are showing your youth, Duchess. Try showing me how smart you can be."

Rina nibbled her bottom lip, thinking.

"Okay, you don't *know* anything," Rina said. "But you can guess."

Krell shrugged. "Whatever my poor guesses are worth."

"What's in the south?"

"You can read a map as well as I can, Duchess."

She resisted the urge to draw her sword and stab him.

"You said the northern path fills an empty palm," Rina said. "That sounds like if I go north I'll get money or something."

"Perhaps," Krell said. "But consider the Hand of Death." He gestured to her gloved hand.

She looked down at her hand, didn't need to remove the glove to perfectly picture the skeletal tattoo on her palm. Her other palm was blank.

Empty?

"A tattoo," Rina said.

"For an ink mage, bare skin is a blank canvas, unused," Krell said. "Empty."

Rina considered. Talbun had told her there might be a tattoo in the Great Library of Tul-Agnon to the north. Something that might have to do with the gods. Her interpretations of Weylan's journal had been as frustratingly vague as Krell's prophecies.

The sons of bitches who run the universe could save a lot of time by just being clear about what they want.

"If there's a tattoo in the north, then where is it? What does it do?" Rina asked. "Why is it important?"

Krell shook his head. "I have told you all I can. Go now, Rina Veraiin. Go and make your choices."

CHAPTER THIRTY-SIX

Empress Mee Hra'Lito sat cross-legged on the elevated platform in the grand throne room. The advisor kneeling before her looked pained to delivery his litany of bad news, but such was his lot.

"The outlying provinces continue to report rumblings of insurrection," reported the advisor.

The empress pinned him with a cold look. "Define *rumblings*."

"The food shortages have aggravated an already volatile situation," the advisor said. "But at the moment, local militias still maintain order."

Local militias were not as able as imperial troops. Under other circumstances, Mee would have sent a company of imperial troops to squash any uprising, but every last warrior was currently on one of ten thousand ships crossing the sea to Helva.

"When you say 'at the moment,'" Mee said, "you mean that the situation is . . . fluid."

"I regret to say that indeed the situation can change at any time," the advisor said.

"And the militia will no longer be able to control the uprising?"

The advisor looked embarrassed. "The militia will likely *join* their uprising, highness. The people are starving."

"And what of the capital?"

"Calm. But unrest is coming."

"And the Imperial Palace?"

"Secure, highness. The gates of the outer walls and also those of the inner keep have been sealed. Your personal guard is a thousand strong and will defend the palace to the death."

"How long do we have?"

"There is no way to accurately—"

"How long?"

Again, the advisor looked pained. "If we're lucky, four or five months. The people only just now begin to suspect the situation. Empires do not collapse overnight. If our forces are victorious in Helva, that news alone might be enough to avert catastrophe."

Mee raised an eyebrow. "And if we're not lucky?"

"A matter of days," the advisor said. "The least spark could spawn an inferno, a rumor into a riot."

"What happened to us?" Mee hadn't meant it as an actual question. She teetered on the edge of despair, and the words had just slipped out.

"We tried to hang on to the conquered lands too long, expended too many resources," the advisor said. "And then we were too slow to turn our might toward Helva. The half measures in Klaar were because we were afraid to commit more resources. We should have struck sooner, and with more confidence."

Mee gathered her wits, lifted her chin. Aloof. Regal. "General Thorn will triumph. Perran will return to glory."

The advisor bowed low, forehead touching the floor. "As you say, highness."

"Have we had further word from the general?"

"Not since his routine contact two days ago," the advisor said. "But one of your court magicians monitors the scrying crystal at all times should he attempt to contact us."

"Then there is nothing for us to do but wait," Mee said. "And to pray."

◆　◆　◆

General Thorn stood on the deck of the fleet's flagship, watching the gray sea toss the thousands of ships all around him. The black clouds overhead were thankfully receding. Two nights ago an unexpected violent storm had come up from the south, battering the fleet. Ship-to-ship communication—a complicated system of colored flags—confirmed they'd lost nearly eighty ships in the typhoon. Considering the fierceness of the storm, it could have been much worse.

In all of Perran's long, glorious history, no military scheme of this magnitude had ever been attempted. Ten thousand ships. As a young officer during the colonial campaigns, he would never have dreamed of such a thing.

The invasion of Helva was necessary to the survival of the Perranese Empire. But the truth was, Thorn would have lobbied for it anyway. The greatest war in human history, and Thorn would forever be known as the one who'd won it. There would be songs and stories, of course. Flattering statues of him. He was well aware of his own vanity and didn't care. He would practice modesty if he failed.

Actually, he would kill himself if he failed. Honor would demand it.

But he didn't plan to fail.

Success depended on a thousand little things going right, and at the moment more than anything he wished for some intelligence, and being on a ship at sea made gathering up-to-date intelligence problematic.

Still, there were ways.

A junior officer approached Thorn and saluted.

"The magician has made contact with the scout ships?" Thorn asked. They'd sent out scout ships a few days before the main fleet had departed Perran. Hopefully Thorn wouldn't be invading blind.

"As you ordered, sir," the officer said. "Our ship has spotted a cargo ship coming out of Kern. They report they should be able to close on it today and get prisoners for interrogation."

"Excellent," Thorn said

It would be impossible to keep ten thousand ships secret forever, but the longer the better. Prisoners from the ship out of Kern might tell him how far up the coast information had traveled, if at all. Catching the city of Sherrik by complete surprise would of course be preferable, but in the long run it didn't matter. There were not even half the number of fighting men in the southern part of Helva to oppose Thorn's landing. His spies had been confident about that. Pemrod would send troops, of course, but too few and too late.

"When the scout ship has prisoners, inform me immediately," Thorn said.

◆ ◆ ◆

The captain had told them to keep the weapons out of sight. Barazz wanted them to look helpless, a merchant ship fleeing for its life. Alem kept glancing into the coiled stack of rope where he'd hidden his crossbow and quiver of arrows. The others had done likewise, all of Barazz's crew going about the business of sailing the *Witch of Kern* but none ever getting too far from a hidden cutlass.

Alem had been standing at the railing all day, watching the Perranese ship draw slowly but relentlessly closer. When it had gotten close enough to see details, Barazz had confirmed everyone's fears. It was a Perranese vessel. The accordion sails and sleek, narrow design left no doubt. A smaller ship than the *Witch of Kern*, but faster for it. The men on the deck of the Perranese vessel looked like they were bunching along the rail, weapons and rope and grappling hooks ready for the ensuing clash.

"Don't let them cross," Barazz said, suddenly behind him. "They'll get close and throw across the grappling hooks. If the hooks catch, they'll pull the ships together and send everyone they have across. Pick them off with the crossbow if you can. I have another bowman in the crow's nest."

Alem swallowed hard. He'd told Barazz he'd handled a crossbow before, and somehow the captain had the idea he was some sort of expert marksman. Alem wanted to tell him he was no warrior. He'd been practicing with the crossbow but was far from an expert. He would do his best but—

"Don't let them cross," Barazz ordered.

"I won't," Alem said.

The Perranese ship was almost even with them now. Alem could see the grim faces of the warriors on the other deck. They didn't seem afraid or eager or anything at all, really. That they would board the *Witch of Kern* and assault her crew was simply a matter of their existence.

Alem felt an urgent need to pee.

Maurizan appeared at his side, her brace of long daggers on her belt hidden by a long cloak. The gypsies had a signature fighting style, a dagger in each hand. They danced and dodged around their opponents, knives twirling in some lethal ballet.

"Feeling better?" Alem asked.

Her eyes flicked to his then back to the other ship. "My churning gut has been replaced by battle nerves. Probably some kind of survival instinct."

Survival. The word jarred Alem. His first sea battle, and he would either live or die.

"I'm sorry," Alem said.

Maurizan looked at him again, more piercing this time. "What do you mean?"

"I don't know what I could have done differently," Alem said. "But I'm sorry about the way it ended between us. Sorry I hurt you."

She looked back out to sea. After a moment, she said, "No. I was foolish. You always belonged to another. I made myself think I could change that."

"If it helps at all, I know what that feels like now," Alem said.

"It doesn't help."

Maurizan tried to smile and failed, and somehow that hurt Alem more than if she'd scowled at him.

A swell suddenly pitched the two ships closer to one another. Alem saw men readying ropes and lifting weapons. The *Witch of Kern* tried to veer off, but it was too late. Arrows flew from the other ship and clattered on the deck and among the rigging behind Alem.

Nobody had said the words *go* or *charge* or anything. They were just suddenly fighting.

He grabbed his crossbow, aimed at one of the men holding a coil of rope and twirling a grappling hook over his head. The deck dipped as Alem shot, and the bolt sped over his target's head, hitting a different man behind him in the thigh.

Damn it. Alem scrambled to crank the crossbow and reload.

The warrior with the rope let the grappling hook fly. It clanged short against the gunwale and fell into the water. The warrior rushed to reel it back in.

Alem set a new bolt into the firing slot.

The other ship was ridiculously close now, and a dozen Perranese warriors swung out of the rigging on ropes over Alem's head to land on the deck behind him. The sailors behind him roared a battle cry, and the racket of steel on steel filled the air as hand-to-hand fighting erupted. A grappling hook clanged home to Alem's left, caught on the railing, the rope pulling tight.

Maurizan rushed to the railing, one of her long daggers in her hand. The iron stem of the grappling hook was long enough that it forced her to lean out dangerously over the water to reach where the rope was connected. She sawed on it with the dagger.

Across the narrow gap between ships, Alem saw one of the warriors raise a bow and aim it at Maurizan.

Alem lifted his crossbow. He remembered the bobbing motion of the ship, took aim, and held his breath. He timed it for the upswell and fired.

The bolt caught the warrior in the shoulder, spinning him back into the men behind him. Other warriors surged forward to take his place, brandishing weapons and ropes. More grappling hooks flew across the gap.

Maurizan finished cutting away the first grappling line and ran to another. Alem cranked the crossbow.

Another half dozen Perranese warriors swung across on ropes. Others were already attempting to haul in the lines connecting the ships, pulling them closer.

Alem aimed at one of the warriors with rope in his hands, and shot. The bolt pierced the man's breastplate in the dead center. He dropped the rope, screaming, and fell back.

"Alem, look out!"

Tosh's voice? Alem turned to look and—

Bodies smashed into him, knocking him to the deck. Legs all around him, the barefoot sailors and the booted, armored Perranese warriors. Steel clashed above. Below, a knee hit him in the side of the head. Somebody tripped and fell over him. A stab and a scream; others moved in to join the fray. Somebody stepped on his hand.

Get out of here, thicko, before you get trampled.

Alem spotted an opening in the legs and crawled on his belly toward it.

A scream and a sailor hit the deck hard next to him, his eyes rolled back.

Alem pried the cutlass from the dead man's hand. He had no idea how to use it, but standing around slack jawed wasn't an option. He swung at the nearest pair of armored Perranese legs. The blade bit deep in the leather part of the armor behind the warrior's knee. He screamed and toppled, crashing into the deck. A sailor on top of him finished the job, jabbing a dagger into the warrior's throat.

Alem scrambled to his feet, cutlass raised to ward off whatever came next.

A Perranese warrior lunged at him. Alem was barely able to bring the cutlass around to block. The warrior pressed his attack, and Alem backed away quickly, swinging the cutlass back and forth, trying to fend off the blows. He was clearly outmatched and wasn't going to last long. The warrior was already batting aside his defenses with little effort.

One of the twins crashed in from the side, bringing her sword down in a two-handed strike. Kalli—the one with the long scar on her face—hacked at the Perranese warrior, penetrating armor, blood gushing. He screamed in pain and tried to bring his sword around to parry, but she was already laying into him with another savage chop. The blow caught him on the shoulder near his neck, blood spraying, and he went down, eyes bulging.

"Thank you," Alem said, but Kalli was already moving on, throwing herself back into the thick of the battle.

Back at the railing, Maurizan sawed frantically at a grappling line with her dagger. Alem was alarmed to see three other hooks caught on the railing within twenty feet of her. The warriors across the gap hauled on the lines, drawing the *Witch of Kern* closer. Soon they'd be able to leap across easily. Sailors ran to the other lines, tried to cast them off.

A volley of arrows flew from the Perranese ship. One missed Maurizan by an inch.

The others didn't miss.

The arrows fell among the sailors attempting to cast off the grappling-hook lines. They twitched and died, falling to the deck, still uselessly clutching the arrows protruding from chests or necks or bellies.

Alem rushed to one of the lines, hacked at it with the cutlass. It wouldn't be fast enough, he realized. They were tossing across lines faster than he could cut them. They'd soon pull the ships together, and the rest of the Perranese would storm across and overwhelm them.

The line Alem was cutting suddenly went slack and fell into the water, but not from his end. He looked up, saw the Perranese hurriedly cutting the lines on their side. A ragged cheer went up from the sailors behind Alem. He turned to see them putting down the last of the Perranese warriors. Bodies from both sides littered the deck.

Barazz appeared at the railing next to Alem. He was covered in blood, one red hand still clutching a cutlass. He pointed out to sea past the prow. "There."

The three ships were surprisingly close, triangular sails white and bright against the blue sky, sleek hulls slicing the waves as they headed directly for the *Witch of Kern*.

"Who are they?" Alem asked.

"They fly the flag of Sherrik," Barazz said. "The duke's flag. Luck is on our side. A few more minutes and we would have been dead."

Maurizan and Alem exchanged nervous, relieved smiles.

"Maybe they will escort us in," Barazz said. "I'd sure feel safer if they did."

Alem looked back at the carnage on the deck. The fight had taken its toll on the crew. A number of sailors lay dead. Alem spotted Tosh, who bled down one arm, but the wound didn't seem critical.

He sighed with relief but then saw Kalli kneeling next to her twin sister. Nell lay on her back, eyes open and glassy. Those eyes would never see anything again.

CHAPTER THIRTY-SEVEN

Rina and the rest of them hadn't expected to catch up with Count Becham's party so soon.

They also hadn't expected to find the army camped across the road in front of them.

They'd crested a small hill and had reined in their horses upon seeing the army. At least a thousand men, horses and supply wagons.

"Royal banners," Hark said. "Troops from Merridan."

"Why here?" Rina asked.

"Maybe they heard you were coming," Brasley said.

Rina frowned at him.

"A joke," Brasley said. "Suddenly everyone hates jokes now?"

"Riders," Talbun said. "Heading this way."

Four men in full armor galloped toward them. One carried a royal military banner. The halted in front of Rina, and the one wearing an officer's ribbon lifted a hand in greeting. "Duchess Veraiin?'

"I'm Duchess Veraiin," Rina said.

"Well met, your grace. We've been expecting you."

"See?" Brasley said from the side of his mouth.

"Shut up," Rina whispered back. To the officer she asked, "Expecting me how?"

"Count Becham preceded you," the officer said. "As you see, we're bivouacked below. Tents have been prepared, and General Inshaw invites you to join him for a feast tonight."

"A feast?" Rina raised an eyebrow. "The general's army travels well."

"The general is a champion of civilization, even in the wilds," the officer said.

"Tell the general we will be happy to join him," Rina said.

The officer saluted again, and then he and his men rode back down the hill.

"Where's this army going, I wonder," Hark said.

"We'll ask General Inshaw. Come on." She spurred her horse down the hill toward the camp.

◆ ◆ ◆

They sat at a long table, laughter and conversation filling the grand tent. The encampment had more of a holiday feel than of an army off to war. As honored guests, Rina sat to the general's right at the head of the table, Count Becham to the left. Bishop Hark, Sir Gant, Brasley, and Talbun occupied the next seats down the line, followed by various junior officers.

"Five thousand men to Sherrik, you say?" Hark held out his cup, and a servant behind him leaned in to refill it with wine.

"Yes, by barge. But that will only take them so far. They'll need to strike out across land before hitting the white water."

General Inshaw had probably been a powerful figure at one point in his life, but now, in his early sixties, he'd gone bald and fat, and he seemed to think a constant flow of red wine instrumental to conducting any good military campaign. His defining feature was an enormous white moustache that curled at the ends like boar tusks. He'd been all too delighted to host a duchess, a count, and a bishop for a feast far too elaborate for an army on the march. The man seemed to think he'd gone far too long without the jolly good fun of a good old-fashioned war, and it was about time another had come along.

"Will that force be large enough to hold the city?" Rina asked.

Since arriving at Inshaw's camp, Rina and her party had been inundated with news of the incoming Perranese fleet. Reports from various spies conflicted. Some said the Perranese were sending a small expeditionary force. Others warned against an all-out invasion, and a few said there was no fleet at all and the whole thing was a complete hoax.

"More than sufficient, I should think," Inshaw said. "Sherrik's walls are high and its gates thick. With our men reinforcing the duke's, I imagine they can withstand a siege indefinitely."

"Is it to be a siege, then?" Brasley asked.

"That's what I would do if I thought it would be a short one," the general said. "Capturing Sherrik gives them a deep-water port and a strong foothold on Helvan soil. With Sherrik in their hands, they can resupply in relative safety. The trick is speed. The longer a siege lasts, the less likely the Perranese are to succeed. It's why I successfully lobbied Pemrod to send as many troops as possible. The Perranese might have overwhelmed the walls in a few days, but an extra five thousand fighting men will put a stop to that. Whether our men get overland to Sherrik in time is the only question."

Rina felt her eyes glaze over. These were important details, she supposed, but this talk was *dull*. She mentally thanked Brasley for engaging the general in this line of conversation so she didn't have to.

"Forgive me, General," Brasley went on. "But why shouldn't the Perranese land anywhere up or down the coast and just start marching inland? Why throw themselves at a fortified city first?"

Inshaw smiled tolerantly. "I take it you're not a military man, Baron Hammish."

"No, sir. I'm a drinking man." Brasley gestured to his cup, and a servant scrambled to fill it.

The general laughed. "A man after my own heart. Allow me to explain. Landing a large army at some desolate patch of beach does have the advantage of no opposition. But that would leave the Perranese forces exposed, with no stronghold to fall back to. They tried something similar in Klaar but on a much smaller scale. A terrible scheme, in my opinion. Imagine launching an invasion from a frozen, isolated wilderness like Klaar." He mustered an apologetic smile for Rina. "No offense, your grace."

Rina returned an equally perfunctory smile. "None taken."

The general had already turned back to Brasley. "Failing to take Sherrik not only means no stronghold for the Perranese; the duke can also harass him from the south. Then ships from Kern can sweep down from the north and pinch the bastard savages in the middle." Inshaw slurped wine and shook his head. "No, the Perranese will attempt to take Sherrik, then dig in and fortify. I shudder to think the cost of blood to throw them out if they do that. Fortunately, we have no plans to let that happen."

"It's my understanding you're *not* on your way south to reinforce Sherrik," Count Becham said. "You're going to Kern instead. Why?"

"Ships," Inshaw said. "I've been charged by Pemrod to commandeer as many ships as possible. Another brilliant idea of mine. If the siege hasn't started yet, we can resupply and reinforce Sherrik much faster by sea. If the Perranese beat us there, then we can still engage their blockade more efficiently from Kern."

"You seem eager for it," Rina said.

Inshaw waved for the servant to refill his cup again. "No true soldier is *eager* for war, your grace." This was something the general seemed obligated to say but clearly didn't mean. "But a man trains himself, trains his men, studies all the historical strategies at the war college. I'm glad that I've honed these skills all of my life on the chance they might be needed . . . which they are now." He drank deeply, smacked his lips. "My only goal is to perform my best for my king and his people."

"Admirable sentiments," Rina said.

She glanced down the table. Gant caught her eye. He didn't seem any more interested in what the blowhard general was saying than she was. Rina understood his look and nodded curtly. *Yes, I'll meet you later.*

Inshaw stood abruptly, tilting on unsteady legs and thrusting his cup into the air. "To Helva and the king!"

Everyone else at the table lunged to their feet, likewise lifting their cups. "To Helva and the king!"

◆ ◆ ◆

Rina returned to her tent, startled when she discovered Talbun waiting within.

"I hope you don't mind," Talbun said. "But we need to decide some things."

"Oh? What's to decide?" Rina's eyes darted around the interior of the tent as if expecting an ambush. An absurd thought, but she hadn't been expecting the wizard and was caught off guard. A narrow cot, a camp stove, a small table, and a chair. Nothing untoward. Talbun sat in the chair, refilling a cup in one hand from a pitcher of wine in the other.

"Don't be obtuse," Talbun said. "We know each other now. I'm not going to do anything to you. And I know you wandered off to speak to Ferris Gant."

Rina cleared her throat and felt silly. "Are we friends, then? Do we share our secrets?"

"I haven't had a friend in a century." Talbun considered for a moment as if the idea were something just now being presented to her. "But for lack of a better term, yes. I hope we are."

"Okay," Rina said. "I suppose I need as many as I can get."

"Then sit," Talbun said. "And talk."

Rina spotted her saddlebags at the floor of the cot. She opened them and fished around for a chuma stick, found one and lit it from a lantern hanging from a tent pole. She sat on the cot, crossed her legs, and puffed.

"Gant says Pemrod wants me to come back to the capital with him," Rina said.

"How is he able to communicate with Merridan?" Talbun asked.

Rina shrugged. "He says he has a way."

"Probably scrying crystals," Talbun mused. "Nothing terribly complicated if you have the gold to pay for it."

"I doubt money is a problem for the king's grandnephew," Rina said.

"Are you going?"

"To Merridan? No," Rina said. "Or if I am, not because Gant wants me to. Certainly not to please Pemrod, the old bastard. He wants to start the whole matrimonial process. I don't think he believes in long engagements. Probably he's just impatient. He's used to getting his way."

"North fills an empty palm," Talbun said.

Upon leaving the temple, Rina had related to Talbun and the others what High Priest Krell had said to her. She'd hoped for insight, but her friends' guesses weren't any better than her own. Applied in some ways, Krell's words seemed plain. Considered other ways, cryptic.

"I don't see how marrying Gant fills an empty palm," Rina said.

"Well, it's all supposed to be figurative, isn't it?" Talbun said. "Filling an open palm could just mean giving something to somebody. If you *give* your hand in marriage . . . It's a stretch, isn't it?"

"Why don't gods just come out and say what they mean?" Rina frowned around the chuma stick in the corner of her mouth and puffed angrily.

"An old and long-dead philosopher friend of mine explained prophecies and other such divine edicts like so," Talbun said. "It's not so much what the gods tell you as it is how you react to it. They dazzle you with some enigmatic words and bewilder you and see what you do. We're all just human dice the gods throw to see how we tumble, to see if we come up sixes or ones."

"So I'm a die that's been tossed?"

"That's the theory," Talbun said. "And Mordis watches to see how you'll land."

"South pays a debt," Rina said. "I suppose it's too simple to think that I can go south and do something—whatever it is—and that will fulfill my obligation."

"Or maybe the trick is that it *is* so simple."

Rina chewed the chuma stick, puffed. "For an all-powerful wizard, you're not so much help."

Talbun grinned. "I did bring you some wine, but I drank it all."

"It's the thought that counts."

South pays a debt. Rina blew a long gray stream of chuma smoke into the air and thought about that. If Alem had gone with Tosh, then he'd be somewhere in the south. She wished Alem were here. She felt something hollow and gnawing in her chest whenever she thought of him. It seemed unlikely the gods were interested in Rina's love life. Alem might be somewhere in the south, but that was a coincidence, not an answer. Krell guessed the path north had something to do with another tattoo, but Krell so much as admitted he didn't actually *know* anything. And if the tattoo were anything like the one on her other palm, then she didn't want anything to do with it.

She didn't want to be thrown like dice. She didn't want any of this.

"Did you really drink all the wine?" Rina asked.

"I was only fooling." Talbun filled a cup and handed it to her. "Here."

Rina tilted her head back, finishing the wine in three big gulps. It burned her throat. She wished it would burn everything away, her desperate need to see Alem again, all these stupid tattoos, and red eyes lurking in the shadows of her dreams.

CHAPTER
THIRTY-EIGHT

Tchi sat on his horse just within the tree line on a low rise west of the road. He had a clear view of the army encampment below. His smaller force hid in the woods behind him. The spy sat on another horse next to him. The commander had three choices and didn't like any of them.

According to the spy, Duchess Veraiin had left Klaar with a small party and had taken refuge in the army camp. The first choice was simply to watch and wait, although Tchi doubted he could hide five hundred men for long.

Which led him to the second choice. The moon would set soon, and under the cover of darkness, he could take his force in a wide circle around the camp, putting a bit of distance between them. He'd task the spy and his men with keeping tabs on Veraiin's movements. It was the safer course, but the risk was that his men would be too far away to take action should the duchess become vulnerable.

The muted clank of armor in the darkness caught Tchi's attention. His hand fell to the hilt of his sword. "Password."

"Bone breaker," came a guttural voice from the darkness.

A second later a burly sergeant stepped into the moonlight with two men behind him. His one good eye gleamed a hard challenge to any who met his gaze. His other was covered by a black eye patch. His face looked carved from some gray stone. Instead of the long, curved sword usually favored by the Perranese warrior, a short, heavy, double-bladed war axe hung from his belt. His name was Yano, and he'd seen two decades of action in the colonies before the Empire had been kicked out. He considered the officers—including Tchi—wet behind the ears, and his attitude constantly rubbed up against insubordination. Tchi had been tempted on a few occasions to reprimand and demote the man, but the men under him were the best, and fiercely loyal to him. Tchi needed the insolent bastard.

"Report, Sergeant."

"Their scouts are lazy and inexperienced," Yano said. "They might stumble over us eventually, but we're safe for the time being. Being attacked doesn't seem to have entered their thinking. No defenses. The usual sentries. Nothing impressive. It's almost like they're asking for it."

Which brought Tchi to the third option: attack. The object would not be to defeat the enemy. The forces in the camp outnumbered Tchi's men two to one. But a raid to capture the duchess might work. Surprise would be on their side.

But Tchi didn't like the risk. There was risk in any military engagement, of course, but the Veraiin woman was an unknown. If the stories were true, then it was unlikely she would meekly let herself be kidnapped.

Then there was the fact that nobody had actually ordered Tchi to take the woman. Left to his own devices, it was up to Tchi to decide how best to use his forces in aid of the imminent invasion fleet. The army camped below might be on its way to reinforce Sherrik, in which case harassing them might be the right thing to do.

Yano must have read the hesitation on Tchi's face.

"So, do we attack, Commander?" the sergeant asked.

Tchi frowned. "I'll let you know my decision when I make it, Sergeant."

Yano turned his head and spit. "As you say, sir."

"How many horses do we have?" Tchi knew the answer but wanted to show he was considering all the possibilities. He winced inwardly at the need to do so.

"Fifty," Yano said. "But I wouldn't take a few of those packhorses into battle. Call it forty-five."

"How would you do it?"

Yano peered down at the camp, scratching the stubble on his chin. He pointed. "They've bunched all their horses together on our side. Easier to water and feed them like that, I guess, but stupid. Provides cover for us. We send our quietest men to take out the sentries, then our men on foot can hide among the horses and wait for our riders to storm in. Tossing torches at some tents will add to the confusion. They'll waste a lot of time getting their pants on. Our riders can cover the men on foot as we pull back, and we can run off their horses too. By the time they organize a pursuit, we would be long gone. They might not even bother. It's a pretty sloppy outfit. My only wish would be to know where the woman is. Searching from tent to tent drags things out. Not the best for this sort of thing."

Tchi turned to the spy. "You're sure she's down there?"

"Saw her enter the camp with my own eyes," the spy said.

"Send for the wizards," Tchi said. "Tell them I might have work for them. Sergeant?"

"Sir?"

"Pass the word among the men. We'll go in after the moon sets."

"Yes, sir."

Sergeant Yano's salute was very nearly respectful.

CHAPTER THIRTY-NINE

Far in the eternally frozen north, high on a lonely peak in the Glacial Wastes, the Temple of Mordis drew the faithful. The ancient black pyramid had long been an important symbol for the order, a place of reverence, the mother temple of the entire cult.

A dozen of the faithful trudged up the worn steps of the Skyway of Eternity in the dark, a zigzagging line of torches.

Foot traffic to and from the holy place had picked up considerably since the Great Reconstitution. Bremmer watched them come from the steps of the temple. Climbing the lonely path had once been a tedious obligation designated to lesser priests to keep them busy and test their patience. Now everyone wanted to do it.

Understandable, really, Bremmer thought. *When your god comes back to life it's kind of a big deal. Okay, maybe "back to life" is not quite the way to put it. Back from the realm of the gods? Back in his old body?* None of it quite sounded reverent enough.

How to talk about these sudden and groundbreaking changes in the order itself was part of Bremmer's new job. As the priest who ushered in Mordis's return, he was immediately raised to abbot of the mother temple, a title invented specifically for him. That someone so young and inexperienced should be granted such an honor took him completely by surprise.

But over the following few weeks it had become clear that the cult elders were more than happy to keep the newly returned god at arm's length while they scrambled over ancient tomes and other church documents to determine just exactly what it meant to have the god they'd worshipped for centuries walking among them. Bremmer understood all too well that he was considered expendable. Anger Mordis, and he lashes out to crush those around him? No problem. It's just Bremmer.

Bremmer didn't care. He was devout. If he burned at the hands of an angry deity, then it was meant to be. In the meantime, he alone acted as the liaison between the cult and its god. It was a position of honor and power, and he didn't plan to let this opportunity go to waste.

In the meantime, the most pious of the order made the arduous journey up the Skyway of Eternity to hear the wisdom of Bremmer, delivered twice daily in the evening sermon. Well, sometimes it was a sermon. Other times more like a lecture, and on occasion, a sort of roundtable discussion.

Bremmer was still getting the hang of it.

The temple was now off limits to all but Bremmer, and Bremmer himself entered only when summoned.

Skilled priests had hauled tools and building materials up the Skyway to refurbish the outbuildings. There had even been talk in housing a permanent garrison of monks, as the order had done in days of old. The elders seemed optimistic. The Cult of Mordis was not a popular religion by Helvan standards, and many in the order saw the return of their god as fodder for a membership drive.

Fools. Don't they understand what's happening? Don't they know something big *is coming?*

Of course they did. It was simply that they didn't know how to react. The entire order was in a state of shock.

Mordis has returned!

Whatever that meant.

Bremmer was cold.

He escaped the bitter wind into the largest of the stone buildings, where novices scurried to prepare the evening meal. The hall was wide enough for two long wooden tables. There were fireplaces at either end of the room. Other novices stoked them periodically. After the meal, the tables would be shoved to the walls and the chairs turned to face Bremmer for the nightly sermon.

Bremmer paused to observe one of the priests skilled in woodwork. He was carving a figure into one of the great wooden support beams in the center of the hall. He looked up at Bremmer and smiled.

"I think it's coming along well, don't you, Abbot Bremmer?"

"You're doing a good job." Bremmer made a point of saying "good job" to anyone he could, even just a novice washing the dishes. It was ridiculously easy and seemed to mean a lot to them for some reason.

"It's my honor to carve the likeness of the martyr Glex," the priest said. "All will remember his sacrifice, which made the Great Reconstitution possible."

Yeah, he did a great job lying there and bleeding.

"Don't carve too much away from the belly," Bremmer said. "Glex was fat."

The new group of priests arrived, and they were given something warm to drink and promised food. They were assigned places to sleep. Bremmer uttered perfunctory words of welcome. Abbot Bremmer was a celebrity in the order. They were pathetically gleeful to see him, to hear his words, to know they would serve Mordis under his watchful eye. Wide-eyed fools could not get enough.

Bremmer loved every second of it.

The hall filled with all the priests at the top of the mountain. Nearly a hundred of them crowded at the long tables, spooning in weak broth and eating brown bread and turnips. The way they talked, one might think they were at a fancy feast, dining on pheasant and drinking the finest brandy. There was a peculiar kind of excitement in the air. The priests were animated, talkative, enthusiastic.

For so long they've been the dour priests in the black robes. Everyone hates them. Not now. Now it's . . . different.

The meal ended. Novices swarmed in to clear the dishes and push the tables back. Priests eagerly scooted their chairs into rows to face the fireplace on the south wall. This was the big payoff, what they'd climbed so many steps in the brutal cold to hear.

Abbot Bremmer was about to speak.

He waited in a room adjacent to the kitchen. He could hear the chairs scraping on the stone floor. Bremmer still wasn't sure what he would say to them. Generally, he played it by ear. He liked to start with a few obvious platitudes to warm up, basic stuff about how being called to serve Mordis was a lonely but important calling, that sort of thing. Something poignant always occurred to him as he went along.

An impossibly young novice approached him, timid as a rabbit. "Sir . . . uh . . . Abbot Bremmer, sir. They're ready for you."

"Have the fires burned low?" Bremmer liked it when the lighting was low and mysterious, his eyes shining from beneath the shadow of his hood. He assured himself it wasn't vanity that spurred such drama. The younger priests listened better when they were on the edge of their seats.

"We stopped adding wood to the fire halfway through dinner," the novice said.

"Very well." Bremmer stood. "Let it begin."

He went out to the main hall, and hushed whispers rolled through the assembled priests. Bremmer stood in front of the low fire and raised his hands.

"Welcome to the mother temple," Bremmer said. "The cradle of the Cult of Mordis."

The assembled priests bowed and in unison said, "Peace and rest."

Peace and rest sound much better than death, Bremmer mused. *So much in life is a matter of pleasant phrasing.*

"Long have we labored thanklessly, just as our god has worked thanklessly throughout the ages," Bremmer said. "Praise be to Mordis. Praise be to the thankless tasks. The servant who toils for need and not for praise serves twice as well."

This was all still pretty standard stuff. Nobody was keen on death. The virtues of doing a thankless—but necessary—job were a popular theme among the brethren.

"There would be no life without death," Bremmer went on. "We are part of a never-ending cycle. The sunset to the sunrise. The final winter. The cool relief of night. We are death. Men fear death, and so we are shunned. But with death there is release and an end to suffering. The mouse dies to feed the owl. The old die to make way for the new. Ideas die to make way for purer thought. We are the facilitators. We are transition."

Still pretty standard stuff. If he didn't stumble on to something new pretty soon, it was going to be a long night.

He lowered his hands.

The priests waited anxiously, leaning forward, eager for Bremmer's next words.

Bremmer turned his head slowly, eyeing the congregation. "What a lot of bullshit, huh?"

Scattered gasps. A stunned murmur ran through the crowd.

"Everything I said was true. The release, the transition, all that." Bremmer waved his hand dismissively. "Sure. Of course. But a *change* has come. Something has happened to remind us that Mordis is fundamentally different from the other gods. He has returned. That is the Great Reconstitution. A return. But have any of you considered the *manner* of his return? Have you considered what it *means*?"

More murmuring. This time curious. They weren't sure where Bremmer was going with this, but they were intrigued.

"Mordis is the gatekeeper," Bremmer said. "Every god promises his or her faithful a place in their own version of paradise, but how do you get to paradise? You have to die first, don't you? Mordis is the one who ushers each and every soul from this life to the next. Death is his province. No follower joins his god in the afterlife except when Mordis facilitates it. Many philosophers have mused that this makes Mordis a servant of the other gods. I see things . . . differently."

He waited and let the silence stretch. The only sound was the pop of the fire behind him.

"Mordis is not a servant of the other gods," Bremmer said. "Mordis is a *check* on the other gods."

Excited talk as the priests turned to one another. Bremmer's notion was not original. Fringe scholars in the order had suggested such notions centuries ago, and Bremmer had stumbled upon the readings in the order's archives. He'd found it only a peculiar curiosity at the time, but now, as he spoke, he felt a tingle down his spine. He was on to something. Bremmer felt he was glimpsing some tiny part of a greater truth that was slowly revealing itself.

He wasn't just delivering a nightly sermon. He was *discovering* something.

"Remember, the mother temple is not just a temple," Bremmer went on. "It's a tomb. For centuries Mordis's remains were kept here. Bones and dust. The remains of a *person*. Let me say that again. We don't know who he was. That's lost to time. Perhaps he was a powerful sorcerer, maybe a king, maybe a wise man. Whatever else he was, he was a person *just like you and me*."

The priests buzzed excitedly. They were approaching some emotional peak.

"Unlike any other god, Mordis started as a person, a human." Bremmer let his voice rise. "In each of us, in me and in you, there is a spark of that, something small, a seed, the same thing inside of us that was in that human who became a *god!*"

The priests were almost on their feet now. Bremmer's words had awakened something in them, not just piety, not just fate, but some dormant pride they hadn't even known was there.

"This is the time of Mordis!" Bremmer shouted. "And that means it's *our* time too. In each of us is the potential, maybe distant and remote, but the very real potential to be more than we are." He lifted his hands, voice filling the hall like thunder. "To walk as equals among the gods!"

The priests sprang to their feet. The cheering was so loud and sustained that it shook the dust from the rafters.

EPISODE SEVEN

CHAPTER
FORTY

Giffen's eyes flickered open.

It didn't help. He closed and opened his eyes again.

Darkness.

He remembered the tavern and the gorgeous red-haired woman. The fight. Something smashing into the side of his head. He ached all over, bruises and scrapes covering him head to foot.

And he was cold.

He felt himself up and down, discovered he wore only a loincloth. He felt around some more. Dirty stone floor. A pile of straw behind him.

Ah, yes, the dungeons. Well, that's just typical.

He explored his cell. Small. Stone walls on three sides, and a heavy wooden door on the fourth. A bucket for his waste. There was a small window in the door. Giffen put his face to it but saw and heard nothing in the hall beyond, where it was equally dark.

Giffen returned to the pile of straw, curled up, and waited.

Most of his best operatives had been in the tavern. There were others who served him, scattered about the city, but none with the wherewithal to break him out of the dungeons, even if they knew he was here.

He needed some kind of plan. Giffen was a great believer in his own cunning, but nothing sprang to mind.

A couple of hours passed, or maybe it was only thirty minutes. He hadn't realized how difficult it was to mark time in total darkness.

The distant turn of a lock, the clank of a chain.

Giffen stood, cocked one ear to listen.

Boot heels on the stone floor echoed, a glimmer of orange light in the little window. It grew brighter until it was obvious there were people standing right on the other side. The jingle of keys and the tumble of the lock. The door creaked open slowly on rusty hinges. Torchlight and jagged shadows flooded the cell.

Two armored guards appeared. One carried the torch. Both carried swords.

"Move back," one of the guards told Giffen.

"I demand to see—"

"Get the fuck back," the guard said.

Giffen stepped back until his back touched the wall opposite the door.

The guards moved from the doorway and a woman appeared, took one step into the cell, stood primly with hands folded in front of her.

Giffen didn't recognize her. "Who are you?"

"I'm the woman who has your old job."

Giffen sneered. "The whore peddler."

Stasha Benadicta's smile was tight and controlled. "Just so."

"Where is the duke's brat?" Giffen asked. "Didn't she want to come herself to gloat?"

"She's away," Stasha said. "She doesn't even know you're here."

Giffen waved her away with the back of his hand. "Then piss off, slattern. I'm sure your better has plans for me upon her return."

"The duchess might be away for a while," Stasha said. "Whatever happens to you is up to me."

That gave Giffen pause. "Oh?" He had an animal instinct for self-preservation, and something told him this wasn't good news.

"Tell me what it was like," Stasha said. "When you slipped the knife into the duke. Did you feel pleasure? Were you proud of yourself?"

Giffen shrank into the corner of the cell. This was bad. He fell back on defiance. "I don't answer to you."

"Don't you? You're going to tell me the names of the rest of the traitors in the city. Then we can be rid of you once and for all."

Giffen's mind raced. "I'm more useful to you alive than dead. Your murdering whore and her men killed all of my minions. There are none left. But I know the plans of the Perranese. I can tell you what they'll do next. Harming me would be foolish."

"You will tell us how many traitors remain in Klaar," Stasha said. "Their names and where they can be found. Lubin?"

She stepped aside, and a gigantic bruiser entered the room.

"Wait!" An edge of panic in Giffen's voice. "Don't do anything rash."

"Lubin, beat this man," Stasha said. "Don't stop until he's told you the name of every traitor he's employed. Do you understand?"

A lopsided grin spread across the bruiser's face. "Yes, ma'am."

"But don't you see that would be a waste of time?" Giffen said, suddenly desperate. "I've told you there aren't any more traitors. This lummox would be beating me for nothing."

The smile on Stasha's face was warm and genuine this time. "That's fine too."

CHAPTER FORTY-ONE

The screams.

Bishop Hark's eyes popped open. The feast had gone later into the night than he would have liked. He'd always gone to bed early, risen with the sun. Dumo frowned upon the man who frittered the day away, favored he who made hay while the sun shined.

More screams. The clash of steel. The animal scream of horses.

Yes, something was definitely amiss.

He sat up in his cot, blinked, looking around the tent. He'd gone to sleep in his breeches and undershirt. That would have to do. No time to don armor, and only Dumo knew where his lazy squire had gone to. He pulled on his boots and grabbed his mace.

Hark stepped out of his tent and into chaos.

A half dozen tents on his row burned, flame and smoke swirling into the night. Half-dressed soldiers ran in random directions, shouting to one another, each more bewildered than the next. A junior officer appeared, trying to bring some kind of order to the madness, but with little success.

Blast it! I wish I had my horse.

It had been years since he'd been in a major battle, but Hark preferred to fight from horseback. He wished he hadn't let his idiot squire take his mount away to be fed and watered with the other horses halfway across camp.

More screams and shouts two rows over in the tent village told Hark he was only on the edge of the conflict.

The high-pitched whinny and snort of a charging steed drew his attention.

A warrior rode toward him, sword raised high to deliver a death-blow. Hark recognized the style of his opponent's armor immediately, the overlapping plates of metal on his arms and legs, the flared helmet. Perranese. Hark had lived through the occupation of Klaar, and there was no mistaking the trappings of the enemy.

The mounted warrior was about to ride him down when the bishop moved—not to one side, but sideways in front of the charging horse. He grabbed the reins, and they almost jerked out of Hark's hand as the horse thundered past, but Hark hung on with a white-knuckled grip.

The horse's head wrenched to one side, tossing the rider from his saddle. He clattered along the ground, dirt kicking up, weapon flying away. Dazed, the Perranese warrior lurched to his hands and knees, trying to orient himself.

Hark didn't give him the chance. He moved in fast, swinging the mace down hard with both hands, crushing the man's helmet and skull. He went down, legs twitching, and Hark finished him with a second blow.

The bishop mounted the man's horse and spurred it toward the heart of the battle.

Hark saw that the fiercest fighting focused on the tents two rows over, where the ladies were sleeping. A coincidence? Or a deliberate attack on the duchess? It didn't matter. She was in danger. He raised his mace and rode faster.

A line of foot soldiers in Perranese armor stormed across his path. The horsemen must have been clearing the way for them. Hark wondered how many. Was the entire camp overrun?

He swung the mace just as one of the warriors turned to him, lifting his sword. The bishop caught him square in the face, nose flattening, teeth shattering, blood splashing to both sides.

On the backswing, Hark smashed another one on the collarbone, the crunch of armor and snap of bone clearly audible above the din of the battle.

Most of the Perranese troops swarmed past him, but a few stopped to engage, trying to hack up at him with their curved swords. He batted their blades away with the mace, maneuvered the horse away, but took a shallow slice down his thigh. He winced, immediately lamenting he hadn't paused to put on his armor.

Hark swung wildly. Everywhere the mace rose and fell, skulls caved in and bones broke. He smashed open a hole in the ring of soldiers and was about to urge the horse through.

An intense blue light exploded with a crackling roar two rows over among the tents, blinding all who saw it.

The light seared Hark's eyes, and the world disappeared in a flash of white.

◆ ◆ ◆

The smell of fire brought Talbun immediately awake.

She threw the covers back and bolted from her cot, nude, and grabbed a thin robe, cinching it at the waist. Stepping into velvet slippers was faster than lacing up her boots.

Talbun swept the tent flap aside and stepped out into a battle.

A wave of Perranese warriors crashed into a line of royal troops. Swords clashed against armor. Men screamed. An entire row of tents across the row from her was completely engulfed in flame.

Most of the king's men went down immediately, a few others striking back at the Perranese before being overwhelmed. The few remaining turned and fled. There seemed to be no leadership among General Inshaw's men at all, no officers to rally them. They ran, dozens of howling Perranese warriors on their heels.

In the blink of an eye, a score of the invaders pressed close to her. Their swords sheathed, they ringed her in, hands up to make a grab for her in case she tried to dart past.

No, thank you. If it's all the same to you gentlemen, I don't feel like being taken prisoner this evening. Especially if it had been a while since they'd had a woman.

Rapid-fire syllables flew from her mouth, and her right fist became a ball of orange flame. She lunged at the closest warrior, punched him in the face, his flesh sizzling as he fell back screaming.

They were already coming at her from the other side. She swung her fist back, the flames flaring. The Perranese warriors fell over one another to get out of the way. Another who made to leap at her from the other direction hesitated when Talbun brandished the flame fist again.

They had her surrounded, pausing, not quite willing to risk the fire.

Another warrior rode up, abruptly reining in his horse. He was a tough-looking customer with a patch over one eye, the sort of man who might eat a handful of rocks for lunch. He pointed a lethal-looking war axe at his men and bellowed his displeasure in their native tongue. He didn't bother to see if they obeyed before turning the horse and galloping away toward some other part of the battle.

Fairly easy to guess what the man's orders had been—the circle of warriors immediately rushed her. She smashed a warrior in the face with her fire fist, and he spun away screaming and clawing at his eyes.

Others grabbed for her.

They still haven't drawn weapons. They want me alive.

They grabbed her from all sides, awkwardly trying to hold on to her while simultaneously dodging the fire fist. She clouted one on the ear, burning away his hair and half of his flesh on that side of his head.

There were hands all over her now. Her robe ripped open, exposing her. Hands on her legs trying to lift her. Two of them had hold of her right arm, bending it away so she couldn't use the flame fist against them.

I hope none of the king's men is nearby. If they are, I'm sorry for this.

She spat the words to another spell. A ball of blue light surrounded her. When she uttered the final word, the ball expanded with a roar, and the entire world seemed to fill with blinding light.

Talbun blinked, spots in front of her eyes. For a moment she panicked, thinking herself blind, but slowly the world came back into focus.

The bodies in a ten-foot circle around her were nothing but ash. Beyond that, the bodies were more recognizable but still charred and smoking. Talbun lifted her head, scanned the area. The ground was scorched ruin for a hundred feet in every direction. Even the tents that hadn't already burned were blasted flat.

Weylan, you had a few surprises in your spell book, didn't you, you cranky old son of a bitch?

She trudged through the ash, careful to step over and around the scorched corpses. In the distance, the sound of screams and the ring of metal on metal told her the battle raged on in some other part of the camp.

Talbun knelt next to one of the bodies that wasn't so badly damaged and took a dagger from the dead warrior's belt. She stood, dagger held at the ready, her other hand clasping her robe closed in front of her. Her eyes darted around the burning camp. She braced herself.

No more enemies came at her, at least not at the moment.

She moved in the direction of Rina's tent, walking at first and then breaking into a run.

◆　◆　◆

Brasley woke up in the narrow space between tents when he heard the racket. He'd crawled out of the tent to vomit and hadn't made it back before passing out. It had been a long night of drinking.

At first, Brasley thought all the noise came from the soldiers breaking down the camp. He had a vague memory of General Inshaw saying the army would march at dawn.

Dawn certainly does come early these days, he thought, rubbing his throbbing head.

He stumbled to his feet, and the fog in his brain cleared. He smelled smoke. Screams split the night.

Oh, shit. They aren't breaking camp. This is . . . something else.

He stumbled to the front of his tent, blinked at the spectacle before him.

The row of tents across the aisle was in flames. Against the fiery background, armored silhouettes flung themselves at one another, swords crossing, the ring of metal blades against armor rising above the screams of the dying.

Brasley recognized the overlapping shingles of armor and the flared helms of the Perranese.

What the fuck are they *doing here?*

Inshaw's men were fighting them toe-to-toe. To Brasley's untrained eye, there didn't seem to be any battle strategy. Just men slamming into one another, swinging blades, some falling and bleeding and yelling.

He knelt next to a slain soldier and pried the sword from his hand, a long blade with a plain guard, unadorned but solid. He backed into the shadows between the tents, hoping not to be spotted. If the battle passed him by, that would be just fine.

It almost worked out that way.

A few dozen of General Inshaw's cavalry crashed unexpectedly into the fray, horses rearing and smashing aside Perranese foot soldiers. The horsemen erupted from between the tents on either side of Brasley's hiding place, their pikes scattering the Perranese warriors. In seconds, the entire battle had shifted to another part of the camp.

The bodies of dying men writhed in the wide, muddy aisle between the tent rows. Brasley stepped out of his hiding place slowly, ready to turn and run if need be. The smell of blood and loosened bowels hit him hard.

A figure came toward him, and he wheeled, bringing his sword up.

"It's me," Talbun said.

Brasley almost didn't recognize her. Hair mussed and matted, torn robe held closed in front of her with a little fist. She gripped a dagger tightly. Her bare feet were covered to the ankles in grime, a mix of blood and mud and feces, the standard unsavory mix of any battlefield.

"What's happening? Have they invaded again?"

"I don't know," she said. "Have you seen Rina?"

"I haven't seen anyone. Just you."

A column of Perranese soldiers spilled from between the tents fifty yards up the aisle. They jogged across, but the last two spotted Brasley and Talbun and broke off to run toward them.

"Oh, fuck me," Brasley said raising his sword.

Brasley and Talbun stood close to each other and braced for the attack.

The first Perranese warrior thrust, and Brasley smacked the sword aside with his own. He brought the blade back just in time to parry an attack from the other one. He gave ground, completely on the defensive.

I'm not going to last long two against one. He was acutely aware of the wizard at his side. *So . . . yeah . . . some kind of awesome magic right about now wouldn't be the worst thing.*

The galloping thud of horse hooves in the mud grew suddenly loud behind him. A spilt second later the horse was right next to him, a thick arm sweeping down and smashing a mace on the helmet of the closest Perranese.

The warrior's helmet crushed almost flat, brain and blood oozing from beneath as the man toppled over, dead before he even hit the ground.

The second warrior turned and ran. A futile effort.

Bishop Hark rode him down, smashing him in the back of the head. A sickening crunch of armor and skull.

Hark turned the horse back toward Brasley and dismounted in front of him and the wizard. "Are you okay?" He let the horse wander off. There were no more foes in sight.

"Thanks to you," Talbun said.

Brasley frowned. "I helped too, you know."

The ground suddenly shook. A score of Perranese warriors on horses rode straight down the aisle toward them. Brasley and the bishop brought up their weapons, stood shoulder to shoulder.

The horsemen split apart and rode around them, followed by dozens of Perranese foot soldiers. None raised a weapon. Soon they were gone as fast as they'd arrived, not even sparing a glance for Brasley, the bishop, and the wizard.

Brasley gawked. "Didn't they *see* us?"

"They were ordered to withdraw, I'm guessing," Hark said. "Either they were losing the battle, or they accomplished whatever they came here to do."

Brasley's eyes went wide as he looked back down the row of tents. "Rina."

CHAPTER
FORTY-TWO

She hadn't really been asleep, just barely dozing, skimming the surface of slumber. Rina's mind raced. So many problems. Too few solutions.

And the eyes. If she fell asleep, she risked the eyes.

She sat up, swung her legs over the cot, bare feet on the cold grass. The tent left much to be desired as far as creature comforts. She'd pay real money for a feather bed in a warm inn.

She chuckled. It was something Brasley would say. She wished his tent were closer. Maybe he was still awake. Rina wanted somebody to talk to. As duchess, etiquette demanded someone of her rank had a tent closer to the general's, but she had no desire to see Inshaw.

I'm not that *desperate for conversation.*

The man had been a tiresome blowhard all through dinner, constantly touting his alleged military prowess. She'd thought Brasley was doing her a favor by engaging the man in conversation until she realized Brasley was simply drunk.

That made her laugh again. She had only a few friends, but Brasley was one of them.

Who would ever have guessed that?

Tosh was something of a friend, as was Klarissa, the de facto leader of the gypsies. Meeting Talbun for the first time had been completely intimidating, but she was growing fond of the woman. Rina wasn't quite ready to define Stasha Benadicta as a friend, but the woman was certainly somebody Rina respected and trusted.

And then there was Alem.

Where was he now? What was he thinking? She hoped he was safe.

The thought she might never see him again created a sickly, heavy feeling in the pit of her stomach.

The chances of her going back to sleep now were zero.

Rina stood and stretched. The night air was cool and broke her skin out in gooseflesh. She wore only a thin silk shift and a man's pair of underwear. She'd quickly found her own underwear incompatible with armor.

She dug through her pack, found a chuma stick and stuck it in the corner of her mouth, realizing there was no way to light it, no lit candles or lanterns in her tent, and she didn't want to fumble in the dark for flint. The only light came from the outside, a campfire or torchlight leaking in through the crack in the tent flap.

Rina blinked at the light, noticing for the first time that it seemed a little . . . off. Torchlight flickered orange red. This light was a bright pink, shimmering strangely like some kind of rapid blinking.

She cautiously eased aside the tent flap.

A glowing pink hummingbird the size of her fist floated in front of her, its wings a bright blur.

Rina stepped back, startled.

The bird was translucent, obviously magical. She had no idea what it was doing here. It bobbed and fluttered but didn't follow her into the tent.

When she took a step forward, it backed away, hovering and waiting.

Uh . . . okay.

Rina moved forward slowly in an attempt to slip around the hummingbird. It backed away from her immediately, and she froze. The bird didn't seem frightened. Nor did it act hostile. She experimentally reached out her gloved hand, and the bird backed away. When Rina withdrew her hand, the bird floated back into position.

Rina walked toward it, exiting the tent, and the hummingbird backed away, maintaining a distance of about three feet.

The aisle between the tent rows was deserted. Not a sound.

Looking back down the aisle, she saw a pink trail like glowing dust hanging in the air. It led to the hummingbird. Rina turned and jogged away. She looked back over her shoulder and saw the hummingbird following, still maintaining its distance. The glowing pink dust trailed behind it.

Rina zigzagged as she jogged, and the bird followed, the pink trail zigzagging along with it.

It's laying down some kind of trail. But why? To what?

Rina ran in a circle, and the hummingbird drew a pink circle in the air.

Her eyes widened and her breath caught.

To me. It's a trail leading to me.

Rina could not immediately think of a scenario in which this was a good thing.

She turned abruptly, looking behind her and going into a fighting crouch as if she expected some dire creature to be sneaking up from behind. The aisle was empty save for the pink trail. Quiet tents and the damp night.

She grew acutely aware that she wasn't really dressed, not properly, no armor or weapons. Not even boots.

Because you wanted to play with the pretty magic hummingbird. Idiot girl.

She stood poised for trouble, feeling equally ready and foolish. It was the middle of the night. Nothing stirred. The obvious course of action was to go to Talbun and consult her about the hummingbird. Maybe she would know what the thing was for. Wizardry was her business, after all. If anyone would have answers, it would be her.

As she pondered this, something moved at the other end of the aisle, stirring in the darkness between tents.

Rina tapped into the spirit.

Her eyes immediately absorbed all available light, allowing her to see clearly in the distant darkness. The vague, shadowy shapes resolved clearly into armored men—at least twenty—skulking in the spaces between the tents.

She assessed the situation in a split second.

And ran toward them.

Realizing they'd been spotted, the warriors abandoned stealth and charged her, armor clanking as they sprinted down the aisle.

As always when she was tapped into the spirit, her eyes saw everything, mind cataloging every detail. None had drawn their weapons. She discarded the wild possibility they'd all simultaneously forgotten they had swords. That meant they had orders not to use them, which meant Rina was to be taken alive. Too bad for them. She didn't value their lives quite so much.

She also noticed many pieces of their armor were tarnished and even dented, pocked with rust in places. These were not fresh troops with new equipment. Rina's guess was that they were left from the force that had landed in Klaar.

In her mind, she processed each of these thoughts methodically, but to the outside observer she was a blur of motion, the lightning-bolt tattoos on her ankles lending her incredible speed.

She dove under the lead warrior's sluggish grab for her, tucked and rolled, reaching as she came out of the roll to pluck the sword from the man's scabbard. Rina sprang to her feet, spun, a backhanded swing opening the man's throat before he even knew his sword was missing.

Rina turned to the others coming for her. One was already reaching to grab her, and he lost the arm a split second later. She wheeled to her right and hacked down two more attackers. The sword flashed and spun in her hands, striking, biting, slashing. The air filled with screams and a bloody mist. It spattered hot across her face.

Another group of warriors surged from the tent rows to support the first group.

So many.

Rina felt the drain, knew she'd soon have to either break off the fight or replenish her spirit. The latter would mean taking off the glove.

They rushed her from three directions at once. She opened bellies and slashed through helms. With the strength from the bull tattoo, their armor might as well have been jewelers' foil. One managed to get close enough to lay a hand on her.

He lost it at the wrist.

Rina guessed a few of them must have abandoned the plan to take her alive, because they drew weapons. Or maybe they were just tired of dying in droves. And once the rest saw their brethren loosing steel, they all did.

Now they crowded in on her, slashing and trying to thrust, but they couldn't get past her defenses. Kork had taught her well. She parried, lunged, and caught one in the throat. He went down, and another warrior stepped over the twitching body to take his place. He died a second later, but Rina took a long, deep gash on the forearm.

As quickly as the pain flared, Rina locked it away. She felt the wound tingle as the healing rune went to work, saw the gash close up, new flesh knitting over the damaged area. Even as it healed, she took another long gash down her back. She twisted, stabbed her attacker in the face, then turned back to the men in front of her, slashing left and right, fountains of blood punctuated by the warriors' death cries.

Rina's entire body was red and slick.

Above her, the magic hummingbird bobbed and hovered along with her as she moved, its bright pink trail obscene amid the carnage.

Rina was intensely focused on her attackers, but a peripheral awareness took in new developments transpiring in the camp. The clamor of fighting and men shouting, the acrid stench of something burning. She glimpsed flames three rows over. Tents on fire.

Inshaw's men had joined the fight at last, but whether any were close enough to help, Rina couldn't guess.

A jab deep into her thigh made her stumble back. The blood ran hot down her leg. The warriors sensed the severity of her wound and pressed in, redoubling the savagery of their attack. Rina went on the defensive, batting aside their sword thrusts, favoring the wounded leg as she gave ground. She felt the healing rune go to work, but she also felt her well of spirit running dry.

Another blade grazed her shoulder and drew blood. Another thin slice across her belly.

It's just like the battle in front of the temple gate. There's too many. I can't make it through this unless . . .

Rina bit the thin silken material at the end of her middle finger and tugged the glove off with her teeth.

She waited for the next warrior to lunge, sidestepped the thrust, and grabbed his wrist. The effect was immediate, skin on skin, the Hand of Death draining the man's spirit. He screamed as Rina knew he'd never screamed before, his very essence ripped away.

She parried three more attacks as she drained the man, thrilling to the spirit that filled her even as she felt sick at the hideous thing she was doing. A greasy layer of distaste wrapped around the pure, bright energy that filled her.

Rina released the man, his husk falling and tripping the next warrior who moved in to attack. She caught his throat on the way down and drained him as well.

The bones in Rina's body hummed with the spirit. There was a mad glee in her trying to surface, but a saner part of her feared letting it out. This wasn't what she wanted. It wasn't who she wanted to be.

And yet the part of her that yearned for more was undeniable. She would drain everyone here if she could, revel in the intoxicating power of the spirit. She wanted the power like nothing else she'd ever wanted before, and knowing that made her realize how dangerous the magic was.

She was of two minds. Rina Veraiin wanted the power. But she wished she were the type of person who didn't. She wanted to be good. She wanted endless spirit. She wished none of this had ever happened. She relished that it had.

The Perranese warriors came at her again, and she added to the pile of bodies surrounding her. She swung her sword and heads flew from necks, tumbled through the air, disbelief on the faces of their owners.

Rina stomped through the bloody mud, grabbed another warrior and drained him. Everywhere she swung the sword, death reared its bloody head. The Perranese fell back before her now. Only death could be the result of continued conflict. They backed up, stepping over the bodies of their comrades, swords up in the feeble pretense they might be able to oppose her.

Rina plunged into the middle of them, her sword rising and falling and cutting a red path. They would all die. The spirit sang a song of power in her ears. Rina danced to the tune, each move sending another warrior to his end.

The mob of warriors split and ran, fleeing between the tents on either side of the aisle, scattering like children in a game of tag. When the aisle cleared, she saw the horsemen at the end, galloping toward her.

Come and die, then. She realized how eager she was for their blood. She didn't care.

The two lead horses were each riding double. The first horseman sat straight backed in the saddle, a lean no-nonsense face. Rina wasn't familiar with Perranese military insignia, but a red band with three slashed circles around his arm probably marked him as some kind of officer. The man mounted behind him was older, with braided moustaches and flowing silken robes. No armor. Definitely not a warrior. The rider of the other horse was burly and gruff, an eye patch over one eye. The man holding on to him from behind wore similar robes to those of the man with the mustaches, but was younger and round faced. He held one hand aloft, a glowing pink globe around it. The pink trail stretched from his hand to the hummingbird like a leash.

Wizards.

The round-faced wizard waved his hand, and the pink trail and hummingbird dissolved and vanished. The other wizard began chanting arcane syllables.

Rina ran. Whatever spell was coming, she wanted no part of it. She ran fast, the lightning-bolt tattoos sizzling with spirit.

She felt the spell hit her, like a blast of wind that tingled with eldritch energy. Immediately she felt as though she were made of lead. The strength from the bull tattoo kicked in to compensate, but she felt herself being pulled down to the ground, like the sudden increased weight of her would sink her into the soft ground up to her knees.

Fighting the spell was again draining her spirit. Instead of running, she turned to fight.

The riders pursued but kept their distance, letting the wizards do the work. The one with the moustaches kept chanting, maintaining the spell.

Rina flung her sword at him.

It flashed end over end. With the bull's strength behind it, the sword closed the distance in an eyeblink. The two men on the horse barely had time to dodge aside, the wizard yelling and tumbling from the horse, hitting the ground with a dull thud. He seemed unhurt, but his concentration had been shattered, and he'd lost control of the spell.

Rina felt the weight fall away from her. She ran.

Toward them.

Attack felt better than flight. It felt right.

It felt good.

Four other riders surged past the wizards, charging her.

Rina ran and jumped, leaping into the saddle behind the first rider before he even knew what was happening. She grabbed the back of his neck and squeezed, felt and heard the bone snapped. She tossed the corpse aside and grabbed the reins, wheeling the horse around to face the others. The others turned their horses to run.

Rina stood in the saddle, perfectly balanced, and leapt from one horse to the next, knocking the rider out of his saddle. She grabbed a dagger from the man's belt as he fell, turned, and let it fly.

The blade buried to the hilt in another warrior's eye, and he went down screaming.

She turned toward the other wizard.

The warrior with the eye patch shouted over his shoulder at the round-faced spell caster. "Do something, you fat idiot!"

Rina spurred the horse straight at them.

She had to give the fat wizard credit. The terror on his face was plain, but he hung in, carving magical symbols in the air, spitting out the words of whatever spell he'd picked from inside his brain.

It didn't hit her physically as the last spell had. It was more a blow to her mind. The world blurred. As heavy as her limbs were before was how her mind felt now, clouded and sluggish. Everything slowed.

Darkness seeped in from all sides and then she was floating and—

—then the world—

—sight, sound, touch—

—vanished.

CHAPTER
FORTY-THREE

Brasley stood in the smoking ruins of the camp, holding his horse's reins. The wounded were still being carried to the overworked surgeon's tent. The sun had been up less than an hour. He watched Talbun and Hark approach, also leading horses, careful to step around the dead bodies.

It was starting to smell bad. It would get worse as the sun climbed higher.

Talbun's tent had burned along with all of her possessions, but she'd managed to scrounge some clothing, men's tan breeches tucked into loose-fitting boots. A cream-colored man's shirt, cinched at the waist with a belt. She still had the dagger she'd picked up during the battle, hanging in a sheath from her belt. A dark-green cloak, clasped at her throat and thrown open, hood back.

Give her a bow and quiver and she'd look more like a poacher than a wizard, Brasley thought. *A very pretty poacher.*

The bishop was decked out again in his full plate armor. He had a grim look on his face. His squire had been slain during the battle.

They stood in a small circle among the dead. Some of the tents still burned, and black smoke wafted past them.

"Did you find out about Rina?" Brasley asked.

"Nobody has seen her," Talbun said. "And a woman's body would stand out among the dead."

"The fires. Maybe . . ." Brasley didn't want to complete the thought.

"I checked her tent," Talbun said. "It's not one of the ones that burned. And all her things are still there. They've taken her."

Brasley shook his head. "No. I mean, how? With what she can do, how's it possible?"

"Magic."

Magic. Well, she's a wizard. Magic is probably her answer to everything.

They all let that sink in a moment.

"What did you find out, Bishop Hark?" Brasley asked.

"Inshaw is dead," Hark said. "The senior captain is taking command. He seems less a fool than Inshaw, at least. He's ordered the banquet tables and other useless gear abandoned, so they can make a faster march to Kern."

"They don't intend to pursue the Perranese?" Brasley asked.

"It appears not," Hark said.

"Then it's just us," Brasley said.

Talbun and the bishop exchanged glances.

Brasley frowned. "Okay, is there a reason we *wouldn't* go after her?"

"We don't even know she's still alive," Hark said.

"They could have killed her here," Brasley said. "Why kill her, then haul off her body?"

"A fair point."

"The better point is that there are a few hundred of them," Talbun said, "and only three of us."

"Are you a wizard or not?" Brasley said crossly.

"And what would you know about it, boy?" Something fierce and impatient lit her eyes. "I've taken on armies in my day, but I've always chosen the time and manner of such confrontations." She gestured at her borrowed clothes. "I'm not exactly in top form right now."

Some wizard. Can't go into battle without the right outfit.

"Let's not bicker." The bishop sounded weary. "The question still lies before us. What shall we do?"

Talbun sighed. "There's something important—*critically* important—at the Great Library in Tul-Agnon. I think Rina would want me to fetch it. If it's even possible. It's one of the reasons we set out from Klaar in the first place."

"Whatever you find is pointless without Rina," Brasley said.

Talbun hesitated. "Perhaps."

"Look, I'll just go myself then," Brasley said. "And you can do whatever you want."

"No," Talbun said. "You have to come with me. You know how to negotiate the nobility. She told me she has faith in your ability to talk fast and to trick your way along. Also, I've been away from court politics for nearly a century, and we'll need help talking our way into the library. It's why she wanted to bring you."

"I thought it was because she trusted me."

The wizard shrugged. "That too."

"I'm not just abandoning her."

"And if you can track them, and if you catch them, and if she's still alive, what do you hope to accomplish against so many?" Talbun asked.

"I don't know. Something. I can hang back and wait for an opportunity," Brasley said. "Or find her and come back for some of these king's men to help me get her back. Anything is better than trying nothing."

"I'll go," Hark said.

Brasley blinked at him. "You'll go what?"

"I'll go after her," Hark said. "That many men will leave an obvious trail. It won't be difficult to catch up."

"And then what?" Brasley asked.

"Same as you. I'll think of something."

"It's a good compromise," Talbun said quickly, trying to bring the subject to a conclusion.

Brasley rubbed the back of his neck. "I don't know. I don't like it."

"Let me go." There was an urgent sincerity in the bishop's voice. "I pledged to help her, and I don't feel like I've been very helpful so far."

A pause. Brasley briefly met the bishop's eyes. A curt nod.

"It's settled then," Talbun said. "The direct route is through the wilderness to Tul-Agnon, but going to Merridan and then taking the river up is faster." She turned to Hark. "Good luck."

"Thank you."

"Bring her back," Brasley said.

"I'll do my best," Hark said.

"I'll tell Becham we'll be joining his party for the capital." Talbun led her horse away.

"Bishop."

Hark looked up. "Baron Hammish?"

This time Brasley held the man's gaze. "I don't want to hear you'll do your best. I want to hear that you're bringing her back, that you'll find a way."

"As long as there's life left in my body," Hark said, "I'll bring her back."

CHAPTER FORTY-FOUR

Sherrik's waterfront roiled with chaos.

The duke's ships had escorted the *Witch of Kern* into port. Tosh and all aboard had breathed a sigh of relief when the ships had appeared to drive away the Perranese raiders. The joy had evaporated rapidly upon seeing the turmoil of the Sherrik wharves. The few ships still in port were scrambling to provision and cast off before they were trapped by the inbound Perranese fleet.

Rumors spread through the waterfront like a virus. The Perranese had five hundred ships. A thousand ships. Two thousand. They were coming to burn the city. To loot the city. To enslave the population. To rape all the women. To murder everyone.

Under normal circumstances, the Sherrik waterfront saw a thousand ships coming and going each day, trade from all coasts, exotic gems and curiosities up from the Red City, spices from as far as Fyria. Sherrik grew fat on the tariffs. Now the port hosted just over twoscore ships, stragglers frantic to push off and be gone before the city came under siege. Even with so few ships in port, the piers were crowded and hectic. Scared citizens attempting to book passage on the last ship out. Opportunistic hucksters selling provisions at five times the normal price. Desperate ship captains trying to find qualified hands to fill the gaps in their crews.

Sherrik was a city teetering on the edge of war, and the last of the rats scurried to desert what they suspected was a sinking ship.

Between the waterfront and the city proper were the great stone walls that rose sixty feet high and circled all of Sherrik. Seven cobblestone roads led from the waterfront through seven arched gates and into the city. On a normal day, trade goods streamed at a steady rate through all seven portals. Now only the middle gate was open, the portcullises lowered and iron doors closed on the other six. Any minute the city would seal itself.

Tosh pushed a handcart with four barrels of water on it. There was an additional barrel filled with rum, which he planned to sample immediately upon escaping this madness. Alem followed him closely with another handcart and another three barrels of water and a case of hardtack and beef jerky of dubious quality.

Barazz had sent them into the city to gather whatever provisions they could, the priority being water. They could go on half rations, but they couldn't make it to the Red City without water. Tosh and his people had gone to the center of town, where water could be had for free at a community well.

However, they'd had to pay outlandish prices for the barrels and the handcarts.

They passed through the middle gate and headed down the pier to the *Witch of Kern*. Maurizan and Tosh's girls flanked them, hoping swords and daggers and tough glares would discourage anyone who wanted the barrels.

This place is minutes from full-blown panic, Tosh thought. *We've got to get back on the ship and get out of here.*

They passed a fat, sluggish cargo ship, and Tosh thought they'd made it. The *Witch of Kern* was in the next berth.

Then a half dozen burly sailors stepped out to block them.

"How much for the barrels?" The leader was tall and tan, gold hoops in his ears. "We'll give you double whatever you paid."

Kalli's hand fell to her sword hilt.

"Thanks anyway," Tosh said. "We're not selling."

The sailor with the gold hoops put his hand on one of the barrels. "I'm not asking. Maybe we take them for nothing."

"And maybe you'll lose that fucking hand, cocksucker," Tosh said.

The men behind the leader with the gold hoops stirred and grumbled, pulling short knives and belaying pins.

Shit. Sixty more seconds and we'd be on the ship. Now it has to get ugly.

"Tough talk for a man with a bunch of pretty-girl bodyguards," Gold Hoops said.

Maurizan drew her daggers. "You die first. For water. Is that how you want to be remembered?"

He grinned at her. "Maybe we'll take you *and* the barrels. It gets lonely at sea."

There was a tense moment. Tosh could feel it; the air itself tightened, the two parties facing each other on the pier, coiled to strike, muscles taut. In the next second, he'd hear the hiss of blades drawn from sheaths, and they'd be at it.

Instead he heard a booming voice from down the pier. "Stand aside, you men."

The one with the gold hoops turned to see Barazz fast walking toward them, his hand on the hilt of a sheathed cutlass. Ten members of his crew strode behind them, all meaning business, naked blades in their hands. Barazz's message was clear. Get out of the way or get killed.

Gold Hoops gestured to his men to stand back, a sneering grin on his face. "Sure. No problem here. We were just talking."

Tosh hurriedly pushed the cart past them, Alem and the others following. Crewmen took over the barrels and began hauling them up the gangplank.

"Thanks for fetching these," Barazz said to Tosh.

"I wish it could be more."

"It's enough to get us to the Red City," Barazz said. "How bad is it in there?"

"Bad," Tosh said. "I guess a lot of people have fled the city because they're starting to loot the empty houses. Have you ever been in a city under siege? A long one?"

"No," said the ship captain.

"Neither have I," Tosh said. "But I've heard stories. If it goes on too long, they'll eat the dogs and cats first. Then rats. Then each other. I hope we're not sticking around."

"We'll shove off as soon as these barrels are loaded."

"Suits me," Tosh said. "A shame. I always wanted to see Sherrik. Just not like this. Maybe someday I'll get back this way and—"

A surge in the crowd noise drew their attention back to the city walls.

The crowd boiled around the last open city gate, people pushing and shoving. Screams. Panic.

The chain-link clank of the portcullis lowering rose above the crowd noise and thunked into place like the final nail in a coffin. The people went mad, the frenzy redoubling as the iron doors thudded closed behind the portcullis. Sherrik was officially sealed. People inside would stay there. People outside would have to fend for themselves.

Suddenly cut off from the safety of the city walls, the hysterical crowd turned their attention to their last possible refuge.

The ships.

The mob stormed down the pier like a living thing of a thousand seething parts. Men and women with hastily packed bags and bundles on their shoulders. They pushed their way to the fat cargo ship in the first berth and attempted to go up the gangplank. Armed sailors stood in their way at the top. Shouting. People holding up bags of money. Pushing. Threats.

The first man knocked off the gangplank sparked the rest of the mob to push forward. More sailors appeared to push them back. A woman fell and then another man. The crowd pushed past the sailors blocking the top of the gangplank and soon crawled over the deck like ants. Weapons were drawn. Blood spilled.

"Get that last barrel aboard," Barazz shouted. "We're going. *Now.*"

Already some on the ground were looking to the next ship.

They were about to pull up the gangplank when the ruffian with the gold hoops in his ears and his men appeared at the bottom. "Take us."

"That a joke?" Barazz asked.

"We know you're shorthanded," Gold Hoops said. "Don't be stupid. We're all experienced hands."

"Who's in charge?"

"I am," Gold Hoops said. "These men'll do as I tell 'em."

Barazz turned to look up at the rigging. He waved his hand, then pointed at Gold Hoops.

A crossbow bolt shot from the crow's nest and buried with a *thuk* in Gold Hoops' chest. He grabbed at it, eyes wide, stumbling backward, halting steps before he fell and tumbled off the other side of the pier and into the water.

Barazz repeated his question to the other five men. "Who's in charge?"

"You are," said one of the smart ones.

"Then cast us off and get up here."

Within seconds the gangplank had been hauled up and they'd pushed off. Barazz shouted at the men in the rigging. He wanted full sail and out of this harbor with all possible speed.

The crowds lined the pier now, shouting and waving for the *Witch of Kern* to come back. A woman held up a baby for all on the ship to see.

"Can't we take them?"

Tosh looked to see Alem had joined him at the railing. He waved at the crowd, all of them along the pier and up and down the wharf. "All of them? There are thousands."

"We could take some."

"How do you choose?" Tosh asked. "Who lives and who dies? There's a war starting. It will get much uglier than this."

Somehow a fire had started on the cargo ship. Black smoke filled the air. Some of the men and women on the pier leapt into the water, trying to swim after the *Witch of Kern*.

"I feel sick," Alem said.

"Well," Tosh said, "you have to be alive to feel sick."

CHAPTER
FORTY-FIVE

Tchi sat on his horse and watched the three riders approach.

"You should kill her now." Yano sat on the horse next to Tchi's, also watching the riders come.

"If we have to, we will," Tchi said. "Right now we don't have to."

Yano turned and spat. A moment later he said, "When the wizards sent the demon and that great flying lizard, that was to kill her, wasn't it?"

Tchi bit off a sharp retort. Yano would take Tchi's losing his temper as some petty victory. "I saw an opportunity and took it."

"Lost good men taking that opportunity."

"Then I'd think you'd cherish our prize more highly," Tchi said.

Yano grunted. He wasn't sure if Tchi had made a good point or not.

The three riders had almost arrived. They didn't look particularly harried, and Tchi took heart in the thought.

"She's dangerous." Yano was evidently not quite prepared to let the subject go.

"Yes," Tchi said. "Otherwise she would not be the object of our attention."

Another grunt.

"The wizards have her under constant observation," Tchi said. "They've bound her and have spelled her to sleep. We'll take her south to Sherrik and turn her over to the commander of the invasion. They'll have people who can interrogate her properly. More important, the girl possesses a unique magic. The imperial sorcerers will want to examine her."

When Tchi didn't even get a grunt, he figured the matter must be at last closed.

The riders reined in their horses before Tchi and saluted.

"Report."

"No pursuit, sir," said one of the riders. "We stung them badly, I think. Caught them utterly by surprise."

"Well done, Corporal," Tchi said. "Pass the word that we're moving out again in an hour."

They saluted again and galloped away.

"Sergeant, take two squads and scout the roads ahead," Tchi said. "I want the fastest path south possible, but obviously we need to avoid towns and large villages. We'll be spotted eventually. There are too many of us. But later is better than sooner."

Yano hesitated.

"You have your orders, Sergeant."

"Commander Tchi, I would like to go on record as saying I don't agree with the order to keep the woman alive. She's an unknown. Maybe our wizards can keep her under wraps. Maybe not. It's a bad risk."

Tchi's back went stiff, the muscles in his jaw working with anger. "Your objection has been noted. Shall I call back the corporal so you have a witness?"

Yano grinned crookedly, showing yellow teeth. "Don't bother. I trust you, Commander." The sergeant spurred his horse left at a trot.

◆ ◆ ◆

A two-wheeled cart had been hooked to one of the packhorses, Rina Veraiin dumped in the back. She'd been gagged and blindfolded and bound by heavy chain. Prullap and Jariko had been ordered to stay with her around the clock, to use their magic to keep her asleep and alive.

"A simple sleep spell." Jariko *tsked*. "Here we are summoning demons and great winged beasts, and one of the most basic incantations was all that was needed."

"Not quite," Prullap said. "You have to be within sight of your target to cast it, and let me tell you, that was no fun."

"I know," Jariko said. "I was there."

"You fell off your horse," Prullap said.

"I *know*," Jariko said. "I was *there*."

"You didn't see the murderous look in her eyes," Prullap said dramatically, reliving the encounter. "She was coming right at me. I almost soiled myself. If the spell hadn't worked—"

"But it *did* work," the older wizard said. "Calm down. You're making me nervous."

"*I'm* making you nervous. I saw the woman break a man's neck with one hand."

"If she stays asleep, she can't hurt anyone."

"I'm not sure we should keep her like this," Prullap said. "I can keep spelling her to sleep, but what if something goes wrong and she gets loose? The woman is a bloodthirsty animal."

"Don't be a fool," Jariko snapped. "Look at the woman's back."

Prullap already knew what he'd see but looked anyway. They'd ripped her shift halfway down her back to expose the tattoos. The wizards had looked on with wonder, but only Jariko seemed to fully realize what it meant.

"You're looking at power, Prullap. A rare and amazing power that many thought was lost. But it's not lost. It's right here. In our hands."

"In *her* hands," Prullap said. "Which is exactly why I don't want her to wake up."

"Some wizard had to ink those tattoos on her," Jariko said. "She knows who. If we can ferret out the secrets, the potential is unlimited."

"I suppose you could ask her if she were awake," Prullap said. "Oh, wait, then she'd kill us."

Jariko frowned. "Sarcasm ill suits you."

"*Death* ill suits me."

"We are intelligent men," Jariko insisted. "We could figure a way."

"Count me out," Prullap said.

Jariko opened his mouth to say something cutting but held back. *Count him out? Yes, why not? Why should someone with so little ambition share in the power? He's weak. I don't need him.*

"Perhaps you're right," Jariko said. "I have heard some of the warriors express similar sentiments. Just her presence among us makes them anxious."

"I don't doubt it," Prullap said. "Many of their friends and comrades died at her hands."

Jariko sighed elaborately. "Well, so much for dreams of power. Perhaps it is better we focus our efforts on keeping her enchained and asleep. Let others worry what to do with her."

But already the wheels were turning in the old wizard's mind, for the secrets of the ink mage were too tantalizing to resist.

◆ ◆ ◆

The beef jerky was terrible.

The sergeant in charge of the king's stores had been willing to part with a bag of beef jerky, some hard biscuits, and a skin of weak wine. Hardly gourmet fare, but it would last long and travel well.

Bishop Hark sat on his horse just inside the tree line. Low-hanging branches hid him well enough. He held the reins of Rina's horse also, her armor and weapons packed on its back against the chance he actually found her alive and managed to rescue her.

He watched and chewed.

The three Perranese riders galloped across the open land in front of him. Scouts. Hark would need to hang back and stay out of sight until the enemy force felt comfortable they weren't being pursued. He waited a bit, then clucked his tongue, his horse breaking into a trot. He kept to the shadows of the tree line.

Hark uttered a brief prayer to Dumo, nothing deeply personal, just something simple and comforting from one of the novice prayer books.

He hoped Dumo was listening.

CHAPTER FORTY-SIX

The sun sank into the ocean, the waves pink and orange in the dying light. The sea was strangely calm, but Alem couldn't feel it. He couldn't get the images of the desperate citizens out of his mind, how they stood there on the pier, screaming for the ship to return and take them away. He'd killed enemies who'd been trying to kill him. It had been unpleasant, but it also couldn't be helped. Alem had no problem defending himself.

That's what Tosh had suggested they were doing when they left those people, men, women, children. Defending themselves. Couldn't take them all. Barazz had his own crew to think of. It couldn't be helped.

But to Alem, it just felt . . . bad.

It felt wrong.

It couldn't be helped.

They're not dead yet, Alem thought. *They might be locked out of the city, but they can still leave on foot. There are options.* He wondered how many would be killed in the chaos at the waterfront. The war had started and the enemy hadn't even arrived yet.

Alem put his hands on the rough wooden railing, leaned, and watched the sun disappear.

Maurizan appeared at the railing beside him. "It's too hot belowdecks."

Since they'd come south, the heat had amazed them. They'd only just eased into spring, but compared to the bitter Klaar temperatures, the weather was a startling contrast. Alem sweated even in his lightest shirt with the sleeves rolled up.

"You seem better," Alem said.

It took the gypsy a moment to understand his meaning. "You mean the vomiting. Yes, I think I have my sea legs now. Still a bit woozy, but not so bad, really."

She leaned against the railing next to him, her hand an inch from his. The last of the sun was a garish orange blur on the horizon.

"I'm sorry," she said.

"I'll be fine," Alem said. "I just . . . I wasn't prepared to look so many people in the face who were fighting for their lives."

"No," Maurizan said. "I mean, yes, of course. That's terrible. How could it not be? But that's not what I meant. I meant me. How I've been to you. I mean, damn . . . this is harder than I thought. I mean, yeah, you deserve a good slap, but I should have known, right? I mean, you and me. I wanted it so bad I refused to see it. It was her that you always *really* wanted."

Alem closed his eyes, felt a weight descend upon him. "Maurizan."

"No, it's true," she said. "I knew. I knew and pretended not to know because I loved you."

A long moment passed. The sound of the ship carving a path through the salt sea.

"I should have known better," Alem said. "A duchess. Who was I kidding? I should have . . ."

"Settled?" Maurizan asked. "For the cute gypsy girl who was more in your league?"

Alem went red, face hot. "I didn't mean—"

"I don't care," Maurizan said. "I don't care if I'm second choice. It hurt so much to see you with her. I'd take any chance to get you back. If she's a fool, then why shouldn't I benefit? I don't care why. Pride isn't the choice for happiness. I hate to say this, it sounds terrible, but I can't help it. I've started talking now and I can't stop no matter what."

Alem desperately wished she would stop.

Desperately wished she wouldn't.

"It's almost better this way," Maurizan said. "Because you left me for her, and now you've come back to me broken, and that's easier. Because I can save you and comfort you and make you forget how badly you hurt. That's terrible, but I don't care. I can be the one who picks up the broken pieces she left behind, and I'm so selfish that all I can think is that I'm glad. Glad she hurt you, so I can be here for you now. And I have to say this so you know. So it's honest."

Alem felt sick and dizzy and couldn't believe that feeling this way wasn't all bad. He didn't really know how to feel at all.

She moved her hand a fraction of an inch so her pinky finger intertwined with his on the railing.

And he didn't say a thing. What could he say?

But he didn't move his hand.

EPISODE EIGHT

CHAPTER
FORTY-SEVEN

At first, Alem thought the sun was rising in the wrong place, but the bright blur on the horizon was the Red City catching the morning light. The collection of low buildings spread along the coast had been constructed of some native stone from a quarry inland that was red like clay but hard like granite. The city's original architects had favored broad blocky buildings, squat pyramids, and wide domes over soaring towers and spires.

Strong winds and fair weather had carried them south from Sherrik in just nine days. Everyone's mood had brightened considerably. Alem found himself eager for dry land. When he'd boarded the ship in Kern, some vague feeling of adventure had stirred in him. Now the vessel was simply a small, claustrophobic place with bad food. He watched eagerly as the shore drew closer.

Whereas Sherrik had one huge centralized waterfront, docks in the Red City could be found all along the coast. Barazz had told Alem that the city was long and thin and spread along the sea. As the only civilized place in the Shattered Isles, it depended on sea trade as its life's blood. There were quarries and some minor agriculture inland—mostly fruit groves—and a decent fishing industry, but the Red City imported the vast majority of its food.

The *Witch of Kern* tied up at the very end of a long pier at the northern tip of the city. The docks were bustling, much of the traffic refugees from Sherrik or ships that had been bound for Sherrik that now had to change plans.

Alem was considering heading down the gangplank when Tosh caught up with him.

"Decided?" Tosh asked.

Alem turned his head to look at the Red City, at least what he could see from the deck. The people hustled along the walkways. They wore loose light clothing because of the warm weather, sleeveless in some cases. Women wore silky, billowy pants bunched at the ankles. Footwear consisted mostly of sandals with lots of leather straps. Some carried baskets balanced on their heads. Men seemed to favor close-cropped beards without moustaches. Hats ranged from turbans to big felt thimbles, perched at jaunty angles. The place and its people looked exciting and mysterious and exotic.

It seemed like a place to visit, not to stay.

And anyway, his friends were going off to do something that would help Rina. Putting their lives in jeopardy for her. How could he not lend a hand?

Because she could give a damn about you.

Don't be a petty, pig-headed thicko.

He turned back to Tosh. "I want to come."

"Then don't go far." Tosh gestured at the smaller boats along the dock. "As soon as I hire and provision one of these little island hoppers, we're going."

"How long?"

Tosh squinted at the sun. It was still fairly early. "I'd like to be out of here by lunch."

"Okay. I'll have a look around and be back by then." After all, to come all this way and not at least have a quick look seemed a waste.

"Take somebody with you." Tosh grinned. "Take Maurizan."

Alem frowned.

"It's a strange city. Safety in numbers."

"My bodyguard?" Alem said.

Tosh laughed, and Alem went in search of the gypsy.

◆ ◆ ◆

Merridan's southwestern suburb stretched shabby and poor to the docks along the river where the paddle-wheel boats tied up. River traffic to and from Tul-Agnon to the north accounted for both a steady flow of commerce and passengers. The river was also a connection to the villages and towns south.

The paddle-wheel boat was a century-old invention of the Tul-Agnon scholars who'd figured the best way to configure the gears to allow four or five men to turn a capstan and sufficiently power the paddle to propel a large boat upriver against the stiff current. An arrangement with the nobles who ran the capital's dungeons provided the manpower. Those convicted of lesser crimes could work off their time on the boats.

Count Becham had used his authority and influence to secure space on the next outgoing boat. Doing this involved putting off a couple of very cross spice merchants, but Brasley couldn't quite bring himself to feel bad for them.

My father-in-law is an important man, after all, Brasley thought smugly. *Rank hath its privileges.*

Brasley watched the boatmen push away from the deck with long wooden poles, and four shirtless men in ankle chains shuffled to the capstan, took their positions, and started turning it, walking a slow circle. It was tough at first, but then the paddle wheel at the stern of the thirty-foot boat began to churn and a minute later, they were slowly making their way upriver.

The boat was flat bottomed, half as wide as it was long, with a low pilothouse in the center. The captain manned the wheel from the flybridge atop the pilothouse. He was an unshaven, spindly man who smelled like cheap wine and hadn't been pleased about putting off two legitimate passengers to make room for Brasley and Talbun.

Brasley didn't think the captain really cared so much about the other passengers. He just didn't like being pushed around by a count and a baron. *Tough shit. What's the point of being a baron anyway if I don't get my way once in a while?* Although Brasley had to admit it had been Becham's clout that had done the trick, not his own. He'd caught the captain shooting him dirty looks more than once. *Some people simply don't respect authority.*

They weren't advertising that Talbun was a wizard, but Brasley suspected the captain wouldn't much like that either.

Most of the deck was crowded with various cargo, crates, and canvas bags, stacked and lashed tight. There were a dozen other passengers aboard, all currently claiming a spot, unrolling bedrolls or finding a quiet nook between stacks of cargo. These were people who'd paid the cheap rate for deck passage. The weather was mild this time of year, so it was a good bet, but if it rained, then these people would be in for a miserable voyage.

Brasley followed Talbun belowdecks. There were three cabins. The two forward would have been considered closets in Castle Klaar. One belonged to the captain, the other to the first mate. Brasley and Talbun headed to the third cabin aft.

Small. Very small. A bed barely big enough for two. A narrow desk that folded up into the wall. A three-legged stool. At least they had a porthole. Some fresh air would definitely help.

Brasley gestured extravagantly at the tiny cabin. "Your first-class accommodations, milady."

"Don't knock it," Talbun said. "It beats walking, and my ass is so sore, if I never see another horse again it'll be too soon."

"I suppose I get the floor."

"Don't be a prude," she said. "Share the bed if you like."

"You trust me?"

Her smile was cold, didn't touch her eyes. "I don't need to trust you. I'm old enough to be your great-grandmother. I have no fathers or brothers to worry over my virtue, and I don't particularly care what people think. I'm also one of the most powerful wizards in Helva. Try to guess what I might do if you annoyed me somehow."

Brasley raised an eyebrow. "Turn me into some sort of newt or frog, I expect."

"Slightly cliché, but you get the gist. Did you pack something to drink?"

"Several somethings," Brasley said. "It's four days to Tul-Agnon. This tub makes a number of stops I'm afraid, cargo and whatnot."

"Well, whatever you've got, break it out," she said. "Because I'm bored already."

◆　◆　◆

Darshia chased him down the narrow alley, Lish close behind her.

Lish was young and gap-toothed, skinny. She hadn't really been Wounded Bird material in Darshia's opinion, hardly pretty. Cute in the right light maybe, wild and frizzy brown hair. But she was quick with the sword and liked to practice, and seemed more comfortable holding a blade than holding a man. A good companion for this kind of work.

Giffen had been persuaded to give up the names of his agents around Klaar. For the past two weeks Stasha Benadicta had been directing the operation to dig out the last of the rats from the bowels of dank taverns and hidden safe houses. She wanted to give Rina Veraiin a traitor-free city upon her return.

The burly man fleeing from her now was theoretically the last of Giffen's henchmen. They rounded a corner, and the alley dead-ended at a thick wooden door. The man slammed a big shoulder against the door, but it wouldn't budge. He turned quickly, drawing a short sword, and went into a fighter's crouch, a determined scowl on his face.

"So the Birds of Prey finally caught up to old Bolger, eh?" He waved the sword in front of him. "You want me, you'll pay the price in blood, ya cunts."

Darshia paused, wanting to approach the man carefully, but Lish rushed past her, charging and thrusting her blade.

Bolger swatted her sword aside with his own, stepped in with surprising speed, and smashed her square in the mouth with a fist. Lish stumbled back on noodle legs, dizzy, spitting blood. Bolger followed with his own sword thrust, but Lish collected herself just enough to parry it.

Darshia was already moving, swiping at him from the other side. Bolger had to break off his attack on Lish to block her, but she feinted high and went low. Her sword tip sank three inches into his upper thigh. He screamed and staggered back, slapping a hand over the wound.

Lish had recovered and came back at him. He tried to bring the sword around but was too slow this time. Lish's blade struck deep between two ribs. He grunted, stumbled back against the door, and slid to the ground, dropping his weapon. It clanged on the cobblestones.

"You . . . bitches." He'd gone white.

Lish stepped in and put her sword through his throat. Bolger's eyes rolled up, and it was finished.

Darshia bent, wiped the blood from her blade on Bolger's breeches. "Search him."

Lish knelt next to him, pulled a purse from his belt and opened it. "Oi, look here. Two silvers and a gold. Never seen a gold coin before."

"Somebody must have paid him off for some dire deed." Darshia smiled. "Keep it."

Lish grinned wide, showing the gap in her teeth. *Might be cute to a certain kind of man*, Darshia mused.

Lish went through Bolger's vest pockets. "He called us Birds of Prey. What's all that then?"

"You haven't heard? It's what they call us now."

"They who?"

"I don't know how it started," Darshia said. "Somebody made a connection. 'Birds' since we used to work at the Wounded Bird and 'prey' since we prey on guys like this, I guess." She gestured at the dead man.

"I like it," Lish said. "Better than being called 'them whores' all the time."

"Fair point."

"Hey, now, look here." Lish pulled a folded parchment from inside the man's coat. "This anything, you think?"

"Read it."

Lish shrugged. "Don't read."

Darshia took it and turned it over in her hands. It was sealed with wax. She almost opened it, but stopped herself. She didn't want to make whatever might be written within her problem. She'd had enough hunting down greasy oafs in back alleys. She'd had enough of righting whatever wrong Giffen had done to Klaar. Let somebody else have a turn.

"We'll take it to the steward," Darshia said. "She'll know what to do with it."

CHAPTER
FORTY-EIGHT

Alem was surprised the most by the completely new aromas.

Exploring randomly, he and Maurizan had crossed through a large arched gateway, the path beneath them paved with a brilliant blue tile. On the other side, they'd found themselves in a bustling bazaar with men and women selling every sort of thing imaginable. They passed a tent in which there were stacked cages of small furry animals neither of them had ever seen before. A turbaned man in a long yellow robe held one of the animals out to Maurizan as they passed by. The creature was like an odd, elongated squirrel, with big yellow eyes and a long, ringed tail. The man spoke in a foreign tongue and was either assuring her the animal would make a fine pet or telling her how delicious it would be skinned and fried.

But it was the food section of the bazaar that won Alem over. Smells hit him that made his mouth water, smoke and the sizzling sound of various grilled meats competing for his attention. After a lifetime of boiled cabbage and potatoes and bland fish, the exotic spices that hit him were too intriguing to resist.

They paused at a stall and purchased two chunks of brown glazed meat on a stick for a copper coin. They brought the meat to their mouths, both pausing and looking at each other as if waiting for the other to go first.

They laughed.

"You don't think this is the big yellow-eyed animal with the ringed tail, do you?" Maurizan asked.

"Too late now," Alem said. "We've already paid for it."

"Together?" Maurizan said.

"On three."

Alem counted and they both bit. The meat was juicy and the flavor exploded in his mouth. He'd never tasted anything so instantly enjoyable.

A second later the spices hit.

The heat started from a long way off, but soon his mouth was on fire. He looked at Maurizan. Her eyes were watering, a look of panic on her face.

"Dumo help me, I'm going to die," she said.

The stall next door sold a light and surprisingly cold beer. Four coppers bought them two enormous tankards. They each gulped down a third of the brew without stopping.

"Well, we can't let money go to waste." Maurizan grinned and took another bite of the meat. Her face went red, sweat on her forehead. She immediately gulped more beer.

Not to be outdone, Alem took another bite too, with the same result. By the time they had finished the meat, both were sweating and laughing. Passersby shook their heads at the silly foreigners. Their mouths were still burning, and they were forced to buy two more tankards of beer.

By the time they were finished, they were giggling as they moved farther into the bazaar. Maurizan spotted a stall with brightly colored silk scarves and tugged on Alem's sleeve to pull him along.

"Which do you think?" She held up a scarf in each hand.

"The green," Alem said. "Goes with your hair."

She smiled and wrapped the scarf around her head in the fashion she'd seen on the other women in the market. "This is nice. Just shopping like this. You know . . . well, I mean we never did anything normal, did we?"

"What do you mean?"

"The first time we met, you were literally saving my life," Maurizan said. "I mean, I'm not saying you arranged that just to impress me, but you were off to a pretty good start. After that, we went from one situation in which we almost died to the next situation in which we almost died."

"You do remember we were recently in a ship-to-ship battle on the high seas and barely escaped a city before it came under siege, right?"

Maurizan rolled her eyes. "Okay, well, yeah. But the voyage since has been pretty calm and . . . look, I'm trying to say that this is nice, and I'm not saying it for any reason." She looked away, awkward now. "I mean, I'm not trying to do anything or get anything. I just wanted you to know because . . . okay, I don't really know why. Shut up."

Alem was about to say something when the scarf merchant approached her, grinning with charm. He seemed to be telling her she could get a special price if she bought three. They both started talking in two different languages, and Alem took the opportunity to drift to the next stall.

Jewelry, necklaces and pendants. Bracelets and brooches.

"And what can I interest you in today, young master?"

Alem looked up into the face of an old, bald man, white beard neatly trimmed. The man's eyes were such a dark brown they were almost black. His smile showed a gold tooth on the left side.

"You speak my language," Alem said. The accent was heavy but not a problem.

"Yes, when I was younger, I took my wares across the seas. Now my sons travel and I tend to business here." The old man gestured to

Maurizan, who was still dickering with the scarf salesman. "Something pretty for your young lady, perhaps?"

Alem reddened. "Just a friend."

"A shame. Such red hair. So striking."

Alem cleared his throat. "Yeah."

"But a friend is a good thing too." The merchant drew Alem's attention to a gleaming pendant at the end of a thin leather strap. "Mother-of-pearl. See how it catches the light. Surrounded by these white gems, not diamonds, I'm afraid, but well-cut quartz. Highly polished. Very nice craftsmanship. Very pleasing to the eye."

It did look nice, but Alem shook his head. "I can't afford it."

"Five silvers anywhere else," the old man said. "But not here. I have the best prices in all of the bazaar. For you, only three silvers."

"I'm sorry."

"Please, think how happy the young lady would be. So pretty. Two silvers."

"Really, I can't." Alem turned to leave.

"One silver, young master. Such a deal has never been struck in the history of the bazaar!"

Alem paused.

The old merchant looked at Maurizan again then back to Alem. "I was young once too. Take this deal, young master."

"I told you, she's just—"

"Yes, yes, a friend only. You are kidding yourself. You are young and healthy. The wise men say the flower that blooms today wilts tomorrow. So pick your flower today. The advice is free. The pendant only a single silver piece."

Alem glanced at Maurizan and saw she was concluding her business with the scarf merchant.

He hastily pulled a silver from his pouch and traded it to the old man for the pendant. He stuffed it into a pocket just as Maurizan approached.

"You're buying something?" she asked.

The old merchant said, "Alas, I tried to tempt this young master with my wares, but he has an iron will." He winked at Alem.

Alem grinned at the man. "Thanks anyway."

They moved away from the stall.

Alem noticed Maurizan's hair had been pulled back into a long ponytail and secured with the green scarf. The end of the scarf draped over her shoulder. With her hair pulled back, he noticed that her neck was slender and long. Graceful. Her white skin gone a little pink from the sun. Her ear was perfectly shaped, pierced in the lobe with small green gems.

"What is it?"

Alem blinked. "What?"

"You're looking at me."

"The scarf," he said quickly. "I'm glad you got the green one."

She smiled, looked away, nudged him in the ribs. "Come on. We're late for the boat. Tosh will be pissed."

♦ ♦ ♦

"You're late," Tosh said.

Alem and Maurizan exchanged grins and failed to hide them. Tosh couldn't quite bring himself to be irritated. After all, it was his idea in the first place for Alem to let Maurizan tag along. Whatever love pangs Alem might have been feeling for Rina, it looked like the gypsy girl might be the cure.

But what do I know? Tosh thought. *Not my business anyway.*

"I got no problem leaving *his* ass behind." Tosh nodded at Alem. "But we can't go any farther without you, Maurizan."

"Oh." Realization on her face. "I suppose you want to see it."

"The captain will want to see it if he's going to lay in a course." Tosh gestured to the other side of the dock.

Alem and Maurizan turned to look. There was no ship there. They looked back at Tosh.

"Look over the side," Tosh told them.

They went to the edge of the dock and looked down.

Maurizan looked back at Tosh, frowning, eyes asking, *Are you kidding me?*

Tosh understood the reaction. The *Witch of Kern* was a floating palace compared to the weather-beaten forty-eight-foot scow schooner he'd hired. It sat low in the water, flat bottomed to negotiate the shallows between the islands. It was a decade past its last coat of paint, sails hanging limp and dirty.

"Bigger ships can't go where we need to go," Tosh explained. "And most of the captains of the smaller ships thought I was crazy when I told them where we were trying to get to."

"This captain is braver?" Alem asked.

Tosh shrugged. "This captain is more . . . colorful."

"I don't like the sound of that," Maurizan said.

Tosh grinned sheepishly. "Wait until you meet him."

They climbed down the ladder and boarded the scow. Kalli and the others were hauling provisions below deck, food, water and spare weapons. *I hope it's enough. Rina was kind of vague about how long this would take.*

"It looks like one good wave would knock this tub to splinters," Maurizan said.

Tosh waved away the concern like it was nothing. "She's solid stem to stern." *I hope.*

Alem threw his pack over his shoulder. "I guess I'll find a spot below and get comfortable."

"Cramped down there, and the captain says it gets hot and stuffy," Tosh said. "He suggests grabbing a spot on the deck where you can get some fresh air."

"Fine." Alem headed forward, stepping around a pile of netting and over a poorly coiled stack of rope.

Tosh looked up. "Ah. Here comes the captain now."

Maurizan followed Tosh's gaze upward. The skinniest man she'd ever seen shimmied down the narrow mast, jumping the last few feet and landing on the deck in front of her. He was the same height as the gypsy girl, all ropy muscles and dark, leathery skin. His nose had been mashed flat, and when he grinned there was a gap where his two front teeth should have been. He was barefoot, shirtless, pants cut off just below the knees. He looked more like a castaway than a boat captain.

"Miko." He tapped a thumb against his bony chest, indicating himself. "Captain Miko. I captain. I also crew and cook." He laughed at this like he'd made the greatest joke in the world.

"Show him the map," Tosh said.

Maurizan hesitated, eyes darting to Miko then back to Tosh. Then she reached into the waistband of her breeches and came out with a folded piece of parchment. She handed it over to the captain.

He unfolded it and squinted. Tosh moved to look over his shoulder.

"Oh, you want go see the fish man, yes?" Miko said. "And the water ghosts?"

The captain's accent was thick, so Tosh thought he might have heard him wrong. "Fish man?"

"Yes, yes." Miko wiggled his hand through the air to mimic a fish swimming. "Fish man."

"You've seen a fish man?" Maurizan asked.

"No, no. Is legend," Miko said. "Always others see. Somebody say fish man, and so you ask, you see? But always friend of a friend." He grinned at this. "Same with water ghosts. Legends and tavern talk."

Tosh drew the captain's attention back to the map. A dotted line went from the Red City, winding its way in and around the smaller islands to a spot almost right in the middle of the Scattered Isles. Tosh pointed at the map. "Why not go a more direct route?"

"Many problems. Many bad things," Miko said. "Sharp rocks. Bad currents. Cannibals. Maybe map show the safe way. Avoid the bad things."

Yes, avoid the bad things. That would be nice.

Miko gestured at the sky. "Come. Hurry. Cast off before storm comes."

"Storm?" Tosh looked at the sky but didn't see anything. "Maybe we should wait for it to pass."

Miko laughed again. "Storm season. Wait for no storms, then we wait a long time. Go now in between storms."

Miko used a long pole to push away from the dock then ran aft, skipping over crates and cargo like some scurrying animal. He took up his position at the tiller. He yanked a rope, and a small sail all the way forward dropped into position. It caught just enough wind to ease them away from the dock.

Miko cackled from his perch on the stern, one hand on the tiller. "Fish man, fish man, we are coming to see you."

"Is this going to be okay?" Maurizan asked. "With him, I mean."

Tosh sighed. "Oh . . . probably not."

CHAPTER
FORTY-NINE

Talbun rolled over beneath the covers, her hand finding Brasley. It slid down his flat stomach until she found what she wanted between his legs.

Brasley's eyes popped open. *Again?*

The wizard worked him with her hand until he was erect, then whispered, "Get on."

They'd always tried to be quiet about it. It was a small boat.

The first night aboard, Brasley had dutifully kept his distance, sleeping on the far edge of the bed so as not to disturb the wizard. Without a doubt, Talbun was one of the most beautiful women he'd ever seen, but above all else, Brasley cherished his own hide. He didn't want it fried by one of the woman's dire spells.

The second night, she'd scooted close to him in the wee hours, had thrown a naked leg over him and begun kissing his ear. Disappointing a wizard was not a risk Brasley had been willing to take, and so he'd risen to the occasion. Twice.

What had surprised him most was the pang of guilt he'd felt, being a married man and all. He'd married Fregga strictly as a matter of self-preservation. Yes, he was fond of her, but the idea he might alter his behavior one whit when nobody was looking was a foreign notion to him. Certainly it wasn't his intent to hurt the woman's feelings. That she might be hurt bothered Brasley, he suddenly realized. Obviously, discretion would need to be—

"Pay attention to what you're doing," Talbun whispered.

Oops.

He crawled in between her legs, took himself in hand and aimed, easing himself inside. The familiar resistance, then the sweet welcoming slide the rest of the way. She crossed her ankles at the small of his back as he found his rhythm, her fingers gripping his back hard, digging in, her breath hot on his cheek. She bit his earlobe and kissed a trail down his throat.

Brasley picked up speed.

She trembled beneath him, slightly at first, then went rigid, arching her back and pulling him tight against her.

"Now," she whispered hoarsely. "Now."

He thrust three more times then finished, gritting his teeth to keep from moaning loudly. He rolled off of her, panting, a sheen of sweat cooling his skin in the night air that came through the small porthole. Gray morning seeped in. The sun would be up soon.

Somewhere on the deck a bell rang. The prisoners working the capstan changed shifts.

"Docks ahead," called the captain. "Make ready with the lines."

"We're getting into Tul-Agnon early," Talbun said.

"The way he works those prisoners, I'm surprised the paddle wheel doesn't shoot us into the sky," Brasley said.

"Suits me. The boat is so cramped. And I want a bath."

Brasley cleared his throat. "Listen, about what we've . . . how we've been . . ."

"I used to have an entire tower of loyal men at my disposal when I guarded the Kashar Temple. I have needs, and it's been a while." She patted his cheek like someone might scratch a dog behind the ears. "You just helped me scratch an itch. Don't worry. You did an adequate job. That should hold me for a while."

"Ah. Well, that's . . . good. It's just that I'm married. So . . ."

"I know," she said. "That's why I decided it was safe. I like knowing you have a wife with a claim on you. Makes it less likely you'll cling to *me*. Not really the sort of thing I'm looking for."

"Of course." Brasley felt it possible he'd been slightly insulted.

Mostly he just felt relieved.

"Let's get dressed and pack as fast as we can," Talbun suggested. "I want to be the first off when we tie up."

They hastily dressed and shoved their few possessions into their packs and were on deck within five minutes.

The first thing Brasley noticed were the docks looming closer through the early morning fog, the grim silhouettes of men waiting to take the riverboat's lines, stacks of cargo behind them waiting to be loaded.

A second later the fog cleared, and he noticed something else. A lone mountain looming extraordinarily close. Except it wasn't a mountain.

It was a fortress.

He blinked at it, the fog closing in again, obscuring his view. He'd had a quick second to glimpse columns and high walls and towers, huge arched windows leading onto stone balconies. Surely such a place had been centuries in its construction, generations of builders raising their children to continue and finally complete the task. An undertaking from a lost age.

"Your first time seeing the library?" Talbun asked next to him.

"How can *that* be a library?"

"That's what it is now," Talbun said. "It was built by an ancient wizard of the Mage Wars to withstand the ending of the world."

"But the world *didn't* end."

Talbun shrugged. "Some wizards figure better safe than sorry."

He looked at her, saw the grin. "You're messing with me."

"Only a little," she said. "He built it in anticipation for some cata-clysm that never came. He was the mage responsible for the Scattered Isles, after all, so perhaps he feared some kind of retaliation."

"Castle Klaar could fit inside of it ten times," Brasley said.

"Twenty," Talbun said.

The riverboat's crewmen tossed lines to the men on the dock, and as soon as the vessel was secure and the gangplank slid into place, Talbun was the first to disembark as promised, Brasley right behind her.

The streets beyond the riverfront bustled with activity. The fog was clearing, and no matter which way Brasley turned his head, he could still see the enormous fortress from the corner of his eye. It loomed over everything, casting a shadow over the city. They maneuvered in and out of the crowd. Brasley hurried to catch up with the wizard. She knew where she was going and walked fast.

"Are we headed someplace in particular?" Brasley shouted after her.

"Town Square," she called back over her shoulder. "We can find a good inn there, and it's a short walk to the university. It's been twenty years since my last visit, but I doubt much has changed."

"Why are we going to the university?"

"Because the scholars control the library, and we have to ask their permission to enter," Talbun explained. "You still have that letter Count Becham wrote for us, yes?"

Brasley patted his vest pocket. "Right here."

"Good."

"It's early in the day," Brasley said. "We could skip the inn and go directly to the university."

"I want a new dress and a bath," Talbun said. "I'm not going to an audience with university scholars smelling like a river barge and sex sweat. They're rather big on cleanliness."

"Good point."

◆ ◆ ◆

Talbun had said the scholars were big on cleanliness. Brasley took this to mean they were fussy little bureaucratic nebbishes bent on making his life miserable. The sole job of each squinting, sneering clerk seemed to be to keep him from getting to the next squinting, sneering clerk down some other hallway, hunched behind an identical small desk.

Brasley and Talbun arrived at the fifth such clerk at the fifth such desk. He wore a variation of the same outfit as the others, what Brasley had come to think of as the university uniform, a heavy velvet robe of deep green and a shapeless black hat leaning to one side or the other. Each of the clerks had a gold cord draped over his shoulders, some thinner, others thicker. Some were knotted at the end, and others had two or three knots. Brasley thought the knots might signify rank or experience, but he hadn't asked, and nobody had volunteered to explain.

The man before him now had the most knots so far, three on one side and four on the other. Brasley hoped this meant they were finally getting somewhere.

"Yes?" the clerk said. He said yes in the same way someone might say, "Please don't use my hat to wipe your arse."

Brasley smiled. It hurt, but he did it. "My good man, we were told this was the desk where we might apply for library access in the sense of—"

"Downstairs. North Hall. Third door on the left," the clerk said crisply.

Brasley's smile wavered, but he heroically held on to it. "That line— where we started the afternoon, I might add—is for *normal* library access. We are seeking entry to the upper levels."

"Ah." The clerk looked pleases. "We do not allow access to the upper levels. Good day."

"So we were informed by the previous two clerks," Brasley said. "We went back and forth between them a few times for reasons that did not seem clear."

"Then I'm *sure* they informed you an appropriate letter of introduction from a sufficiently high-ranking official must accompany any such request."

"They did not," Brasley said. "But the fourth clerk did."

"Then you are well aware."

"Yes."

"And do you *have* such a letter?" he asked.

"Indeed we do," Brasley said.

The clerk's frown was so deep, it seemed to pull his whole face down. Apparently Brasley had delivered upsetting news. "Then why didn't you *say* so?"

"I just did."

The clerk held out his hand, snapping his fingers impatiently. "Fine. Fine. Let's see the letter."

Brasley handed it over. He cast a sideways glance at Talbun, who stood stoically and uncharacteristically silent.

What's the matter? Don't you have some kind of spell of obedience you could cast on this fool?

The clerk scanned the letter, lips moving as he read silently.

The clerk's eyes flicked up to Brasley's. "Count Becham?"

"Yes."

Brasley could see the name worried the clerk. This wasn't something he could pass off easily.

"And your name?" the clerk asked.

"Brasley Hammish."

"Lord Hammish, as I'm sure you understand, we can't just let anyone—"

"Baron."

The clerk blinked. "What?"

"It's Baron Hammish."

Now the clerk looked worried. "Ah. I see. Baron of . . . ?"

"Klaar."

The clerk no longer looked worried. "Baron Hammish, as you might be able to guess, the upper levels of the Great Library represent not only a rich archeological chronicle of past centuries but also a potential treasure trove of magical—"

"I should also mention Count Becham is my father-in-law," Brasley said.

The clerk looked worried again. "Excuse me." He stood. "I must take this to a higher authority."

The clerk crossed the room, knocked on a door, then entered after a muffled voice told him to come in.

"You could have helped," Brasley said from the corner of his mouth.

Talbun smiled tightly. "You're doing fine."

"I'm just saying, I thought an all-powerful wizard would be more help."

"What's *that* supposed to mean?" Some heat in her voice.

Brasley held up a hand, placating. "Nothing. Never mind. I just thought—"

The clerk returned, gestured to the door behind him. "Lord Minn will see you now." His nod was like a reluctant bow, as if he hated himself for doing it. "Please go in."

Brasley and Talbun walked past him into the room beyond. The door clicked shut behind them.

A much bigger desk. The man behind it looked far more important that the previous clerks. He stood. His robes were soft and beige, but he wore a sash of the deep green that Brasley associated with the university. A gold cord around one shoulder with multiple knots. Brasley didn't bother to count. Minn was bald, a smudge of gray moustache under his nose, short, and approaching chubby.

"Welcome, Baron Hammish," he said. "I'm Lord Minn. Let's discuss your situation."

Minn gestured to two chairs. Brasley and Talbun sat.

"I understand you wish to go to the upper levels of the Great Library," Minn said.

"Yes," Brasley replied.

Minn looked down at the piece of paper in his hands. Brasley realized it was the letter from Becham he'd given the clerk.

"Naturally, we respect Count Becham's position in Pemrod's court," Minn said. "I understand he's your father-in-law."

"Indeed."

Minn held up a finger. "A moment."

He turned to a wall of shelves behind his desk. Piles of parchment. Scrolls rolled and stacked in cubbyholes. Thick leather books. He picked a large scroll and unrolled it on the desk. It was well worn and old. Brasley and Talbun leaned forward to look at it.

It was a detailed sketch of the Great Library.

A narrow road led through a gate in the fifty-foot-high stone wall. Someone had drawn a tiny wagon and team of horses to give the drawing scale. Brasley had to squint to see them. The structure was roughly pyramid shaped, flat on top, occasional towers, spires, or landings breaking the symmetry. Numbered lines written in tight neat printing out to the side indicated each level of the massive fortress.

Minn gestured at the diagram. "As you can see, there are eighty-one levels to the Great Library. The first two floors make up the library proper, where university students may study the histories and the ancient arts. High-level scholars act as curators."

"So I've been informed," Brasley said, trying not to sound bored.

"In recent centuries, scholar-explorers have mapped and cleared the next five levels," Minn said.

"I'm sorry," Brasley said. "Cleared?"

"Some believe the master wizard who built the fortress meant for it to be a city unto itself, sealed from the rest of the world," Minn explained. "This is just a theory, of course, but dangerous and multiple wards had to be removed level by level by our best mages. This is one of the reasons for the seemingly slow process. Exploration must progress slowly and methodically. Since the university was founded nearly five hundred years ago, we've lost three hundred ninety-one scholar-explorers. You'll notice I have the exact number memorized. Safety for our people is a constant concern."

"Commendable and understandable," Brasley said. "May I ask—not that I don't find it *fascinating*—why we are being treated to this history lesson?"

"Undertaking an expedition into the Great Library's upper levels is one of the most dangerous things anyone can do," Minn said. "And yet all exploration would come to a halt if not for the intrepid curious who wish to take the risk."

"I'm not sure I understand," Brasley said. "You discourage people from exploring the upper levels, but you need them?"

"We don't want people risking themselves frivolously," Minn said. "But we're even less keen to risk our own people. It's rather silly for a man to spend a decade training himself to be a bona fide scholar only to fall down a hole while exploring the upper levels. Making arrangements with outside parties has proven profitable and less perilous for university personnel."

"I presume there is some sort of nominal fee for entering the library," Brasley said.

"There is no fee for taking an expedition into the Great Library."

Brasley narrowed his eyes. "I am pleased and suspicious."

Minn smiled. "There are other ways the university is compensated. Should you venture into a new area, we require that you map it. This will aid future exploration. Additionally, all artifacts of a magical or historical nature are automatically property of the university. An appropriate finder's fee is awarded to the expedition, depending on the value of the find. These awards range from nominal to generous. May I ask the nature of your expedition?"

"We seek information pertaining to ink mages," Brasley told him.

"Ah. That's not a subject much in vogue anymore at the university," Minn said, "but I'm sure we'll be able to dig up a junior scholar who might serve as your guide."

"Guide?"

"All expeditions are required to take a guide through the explored levels," Minn said. "These keep you from retrodding ground that's already been picked over. The guide will turn back as soon as you reach unexplored territory."

"This guide is to be paid by the expedition, I imagine."

"Yes. Negotiate whatever fee is mutually acceptable to both parties," Minn said. "May I ask why ink magic is the particular field that has caught your attention?"

Brasley gestured to Talbun. "My associate might be able to answer that better than I. She's—"

"Baron Hammish's assistant," Talbun interjected quickly. "My name is Esthar."

Minn nodded to her. "A pleasure."

"You may have been told that the baron hails from Klaar," she said.

"Yes, so I was told." Understanding lit Minn's eyes. "Oh. The duchess."

"Just so."

"I had thought the stories . . . exaggerated," Minn said.

Talbun shook her head. "No. As you can imagine, Duchess Veraiin is anxious to unearth any lore about the tattoos and their history. Baron Hammish is here to lend his authority to the enterprise, but I'll actually be cataloging any information we'd be able to gather."

Minn nodded, drummed his fingers on his desk. "Well, in light of our discussion and your excellent credentials, I feel it is appropriate to grant your request to send an expedition to the upper levels."

Brasley beamed. "Excellent!"

"We should have an opening in eleven weeks."

Brasley's smile fell. Hit the ground. Shattered into little pieces.

"Eleven weeks?"

Minn looked pained. "Alas, we must space the expeditions in a way that they are not tripping over one another in their explorations."

"This is most disappointing," Brasley said.

Minn took a leather-bound ledger from the shelf behind him, opened it, and slid it across the desk to show Brasley. "As you can see, we're totally booked for the foreseeable future. Really, my hands are tied."

Brasley leaned in, squinted at the ledger, and memorized the first three names on the list.

He sighed dramatically. "Count Becham will be most displeased. Those at court who've taken an interest in this project won't like hearing about the delay."

Brasley had hoped Minn would infer he was talking about the king. As lies went, it was fairly brazen. *Well, really, what's the point in lying if one can't be brazen once in a while?*

Minn held up his hands, palms out. "Well, now let's not be hasty, Baron Hammish. Here's what I can do for you. Okay? How about this? If one of the other expeditions cancels for any reason, I can slot you in their place. That's within my authority, and I'm happy to do it for you. And for Count Becham, of course."

Brasley rose slowly, chin up, and looked down on Minn with all of the haughty bearing he could muster. "I suppose it will just have to do."

◆ ◆ ◆

"You did *what*?"

"Keep your voice down." Talbun looked around the inn's common room, but even though it was crowded, nobody took notice of them.

"Why do you think I didn't want to give my name at the university? Scholars have long memories."

"I don't know. I thought you were just being mysterious," Brasley said. "I didn't know you'd stolen something from the Great Library."

"Will you keep your voice *down*?" She glared.

"Okay, okay."

A serving woman arrived with two tankards of dark beer and a quill and an inkwell, which she set in front of Brasley.

"What's that for?" the wizard asked.

"I want to write down these three names before I forget them." Brasley dipped the quill into the ink then scribbled on a scrap of parchment.

"What names?"

"The first three names in the ledger Minn showed us," he said. "What did you steal, anyway?"

"A spell," she said. "It is said that the master wizard had over five hundred acolytes, each a powerful mage in their own right. There's *a lot* of powerful magic to be discovered in that place. I figured they wouldn't miss one little spell."

"Which spell?"

"None of your business."

"If there is so much magic up there, then why aren't they pulling it out left and right?" Brasley asked.

"Because wizards can be real assholes, and most of them hate people messing with their stuff, even centuries after they've died," Talbun explained. "Booby traps are common, and magical booby traps are particularly nasty."

They both paused to take large gulps of beer.

"Why did you write down those names?" she asked.

"Because these are the leaders of the next three expeditions heading for the upper levels."

"So?"

"So you heard what Minn said. If there is a cancellation, we get the slot."

"Please. What are the chances of . . ."

He smiled.

"You have some kind of *plan*, don't you?" she said.

"It's a work in progress."

"You have some kind of sneaky bastard plan because *you* are a sneaky bastard."

Brasley frowned. "That's not quite how I'd put it, but yes."

Talbun gulped beer. "Okay, let's hear it."

Brasley read the first name from the list. "Kalrick Vishnae."

"I've heard of him," Talbun said. "A powerful sorcerer from somewhere out west, I think."

"As we've already labeled wizards as dangerous and ill tempered, we should probably cross him off the list." Brasley drew a line through the name with a quill. "Not looking to incur the wrath of the wrathful."

"A wise policy," Talbun agreed.

"Likewise, Count Ahlruck seems to be someone of importance, if the title is any indication, so let's give him a miss as well." Brasley crossed through the name. "That leaves us with somebody named Rell Blummand."

"Never heard of him," Talbun said.

"Perfect."

"Now what?"

"Now we arrange for some appropriate calamity for our dear Master Blummand."

Talbun hoisted her tankard in salute. "I wondered what Rina saw in you. Now I get it."

Brasley shrugged. "What's the point of being a liar and a cad and a womanizer if one can't . . . You know, I forgot where I was going with this."

"Never mind," Talbun said. "Just drink your beer."

They clunked their tankards together and drank up.

CHAPTER FIFTY

They'd dodged three storms since leaving the Red City, the captain seemingly everywhere at once on the scow schooner, hopping around like some emaciated tree frog, pulling ropes, tugging on the tiller, and cackling at his own jokes. He'd squint at a smudge of cloud on the horizon, declare a storm was approaching, and alter course.

Miko had done his best to follow the map's course, and it quickly became clear why a bigger ship such as the *Witch of Kern* wouldn't do.

The Scattered Isles were a mess, at least from the point of view of anyone trying to navigate them. The narrow passages between the islands were littered with rocks humping up from the water in unlikely places. At one point, they'd taken a channel between two islands so narrow that Alem could almost reach out and touch the hanging palm fronds from a tree that grew out at an angle over the water.

When they'd later come to a patch of what seemed like open water, Miko had sent Alem to the prow and had ordered him to watch the depth. "You yell if too shallow. Okay? You tell Miko quick or bottom rip out of boat and we sink good and fast, yeah, yeah."

Through the crystal blue water, Alem had watched with alarm as a reef rapidly came up from the bottom of the sea. At one point there was barely three feet of water between the bottom of the scow and the craggy reef. Alem had breathed a sigh of relief when they'd hit deep water again.

So far, the gypsy's map hadn't steered them wrong.

"What's he looking at?"

Alem turned away from the islands he'd been watching, to look up at Maurizan. She wore one of the blousy pairs of pants she'd purchased in the bazaar but had cut them off at the knees to combat the heat. She wore her lightest blouse, bright yellow cotton, the long sleeves rolled up, knotted above her belly button. The sun had turned her skin pink and had brought out the freckles across the bridge of her nose.

She looked beautiful in such a completely different way from Rina.

No wonder men like Brasley have such a hard time settling on just one woman.

But Brasley was married now. Would that change him?

"Did you hear me?"

Alem blinked. "What?"

"I asked what you think he's looking at."

Alem looked back at the tiller. Miko balanced on the stern gunwale, bobbing with the waves, hands cupped around his eyes as he stared into the distance.

"He's usually laughing about something, but he's not now," Alem said. "Which worries me."

"Let's ask him," Maurizan suggested.

They went aft, stepping over Kalli, Lureen, and Viriam, who lounged on the deck in the sun, heads resting on coils of rope. Barefoot. They wore men's breeches rolled to the knees and blouses knotted in the same fashion as Maurizan's.

"Aren't you hot?" Kalli asked Alem as he passed.

"There's a good breeze," Alem said. "But yes."

"Then get that shirt off," Lureen said. "Show us what you've got."

The other two giggled. Alem went red to the ears.

Maybe they'll just think it's sunburn.

They laughed harder.

Nope.

Alem hurried along aft.

"Alem."

He looked back at Maurizan.

"If the bullies are picking on you, just tell me." Maurizan grinned. "I'll protect you."

Alem frowned. "Hilarious."

Maurizan laughed, caught his sleeve. "I mean, you do know they look at you, right?"

"What? That's ridiculous."

"Don't get too big headed," the gypsy told him. "You're basically the only game in town. Miko looks more like a wrung-out piece of leather than a man. They're just looking. To pass the time."

"What about Tosh?"

Maurizan shook her head. "Too complicated from their time at the Wounded Bird. He's more like a big brother or something."

Alem managed a grin. "Looks like I'm not going to be lonely on this trip."

Maurizan's smile dropped. "The way this boat tosses around, it would be real easy for me to bump into somebody and knock them overboard."

"Maybe we should just go see what Miko is looking at," Alem said.

"That's a good idea."

At the tiller, both of them looked up at the captain. He hadn't moved from his spot, still staring into the distance.

"What's the word, Miko?" Alem asked.

Miko said nothing.

Alem looked at Maurizan. The gypsy shrugged.

Alem raised his voice. "Miko. Is it another storm?"

"Yes," Miko said.

"Can we go around it like the others?"

"No."

"No? What do you mean no?"

"The others ones we go away from," Miko said. "This one gets us."

"What if we change course?"

Miko shook his head. "This one gets us."

Tosh was coming now, stepping over the women and heading aft. "What's going on?"

"Storm."

"Can we avoid it?" Tosh asked.

Alem shook his head. "Apparently this one gets us."

"Then we should put in somewhere," Tosh said.

Miko pointed at the closest island off the port side. "Cannibals." He pointed starboard. "Cannibals."

"Are you serious?"

Miko gestured at his own body. "Skin and bones." He reached out and pinched the fleshy part of Tosh's upper arm. "Good meal."

Tosh jerked his arm away. "Stop that. That's fucking creepy."

"What do we do now?" Maurizan asked.

Miko pointed a bony finger at the deck. "Everything loose. Tie down or get below."

Tosh turned to the women lounging on the deck. "Kalli, get 'em up. We've got weather coming. Batten down the hatches."

They all scrambled to clear the decks or lash down the bigger crates. Miko stayed at the tiller, leaning into it, pointing the scow into the wind. The clouds had seemed far off, but the cold rain lashed them sooner than expected, thunder rolling across the sky. Lightning illuminated the insides of black clouds. What had been a bright sunny day less than an hour ago was now grim and gray and dark.

The sea tossed the scow, waves splashing over the gunwale.

Maurizan and Alem clung to a lifeline. Her face looked terrified.

"Alem," she shouted over the wind and crashing waves.

"Yes?"

"I'm not the best swimmer."

"That doesn't matter," Alem said. "We're just going on a little ride. Miko will bring us out on the other side and we'll just be a little wet is all."

It was now so dark it might as well have been night. He saw her frightened face in the next flash of lightning. And the next crack of thunder was so loud, it sounded like it was five feet over their heads. Maurizan jumped and grabbed his arm. The rain came in almost sideways, stinging and cold.

The scow rose alarmingly with each wave, nearly pointing the prow straight up at the sky, then crashing down again on the other side so hard, Alem thought the boat might be smashed to kindling. Somehow they stayed afloat.

A wave crashed over the side, knocking Maurizan and Alem from their places in a rush of foaming seawater. They lost their grips on the lifeline. Maurizan screamed. Alem grabbed for the rope again with one hand, barely caught it. With the other hand he snagged Maurizan's ankle as she tumbled toward the edge of the boat. He pulled her back, and she clung to him shivering and coughing.

Alem's hand went into his pocket, came out with the necklace he'd bought for her at the bazaar. He put it around her neck. "Here. I got this for you." Maybe it would take her mind off of their imminent deaths.

Maurizan couldn't see it, felt the pendant in one hand, trying to guess its shape.

"What is it?"

"Something pretty," Alem said. "You can have a better look at it when this is all over."

"Do you remember the first time we kissed?" Maurizan had to put her mouth almost against Alem's ear to be heard over the wind and the crashing waves.

"In a storm," Alem said.

She took his face in her hand and pulled it down, kissed him hard, desperately. She tasted like salt water, but it didn't matter. Their tongues snaked into each other's mouths, and they held each other as if it might be the last thing they would ever do.

Another huge wave slapped across the deck, smashing a line of crates that had been lashed to the deck. They went over the side but were still attached to one end of the rope. They dragged along in the water, and the scow listed badly in response, the deck pitching at a terrifying angle.

"Cut it loose!" Miko screamed from the tiller. "Cut it! Cut it!"

Alem let go of Maurizan and lurched toward the line, waves crashing down on him, one hand falling to the knife on his belt. He went to one knee, used the knife to saw at the rope where it was pulled tight against the gunwale.

In the next flash of lightning, he saw something in the water, a white shape maybe six feet long, something just below the surface. The next display of lightning lasted longer, jagged blue lines crackling across the sky. Alem took a better look. Arms and legs. The shape of a person swimming alongside the scow.

Alem heard Miko's crazy voice in his head: *The Fish Man.*

You've got to be kidding me.

"Cut it!" Miko shouted. "Cut it, you fool!"

Alem returned his attention to the rope. The knife was wet and slick in his hand. He fumbled it. It bounced once off the gunwale and vanished into the dark sea.

Oh . . . shit.

Maurizan was at his side in the next instant, handing him her dagger handle first. "Use this!"

He sawed the rest of the way through the rope, and it pulled apart, leaving the crates in the scow's wake.

The boat righted itself. The deck under their feet tilted back into position abruptly, and Maurizan staggered, arms wheeling to find balance. She lost her footing . . . and went over the side.

A stab of horror jolted Alem's heart. "Maurizan!"

And without thinking he was over the side after her.

He went down into the cold water, kicked, came up again, sputtering. "Maurizan!"

Alem saw a gleaming pinprick of light on the water in the next flash of lightning.

The pendant.

He kicked toward her.

"Alem!"

"I'm coming."

The white shape streaked past him toward Maurizan. The Fish Man scooped her in one arm as he past, and Alem saw her terrified eyes, hands reaching out for him as she disappeared into the night.

"Alem!"

He opened his mouth to answer but a wave slammed down onto him from above. He was pushed deep, lungs burning. At first he didn't know which way to swim, but then he saw a blur of lightning above like something from a fading dream.

He kicked hard, broke the surface, and gasped for air.

Alem turned his head in every direction, but there was no sign of Maurizan or the scow.

Only towering waves and the wide angry sea.

CHAPTER FIFTY-ONE

Talbun and Brasley stood before the immense gates of the Great Library. Standing this close, it was dizzying to look up at the edifice that seemed to stretch endlessly into the sky. Now that he was here, Brasley realized what should have been an obvious flaw in his plan.

He had *zero* desire to enter the Great Library.

And yet that's just where he was about to go.

There was a small guardhouse to the right of the gate. A man in university livery and leather armor emerged and waved Talbun and Brasley off the side of the road. "You're not clear to enter yet. Please allow other traffic to pass."

Brasley waved at the man. "Yeah, yeah."

Scholars in green robes went in and out of the gate. They didn't seem to have any problem walking around the cart, but Brasley didn't want any trouble. He took the goat by the reins and led him to the side of the road to get out of the way.

A goat cart. Not in a thousand years had Brasley expected to buy a goat cart. When Brasley had realized he'd need to outfit himself for the expedition inside the Great Library, he'd been directed to a market just outside of the library's gates that specialized in such things: lanterns, food, water, rope, mapping materials, various tools for the ardent treasure hunter.

It was a lot to carry.

The solution had been the goat cart, a staple of library expeditions for over a century.

It had been explained to Brasley that the library was like a great city in some ways, with wide avenues and soaring arched ceilings. Lots and lots of room, enough for a team of wagons. But in other areas, passages were no wider than an ordinary doorway.

The wooden goat carts were six feet long but only two feet wide. The goats were a domesticated version of a sturdy mountain breed, and the curved horns of the brown animal standing next to him came up to his chest.

He named the goat Titan in memory of a horse.

"Baron Hammish!"

Somebody was yelling his name. Brasley turned to see a pimple-faced youth running toward him, his green university robe hiked up so he could move fast, a leather pack over one shoulder. He wore a gold cord around his shoulders with no knots.

The youth stopped in front of him, bent to put his hands on his knees, panting. "I'm your guide, *pant, pant*. Name's Olgen. *Pant, pant.* Thought I might be late." He straightened and smiled crookedly. "Hate for you to leave without me."

"We can't leave without you," Brasley said. "It's against the rules to go without a guide."

Olgen scrunched up his face as if it were taking Brasley's words a long time to get from his ears to his brain. "Oh yeah."

Brasley sighed. "And how is it we are so privileged to have you as our guide, Olgen?"

"My area is tattoos and ink magic," Olgen said. "It's a branch of the historical study of the Mage Wars. Hardly anyone specializes in the study of the tattoos themselves. I'm only a first year, but don't worry. I know my stuff."

"Excellent." *We're doomed.*

A coach drawn by a single horse pulled to a stop next to them. The door opened and Lord Minn stepped out.

"Lord Minn," Brasley said. "I hadn't expected you to see us off in person."

"I see off all of the expeditions," Minn said. "I see you have your goat and cart."

"A magnificent beast full of vim and vigor."

"Ah. Yes." Minn's eye shifted to Olgen. "And also your guide."

"His vim and vigor has yet to be determined."

"I must admit, I was surprised when a slot opened up so soon," Minn said.

"Fortune has indeed smiled upon us," Brasley said.

"Strange that Rell Blummand and his entire expedition should suddenly all come down with dysentery. I was told they were all having a last meal together in celebration of their expedition and perhaps got a hold of some bad fish."

"Alas that our good luck should be predicated on his unfortunate circumstances," Brasley said. "We wish him and his party a speedy recovery."

"Hmmm. Yes. Well, in any case, good luck, sir, to you and your assistant." Minn waved at the soldier in front of the guardhouse. "They're clear! Let them through."

"Farewell," Brasley called to Minn over his shoulder.

Talbun walked next to him as Brasley led Titan through the gate. No turning back now.

"You've been in here before, right?"

"Yes," Talbun said.

"How long do you think this will take?"

"There's no way to know," she said. "The place is vast."

"Can you guess?"

"Let me put it this way," Talbun said. "Last time, we ended up eating the goat."

CHAPTER
FIFTY-TWO

Tchi had ordered one of the wizards to watch the duchess at all times. They took shifts, constantly renewing the sleeping spell as they headed south.

Jariko had pretended to agree with Prullap: It was far too dangerous to try to get the secrets of ink magic from the captive. Prullap had been relieved.

But secretly Jariko made his own plans and had concocted a potion that would help him. He'd had most of the ingredients with him and had found the rest growing wild in the forest.

Jariko went to relieve the other wizard, two guards in tow.

As the junior wizard, Prullap had been stuck with the night shift. Jariko found the man, hunched at the dwindling campfire, bleary eyed. The two guards with him leaned against nearby trees. They looked tired too. Although they all knew the duchess was dangerous, guarding her sleeping body had become routine.

"The night passed without event?" Jariko asked.

"Yes," Prullap said. "I am dead. I just want to sleep."

"Go, then. I'll take over."

"It's time to renew the sleep spell. Shall I do it before I leave?" Prullap offered.

"I'm just as capable of renewing the spell as you are. Go on. Get some rest."

Prullap shrugged and motioned for his guards to follow as he departed.

Jariko watched him go. He watched another minute after Prullap disappeared into the trees toward the main body of the camp. It had been Jariko's suggestion to Commander Tchi that the prisoner be kept on the edge of the camp instead of in the middle. He'd told Tchi that if by some circumstance the duchess managed to get free, then Jariko would be able to wield his most powerful magic without endangering the men. The gruff one with the eye patch had spoken against the idea, but Tchi had overruled him.

What Jariko had really wanted was privacy.

He motioned to the two warriors. "Come with me."

They followed him to the cart where Duchess Veraiin slept, still bound by chains. He looked down at her a moment. She looked young and peaceful, oblivious to what was happening to her.

He'd remedy that soon enough.

"Bring the cart," he told the men.

They looked at each other, then back at the wizard. "We have no orders to move her," said one of them.

"The orders were given to me, and now I'm telling you," Jariko said impatiently. "Stop wasting time. We're trying something new today."

Strictly speaking, the wizards were not in the military chain of command.

But a wizard was still a wizard. They took hold of the little cart on each side and followed Jariko deeper into the forest.

When he thought they'd gone far enough, he told them to halt.

"Sit her up."

He had to hurry. Prullap was right about one thing. The spell would wear off soon. And then he'd be in peril.

The soldiers sat the duchess up in the back of the cart. Her head flopped to one side.

Jariko took a glass vial from his pouch, uncorked it. He held Veraiin's head in one hand, forced the vial between her lips, and emptied the dirty brown liquid down her gullet. He massaged her throat to make sure she swallowed every drop.

If Jariko timed it right, the potion would take effect just as the sleep spell wore off. Some bit of overlap was to be expected, but the effect would be eventually as desired.

Now to wait. It wouldn't be long.

◆ ◆ ◆

She felt like she'd been swimming through a dream for a long time.

A world of swirling images had closed over her like an arctic sea, dimming light, muffling sound. Afloat.

At times she felt herself floating upward, no longer simply adrift, but speeding to the end of something, and she'd reach, so close, mere inches from her fingertips. And just when she thought she might break through to the surface, she was pushed back down into the depths, sent tumbling, a cottony veil pulled down over her eyes.

This time there was a light. It was so far above that it could not possibly have anything to do with her, but some current took her, and she began to move toward it.

Rina picked up speed, hope blooming, the light glowing closer. She felt weightless, paddling toward it. The cold sea above her receded and—

Her eyelids opened slowly.

Rina would not have been surprised to hear them creak as if on rusty hinges.

A strange face hovered before her, an old man, long moustaches, obviously Perranese.

She tried to reach out, grab his throat. Her arm refused to obey. She tried to sit up, tried to kick him, anything. Her muscles refused to obey. She tried to scream. Her mouth didn't even tremble.

"Good," said the old man. "You are awake. I can't very well question you while you slumber, can I? But the potion makes you equally helpless, yes? You are paralyzed and will stay that way. I am Jariko, a Perranese wizard. But all you need to really know is that I am your master now."

Jariko drew a dagger and brought the tip to within a fraction of an inch of Rina's eyeball. "Your fate is completely a matter of my whim. I can see in your eyes that we understand each other."

She tried to flinch away but couldn't.

Her body sat limp in the cart, head lolling to one side, but within her a panic raged. She reached for the spirit, but it was as if some elastic barrier had stretched between her and it, forbidding access. She tried to twist her body, move a hand, wiggle a toe. Anything. To no avail.

Rina Veraiin was trapped inside her own body.

EPILOGUE

Far to the north in Tul-Agnon, one of the university's master engineers labored over a hot forge. His name was Wexton. Sweat dripped from every part of him. The project was finished for all intents and purposes, but there was just one bump along the thigh that seemed imperfectly shaped.

Wexton wanted it just right. The man paying him probably did too.

Most journeymen engineers felt themselves too good for the sweaty hands-on work. They poured their efforts into design work, drafting detailed sketches, but left it to the blacksmiths to actually put the muscle into it. Such engineers would never be truly great until they overcame such pretentions.

Working the metal itself told him things he could never have guessed sitting at a drafting table. He developed instincts. A feel for the metal.

And he enjoyed it.

"I'll be finished in a moment, my friend," Wexton said. "You'll be pleased. I promise."

The hulking brute of a man grunted from the far corner of the blacksmith's shop. The man had said he preferred to sit in the shadows because he was always so hot. Wexton rather thought the man was in hiding and didn't want to be seen. Perhaps he was a fugitive.

Not that Wexton cared. The man had gold to spend. He'd given Wexton an extraordinary amount to do the work, with a promise of double upon completion. He'd also paid to have the best steel imported for the job, and there would be enough left over for Wexton to use in one of his own projects.

All things considered, Wexton didn't care if the man had set fire to an orphanage. The engineer was being paid enough to look the other way.

Wexton dipped a ladle into the water bucket and cooled the bit of thigh he was working on. He looked over the entire leg, squinting at every inch of gleaming metal.

It was perfect.

"Come, my friend," Wexton said. "Come and see."

The brute rose from his shadowed corner, balancing awkwardly on one leg, the man's cloak hanging down to cover the stump of the other. With a crutch he managed to hobble over to Wexton.

"Most men would have settled for a wooden peg leg," Wexton said.

"I'm not most men," the brute said. "And I have work to do and no time to hobble on a peg leg."

"Look here at the ankle," Wexton said. "And here at the knee. The pulleys and counterweights. It's perfect. Come, let's try it on, and I'll show you."

The brute unclasped his cloak and let it drop.

Wexton gasped and stepped back.

The man was covered from head to toe in tattoos. Wexton imagined that his missing leg must have been too.

More than that, a light steam rose from the man. His muscles and skin seemed almost to pulse.

"You said you ran hot," Wexton said. "I didn't think you meant . . ."

"The tattoos," he said. "It's like a fire beneath the skin that's always burning. I live with it. Come now. The leg."

Wexton fit the top part of the steel leg to the man's stump. "Lamb's wool. Very soft for your stump. Very comfortable. But let me know if it hurts. We can make adjustments."

"No," said the brute. "It feels good."

The leg was kept in place by a series of straps, around his waist, over his shoulders. Wexton cinched them tight and buckled them. "Too tight? Just tell me."

"No. It's fine."

"Try it out," Wexton said. "You have to sort of swing your hip so the leg will go forward, but it should be perfectly balanced."

At first the leg seemed like a complete failure, and the brute almost fell several times. But he was patient. In five minutes, he found a rhythm, the steel leg swinging out and planting as he walked. In another five minutes, he walked like a man with a severe limp, and five minutes after that like a man with only a minor limp.

"It's wonderful," he said.

Wexton beamed.

"You must be very proud of your work."

"I am," Wexton said. "And I am happy you are pleased."

"It must be difficult," the brute said. "You probably want to tell your peers. To tell them of this accomplishment in engineering. I'm sorry."

Wexton looked at the leg wistfully. He had been tempted to show his colleagues on a number of occasions. He sighed. "It's okay. You paid for my discretion. I'll honor our bargain."

"No," the brute said. "I mean, I'm sorry."

Wexton understood what he meant at the last second and darted for the door, but the man was impossibly fast. He grabbed Wexton's throat and squeezed. A quick snap, and Wexton's body thumped to the ground.

The brute had come prepared. He put on a pair of baggy breeches to fit easily over the steel leg. An oversized boot for the foot. He put his cloak back on and left the blacksmith's shop. He could have been anyone as he joined the crowd on the street, perhaps a war veteran with a slight limp he'd earned in some far-off battle.

The ink mage known as Ankar headed for the Great Library.

He had work to do.

To be continued in Book 3 of *A Fire Beneath the Skin* . . .

ABOUT THE AUTHOR

Victor Gischler was born in Sanford, Florida. He is a world traveler and earned his PhD in English from the University of Southern Mississippi. He received Italy's Black Corsair Award for adventure literature and was nominated for both an Anthony Award and an Edgar Award for his crime writing.

He currently lives in Baton Rouge, Louisiana, and would grill every meal if his wife would let him.

Please join Victor on Twitter for hijinks and nonsense: @Victor-Gischler.